HOMECOMING GIRLS

www.rbooks.co.uk

HOMECOMING GIRLS

Val Wood

BANTAM PRESS

LONDON · TORONTO · SYDNEY · AUCKLAND · JOHANNESBURG

TRANSWORLD PUBLISHERS
61–63 Uxbridge Road, London W5 5SA
A Random House Group Company
www.rbooks.co.uk

First published in Great Britain
in 2010 by Bantam Press
an imprint of Transworld Publishers

A CIP catalogue record for this book
is available from the British Library.

ISBN 9780593066997

Addresses for Random House Group Ltd companies outside the UK
can be found at: www.randomhouse.co.uk
The Random House Group Ltd Reg. No. 954009

The Random House Group Limited supports the Forest Stewardship
Council (FSC), the leading international forest-certification organization.
All our titles that are printed on Greenpeace-approved FSC-certified
paper carry the FSC logo. Our paper procurement policy can be found at
www.rbooks.co.uk/environment

Typeset in 11½/14pt New Baskerville by
Kestrel Data, Exeter, Devon.
Printed and bound in Great Britain by
Clays Ltd, Bungay, Suffolk.

2 4 6 8 10 9 7 5 3 1

For my family with love, and for Peter

A child's life is like a piece of paper on which every person leaves a mark.

Chinese proverb

SOURCES

Books and information for general research:

Hawgood, John A., *The American West: The Revolution in Western Transportation*, Frontier Library, Eyre & Spottiswood, London, 1967.

Sheehan, James Joseph, *History of the Town and Port of Hull*, John Green, Beverley, 1866.

And the free dictionaries by Farlex and Wikipedia for general information on Han Chinese and Old St Mary's Cathedral, San Francisco.

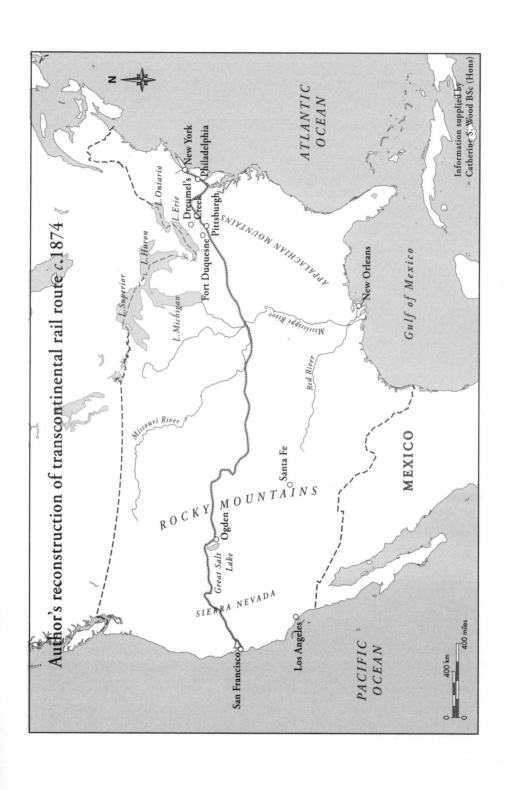

Author's reconstruction of transcontinental rail route *c.*1874

N

ATLANTIC OCEAN

New York
Philadelphia
Dreumel's
Creek
Pittsburgh
Fort Duquesne

APPALACHIAN MOUNTAINS

New Orleans

Gulf of Mexico

L. Ontario
L. Erie
L. Huron
L. Superior
L. Michigan

Mississippi River

Red River

Missouri River

Santa Fe

ROCKY MOUNTAINS

Ogden
Great Salt Lake

SIERRA NEVADA

San Francisco

Los Angeles

MEXICO

PACIFIC OCEAN

Information supplied by
Catherine S. Wood BSc (Hons)

400 km
400 miles
0
0

HOMECOMING GIRLS

PROLOGUE

In the mid-nineteenth century there had been great poverty and distress in the port town of Hull. Cholera, typhus and malnutrition killed off many inhabitants, opium addiction was rife and there were mutterings from the abandoned poor who considered that they suffered much injustice at the hands of the rich and more fortunate. Those amongst them who concluded that they needed to eat and work in order to stay alive and keep a roof over their heads eventually gave up complaining when hunger and apathy sapped their energy.

In those days, two young women on the brink of starvation in a final desperate act took control of their own lives. One, normally quiet and reserved but with a yet undiscovered inner core of steel, became a beacon of hope as she railed against oppression and inequality and spoke up for the rights of herself and others like her; whilst the other, hungry and deprived, succumbed to the lure of a life of comparative ease and became the mistress of a rich and married philanderer.

The consequences of these naive young women's actions were to stretch out for twenty years or more, touching the lives of many and even reaching the shores of America, which for some wasn't quite the land of opportunity – the Eldorado – it was meant to be.

Into this New World a child of mixed parentage was born; of her Chinese mother nothing was known except that she too had escaped from oppression, and about her father there were many questions but few answers. It was to the old town of Hull that the child was returned.

There were many who were curious about her, and wondered about her ancestry. Residents in the port town were used to foreign sailors, brown and weathered, speaking languages that they couldn't understand, whose only English words were *girls* or *room*. Seamen might occasionally come across a Chinese cook, but rarely did people of that nationality arrive in this eastern harbour. Sometimes women were smuggled off the ships, young pretty women, their faces pale with fear, who, speaking with Germanic or Scandinavian accents, begged to be taken back home.

But never young women like her. Rich, beautiful, and with a cool enigmatic glance which defied interrogation. *Oriental*, the gentry whispered as they speculated. They knew her father, of course, or once did, for he was long dead. The Newmarch family was well known in the town, not only for their wealth, but for their industry and charity, and she was part of it. Her family and close friends knew what little there was to be known, but for the rest she was shrouded in a cloak of mystery and intrigue and many stories were told about her. Over the years the tales faded into obscurity as she was accepted as part of the community, until strangers arrived and asked about her, and then they began again, increasing in exaggeration and veiled insinuation.

CHAPTER ONE

March 1874

Jewel watched her cousins from across the floor of the state
ballroom in the Royal Station Hotel: Elizabeth, married for
only an hour, golden-haired, elated and vivacious beside
her new husband; on her other side, her twin, Clara, almost
but not quite her double, palely serene, but, as Jewel knew
well, anxious and fearful at the thought of having lost the
sister who for twenty years had been an inseparable part of
her life.

Jewel swept towards them, her rose-coloured watered-silk
gown rustling and the feathers in her headdress gently tossing
and quivering; she and Clara had been Elizabeth's attendants,
and as they had walked down the aisle of St Mary's Church
she had been conscious that she was turning heads with
her oriental looks, her dark almond-shaped eyes and high
cheekbones. She was aware of her beauty, but it meant little to
her. She had no vanity or pretensions, but was liberated and
worldly.

She took Clara's arm now. 'Come, cousin,' she said. 'Let
these two lovebirds enjoy their dancing. It might be for the
last time; they will be so busy playing house and embroiled in
matters of housekeeping that there will be no time for such
pleasures.'

Elizabeth's husband, Patrick Goodson, not yet used to Jewel's particular brand of humour, frowned a little and glanced at Elizabeth.

'She teases.' Elizabeth laid her hand on his arm and arched her fine eyebrows. 'She is jealous because I have caught the most eligible man in town and there is no one left for her.'

'I say!' Patrick flushed, but was flattered nevertheless.

Jewel gave him one of her inscrutable glances, which confused him even more. He was not a handsome man, being rather thin, with angular features, but Elizabeth had declared him to be masterly in discourse and an accomplished conversationalist. Jewel had not yet heard him say anything to convince her of this, but one thing was for sure: he was very rich, and Elizabeth, having being brought up thriftily by wise and prudent parents, was quite prepared to help him spend his wealth.

'So, Clara,' Jewel said softly as she led her cousin away. 'Now that Eliza has tied herself down, what shall we do? Some adventure is called for, I think.' She drew Clara's arm affectionately into hers as they strolled towards the foyer lounge. 'Something to keep you occupied now that your sister is otherwise engaged.'

'I am bereft!' Clara said tearfully. 'Oh, I'm pleased for Elizabeth, for them both, please don't think that I'm not, but we've—'

'I know,' Jewel murmured. 'You've always been a twosome, but now – well, you're just like me,' she added brightly. 'You're now an only child. You'll be spoilt and indulged by your mama and papa just as I am by mine.'

She looked across the room and raised a hand to Georgiana and Wilhelm, who were chatting to other guests. They were not her birth parents but had adopted her after her father died. Edward Newmarch, whose features and mannerisms were now indistinct in her memory, had been the brother of Martin, the twins' father; they, she always considered, really were her own flesh and blood in spite of her mixed-race background.

After Edward Newmarch's death in America, Georgiana,

who had travelled to that country in search of a new life, had brought Jewel to England to meet her relatives who lived in the northern town of Hull; they were followed by American-born Wilhelm Dreumel, who found that he could not live without either of them, married Georgiana and adopted Jewel. They settled in the town, but were well travelled, making frequent journeys to America and the Netherlands where Wilhelm's forebears were born.

'I don't think that you're spoilt, Jewel,' Clara said. 'But your parents are very liberal, are they not? They have taken you with them on most of their travels.'

'Mm, but not recently,' Jewel mused. 'Oh, I've been to Europe – Italy and France and the Netherlands of course – but I haven't been to America for, what, ten years, and then we went to Dreumel's Creek, not to California as I wanted to.'

Clara smiled. 'Gadabout,' she murmured, and then sighed. 'Imagine having a town named after you. Yet Uncle Wilhelm is so unassuming.'

Jewel nodded. 'He is. He's a darling. But of course it was his land, that's why it's called after him. It was shown to him by a half-breed Iroquois trapper; Papa purchased it and then he found gold. It's quite a large town now, but back then it was a deep hidden valley surrounded by mountains, with the creek running through it. That's what Mama says, at any rate, but I can barely remember it even though I lived there for a while. I was only three or four at the time, and then when I was taken back I was ten and the town had grown. Papa goes regularly, of course, as he has business and property there.'

Jewel's age was a contentious subject. Even her birth date wasn't known. Her mother, Tsui, was Chinese and had lived with Jewel's father Edward; then inexplicably she had left him, giving no reason why and no indication of where she was going. Twelve months later a Chinese woman had brought baby Jewel to her father's house and told him that Tsui was dead, the child was his – which he never doubted – and that if he didn't take her she would be sold.

Georgiana had decided on a date for Jewel's birthday

after the child had cried inconsolably during the twins' fifth birthday party. She had chosen 14 May in the hope that the sun would always shine on that day and they would be able to picnic in a park or by the seaside. After discussion with Martin Newmarch regarding the dates of Edward's departure to America and her meeting him there she had decided that the year of Jewel's birth was probably 1853.

'Dan and Thomas are coming over,' Clara said now, as she spotted the sons of her mother's best friend walking towards them.

'Oh, for heaven's sake,' Jewel muttered. 'Can we escape? If we're seen talking to them here, everyone will put two and two together and start asking us when our nuptials will be!'

'We all know that Dan adores you,' Clara laughed, 'and that Aunt Ruby would love to have you as a daughter-in-law.'

'How ridiculous!' Jewel said scathingly. 'We do nothing but bicker when we meet, and, besides, I have absolutely no intention of becoming anyone's daughter-in-law. Much as I love Aunt Ruby,' she added.

'Ladies!' Dan gave a sweeping exaggerated bow to greet them, whilst his younger brother smiled sheepishly. 'How charming you both look. Absolutely delightful.' He bent over Clara's hand and put it to his lips and then turned to do the same to Jewel, who put both hands behind her back.

'Stop acting the goat, Dan,' she scoffed. 'Posturing doesn't suit you. We prefer it when you are your usual forthright self.'

'Like you, you mean?' he retaliated. 'There's no one more forthright or direct than you, Jewel. But I meant it.' He turned to Clara. 'You look beautiful, Clara,' he said in a softer tone to that reserved and gentle young woman, who flushed and looked away.

'You're embarrassing her,' Jewel reprimanded him. 'It isn't what we expect from friends we've known all our lives.'

Thomas spoke up. 'Well, you do both look nice, and – and don't you think we look handsome, all toffed up in our best?'

Clara nodded in agreement. The young men did look handsome in hired tail suits with yellow spotted cravats and carnations in their buttonholes. Jewel glanced slyly at Thomas and then said lazily, 'I'm not sure if I don't prefer you with sawdust in your hair, Thomas, but yes – I suppose!'

'Take no notice,' Dan told his brother. 'She's no idea of style.' He grasped Jewel's hand, which she had dropped to her side, and before she had chance to protest said, 'Come on. I'll show you how to dance,' and led her away.

'I wasn't aware that you could dance,' she said as they returned to the ballroom, where a circular waltz was taking place. 'And besides, you haven't marked my card. I might be booked.'

'I can't,' he replied, looking with some trepidation at the dancers. 'And I know you're not booked. I saw you run off with Clara before anyone could ask you.'

She hid a smile. Dan knew her so well. 'Let's wait,' she said. 'The polka is next and it's more fun.' She gazed across the room, avoiding his eye. 'I want to tell you something, anyway.'

He looked down at her. His heart skipped a beat whenever he saw her. He'd been fascinated by her since their first meeting when they were only children. He had watched her constantly, gazing at her dark eyes and long black shining hair, and listening to her strange way of speaking, although that accent had gone now. His mother had eventually told him that he must stop staring at her; she was just an ordinary little girl but from another country and with a foreign mother. But the attraction never went away. He was completely smitten, totally enthralled and bewitched by her, even though he knew that his ardour was not returned. To counter his feelings, he pretended a wry nonchalance and occasional antagonistic stance towards her, which fooled nobody.

'What?' he asked.

'What?' She frowned.

'You said you had something to tell me.'

'Mm,' she murmured, and waited for the waltzers to come off the floor. 'Yes, I do, but the polka is about to start. Do you know how to do it?'

21

'No,' he exclaimed. 'Of course I don't.'

'Then follow me,' she said as the music began. 'There are only two steps to remember so it's quite easy. Take my left hand with your right. Raise your left foot behind the right, then a little jump with the right foot, then the second step, hop with your left heel, then the toe – what's the matter?'

'It's impossible,' he spluttered. 'I'll look an absolute fool.'

Jewel laughed. 'No, you won't. No more than any of the other men. Look, they're enjoying themselves.'

'Well, I'm not,' he grumbled and grabbed her arm. 'Come away. This is not what men do. Not men like me anyway.'

'Spoilsport,' she said. 'You're hopeless,' but she allowed herself to be taken off the floor.

Dan wiped his forehead with a handkerchief. 'It might be all right for Elizabeth's new husband to cavort like an imbecile on 'ballroom floor but it's not in my nature.'

'No,' she said thoughtfully. 'I suppose not. But you were the one who asked if I'd dance.'

I didn't want to dance, he thought. I just wanted to put my hand on her waist and hold her hand, but I can't even do that right. 'What did you want to tell me?' he asked sullenly.

'Oh, I suppose it could wait.' She bit on her lip as she considered. Perhaps she should wait until she'd mentioned it to Clara.

'Go on,' he said, anxious now. 'What?'

Jewel gave a huge sigh. 'Well, I'm bored. We've had all the excitement of preparing for Elizabeth's wedding, but what's next?' She shrugged. 'It's all right for you and Thomas. You've got an occupation, a business to run. But I haven't. So I've been thinking. I'm considering going away.'

Dan took a breath. 'Really?' he said casually. 'You're always away. You've only just come back from Amsterdam.'

'That's not far. You can get there in two days.' She turned to look at him. 'I was thinking of a longer trip. To America. And I want Clara to come with me.'

CHAPTER TWO

'Are your parents going?' Dan was both agitated and alarmed. If Jewel went back to America, the place of her birth, she might never come back.

'No,' she replied nonchalantly. 'I shall make the trip alone. Or with Clara if she'll come.'

'You can't!' he said vehemently. 'That's a crazy idea.'

'No, it's not. Why shouldn't I? I've travelled a lot. I know what to do. Women do travel alone. Much more than they used to, although Mama went to America when she was not much older than me. Not a word to Clara, mind. I really shouldn't have told you. Not until I'd asked her.'

Surely Georgiana and Wilhelm won't allow it, Dan thought desperately. 'Clara won't agree,' he said abruptly. 'She's too quiet, too insecure.'

'I don't believe that for one minute. You obviously don't know her. Anyway, if she won't or can't, I'll travel alone.' She gazed at him from deep, unfathomable eyes. 'I'm going, Dan. Don't doubt me.'

Jewel regretted telling him, yet she had felt compelled to. She knew how he felt about her, even though he had never voiced his feelings. But she had wanted to warn him of her impending departure. She wouldn't have wanted him to find out from someone else and be taken by surprise; she owed him that at least, and maybe whilst she was away he would transfer his affections elsewhere.

23

There would be many a young woman who would be pleased to have Dan's attention. He was a handsome man and had good prospects, though he was inclined to be moody. He and his brother Thomas and their father, also called Daniel, owned a manufacturing business that made wooden toys and furniture. They lived in the Land of Green Ginger, an ancient area of Hull, behind a toyshop run by their mother, Ruby, and had expanded their business enough to supply toyshops in the neighbouring towns of Beverley and York.

Jewel turned away, and he caught her arm. 'Allow me at least to escort you back,' he muttered between his teeth.

She nodded. 'But not a word, Dan. *Please.*'

He didn't answer. He was too wound up. He led her back towards where Clara and Thomas were in conversation, gave a cursory nod of his head and left them.

'What's up with him?' Thomas asked with a grin. 'Trod on his toes, did you?'

'Trod on his pride, I think.' Jewel laughed. 'I always say something to upset him. I can't do right for doing wrong; isn't that how the saying goes?'

Thomas raised his dark eyebrows. 'Aye, I believe so. Don't worry about it, Jewel. He's a bit crabby at times. Ma says he gets it from our da's parents. She says they were a dowly pair.'

Jewel shook her head to commiserate, but she knew Dan's moods were not just inherited; they were also down to her and her attitude towards him. But she could no more share anything but friendship with Dan than she could fly to the moon.

Thomas excused himself and wandered off to talk to some other friends, for there were lots of young people there who were well acquainted with them all, as well as older people. Grace and Martin Newmarch, the twins' parents, were prominent citizens and the wedding of Elizabeth had been a talking point for months.

'Should we circulate, do you think?' Clara said. 'Is it expected of us?'

'No,' Jewel said easily. 'Elizabeth and Patrick will do that;

it's their wedding. Let's sit down and people can come to us. Besides, I want to ask you something.'

They sat down side by side on a sofa; their gowns, which had bustle pads and wire hoops sewn into the skirts, rose up to show their white stockings, and shoes which had matching rosettes stitched on them.

'When I go travelling,' Jewel said, 'I will wear neither hoop nor bustle. I shan't wear a corset, either.'

'You don't need to wear a corset,' Clara declared. 'You have such a tiny waist it's quite unnecessary – but travelling? Jewel! Are you to abandon me as my sister has?' Her face creased in dismay. 'Where are you going? And when?'

Jewel squeezed her hand. 'I've got plans,' she whispered confidentially into her cousin's ear. 'I haven't thought them all through yet but I want to go to America and I'd like you to come with me.'

'Oh!' Clara's cheeks went pink. 'Me? You want *me* to come with you? Oh! How wonderful!' She gazed at Jewel. 'Really? Who else?'

'No one!' Jewel said gleefully. 'Just the two of us. What do you think?'

Clara hesitated. 'If anyone else had asked me I'd say we would have to have a proper grown-up person with us, like your mama or Uncle Wilhelm, but I know you'd be perfectly capable of travelling abroad without any older companion.'

'Well, thank you, Clara.' Jewel laughed. 'But we are proper grown-up people and quite able to organize a trip abroad!'

'You are, I'm sure, but I haven't been anywhere at all without Elizabeth.' Her face dropped. 'Or our parents.' She took a breath. 'Whatever will Elizabeth say when she hears?'

'She'll be madly jealous, but she can't be included now that she has a husband who can say whether or not she may do anything! We, dear cousin, are absolutely free. So do you agree?' Jewel was quite astounded that Clara hadn't raised any objections to the scheme.

'Oh yes!' Clara enthused. 'Of course I shall have to ask permission first, but I'm sure my parents will allow it. They've always encouraged us to take every opportunity for a fulfilled life; Mama especially.'

'Of course! How could I forget?' Jewel exclaimed. 'Aunt Grace published a book on the emancipation of women, didn't she?'

Clara nodded proudly. 'She did. Twenty-five or so years ago, when women were very downtrodden, and when she was very poor; before she married Papa.'

'Mm,' Jewel said thoughtfully. 'And that's when she and Mama first met. Mama said that she took Aunt Grace to public meetings and persuaded her to speak up against cheap labour and children being exploited in mills and factories.'

'They were so brave, weren't they?' Clara said quietly. 'They were going in the face of society to try to gain independence. And they did, for themselves and a few others.' She sighed. 'But not for everyone.'

'But for us they succeeded. We,' Jewel declared, 'you and I, Clara, can do whatever we want to.'

'Within reason, you can,' Georgiana said the next day when Jewel broached the subject of travelling with Clara. 'I know you are going to say that because I travelled alone all those years ago it will be easy for you and Clara to do the same. But there were many hazards, and sometimes I acted very foolishly.'

'But today, Mama, we'll travel by ship and train, not by dog cart across America as you did.' She glanced teasingly at Georgiana, whom she had once called Aunt Gianna, but now regarded as her mother. 'You've told me of your adventures so often, yours and Aunt Kitty's, that I know the stories as well as you do.'

Georgiana smiled. Not all of them you don't, my darling, she thought. There are some secrets that I haven't shared. 'We'll have to ask your papa's opinion,' she told her. 'He would be anxious about you travelling alone.'

'But I won't be alone,' Jewel exclaimed. 'Clara will be with me.'

26

'It's the same thing,' her mother said patiently. 'Clara is not a seasoned traveller as you are; and when I travelled to America I had Kitty with me, who was such a sensible girl and attended to all my needs. I know she eventually became a friend, but to start with she was my maid.'

'We won't need a maid,' Jewel said stubbornly. 'We're perfectly capable of dressing ourselves and we can use hotel laundry services.'

'Money?' her mother queried.

Jewel gazed at her pleadingly. 'I'll receive my inheritance when I'm twenty-one,' she said. 'In two months' time! Could I not use some of that?'

'You've thought it all out, haven't you?' Georgiana said. 'How long have you been planning this?'

'Almost a year,' Jewel admitted.

'And can you tell me why?' Georgiana asked. 'Are you restless, Jewel? Is this town not big enough to hold you?' I can understand if it is not, she thought. I recall so well how anxious I was to get away, to explore pastures new. To find myself and what I was made of.

'It's not that I'm not happy here at home,' Jewel explained. 'But when I was young we were always going somewhere different. To the Low Countries or Italy, or to America. And I feel that now I've finished my education I would like to see more of the world.'

'And . . . ?' Georgiana questioned. 'Something else?'

Jewel nodded and looked down into her lap and Georgiana marvelled not for the first time at how beautiful she was, her facial bone structure and slight body coming from her Chinese mother, her forthright attitude from her father and, to some extent, her and Wilhelm's determination that their adopted daughter should grow up to be an independent woman.

'And,' Jewel's voice dropped to a whisper, 'I'd like to find out more about my father and see where he is buried.'

'San Francisco!' Georgiana gazed at her, seeing again the small child who had wept for the father who, although she

27

hadn't been told, had only a few weeks to live. Georgiana had promised Edward that she would take Jewel, and look after her and bring her up as well as she would have done her own children if she had had them; which she hadn't, to both her and Wilhelm's regret. But they loved Jewel as much as if she had been born to them, although they never let her forget her heritage.

Jewel swallowed hard. 'I think it's time that I went, don't you, Mama? I'm old enough now to face it.'

Georgiana came to her and put her arms round her. 'If you feel that it is right, then you must,' she said, with a catch in her voice. 'But we should speak to your papa. After last year's financial crisis, life in America is uncertain. He'll be anxious.'

Wilhelm was indeed anxious. The previous year he had taken a ship to New York after hearing of the panic at the New York stock exchange when it closed for several days after prices tumbled. He had stayed in America for several weeks, taking steps to ensure that his own business interests were stable. All was calm in Dreumel's Creek, but the Marius Hotel in New York had many cancellations following the financial collapse and was only now recovering. He was reluctant to agree with Georgiana when she said she didn't think that it would have any impact on Jewel's intended plans.

'It might,' he said worriedly. 'There are thousands of people out of work and roaming the streets. The country is only just recovering from the Civil War. I'll be anxious about her safety – and Clara's too, of course.'

'They won't be staying in New York,' Georgiana said. 'They'll go to Dreumel's Creek and then to San Francisco. I know,' she said as he took a deep anxious breath. 'It's a long journey, but she has a need to go there and it's not only because of Edward. I feel that she wants to find out about her mother too.'

'Impossible. She'll never do that.' Wilhelm shook his head. 'There are thousands of Chinese in California. We don't even know her mother's full name!'

To Jewel he said, 'If you feel that you must go, then of course

28

you must. But we would like to check your travel arrangements and place money at your disposal, as well as give you names of people you can contact in case of any difficulty.' He saw the stubborn expression on her face; as a child she had always wanted to do things for herself, stamping her foot if she was crossed.

'It's as much for Clara as for you,' he said patiently, and Jewel gave a smile. Never in her life had he been cross with her or raised his voice to her. 'We owe that to her parents at least.'

Jewel flung her arms round him and hugged him. 'You are a darling, Papa. I promise I'll look after her.'

Martin Newmarch was very dubious about the venture at first, though his wife wasn't. She was quite sure that Clara was capable of looking after herself.

'Though I hate to say it,' Grace said in the soft voice that was so characteristic of her, 'Clara has always allowed Elizabeth to make decisions for her. Now is the time for her to flower; she has an inner strength that we have not yet seen.'

Martin smiled, kissed her cheek and murmured, 'Just like her mother, then.'

Elizabeth was furious when she heard. She and Patrick had come back from a short honeymoon in the Yorkshire Dales to find that arrangements were already being made. 'How can you even think of it, Clara? You and I have always done things together!'

'We haven't got married together!' Clara retaliated. 'You didn't ask me to join you in a double wedding.'

'But you said you weren't ready to marry anyone,' Elizabeth complained. 'If you had been we could have done, and gone off on a joint honeymoon.'

Clara shrugged. She was so excited that nothing Elizabeth said was going to make her feel guilty. 'Well, I'm going to America instead of the Yorkshire Dales.' She smiled, and her cheeks dimpled. 'And much as I love it there, I've been before. Many times! Now I'm going somewhere quite different.'

There had been much discussion about their travel

arrangements. Jewel was set on going to San Francisco, but which way they should travel posed a dilemma: by sea from Liverpool to San Francisco, which was a very long journey, or overland from New York?

'Overland,' Clara pleaded. 'But first to Dreumel's Creek. I might never go again, and I would like to see as much of the country as possible. And I do so want to meet Caitlin and Kitty. I've heard so much about them. Besides,' she added, 'if we go all the way by sea we will be with the same group of people for weeks!'

'And they might be terribly boring,' Jewel butted in. 'I quite agree. Across country will be so much more exciting.'

'Then you must promise to be very circumspect.' Wilhelm chewed on his thumb. 'You must not become involved with anyone, but keep to your own company at all times and always do things together, not alone. We will write to Ted and Kitty Allen to expect you.'

'And Dolly and Larkin,' Georgiana interjected. 'They'll want to see you, and they can tell you about Edward's early days in America.'

'We promise we'll be careful, Uncle Wilhelm,' Clara said, and Jewel nodded in agreement. 'Please don't worry about us.'

A week before they were due to depart, Jewel and Clara started to say their separate goodbyes to friends, for they didn't know how long they would be away. Their tickets for the return journey were left open. But they went together one evening to say farewell to Dan and Thomas and their parents.

'I remember the first time I ever came to the toyshop, Aunt Ruby,' Jewel said. 'Mama brought me and there was a smell of toffee and lots of lovely toys in the window.'

Ruby, an exuberant, plump and pretty woman with grey streaks in her dark hair, had been a lifelong friend of Clara's mother. Both born in extreme poverty, they now had quite different lifestyles, Ruby being the wife of a prosperous tradesman and Grace an equal partner in her marriage to

Martin and in their philanthropic work, but they had remained firm friends.

'You're so brave,' Ruby said. 'I couldn't possibly travel away from home like that.' She cast a glance at her husband, Daniel, who was sitting by the fire.

He looked up at the two young women. 'Especially not to America, she couldn't.' His voice was rather sour, Jewel thought, but then he was sometimes rather grumpy in her presence, and offhand when he spoke to her. It seemed to be only she who had this effect on him, as Clara said he was always friendly towards her, but she accepted that some people regarded her as foreign because of her looks.

Dan barely spoke to either of them, but Thomas, so like his mother, was full of enthusiasm. 'Golly, to think of you going to America, Clara! We'll miss you; both of you,' he added. 'Though we're used to you going off on your travels, Jewel.'

'But it won't be 'same without you,' Ruby agreed. 'And Elizabeth a married woman now. Everything's changing now that you're all grown up.' Her eyes filled with tears. Ruby cried and laughed easily in equal measure. 'What a silly I am! I'm happy that you're doing something so exciting, yet sad that you're going away.'

'Oh, Ma!' Thomas laughed. 'They'll be back before you realize they're gone, and they'll be just 'same as they are now. Won't you, Clara?'

'Of course,' Clara said consolingly, patting Ruby's shoulder. 'Of course we will!'

Jewel gave a slight smile in Ruby's direction and then glanced at Dan. 'I don't know,' she said huskily. 'I don't honestly know.' She gave a little shrug. 'Who can tell?'

31

CHAPTER THREE

Dan sat in the chair opposite his father after Jewel and Clara had left. He bit on his fingernails and stared into the fire.

'Go on then,' his father said at last. 'Spit it out. Summat's troubling you.'

Dan shook his head. 'Nowt,' he said, taking a deep breath.

'Shall we go and wave them off at 'train station?' his mother said.

'Not if it's during 'week we won't,' her husband said abruptly. 'We've work to do. It's not everybody who can go gadding off to other countries. Some of us have to earn an honest penny and can't go gallivanting 'world over like some folk.'

Ruby and Thomas both looked at Dan but he kept his eyes lowered and muttered, 'I shan't go.'

Thomas grimaced and was about to say something, but his mother cast a glance at him and shook her head. Later she whispered to him that Jewel and Clara were catching the ten o'clock train bound for Liverpool on Friday.

'See if you can arrange an errand or a delivery or something,' she said. 'You can mebbe make a quick detour to 'station to see them off.'

Thomas grinned. 'Thanks, Ma. I'll try. I'd like to see Clara off. She's that excited.'

'You'll miss her, won't you?' his mother said.

'Aye, I will.' He looked pensive. 'We've allus been – such pals.'

He and Clara and Elizabeth had shared their childhood, being the same age, but it was Clara with whom he had had an affinity. Dan and Elizabeth had squabbled over the same toys until Jewel had come along and captivated Dan. But now they were both going away and Thomas wondered who he would talk to and discuss the issues of the day with. Not his brother, for Dan was inclined to be opinionated and not open-minded enough to have an intelligent debate. As for his father, he had been increasingly irritable lately and not easy to talk to; he was sure his mother had noticed it too for she always seemed anxious when his father was around, trying to please or pacify him.

Ruby was indeed worried about her husband and had tried on several occasions to ask Daniel what was bothering him. She had been brusquely rebuffed, though, which generally brought tears to her eyes and apologies from Daniel.

'It's nowt,' he had said. 'You're imagining it. Give over, Ruby. I'm all right.'

She knew that he wasn't. His moodiness had grown worse over the last year and she worried that he would become like his mother, who had been a most disagreeable woman, always niggling that she had come down in the world and that her husband wasn't given his rightful dues. Because of her attitude and the lack of available work, Daniel had left home when he was seventeen and got a job at sea. Whilst he was away his mother had taken her own life by jumping into the Humber, and Ruby knew that in some way Daniel blamed himself for it.

On the Friday morning that Jewel and Clara were due to depart, both Thomas and Dan were up earlier than usual, for once coming down to breakfast before their father.

'Thought I'd deliver to Grants in Beverley this morning, Da,' Thomas said cheerfully when Daniel appeared. 'Everything's ready for me to box up and then I'll drive over. I'll be back before dinner time.'

'No need for you to go.' His father sat down at the break-fast table and Ruby served him bacon and eggs from the side

33

oven. 'I'll send Morris. We've to finish off them rocking horses for Brownlee. He wants them for Tuesday.'

'Can't Dan help with them?' Thomas was disappointed. 'I wanted to show Mr Grant those new designs of locomotives.'

His father looked doubtful. 'I don't think he'll be interested. He's doing well wi' clowns and circus stuff.'

'I – I mentioned them last time I was over there,' Thomas said eagerly. 'He said he'd tek a look at them.'

'Aye,' his father said reluctantly. 'All right. But get back by dinner and then we can all crack on wi' hosses.'

'Dinner'll be a bit late anyway,' Ruby butted in. 'Half past twelve. I've some shopping to do at 'market.'

Daniel gazed at her and then at Thomas, and gently shook his head. 'You can't pull 'wool over my eyes,' he muttered. 'I know what you're both up to. Go on then. Dan can go to Beverley, and you, Thomas, can tek half an hour to go to 'station. But come straight back. We've work to do.'

Thomas heard his brother draw in a breath. He knew Dan wouldn't want to drive to Beverley, but he had also said that he didn't want to go to the station to see Jewel and Clara off. He pushed his chair back from the table. 'I could go to Beverley this afternoon,' he said, 'if Dan and me work on 'rocking horses this morning.' He glanced up at the kitchen clock. 'It's onny just seven; we've a couple of hours. We've just to finish polishing and fit 'manes. Then there's all of 'weekend for them to dry.'

'Sort it out between you,' his father grunted. 'Now let me get my breakfast in peace.'

Dan crashed his chair back and went towards the door.

'Excuse me,' his mother said. 'Haven't you forgotten summat?'

'Sorry, Ma.' Dan's face was flushed. He came back and pecked her on her cheek. 'Thanks for breakfast.'

Ruby nodded. She knew what was wrong with Dan, but she wouldn't dream of mentioning it. Jewel didn't love him. She thought that probably Jewel didn't love anybody, not yet, but she was not the kind of young woman who would ever tie herself down to anyone quite as demanding as Dan.

When their sons had left, Daniel finished his breakfast and drank another cup of tea, then he too pushed his chair back from the table.

'What is it, Daniel?' Ruby asked quietly. 'What is it that's troubling you?'

Daniel shrugged and reached for his jacket from the back of the chair. 'Nowt's wrong. Don't know what you mean.'

Ruby came and put her arms round his waist. 'I know you, Daniel Hanson. Should do after all these years. Tell me!'

'Nowt to tell.' He avoided her eyes.

She put her hands to his face and turned it towards her so that he had to look at her. 'Truth, Daniel,' she whispered. 'We promised long ago that there'd be no secrets between us. Tell me what's troubling you.'

He sighed. 'It's her. Jewel. It's onny dawned on me over 'last few months that Dan is sweet on her. And . . .' he hesitated, 'I can't bear to think that he might want to marry her.'

'She won't have him.' Ruby's brow furrowed. 'But why would that upset you?'

He closed his eyes for a second. 'Because of who her father was—'

Ruby gasped. 'Not after all these years, Daniel! We've put all that behind us. At least,' she added softly, 'I have. But it seems that you haven't.'

He shook his head. 'I thought I had, but lately – well, it was at Elizabeth's wedding. I saw Dan and Jewel talking together and I thought—' His eyes were moist and she put her arms about him once again. 'If they should marry and I saw her every day, it'd be like a knife in my heart.'

'She doesn't know.' Ruby's eyes filled with tears. 'About me and her father. Why would she? It happened before she was born. It was another life, Daniel,' she whispered. 'We were different people then. Jewel has nothing to do with us. She's a beautiful young woman with a different background. Grace said that she thought Jewel wanted to trace who her mother was and that's why she wants to go to America.'

35

She gazed up at him and knew that she loved him as she always had; but a doubt crept in. Had Daniel always harboured resentment over her having been Edward Newmarch's mistress before she married him?

He swallowed. 'I'm sorry, Ruby. I'll be all right. Once that train has pulled out and I know she's gone.' He gave another sigh. 'I just hope that she doesn't come back.'

Ruby pulled away. 'And what about our son? Are you onny thinking about your own feelings? What if Dan does love Jewel? What about his hurt? You've forgotten, Daniel, about the hurt you felt when you thought I was going to leave with Edward.'

'I haven't forgotten,' he said quietly. 'I remember very well and I wouldn't want Dan to feel as I did. But you didn't go with him.'

'I didn't go with him because I loved *you*.' She tapped him on the chest with her finger. 'So be gentle with your son. He might be feeling 'same way as you did. The difference being that Jewel *is* leaving and leaving Dan behind.'

Clara lived with her parents in High Street in the heart of the old town, close by the River Hull. The three-storey house had once been owned by a shipping merchant and his family who lived there before removing to a life on the coast in Holderness. It had then been turned into offices before being put up for sale. Grace, who had known the house from when she was young, was desperate for them to buy it and turn it into a home again.

Clara's bedroom window at the back of the house looked over the river where the ships and barges came in and out of the Humber estuary, the larger vessels passing the wooden wharves and continuing on towards the Queen's Dock in the centre of the town, one of the largest docks in the country.

She loved to be at the centre of things, as her mother did too. The market was only a short distance from their home, and before Elizabeth's wedding Grace and her daughters

36

would walk there most days. When Martin was free he took them to the theatres in the town, of which there were many, and every October they visited the Hull Fair, always a great source of entertainment. Now, Elizabeth had left them to start her married life with Patrick, and although Clara knew she wasn't yet ready for wedded bliss, she missed her sister's companionship and excitedly prepared for her journey to fill the gap in her life.

Jewel and her parents lived on the edge of the town, in Albion Street, a street of elegant mainly Georgian town houses which Wilhelm had much admired when he first came to Hull. Within walking distance there was a subscription library, museums and public rooms, venues for philosophical debating societies of which Wilhelm was an enthusiastic member, and which almost made up for the fact that he missed his American homeland, willing though he had been to sacrifice it for the sake of Georgiana and Jewel in particular, so that she could be near her natural family.

In preparation for their forthcoming journey Jewel and Clara constantly sent messages across to each other's houses, by maids or errand boys, but eventually they were ready. In the first week in June the day dawned for their departure, and both households scurried about making last-minute checks on tickets and personal items.

'Come along, come along. We'll miss the train.' Wilhelm urged his womenfolk to hurry. Both sets of parents were travelling to Liverpool with Jewel and Clara. They would see the two young women safely on to the ship the next day and then travel back to Hull.

'We've plenty of time, Papa,' Jewel said. She knew how anxious he was about their travelling to America alone, but although no one would guess from her calm exterior she was bursting with enthusiasm and greatly looking forward to the challenge. Clara, she thought, would be the perfect companion, for she was malleable yet level-headed.

'The cab is here,' Georgiana called as the doorbell rang and the housemaid scuttled across the hall to answer it.

'Goodness!' Jewel said. 'So soon! We're only five minutes from the railway station.'

'Better to be early rather than late.' Wilhelm was in a fluster, which was unusual for him as he was generally so placid. He was also used to catching ships and trains, being such a frequent traveller himself.

'Don't worry, Wilhelm,' Georgiana said softly. 'She'll be perfectly all right. She's very prudent, and so is Clara.'

Wilhelm took a handkerchief from his pocket and wiped his forehead. 'I know,' he said. 'I'm being foolish. But I can't help it.'

Clara and her parents were just alighting from their cab as the Dreumels arrived at the railway station and the two young women waved excitedly to one another. Clara came over and gave Jewel a hug.

'I'm so thrilled!' she said. 'I hardly slept last night. I was up at six o'clock packing my hand luggage. Papa is having a fit, though. He's worried sick!'

'So is mine.' Jewel laughed. 'Now, I suggest we appear to be very calm and composed.'

'And self-assured,' Clara concurred. 'Yes, I quite agree. We don't want them worrying that we're two empty-headed young women with no idea of how to look after ourselves.'

'Which we're not,' Jewel replied. 'Oh, look! There's Elizabeth.'

A smart single-horse chaise had pulled up alongside them and Clara's sister stepped down.

'Is that her carriage?' Jewel murmured. 'Patrick's spoiling her!'

Clara laughed. 'It's compensation to appease her because I'm going to America and she isn't.'

'Darlings!' Elizabeth swept towards them. 'I had to come and see you off even though we said goodbye yesterday. Oh, Clara!' Her face puckered. 'I'll miss you so!'

Clara hugged her. 'I shall miss you too, Elizabeth. I'll write as soon as we arrive; in fact I'll write whilst on the ship and tell you whether I'm seasick!'

Elizabeth sniffled. 'Yes, do. I shall want to know everything. Oh, I'm so envious!' she said plaintively. Then she turned towards the chaise. 'Do you like my carriage?'

'It's wonderful, Lizzie,' Jewel said. 'How lucky you are to have such a husband to spoil you!'

'Yes. I am.' Elizabeth wiped her eyes. 'Patrick is a darling. So very generous.'

'Come along.' Clara's father beckoned them. 'Don't let's miss the train. It's in already.'

You see! Clara's and Jewel's glances said as they watched their fathers scurry about organizing the trunks and suitcases for the porters to carry, but obediently they followed them into the station, where the train was waiting at the platform.

'Wait! Clara! Jewel!'

The two girls turned as their names were called. 'It's Thomas!' Clara said delightedly. 'Oh, Thomas, I'm so pleased that you came!'

'I just had to,' he said. 'It's so important.' He took hold of Clara's hand. 'I'll really miss you, Clara. You too, Jewel,' he said, turning to include her.

Jewel nodded agreeably. Thomas had come to see Clara, of course. She was his special friend. She hoped he would realize just how special she was whilst she was away. 'I'll be walking on,' she told them. 'Papa is getting in a state, though he should know full well that the train won't go without us.'

She left Clara and Thomas to come on behind her, noticing that Thomas still held Clara's hand. She stepped on board behind her mother and Aunt Grace and took a seat by the window. With her gloved hand she gently rubbed the steamed glass. Clara and Thomas were standing near the door and Jewel tilted her head to look down the platform. There were still a few people milling about and porters loading luggage on to the train, but her eye was caught by a tall man standing behind the barrier. It was Dan.

CHAPTER FOUR

Jewel and Clara went on board the *Swift* the following day. They were private first-class passengers travelling for pleasure and not emigrants, some of whom were in lodging houses waiting for the ship's agents to collect them later in the evening ready for the next day's sailing.

Their parents left once they had seen them safely on board, giving them a loving farewell and much advice on what to do in an emergency. They unpacked the personal items they would need on board and arranged the cabin for their comfort during the voyage, which they had been advised would take between seven and ten days, depending on the weather. Then, putting on warm shawls, they went off to explore the ship. A steward had been assigned to look after their needs and he showed them the state rooms and dining room. After that, at Clara's request, he showed them the emigrants' dormitories on the lower deck.

'We're very fortunate, are we not, Jewel, that we can travel first class?' she murmured. 'I wouldn't want to sleep in a high bunk if the weather was rough.'

'It was rough when I first came to England,' Jewel said reflectively. 'I wasn't very old but I remember it clearly.' She turned her thoughts inward and recalled the journey with Gianna, who, she now knew, had been asked to take care of her by her dying father. She felt a sudden tightness in her chest. Though she barely remembered how Edward looked, she could still recall his warmth and love for her, and it still hurt that he was gone. *Papa*, she had cried when Gianna had told her that he had died, and Gianna had wept with her.

'Jewel?' Clara said anxiously. 'Are you all right?'

Jewel nodded. 'Yes,' she said softly. 'Perfectly. I was reminiscing, that's all.'

'Sorry.' Clara took her arm and they followed the steward up the steps. 'I don't want to intrude,' she said, when they came on to the upper deck. 'I realize this is going to be an emotional journey for you, even though you have been back to America before.'

'As a child,' Jewel agreed and thought how intuitive Clara was. 'But we didn't travel to California as we are doing this time. And of course I was so excited then at seeing Caitlin and everyone else we knew at Dreumel's Creek.' She gave a sigh. 'It wasn't until we were travelling home on the ship that I realized I'd really wanted to visit San Francisco too, to see Larkin and Dolly, and Lorenzo,' she added.

'Lorenzo?' Clara leaned on the ship's rail and looked down at the crowds of people on the dockside. 'Italian?'

'Yes.' Jewel laughed, her mood lightening. 'He was my very best friend! His mother kept a grocery store and made the most wonderful bread, and – and' – a sudden memory came back to her – 'I used to eat with them, and she brought food to my father when he was ill. I'd forgotten that until now,' she whispered. 'He was in bed, and she brought him bowls of pasta.'

Clara turned to her. 'It's good to have memories, isn't it?' she said quietly. 'And when we get to San Francisco you'll no doubt recall other events; things that you and your father shared when you were a child.' She smiled. 'I remember the first day I met you. You came to our house and Mama brought you to the nursery to meet us. She said, "Girls, this is your cousin, Jewel." We were amazed because we didn't know we had a cousin; and you were so tiny and beautiful, just like a china doll, that we immediately wanted to play with you. Oh!' she gasped. 'I didn't mean a Chinese doll. I meant one

41

of those pretty ones with porcelain faces like the kind Aunt Ruby sells.'

Jewel gave her a little push. 'I know what you mean, Clara,' she said. 'You should know by now that I don't take offence. But when we get to America there will be others who look like me; there are a lot of Chinese in America. I won't stand out as being so different as I do in Hull.'

'But you're only half Chinese,' Clara said. 'Your other half is very English. Or American.' She laughed.

'Yes,' Jewel said ruefully. 'What a hotchpotch I am!'

There was a sudden blast from the ship's funnel and they both jumped. 'Goodness!' Clara exclaimed. 'We can't be going today!'

Jewel laughed. 'You've heard of blowing off steam? They're getting ready for sailing. Oh, I can't wait. When we wake up tomorrow morning we'll be on our way.'

The sea was calm until the fourth day, when a heavy ground-swell thundered and rolled beneath them and the low grey sky erupted with lightning flashes, making them nauseous and headachy and keeping them to their cabin. The following morning the waves crashed and broke over the deck in white frothy spumes, the sky cleared to blue with white racing clouds, the air became fresher and they ventured on deck once again.

The voyage gave them the chance to get to know each other better even though they had spent so much time together in the past. Clara realized that in spite of Jewel's apparent worldliness she was quite vulnerable. Is it because she's unsure of her background, she wondered? She has no idea who her mother was and can barely remember her father. People were attracted to her and some of the other first-class passengers, mainly gentlemen, singled her out to introduce themselves. But there were others of a more bigoted nature who pointedly ignored her.

Jewel, on the other hand, found that Clara, away from her more forceful twin, had a hidden strength which was not apparent to everyone; she had a calm demeanour and tended to blend quietly into the background when with a group of people.

There was one day when from across the dining saloon came a cutting derogatory whisper of 'mongrel brew' and silence fell like a stone. Clara put her hand on Jewel's knee, for she felt that her cousin was about to rise from the table, and pressed down to stay her.

'My soup is cold,' Clara announced in a clear voice, and a steward came hurrying across, deflecting the confusion. 'I'm so sorry,' she said apologetically. 'I don't mean to be a nuisance.'

'Beg pardon, Miss Newmarch,' he said. 'I'll bring another bowl.'

The conversation at their table continued and the moment passed. 'Some people are so unfeeling,' Jewel murmured. 'Do they not realize that we are all what we are? What our parents made us?'

Clara shook her head. 'They are locked into their own small world,' she said quietly. 'They don't look outside it. You should pity them, Jewel, for their ignorance.'

But I didn't know, she thought as they continued with their meal. I didn't know that this is what happens. It must have happened before, but Jewel has never said. Clara instinctively felt protective of her cousin, who in spite of her beauty had been exposed to such malevolent prejudice.

Later Jewel spoke of it. 'It never happened when I was young, but then my parents were always there. Wilhelm was an American and therefore different and Gianna was very well travelled, so when we visited other countries in Europe we were accepted for what we were. I never thought of myself as being different from anyone else until I grew up. I was about thirteen and out shopping in Hull with Mama. I'd moved a little further down the street to look in a shop window when I heard someone refer to me as a *Chink*.'

She put her small white hands to her mouth. 'I turned to him, this boy, and asked him in a friendly manner, what

43

do you mean?' She gave a wry smile. 'For I honestly didn't know. He was with a group of other boys and although he seemed embarrassed that I had confronted him, one of the others jeered and said, your da's a Chinaman. I said no, you're mistaken, he was English and lived in America.'

She swallowed. 'Then the first one said, must have been your ma then. Maybe she was a Chinese whore.'

'Boys!' Clara said. 'I hope you walked away from them?'

'Mama came along. She'd seen I was being targeted, I think, and she sent them on their way.' She took a breath. 'Mama explained then how some people are very prejudiced about others who look slightly different.' Jewel smiled. 'And she said that also they were possibly jealous because they were so very ordinary and inadequate!'

'Aunt Gianna is such a sensible person,' Clara declared. 'And I'm sure she's quite right. But you won't have those problems in America,' she added. 'As you said, there will be many Chinese there as well as many other cultures.'

Jewel nodded doubtfully. 'Perhaps,' she murmured. 'We'll see. Come on. Let's take a stroll about the deck before bedtime.'

It was a glorious sunny morning as they steamed from the Atlantic Ocean towards New York at the mouth of the Hudson. The ship had first dropped anchor at Castle Garden Island to allow immigrants, looking for a better life in America, to disembark on to a steam tug. Clara was transfixed at the sight of the tall buildings on the New York skyline, and by late afternoon they too were disembarking on to the quay alongside the brownstone counting houses where porters loaded their trunks on to a waiting hansom sent from the Marius, where they were to stay for the next few days. The hotel was owned by Wilhelm, as was another in Philadelphia, where he was also the proprietor of a newspaper business, and one more in Dreumel's Creek, which he still regarded as home.

'Good afternoon, ladies. We're delighted to welcome you.' The manager of the hotel came from behind his desk to greet them when he heard Jewel give their names to the desk clerk.

He gave a bow. 'Is it Miss Dreumel?' he asked, and when Jewel agreed that it was, he remarked that he had been a counter clerk when she had been brought to the hotel for the first time and the under manager when she came again a few years later.

'I was very young the first time,' she said, 'so I barely remember. This is my cousin, Miss Clara Newmarch.' She turned to Clara. 'Clara, this is Mr Brady who oversees the hotel. My name is also Newmarch,' she told him. 'I am Newmarch-Dreumel, but Dreumel is quite all right.'

When pleasantries had been exchanged, Mr Brady asked about the health of her mother. 'Mr Dreumel was here last year during the crisis, but we haven't seen Mrs Dreumel for a while.'

'She's very well, thank you,' Jewel told him. 'She asked me to send her regards to you and hopes you are keeping well. Is business picking up?' She knew that Wilhelm had contacts in New York who constantly visited the hotel to assess how the business was run and if the visitors were well looked after.

'Better than it was,' Mr Brady said, 'although the depression is here to stay a little longer, I fear. Many companies have gone down. But not the Marius, I'm happy to say,' he added.

'This is lovely,' Clara exclaimed a little later, looking round the suite they were to share. There were two beds with satin coverlets and matching pillows, a plush sofa and chair and an escritoire between two windows which looked out over a small square. Two mahogany wardrobes stood against a wall with a dressing table and mirror between them. Another door led to a bathroom with a plumbed lavatory and washbasin, both of which were adorned with a lavish floral design.

'The first time I came here,' Jewel said, 'Aunt Gianna and I came from San Francisco and it was a long sea journey and very rough and I missed Papa very much.' There was a catch in her voice. 'And then . . .' she frowned as she sought to remember, 'Wilhelm was here to meet us, but Gianna was very sad. I think he'd brought her news about somebody. Anyway, we left and set off for Dreumel's Creek.' She paused and thought back.

Then she smiled. 'And we went to see the Iroquois Indians in their settlement; the men were dressed in colourful blankets and wore feathered headdresses. I was taken to play with the children whilst Wilhelm and Gianna went to some kind of ceremony. It's strange,' she added thoughtfully. 'I haven't thought of that in years; oh, I recall Horse and Dekan, they were Iroquois, but I didn't think about why we were there, and Wilhelm and Aunt Gianna – *Mama* – never mentioned it again.'

'What an exciting life you've had, Jewel,' Clara said wistfully. 'No wonder you wanted to come back. But I wonder if you will ever be satisfied with life in Hull after we return.'

Jewel shook her head and answered as she had answered Thomas when he had voiced something similar. 'I don't know. Will I ever be the same person again after this journey? Will either of us be the same, or will we change irrevocably?'

Clara gazed at her, her lips slightly apart. 'I expect to be the same,' she said softly. 'Or do you think that something might happen to change our lives? Is that what you expect?'

The light from outside the window was fading and there was just one lamp lit in the room, which cast a warm glow over the corner where it sat on a table. The rest of the room was in shadow. Her cousin, Clara thought, seemed pensive and inscrutable as if already she was returning to her unknown ancestry.

'Jewel!' she pressed. 'Is that what you expect?'

'I expect nothing,' Jewel whispered in reply. 'The journey is the reward.'

CHAPTER FIVE

They spent three weeks in New York, exploring the wide boulevards, shopping in the modern stores of Manhattan, craning their necks to see the tops of the tall buildings, strolling in Central Park and taking a boat trip around the harbour. They took a steamer along East River to watch the construction of the Brooklyn suspension bridge which had been started four years earlier to connect Manhattan with the borough of Brooklyn and replace the steam ferry. The first tower was almost completed and their guide nodded knowledgeably and said he reckoned that it would take twice as long again to finish it.

A subtle role change crept up between Jewel and Clara that first one and then the other became aware of but didn't immediately acknowledge until at last it was too obvious to ignore.

Jewel was quite used to English people taking a sideways glance on meeting her for the first time, or even whispering behind a hand about her fragile bone structure and dark eyes; but in New York attention was focused on Clara's fair, translucent skin and fine, almost white-blonde hair.

'There are so many young women like me in America,' Jewel remarked to Clara in their room after someone in the hotel had approached to exclaim at Clara's English rose complexion. 'Half-breeds. Whereas here, you are the one who'll turn heads.'

'It's so embarrassing.' Clara flushed, unused to being the

centre of attention. 'And please don't call yourself a half-breed. It's not nice—'

'But true,' Jewel interrupted.

'You wouldn't say it of anyone else, Jewel,' her cousin rebuked her. 'You are of mixed parentage, it's true.' She smiled mischievously. 'You're an oriental pearl with shades of American gemstone and—'

Jewel fell about laughing. 'And Yorkshire grit! I don't mind,' she said soberly. 'It's quite reassuring not to be noticed. To be able to merge into the background with so many other cultures and races.'

For this is what she had observed on this visit, which she hadn't noticed when visiting as a child: that there were many skin shades and accents. Dutch she recognized from Wilhelm's background, Irish from a maid who had worked for them, French from a governess she had once had; she saw Native American people who seemed lost in their own country, and hundreds of Chinese thronging the streets of New York.

'But not so many Chinese women, have you noticed, Clara?' she said after yet another excursion. 'I wonder where they are,' she mused. 'Perhaps they stay within their homes. I'd like to go to Chinatown, just to see what it's like.'

Clara pursed her lips. 'Would they mind, do you think? Or would they be offended at us looking at them in their own place?'

They had observed Chinese cigar sellers out on the streets, peddling their wares from wooden stands where small oil lamps burned, ready to light a purchase. They had seen young Chinese men carrying billboards advertising local hotels or shopping malls, but all of these were in the main thoroughfares and not in Chinatown where the majority of the Chinese population lived.

'I don't see why they should,' Jewel replied. 'We are tourists after all, come to another country to see how the residents live and work.'

Clara was doubtful, but Jewel could be very persuasive and so on the following day, which would be their last before catching the railway train to Dreumel's Creek, they set out for Chinatown.

They had asked the young under-manager, Stanley Adams, for directions, and after a slight hesitation he brought out a map of New York and showed them the way to Mott Street, which he said was the main street of Chinatown.

'You'll be careful, miss, won't you?' he said. 'And don't take any jewellery or valuables with you.' He glanced at their summer hats, muslin gowns and parasols. 'Perhaps, erm, perhaps if you wore something plainer?'

They looked at each other and Clara turned about and headed back towards the stairs. Jewel followed.

'He's just trying to scare us,' she said irritably as they entered their door. 'There's no reason for us to be afraid. It's broad daylight, for goodness' sake.'

'Nevertheless, we might be entering an area where there is not much money. The Chinese we have seen look to me as if they might be very poor. We shouldn't flaunt our possessions. It isn't fair.'

Jewel sighed but took off her hat and put on a plain bonnet and a shawl over her gown. Clara did the same.

'And sensible shoes,' she added. 'Looking at the map it seems to me that it might be a long walk.'

It was indeed a long walk from the Marius and they got lost several times traversing the grid system of Manhattan, but they realized they were approaching Mott Street as the number of Chinese people in the area increased.

They were not prepared for the sight of dilapidated slum dwellings on either side of the narrow street, or for the fact that they themselves were objects of curiosity. Residents were crowded into doorways and windows or sat on the steps of rooming houses as they passed by, and the elusive Chinese women whom Jewel had looked for hid behind beaded curtains which swayed and rattled and reminded Jewel of something from her past but she couldn't think what.

Outside the general stores, which were converted from the lower floors of the tenement buildings, wooden stalls were piled high with strange-shaped vegetables. Some looked like large white carrots, some were a shiny rich purple colour, and others they thought were either thin green beans or spring onions.

Displayed in another store window were dried mushrooms, bowls of preserved eggs, dried shrimps, packets of rice and long thin pale crisp strands which Jewel said were noodles, and bundles of wooden chopsticks tied with string. Outside the store a squat shopkeeper sat smoking a bubbling pipe which emitted a sweet and spicy tang that tickled their nostrils and made them sneeze.

'Do you think it's opium?' Jewel murmured as they waited for a rickshaw and a waggon to pass before crossing the road.

'Yes,' Clara said. 'It is. I've smelled it before.'

Jewel turned an incredulous face to her. 'When?' she asked.

Clara took her by the elbow and turned her about to go back the way they had come. 'I once went with Mama to visit a woman in difficulties and her grandmother was there – the woman's grandmother, I mean – and she was smoking a pipe. It had such a strong smell it made me dizzy. Mama said it was opium and it was very common at one time to smoke it for pleasure and not only for medicinal reasons.'

An elderly Chinese man barred their way. He gave several deep bows and asked in a sing-song, melodic voice if he could help them. 'You want medicine?' he asked. 'You want potion? I take you to my store and give you anything you want for illness, for pain in your joints, ache in your limbs or trouble in your mind.'

'No, no,' they said in unison. 'We're visitors,' Clara hastily explained.

He bowed towards Jewel. 'You are not visitor. You are seeking something.' He shook his head. 'You not find it here. Not in New York.'

There came a sudden call in a language they didn't understand. A Chinese woman was standing in the doorway of a rooming house and beckoning.

'We have to go,' Clara said, but Jewel hung back as if mesmerized.

The man bowed again several times. 'My daughter says I must go in. The soup is ready.'

Jewel stood and watched him shuffling towards the house. 'He could be my grandfather,' she murmured.

'I don't think so.' Clara took her arm. 'He's quite different. His face is a different shape, more round than yours, and why would he be in New York? Wouldn't he be in California?'

Jewel looked back, and then she sighed and shrugged. 'I didn't mean he *was*, or even might be, my grandfather,' she said. 'I meant he was about the age that my grandfather would be.'

'*Great*-grandfather, I should think,' Clara commented. 'He's ancient, much older than my grandparents.'

The incident unsettled Jewel. How did he know I was seeking something, she thought? What did he see in me that told him that? She was pleased that on the following day they were to move on to the next leg of their journey to Dreumel's Creek. And after that? She gave a deep sigh. After that they would begin another journey to take them – her – to who knew what? She was eager and yet anxious; would she find out about her mother, and, if so, in doing so would she also find out more about herself?

Early the next morning they were driven to Grand Central railroad terminus and the manager of the Marius himself accompanied them to see them board the train which would take them on part of the journey to Dreumel's Creek.

Since 1850 there had been an enormous expansion of the railroads, built mainly by Chinese labourers and Irish navvies. There was now over thirty thousand miles of track, but it did not yet run into Dreumel's Creek.

'I wish you a good safe journey, Miss Dreumel, Miss Newmarch,' Mr Brady said, after overseeing the stowing of their luggage. 'You should be in Dreumel's Creek before nightfall, but if there is any delay I recommend that you stay the night in Woodsville; that's the stop where you depart the train and catch the coach for the last leg of your journey.'

They thanked him and settled down; there would be two changes but they would travel by train for six or more hours. They had the compartment to themselves and sat opposite each other so that both had a view out of the window. They divested themselves of their coats and took shawls out of their bags to drape around their shoulders in case of any draughts. Their travelling gowns were plain, with only petticoats beneath them and no hoops, but even so their full skirts touched and rustled against each other. Jewel's was cherry red and Clara's turquoise, and the young women wore co-ordinating bonnets which they removed as soon as the whistle blew and the train began to shunt out of the station.

'I can't read,' Clara said, gazing out of the window. 'Even though I've brought books. I just don't want to miss a thing.'

The environs of New York spread for several miles. New highrise buildings soared into the sky and they craned their neck to see the workers perched like black crows on the tops of the girders.

'I've brought *Little Women*,' Jewel said, taking a book out of her bag. 'Louisa M. Alcott,' she read from the spine. 'It's about a family of American girls whose father went to fight in the war and they and their mother had to fend for themselves.'

'I'll read it after you, if I may,' Clara said. 'I've heard of it. It will be interesting to read it whilst we're on American soil.'

The train headed west on the long journey into Pennsylvania and in mid-afternoon they changed trains to travel towards Fort Duquesne, once a trading post in an area where, a century before, the English had fought the French and the Indians, and now the city of Pittsburgh had put down its roots.

They were travelling through wilderness country towards the Appalachian mountains, where creeks and wooded valleys lined either side of the railroad track and explosive scars showed on the rocky hillsides where engineers had blasted to smithereens anything that stood in their way. The National Road system too was even now snaking its way across the Appalachians to Ohio, although its citizens still preferred the canal routes and tributaries of Lake Erie to transport their goods.

They were travel-weary when they reached Woodsville but both agreed that if there was a late coach to Dreumel's Creek they would get on it and rest the following day.

'Papa has written to the Dreumel Marius,' Jewel said, as they waited for a porter to unload their luggage, 'so our rooms will be ready for us, though I expect that Kitty and Caitlin might want us to stay with them in Yeller Valley. They have a hotel too,' she added. 'You know that Kitty travelled to America with Mama when she first came out here?'

'I recall Aunt Gianna telling us about her.' Clara smiled. 'They had such adventures, didn't they, just the two of them riding across the mountains on horseback! How very daring they were! Twenty years ago how different things were: no trains as far as this but only waggons or dog carts.'

'And no National Road. I think she'd like to come back,' Jewel said musingly. 'She becomes quite introspective when she talks about that time. That's when she met Papa – Wilhelm, I mean; she met my real father some time later.'

The last coach was due to depart in an hour, so they booked their seats and went in search of something to eat, then walked about to stretch their legs before boarding for the last part of their journey. They were very stiff after the long train ride, and the road to Dreumel's Creek, which was originally a waggon trail, had many potholes and deep wheel ruts. The driver was obviously anxious to finish his day in record time and the coach rattled and swayed at breakneck speed, shaking them and the two other passengers about like sacks of old bones.

Jewel gazed up at the towering mountains above them where the sun was slowly sinking, colouring the sky to red, orange and yellow and casting deep shadows on the valley below.

'Up there, look.' She pointed the direction out to Clara. 'That's where Mama and Kitty rode into the valley for the very first time. They didn't come by waggon trail but were shown the Indian way by a trapper.'

'How romantic!' Clara breathed.

Jewel nodded. 'Yes. I do believe it might have been.'

CHAPTER SIX

Jewel slipped into a slight doze, but Clara, wide awake, continued to gaze out of the coach window even though as darkness was falling it was now difficult to see. Ahead of her the road ran in a straight line over the plain and appeared to come to an end against a mountain wall, and she puzzled as to how they would go any further.

As they travelled on towards the apparent end of the visible road, Jewel stirred. 'Are we nearly there?' she murmured.

'I don't know,' Clara said. 'The road seems to disappear into the face of the mountain.'

Jewel smiled. 'Then we are nearly there. When I came back the last time, Mama said that I should close my eyes and there would be magic and when I opened them we would have arrived. Try it,' she teased.

Clara shook her head. 'No. I want to see what happens, for it seems to me we are going to crash into the mountain!'

The other passengers smiled. 'That's what we thought when we came the first time,' the man said. 'And that's what appealed to us. Now we're planning on coming to live here in this hidden valley. It's hidden even though everybody knows it's here. Our names are Bert and Sarah Thompson. Do you live here?' he asked Jewel.

'No,' she said. 'We're visitors from England, but have family friends here. My name is Jewel Dreumel and this is my cousin Clara Newmarch.'

'Are you a relation of the original Dreumel?' Sarah Thompson asked curiously. 'I understand he lives in Europe, or did I hear that he'd died?'

'He certainly didn't die,' Jewel said. 'Wilhelm Dreumel is my father – my adoptive father,' she added.

'Look!' Clara said. 'We're starting to turn. There's a corner after all.'

The horses were slowing, moving only at a trot as a sharp corner appeared ahead of them, and the passengers felt the pull as the driver reined in and steered into the mouth of the mountain, which opened up to reveal a road wide enough for two waggons to pass each other safely. A broad creek ran alongside the road and half a mile further on a stone bridge crossed over it.

'Oh, if only it were not so dark,' Clara began, but as she spoke a thin sliver of silver moon appeared in the night sky and the waters of the creek glinted in its light. So it is a magic place after all, she thought, and I must be careful what I wish for.

The coach pulled up outside the Marius, which was a double-fronted, two-storeyed timber-framed building with a wide overhanging portico supported by a pair of painted wooden columns. A wooden bench was placed on either side of the doors.

The driver got down and opened the coach door. 'Here y'ah, young ladies. The Dreumel Marius.'

The Thompsons stayed in their seats. 'We're going on to Nellie O'Neill's hotel,' they said. 'We've booked a room for a couple of days and are going to look for a building plot.'

'Then we'll see you again,' Jewel said. 'We'll be coming to visit Miss Nellie and Isaac.'

Wilhelm and Georgiana had impressed upon her that they must be sure to pay this particular visit. Isaac had been with the original team when Wilhelm had first come to the valley and begun the search for gold. He was well past his first youth even then and too old for further prospecting, but Wilhelm had employed him as a guard to watch over the camp, promising him a stake in any gold if they should find it, which they did.

Then along came Nellie O'Neill, who was keen to open a saloon bar in what was then a burgeoning settlement. She and Isaac had met previously and in his heyday he had been sweet on her; together they now ran the popular bar and rooming house in Dreumel's Creek. Often they could be heard haranguing one another, but that they were fond of each other there was no doubt.

'We'll go tomorrow after we've rested,' Jewel said as they followed the driver with their luggage up the steps from the boardwalk and into the hotel. 'I just can't wait to see everyone, but especially Kitty and Caitlin. We write, you know, Caitlin and I, and yet I hardly remember what she looks like.'

'You'll recognize her, I expect,' Clara murmured. She was very tired. The day's travelling had exhausted her. Whatever will I be like when we travel to California, she thought?

They were greeted by James Crawford, the manager of the Dreumel's Creek Marius, but he was young and newly appointed and therefore hadn't met Jewel on her visit when she was a child.

'I'm delighted to meet you, Miss Dreumel,' he said, 'and you too, Miss Newmarch. I'd hoped that your father might have accompanied you. I was looking forward to meeting him again.'

'When did you last see him?' Jewel asked.

'When he came to Philadelphia a year ago, during the crash. I'd heard he was in town and approached him, asking for an interview. I was in the hotel trade but wanted to rise up the managerial ladder. He said he'd get in touch if a position should arise.' He smiled enthusiastically. 'And, man of his word that he is, he did! He wrote to me from England offering me the post of manager here. Everybody wants to work with Wilhelm Dreumel,' he added.

'That's good to know,' Jewel said, and thought how like her father it was to take someone on trust after one meeting. She wondered if he had been influenced by the fact that

James Crawford was of mixed race, white and possibly Native American Indian, judging by his raven-black hair and lean face.

They were shown to adjoining rooms on the first floor by a uniformed bell boy and followed by a maid who came to turn their beds down and bring fresh water jugs.

'My room is charming,' Clara called through to Jewel. 'There's a canopied bed with a patchwork bedspread, and a lovely vase of flowers on the bedside table. And muslin curtains!'

'So has mine.' Jewel came to join her. 'Except that my bed-spread is rose and not green like yours. I don't remember any of this,' she said. 'But of course I wouldn't.'

Supper was brought to their rooms: slices of cold chicken, hard-boiled eggs, tomatoes, and a pot of English tea and china teacups to drink from.

'There's Mama's influence,' Jewel said as she poured. 'She said that English tea was something she often longed for when she lived here.'

When they had finished eating they undressed and pre-pared for bed, but first Clara looked out of her window. Their rooms were at the front of the hotel overlooking the creek and she could hear the rush and gurgle of the water. Its source was somewhere high in the mountains and the stream came down first into the neighbouring Yeller Valley, which, Jewel had told her, had also been a secret place, approachable only by climbing the mountain peak and descending the other side until Wilhelm and his team, including Ted Allen, Caitlin's father, had blasted their way through, releasing the waters of the creek which had previously spouted through a narrow opening in the mountain wall and simultaneously finding gold as they did so.

The evening was warm; she could smell tobacco smoke and hear the low gruff tones of men's voices. She guessed that they were sitting on the front porch below them, perhaps discussing the events of the day. It was a comforting, pleasur-able sound, she thought, as she climbed into the feather bed, like old friends joining together in companionship.

They both slept soundly, exhausted by the travelling but waking refreshed. They bathed and dressed and went downstairs for breakfast, where they were served with eggs, bacon, muffins and piping-hot coffee. The day was sunny, with a heat haze over the mountains, so Jewel suggested they first of all visit Nellie and Isaac and then in the afternoon hire a cabriolet to take them to Yeller Creek.

'It's not that it's too far to walk,' she explained. 'But it will be too hot.'

They took parasols and walked the short distance to Nellie's hotel. Jewel explained to Clara that the building was the original miners' longhouse.

'Mama said it was all very basic when she and Kitty first came. There were no facilities at all; the men bathed in the creek, and,' she lowered her voice, 'she and Kitty had to dig a hole in the ground – you know,' she nodded significantly, 'for—'

'A privy, you mean?' Clara had no qualms about such discussions. She had visited enough poor houses in Hull with her mother to know about primitive conditions.

'Yes. And then as the town grew, Papa rented the longhouse to Nellie, added on another storey and it became a rooming house.'

'Fascinating,' Clara said, gazing about her as they walked.

The town was built along one side of the creek, but, where some areas delved back towards the mountains, squares with houses or stores on three sides had been built, with the road running into them and room for waggons or carts to pass or turn. Many of the buildings were raised on stilts and all had boardwalks in front of them, and she guessed that this was a precaution against winter snow cascading down the mountainside or a swollen creek overflowing. New buildings were still going up and some had land in front to make a garden plot.

On the other side of the water, between areas of white fencing, cows and sheep grazed on lush grass and small copses of cottonwood trees were well managed for the animals' shelter when the weather became too hot. Beyond the pasture, the land leading towards the mountains was mainly rough scrub, scanty cottonwood trees clustering more thickly as they climbed the rocky hillside and bleating goats and chickens roaming unheeded.

Across the front of Nellie's rooming house was a sign proclaiming, in large white lettering, *Nellie's Place. Best lodgings in town*. Outside the door sat an old man wearing a wide hat and smoking a pipe.

Rising to his feet as the two girls came up the steps, he tipped his hat, revealing very little hair, and took his pipe out of his mouth. 'How de do, ladies? You looking for h'accommodation? We're pretty full up, but ah reckon we can find a room.'

'We're not looking for a room, Isaac. It is Isaac, isn't it?' Jewel said. It could be no one else, she thought. Though it was over ten years since she had last seen him, she would have known him anywhere.

He rubbed his chin and looked from one to the other. 'Well, I'm danged,' he said. 'Do I know you young ladies? Am I so old that I don't remember?'

'Sure you remember, you old dawg.' A strident female voice came from the open doorway. 'If it ain't Miss Jewel herself.' Nellie, resplendent in purple, came to meet them with her arms outstretched. 'Why, honey,' she said. 'If you ain't the prettiest gel I've seen in a long time.'

She gave Jewel a smacking kiss on her cheek and held her at arms' length. 'Ain't she just beautiful, Isaac?'

She turned to Clara, standing shyly to one side. 'And here, jest look at your friend.' She put out her hand to Clara, who gave her hers. 'My, my! Here's a true English rose. Pardon me, ma'am, but how d'ya get that skin? Is that because of the rain in England?'

Before Clara could answer, Isaac broke in. 'That ain't that little gel I took fishing?' he said, looking at Jewel. 'Why, you were only this high.' He put his hand level with his waist.

Jewel laughed and leaned to kiss his leathery cheek. 'I've

grown a bit since then, Isaac. This is my cousin Clara,' she said, hooking her arm into hers. 'She was just dying to meet you both.'

'I was.' Clara smiled. 'I've heard so much about you that I feel as if I know you both already.'

'Come along in.' Nellie turned towards the door, but Clara glanced at Jewel.

'Could we sit outside? Here on the bench? I'd love to do that, and watch people go by, and the creek, and . . . everything,' she said. 'It seems such a nice thing to do.'

'Sure we can,' Nellie said. 'Isaac, you go along and ask Clemmie to bring out some tea. Proper English tea, mind,' she added. 'With my best china.'

They sat for about an hour whilst Jewel gave the old pair all the details they wanted to hear about Wilhelm and Georgiana.

'I sure do miss them folk,' Isaac said gruffly. 'Bill Dreumel just about saved my life, and as fer Miz Gianna and Kitty, well, they were the best thing to happen to us in Dreumel's Creek, until Nellie came along.' He grinned, and Nellie gave him a little shove with her elbow.

Clara sat half listening to the conversation. She felt the warmth of the sun now high in the blue sky as she watched the activities of the small town. Waggons piled with timber trundled by and women driving dog carts looked up and gave a wave as they passed and either Isaac or Nellie lifted a hand in response. Women with baskets over their arms and small children by their side walked along the dusty road, and Clara guessed that they were going to the general store which she and Jewel had passed on their way here. It had appeared to sell everything anyone would ever need, from butter and cheese to wheelbarrows and sweeping brushes.

They were offered another drink, this time of cold lemonade, and then Jewel said they must be getting back to the hotel, for they were expected for lunch and then they were going to see Kitty and Caitlin.

'You give those gels a great kiss from me,' Isaac said. 'I gave her away, you know,' he told them. 'Kitty, I mean. When she married Ted Allen. Such a little gel she was when she arrived, but what a cook! Saved my life, she did.'

'Everybody saved your life, you old dawg,' Nellie said. 'I don't know how you ever survived without us women.'

'Well, I guess I wouldn't have.' Isaac chewed on his empty pipe. 'Jest a dirty digger is what I was till I was rescued.'

Nellie gave a huge sigh and shook her head. 'You'd never think he was once a handsome buck,' she said softly. 'All the girls in—' She stopped, as if suddenly aware of her listeners, but Jewel and Clara saw the impish affection in her smile as she responded to the grin and wink that Isaac gave her.

After luncheon they asked Mr Crawford to hire them a cab to take them to Yeller Creek, but as Jewel was making the request Clara suddenly said, 'Could we hire a trap? I've seen some ladies driving them and it looks such fun!'

'We have one at the hotel, Miss Newmarch.' James Crawford smiled at her and she thought how very handsome and charming he was. 'We keep it for our visitors. You're very welcome to borrow it.'

'Oh, please!' Clara said. 'Do let's, Jewel.'

Clara had never driven or ridden a horse. Having been brought up in a town where everyone walked unless going on a long journey, it wasn't considered necessary, although, she mused, her sister, Elizabeth, now had her own chaise and managed to drive it around the town.

Jewel agreed, and the trap and a docile pony were brought to the front of the hotel.

'I'll drive,' Clara said, taking the driving seat. 'It looks easy. Ready?' She laughed. 'This is the next part of my adventures. I've sailed on a ship, travelled in a carriage across the plains of America and now I'm driving a horse and trap.'

She raised the whip she had been given and cracked it above the horse's back, and smiled triumphantly as the mare responded by breaking into a trot. They set off down the bumpy road towards Yeller Creek.

Jewel opened her parasol. She had ridden on horseback and had taken the reins of a trap occasionally when she had travelled abroad with her parents, but she thought of transport only as a means of getting from one place to the next and not as something exciting in itself as her cousin obviously did. And yet they were both on a journey. Clara was looking forward, seeking places she had never seen and people she had never known. Whilst I, she mused, I am on a journey into the past in order to find myself.

CHAPTER SEVEN

They drove across the Western Bridge, over the rushing waters of the creek and on to Pike's Road, which took them into the town of Yeller Creek.

This town was quite different from the one they had left behind. Dreumel's Creek was tranquil, and had an air of contentment. It was quiet and peaceful and life appeared to move slowly. It seemed to have always been there, as though it had materialized gradually without pain or distress, discord or labour, and the buildings, the homesteads and the residents had put down their roots and settled themselves into permanence. No one, visiting for the first time, could possibly guess at the hardship that had made it what it was.

Yeller was a bustling, busy town, and here it was as if the stores and workshops, the houses, hotels, saloons and lodging houses, had been hurled up in a great hurry as the new owners rushed in to make their mark. Which they had, but each mark was different; there was no conformity or town plan as there had been with their neighbour.

When the rock was blasted through from the other valley, killing Pike, the man who had lit the touch paper, word soon got around that gold had been found and that good land was available. First came the miners and diggers who struck the rock or panned the waters of the creek in the hope of becoming rich; then came the settlers looking for land to build on or farm. They staked their claims and put up temporary tents and cabins. Not all stayed; those impatient for riches moved on, selling their stakes to others, but those who stayed sent for their families and built permanent structures in which to live.

Inevitably there were some who, greedy for wealth, built more on their plot than was feasible; they put up two or sometimes three wooden buildings tightly packed together, without the benefit of a hand's width between them, sold them to merchants and shopkeepers who had hurried to the developing town, and then moved up the valley and built for themselves on a larger plot.

It was a hotchpotch of a town, although with a certain charm, and anything that was not available in Dreumel's Creek could be found in Yeller, from merchandizing and eating houses to theatres or brothels. Outside the town were sawmills and flour mills, abattoirs and blacksmiths, carpenters, lumber yards and breweries.

Jewel was cool beneath her parasol but Clara, driving, felt her clothes damp on her body. Her bonnet felt hot on her head and perspiration trickled down her face. She drew in with considerable relief when they saw the sign of their destination: *Yeller Creek Hotel*.

It was a similar size and style of establishment as the Marius with its overhanging portico and columns, but the Yeller Creek Hotel had blue-painted shutters at the windows and tubs of bright flowers on each side of the door. The latter was wide open, and they could see a cool dark hall with mirrors on the walls.

They tied the horse to a hitching rail and went inside. Clara took off her bonnet and shook her hair free.

There was no one behind the reception desk, but as they rang the brass bell a girl of about eighteen came running bare-foot down the stairs. Her dark red hair hung in curls down her back and around her fresh and glowing smiling face. She stopped on seeing the visitors.

'Hello,' she said. 'Welcome to Yeller Creek Hotel.' Then

she put her hand up to shield her eyes against the brightness coming in from behind them.

'Jewel! Is it you?' She took a breath. 'Is it really you?'

'Yes!' Jewel laughed. 'It is,' and was almost bowled over as Caitlin rushed towards her with her arms open wide, swept her up and swung her round and round until she was quite giddy.

'How lovely you are!' Caitlin exclaimed as she stopped her whirling. 'How beautiful! Oh my!' She turned to Clara. 'And this must be Clara.' She put her hands to her mouth. 'What an ass you must think me! But I've been waiting and waiting and every day thinking this would be the day when you'd come.' She gazed wide-eyed at Clara. 'It's good to meet you,' she said. 'I'm so sorry for my greeting. I was just overcome at seeing Jewel after so long.'

Jewel stepped towards her and gave her another hug. 'And I'm so pleased to see you, Caitlin. I would have known you anywhere!'

'Sure you would,' Caitlin said wryly. 'My hair is a giveaway every time.'

'As my face is too,' Jewel responded. 'But let me introduce you properly. This as you guessed is my cousin, Clara Newmarch, and this, Clara, is my good friend of so many years, Caitlin Allen.'

Clara dipped her knee, but Caitlin put out her hand and grasped Clara's.

'Oh my,' she said again. 'You sure look so *English*!'

'I know,' Clara said, smiling impishly. 'That's what everyone has said since I arrived. So that's *my* hallmark!'

'Good afternoon.' Another voice came from a doorway off the hall and they turned to see a woman who could have been Caitlin's older sister, but was unmistakably her mother, Kitty.

'Aunt Kitty!' Jewel's mouth trembled and she felt her eyes prickle with tears. 'It's been far too long,' she said. 'Far, far too long since we last met.'

Kitty squeezed her tight. 'It has,' she said. 'We've missed you.' She gave her a kiss on the cheek. 'You were just a bairn when we saw you last and here you are, grown into a beautiful young woman.'

Clara wondered about her accent as she went forward to be introduced. It could be Hull, or it could be a mixture of something else. She dipped her knee and, as if automatically, Kitty did the same.

The older woman laughed. 'Old habits die hard,' she said. 'I haven't done that in many a year.'

'You lived in Hull, I believe, Mrs Allen?' Clara said. 'You were a friend of Aunt Gianna?'

'Gianna! Does she still go by that name? She was Miss Gregory when I first knew her, then Miss Georgiana.' Kitty laughed and Clara could see where Caitlin's exuberant spirit came from. 'I think it was Isaac who first called her Miz Gianna and it suited her so well.'

She put her head to one side and gazed at Clara. 'And you're the daughter of Martin Newmarch and his wife, who was Miss Grace.' She nodded sagely. 'She was much admired when I was a girl,' she said. 'Especially by those of us who had so little. She was quite exceptional. I expect she still is?'

'Yes,' Clara said proudly. 'She is. They both are.'

Kitty glanced from one to the other. 'You're both lucky to have parents who allow you such freedom.' She seemed to give herself a mental shake. 'Come in, come in. Let's have tea and cake and scones and jam and pretend we're in England again.'

'Do you miss being in England, Aunt Kitty?' Jewel asked later as they sat drinking tea in a pleasant room overlooking the creek, with comfy chairs and pictures on the walls.

'No,' Kitty said firmly. 'There's nothing and no one to miss, apart from your mother,' she added. 'And I do miss her. Without Georgiana I wouldn't be here, enjoying what I have. Sometimes I wake up and can't believe what we've achieved. I'm running my own hotel, I own a bakery; I have a handsome husband, a lovely daughter and a fine son.' She smiled. 'And in England I was a servant, just as Ted was. We'd never have accomplished so much had we stayed in Hull.'

She might, Clara thought. My mother did; but then she re-considered. It was Georgiana's influence that had changed her life too. But women have to want to change. They have to feel that desire for themselves and catch hold of any opportunity.

As they were chatting, Ted Allen came in to join them. He had heard their voices as he went through the hall.

'Da! Da. Look who's here!' Caitlin jumped up to greet him, putting her arm round his waist and bringing him forward. She was full of energy, Jewel thought, and did everything at top speed. 'Can you guess who this is?' Caitlin stood her father in front of Jewel, who rose from her chair and smiled at him.

She wouldn't have known him if Caitlin hadn't said. The last time she had met Ted Allen had been when she was ten, but he hadn't been around much as he was always so busy. He was an important man in Dreumel's Creek as well as in Yeller, where he and Kitty had built the hotel, but in any case she and Caitlin had always had so many things to do and play at that she had seen very little of him. One thing she did know was that he had come to America with her father: her real father, Edward Newmarch.

Ted put out his hand. 'Hello, Jewel,' he said, and he still had a trace of a northern English accent. 'It's nice to meet you again. Been a long time!'

Jewel leaned forward and gave his cheek a kiss. 'It's nice to see you too,' she said, her voice suddenly cracking. 'All of you. It's so lovely to be here again with you all.'

Then she remembered he hadn't met Clara and introduced her. 'This is my cousin Clara Newmarch.'

'Ah!' he said, his eyes flickering over Clara. 'Pleased to meet you, Miss Newmarch.'

'Clara, please,' she said.

He nodded. 'I remember your father. I met him a few times when I was working for his brother Edward.' He gave a sudden grin. 'Seems like a lifetime ago. I hope he's well?'

'He is,' Clara told him. 'And he asked to be remembered to you. He's heard of all your achievements through Uncle Wilhelm.'

Ted pursed his lips. 'Has he? The world is not so large after all, then.'

He sat down with them and asked about their journey on the ship and the train.

'The railroad is getting closer to Dreumel,' he said. 'Another couple o' years and it'll be here. Not into the valley,' he added. 'I've seen the plans and they're going to build a station out on the plain, where I dare say another town'll spring up. I've staked a claim already,' he said shrewdly. 'It'll be a good investment for Robert and Caitlin.'

'Have you, Da? Really?' Caitlin was astonished. 'What'll we do with it?'

'Sell it,' he said. 'Or build another hotel.' He turned to Jewel. 'So if you wait another ten or more years before coming back you might find another town. What name will it have, I wonder?'

'I might not wait so long,' Jewel said thoughtfully. 'It depends on what I find out on this journey.'

He looked at her curiously. 'Find out?' he said. 'Are you looking for something?'

'Yes,' she said softly. 'I am. I'm looking to find out who I am. About my beginnings. About my mother.'

Ted Allen whistled softly through pursed lips. 'But that'd mean going to California. That's where your father was when Georgiana found him.' He frowned slightly. 'You know, don't you, that I came to America with him – as his valet?' he asked.

'Yes, I did know,' she said. 'I think I know most of my father's history, though I can't recall when I was told, only that I always knew. Mama—' She smiled. 'Gianna always explained my background and made sure I never forgot it. I'm so grateful to her for that.'

She paused, looking thoughtful, and they all gazed at her, unwilling to interrupt her train of thought, knowing that she had something else to say.

'But,' she went on at last, 'I know nothing of my birth mother. Only that her name was Tsui, and that my father met her in a bar in California where they both worked.'

Ted shook his head. 'I've always found that so difficult to comprehend,' he murmured. 'Your father working in a bar, I mean, knowing him as he once was. But in this country anything can and does happen. Even a leopard might change his spots.'

Jewel gazed at him. Ted, having been in her father's employ, would have seen him in a different light from his friends and family. She had been told by Gianna that he was a good and loving father, and from the little memory of him that remained she knew it to be true.

'But my mother,' she said, thinking out loud. 'That's what I need to know. To find out about her.'

'But you've only just arrived,' said Caitlin. 'You can't go off to California. Not yet!'

'I don't intend to. I want to show Clara this part of the country before we leave, and there's no hurry. We might even come back if my mission is successful.'

Jewel smiled at Clara. Clara had declared when they had first set out on their travels that she wanted to see *everything*.

Caitlin was staring at her with her lips slightly parted. Then she looked at her mother and then her father.

'Da!' she said, and licked her lips. 'Ma! I want to go with them. Can I? Can I go to California?'

CHAPTER EIGHT

'What! Don't be ridiculous.' Ted was completely taken aback. 'No. No, you can't.'

'Why can't she?' Kitty asked quietly. 'If Jewel and Clara can go, why can't Caitlin?'

'Go where?' A boy of about sixteen came into the room. He was tall, taller than Ted, and nearer his father's colouring than his mother's, but he was undoubtedly their son.

'Is this Robert?' Jewel said. 'You won't remember me.'

He shook his head. 'I don't, but as Caitlin has talked of nuthin' else but Jewel coming, I guess that's who you are.'

He raised a hand in greeting, and on being introduced to Clara he blushed to his hair roots. Caitlin grinned roguishly at his embarrassment.

'So where does Cait want to go?' he asked. 'And if she's going, why can't I?'

Jewel took a breath. The last thing she wanted was to be responsible for a boy of Robert's age. Neither, if she was honest, was she totally sure about Caitlin. But fortunately Ted put his foot down very firmly.

'You can't and that's the end of it. Jewel and Clara are off to California and Caitlin wants to go too.'

Robert shrugged. 'Well, I guess I don't want to go anyway,' he muttered, with a look that said quite plainly that the last thing he would want to do was travel anywhere with a bunch of women.

'So can I, Da? Please,' Caitlin asked persuasively.

'You haven't been invited,' he said bluntly. 'It's manners to wait to be asked. Jewel has her plans and they don't necessarily include you. Besides, your ma needs you here.'

Caitlin looked chastened and Kitty said apologetically, 'I'm sorry, Jewel. Of course Ted is right. This is an experience of a lifetime for you and you must continue with the arrangements as you have decided. Now, would you like to look round? The hotel has changed considerably since you were last here.'

When Jewel and Clara returned to Dreumel's Creek that evening the journey passed mostly in silence. Kitty and Caitlin had shown them the bedrooms and dining saloon in their hotel and the coming journey to California was not mentioned again. They were waved off with bright smiles and promises that they would all meet again the following day.

'It isn't that I don't want Caitlin to come with us.' Jewel came through into Clara's room. 'It's just . . .'

Clara sat on the bed and, swinging up her legs, stretched out and sighed. 'I know,' she said. 'Caitlin's lovely, but at eighteen still quite immature. Would we have to look after her?'

'That's just it.' Jewel sat on the edge of the bed. 'I don't know her as well as I thought I did. She's full of fun and enthusiasm, but would she miss her mother if she came with us? I realize that this is an adventure for you, Clara, but—'

'I know why we're here,' Clara interrupted. 'I'm aware of your mission, Jewel, and I appreciate how important it is to you. It's not just a very special expedition for me; it's going to be a life-changing journey for you.'

Jewel patted Clara's arm. 'Thank you,' she murmured. 'I knew you'd understand.' Her smooth pale brow creased into a small frown. 'But I feel so wretched. I don't want to hurt Caitlin's feelings by saying no, but neither do I want to say yes.'

Clara sat up. 'Then don't say anything, not yet. Leave it for a few days until you know her better. She might turn out to be the perfect companion for our journey!'

Jewel laughed, her mood lightening. 'I've got one already,' she said.

During the following month, Jewel and Clara explored the territory and often Caitlin went with them. The two girls had borrowed mild-mannered and sturdy mustangs and Caitlin rode her own spotted Appaloosa, a present from her parents last year, she said, on her eighteenth birthday. She was very knowledgeable about the area and knew the best tracks to take when going up the mountains.

One morning they were standing outside the Marius debating where to go when Caitlin rode up to meet them. She told them she wasn't free to come with them as they were expecting an influx of guests and she'd promised her mother she'd help in the hotel. But she suggested a route where they would find the best view of Dreumel's Creek.

'Go to the end of the valley and cross the water by Lake's Bridge, then follow the path up the mountainside. The horses are sure-footed, so you needn't worry about the steep incline.'

'Lake's Bridge?' Jewel said. 'I didn't know it had that name.'

Caitlin pressed her lips together and gave a little shrug. 'It's what I call it.'

'Why?' Clara asked. 'Why lake? It isn't a lake.'

'Oh no. Not that kind of lake. It was someone's name.' Caitlin's cheeks went pink. 'I used to see him when I was little; except that people said I imagined him.'

'What do you mean?' Jewel said. 'Who was he?'

'He was a ghost.' Caitlin frowned a little, as if waiting for their cynicism or laughter. When it didn't come, she added, 'No one else ever saw him, but Ma said that I did because I was part Irish and probably believed in that kind o' thing.'

'So your mother believed you?' Clara said softly.

Caitlin nodded. 'I think she did, but Da always made fun and so she didn't say much.'

'Who was he?' Clara asked. 'Or don't you know?'

Caitlin bit on her lip, but before she could speak Jewel

interrupted. 'I know who he was! He was the Indian who told Papa about the valley. He brought him here, otherwise no one would ever have found it!'

Clara smiled. 'I believe you, Caitlin. I think he comes back to see if the valley is being looked after.'

'Yes!' Caitlin gave them an all-embracing smile. 'That's what I think too; but the odd thing is that whenever I saw him he was always riding back over the bridge towards the mountain, and he always turned round as he reached the high ridge. I used to wave to him,' she said sheepishly, 'and he always lifted his hat and waved back.'

'What a wonderful story.' Clara's voice was soft. 'I wish I could see him.'

'He might not come any more,' Caitlin said seriously, pleased that someone gave credit to her tale. 'I was only a child and it was when we lived in one of the cabins in Dreumel. It's a store now, run by a Chinese medicine man.' She pointed to a row of shops. 'The one that stands back from the others.'

Jewel and Clara gazed in that direction. 'We'll take a look,' Clara said, and Jewel added that if they were going up the mountain they'd better be moving off as the morning was getting hotter.

'Watch out for black bears,' Caitlin called as she turned her mount to head back to Yeller. 'Keep to the path and you'll be safe.'

'Black bears!' Clara gasped. 'Is she serious?'

'Yes,' Jewel said. 'I'm sure she is.'

They were both wearing large-brimmed hats but even so the sun beat down on their heads as they rode through the pastureland and into the thick scrub, and they were pleased to reach the tree line. The pines here gave green shelter and as they rode higher and the forest grew thicker it became cooler and darker. Presently they reached a rocky clearing and wheeled the horses round so that they could look down.

'Mama came in this way,' Jewel murmured. 'On her very first visit to Dreumel. She told me that she thought it the most beautiful place she had ever seen.'

74

'And so it is,' Clara said softly, almost afraid to break the spell of the moment. Below them the waters of the creek in the valley sparkled in the sunlight, the small wavelets tossing and foaming as they surged. The source was high in the mountains beyond Yeller Valley into which it also ran; down the middle of the township, through a gap in the mountain wall and beneath the Western Bridge into Dreumel's Creek. They couldn't see the town of Yeller as it was hidden by the mountain range, although they could see Pike's Road leading towards it; but Dreumel, with its wooden houses and cabins, its stores and hotels, lay there before them.

'To think that just a few short years ago there was nothing here,' Clara said, after a moment. 'And yet the town seems permanent, as if it's been here for ever. I don't mean like English towns, not like Hull with its old buildings, cobbled streets and ancient heritage, but somehow enduring and settled.'

'Yes,' Jewel said. 'It does. And yet Yeller doesn't. Yeller looks as if it has been thrown up in a great hurry.'

'Why is it called Yeller?' Clara asked. 'It's an odd kind of name.'

Jewel smiled. 'Because of the gold. One of the men who discovered gold in the creek named it Yeller Valley. Seemingly the creek was glistening with the *yeller stuff*!'

They turned about and continued up the track, but now the going was more difficult. The path seemed to be little used and in places all but disappeared, and they had to make detours to avoid fallen trees or duck their heads to dodge overhanging branches.

'I think we should go back,' Clara was beginning, but then as Jewel, who was leading the way, halted and lifted her hand in warning. 'What?' Clara whispered.

'Shh.' Jewel put her finger to her lips and Clara stared about her, her eyes open wide, looking and listening intently.

There was something; but afterwards, when they discussed it, they both agreed that they could say nothing conclusive or significant about the occurrence, or even if there had been

75

one. But they both felt a presence; a whisper in the trees, a sough or faint breath, like a sigh, which encircled them and compelled them, without either saying a word to the other, to simultaneously turn about and return the way they had come.

CHAPTER NINE

The next day they told Caitlin what had happened, but no one else. They knew she would believe that something strange had occurred even though they couldn't really say what it had been.

'It was a sense of a presence,' Clara said.

'An unexplained *atmosphere*,' Jewel added, 'and I'm not in the habit of being fanciful.'

'Do you think it was Lake?' Caitlin asked eagerly. 'Perhaps he's still living in the forests – or at least his spirit is.'

'But why would his spirit stay here, when there are thousands of miles of forests? Oh, we're being silly!' Jewel said. 'It was probably a bear that we heard, and when it saw us, it moved off.'

Clara agreed somewhat reluctantly that perhaps it could have been that, but Caitlin, in spite of not having been there, was more inclined to think that it was Lake returning to his old hunting lair.

'This area once belonged to the Indians,' she said, 'so maybe they are watching over us. Don't tell anyone else,' she urged them. 'They'll laugh, just as they used to with me.'

'Caitlin,' Jewel said, changing the subject, 'Clara and I are leaving at the end of the week. I'm really sorry,' she began, but Caitlin brushed her apologies aside.

'Don't worry,' she said. 'Pa's just bothered about me going anywhere without him or Ma. He's forgotten that Ma was younger than me when she came to America with Aunt Gianna all the way from England. In any case, the hotel is fully booked with visitors for the next few weeks and I probably can't be spared; people are coming to look at land for building new homes and businesses.' But she gave a huge sigh and her lips turned down, and they understood how disappointed she was.

Two days before they were due to leave Caitlin took them on a journey to the end of Yeller Valley and up the mountain range. It was a hard climb for Jewel and Clara, unused to riding such a long way or in such heat, and after an hour they begged to stop and get down to ease their aching muscles and take a drink.

'Sorry,' Caitlin apologized. She seemed not at all bothered about the heat and quite cool beneath her hat, cotton shirt and skirt. 'I keep forgetting that you're not as at home on horseback as I am. I've been riding since I was – oh, I dunno, maybe two or three years old. My first horse was called Hetty.' She turned to Jewel. 'She was once your ma's.'

Jewel smiled and nodded. 'I recall Mama telling me about Hetty.' Then she fell silent as a faint memory disturbed her: the long sea passage to England when she was very young and Gianna telling her anecdotes and stories to keep up her spirits. She remembered, too, feeling very lost and frightened and knew now that it was because she had lost her father; her real father, Edward, not Wilhelm.

They were standing on a rocky promontory and looking down towards Yeller. Clara, whose fair skin was beaded with sweat, said they must move back under the pines to find some shade or they would suffer sunstroke as the heat beat down even through their hats.

They found a sheltered spot beneath the pines and drank from their water flasks and ate some of the food that had been packed for them. Slices of juicy water melon refreshed them and rye bread and beef gave them energy.

After a half-hour rest they moved off again, climbing in single file ever higher until, when they looked down into the valley, Yeller looked like a toy town, the pitched roofs shaped like the serrated teeth of a saw and people mere dots on the ground. They could also see the scars on the lower mountainside where diggings had been made in the search for gold; a broken windlass and abandoned and dilapidated shacks remained, perched at perilous angles, memorials to lost hopes and dreams.

'Why did everyone build so close to each other in Yeller?' Clara asked. 'There's still a great deal of spare land.'

'Well, I dunno,' Caitlin said. 'I guess they like being friendly. Or maybe folks couldn't afford a bigger plot.'

I wouldn't like it, Clara thought. It's like the terraced housing in the courts of Hull where the poor live cheek by jowl with their neighbours and can hear every cough or cry through the walls. It's not healthy, she mused, and neither do I think it's safe to be so close.

The mountain trail was becoming steeper, and when they glanced up they saw that the pines were much thicker. The trees looked impenetrable and they decided to turn round and make their way back again.

'I hope the horses don't find it difficult,' Jewel said nervously. 'The path is very steep.'

'Not they,' Caitlin said emphatically. 'Just let them go at their own pace. They're very sure-footed and can travel for hours.'

Jewel thought that was probably true, but both she and Clara were coming to the end of their endurance, being hot, tired and aching as they clung on down the precipitous and narrow route.

At one point Caitlin, in front, reined to a halt and held out her arm, her hand held high, indicating that they should stop. Fifty yards in front of them a black bear appeared out of the undergrowth and ambled across their path, seemingly oblivious of their presence, even though the horses snorted in fear. Jewel turned round to look at Clara, who puffed out her cheeks and gazed back with wide scared eyes, but didn't dare to make a sound.

'How did you know there was a bear?' Jewel asked Caitlin a little later when the track evened out and wasn't so steep, and she could at last let out a breath which she had been holding in, tight with dread. 'I didn't hear anything.'

'Nor did I,' Caitlin said. 'But my horse did. She was becoming nervous and agitated and I knew it wasn't the route but had to be something else. There are always bears up here,' she added soberly, 'but they're not a menace unless they're frightened or have young with them. Anyway, come on. Another hour and we'll be home.'

Jewel and Clara were so stiff that they could barely dismount, though Caitlin simply sprang out of her saddle. She turned to help Jewel down and then laughed as Robert ran down the steps of the hotel to assist Clara.

'He's in love,' she murmured to Jewel. 'He's been waiting for her.' She grinned mischievously at her brother, who glared at her but kept hold of Clara's elbow as he shepherded her into the hotel. She was glad of his support. She felt as if she might never walk unaided again.

As they sat comfortably drinking lemonade and eating cake which Kitty had ordered for them, Caitlin suddenly excused herself and dashed away, saying she'd seen someone through the window to whom she must speak immediately.

'I'm beginning to think that Caitlin might have been an intrepid companion after all,' Jewel murmured, and Clara nodded in agreement. 'She's quite level-headed; and although she appeared to be unconcerned about the bear, it didn't mean that she was unaware of the danger.'

'You're quite right,' Clara said. 'She knows the area, of course, and what to expect from it. Which we don't,' she added.

Through the glass they could see Caitlin speaking animatedly and enthusiastically to a young man and pointing in the direction of the mountain range they had just traversed.

'But it's too late now.' Jewel shook her head. 'And besides, her father said she couldn't go.'

They decided to go back to the Marius for supper, start their

80

packing for the journey and then spend the next day at their leisure. Caitlin said that she would join them for breakfast and stay for the day, and Kitty said that she and Ted would come over at some time to say goodbye, whilst Robert seemed totally miserable.

'You'll have to put him out of his misery, Clara,' Caitlin whispered out of Robert's hearing. 'Can't you tell him that you've got a young man back home in England?'

'Which she has,' Jewel teased. 'Thomas.'

Clara blushed. 'Thomas is my best friend, after you, Jewel, as you know very well. He's *not* my *young man!*'

'He thinks he is.' Jewel smiled. 'He adores you.'

'As Dan does you,' Clara retaliated. 'He's obsessed by you.'

Jewel shrugged. 'I haven't even thought of Dan whilst we've been away. It's as if we're living in another world.'

Clara didn't answer. She'd thought of Thomas most days and realized that she was missing him. They were of compatible temperaments, enjoyed similar things and didn't necessarily need to talk but appreciated companionable silence. He would, she knew, like to experience America as she was doing, but, also like her, wouldn't want to make it his home. The country was too big for her, so immense and spacious that she felt small and insignificant within it. She wasn't homesick, but she missed all the people she loved and had left behind.

When they left Yeller Valley Hotel she saw Robert, a shadowy figure in the hall; she called to him and said that she hoped he would be able to come and say goodbye before they left Dreumel. She put her small hand in his large one and left it there and said how pleased she had been to meet him and his family.

He blushed and his eyes watered as he bit his bottom lip and she was pleased that she had been kind to him, for he seemed considerably brighter. She guessed that one day he would tell his friends that he had once loved a young Englishwoman and would boast that he thought she probably felt the same way about him.

'I can't start packing tonight,' Jewel said when they returned to her room. 'I'm too exhausted.'

'So am I,' Clara agreed. 'The air is so heavy. Do you think there'll be a storm?' She looked out of the window, but the sky was blue and the sun still shining even though it was starting to slip behind the mountains. 'It would be good to have some rain to clear the air.'

Jewel lay on her bed and fanned herself. 'It would, but I don't think there'll be any.'

'Did you notice how dry the timber was in Yeller?' Clara said, continuing to gaze out towards the creek. 'The buildings, I mean. There was one, I think it was a carpenter's shop, where sparks were falling from the chimney – the stove pipe, I mean – and landing on the roof.'

Jewel didn't answer, but turned her cheek on the pillow and closed her eyes.

'Shall I order supper to be brought upstairs?' Clara said. 'I don't think I can be bothered to change. I have no energy. We could bathe and put on our night clothes—'

'And have a picnic,' Jewel said sleepily. 'Yes, that's a good idea.'

'I'll go down, then.' Clara turned towards the door.

'Ring the bell,' Jewel murmured. 'The maid will come up.'

Clara looked at Jewel, who was almost asleep, and decided to go downstairs and ask whoever was at the desk to send up something light: chicken or poached eggs, bread and butter and a pot of tea. Then she would go outside for a moment to get a breath of air, for there was none in their bedrooms in spite of the windows' being open.

James Crawford was standing out on the boardwalk as if he had had the same notion. He turned when he heard her, and smiled a greeting. He was without his jacket and his crisp white shirt was open at the neck, while his black sleek hair was tied with a cord at the back of his head. He immediately began to button up his shirt.

'I beg your pardon, Miss Newmarch,' he apologized. 'Forgive

my state of undress. I'm not yet on duty and came out for some air.'

'Please,' she said. 'Don't worry on my account. It's so hot, isn't it? Do you think it will rain? Weather as hot as this in England, which I must say is very rare, is generally followed by a deluge.'

He shook his head. 'My instinct is to say that it will not. But I hope I'm wrong.'

She was curious about him. His skin was the colour of dark honey, and smooth. Jewel had said that he was an Indian and Clara wondered how he had come to be in this job.

'Instinct?' she asked. 'Do you set much store by it? As far as weather goes, that is? I know that some people consider that they have a kind of sixth sense, or intuitive impulses.'

He laughed and his dark eyes shone with merriment. He invited her to sit down on the bench outside the door, and seated himself beside her. 'Are you asking me in my capacity as a Native American, Miss Newmarch? For if you are I must answer that my forefathers would say that I have abandoned my ancestry and its culture and adopted the life of the white man.'

'You are teasing me, Mr Crawford,' she objected, but light-heartedly. 'I was merely asking your opinion. And you must have one,' she added wryly. 'As an American, whether or not you are Indian.'

He gazed sombrely at her for a second; then he smiled. 'I can only tell the weather by the habits of the birds and animals. They behave differently, as indeed we do. We scurry home if we think it's going to rain. Our dogs and cats and horses become nervous if there's thunder in the air, and cows and sheep take shelter.

'I was brought up on a reservation,' he went on. 'The very one that Miss Jewel visited when she was a child; there were old men there who could foretell what was coming – wars or weather. My real name is Jim Crowfoot. I left when I was thirteen. I thought that the outside world had more to offer me. I took what work I was offered and made enough money to improve my education and gain a position of trust.'

'Admirable,' she said softly.

He gave a slight shrug. 'But I am still an Indian, a second-class citizen, and – in some people's eyes – unworthy. '

'They are the ones who are unworthy, Mr Crawford,' she said softly, and touched his hand. 'Not you.'

For a moment they gazed at each other; then he broke the spell by standing up and saying jocularly, 'Thank you. But I still don't know if it's going to rain!'

Clara and Jewel ate their supper at a table by the open window in Jewel's room and gazed down at the creek where men were fishing. A few people were walking slowly by: women with shopping baskets and men with spades or leather bags. Waggons and traps were trundling along the road, but it seemed as if the town was closing down, the heat inducing torpor in everybody and everything.

'I'm going to bed,' Clara said at last. 'I shall read for a while.'

'So shall I, in a moment,' Jewel said. 'I feel more refreshed now after my nap.' She poured herself more tea. 'I think that tomorrow I might walk up the road to see the Chinaman,' she said, adding drily: 'He might be a relative!'

'Jewel.' Clara turned from the door to her room. 'You don't have to joke. Not to me. Are you worried about what you might find out about your mother?'

'A bit,' she said, not looking at her. 'No. Not worried. More nervous, I suppose.'

'I spoke to Mr Crawford earlier,' Clara told her. 'He told me that his real name is Jim Crowfoot and that he was brought up on the reservation which you visited when you were a child. He said that some people consider that he's unworthy, because he is an Indian, even though he's educated.'

Jewel sighed. 'They would,' she said softly. 'There's always prejudice against anyone who is different. But it's strange, isn't it? Especially when the country once belonged to his people, and then everyone came and staked a claim in it, the English,

84

the Dutch, the French, even the Chinese, and called it their own.'

'Yes,' Clara said. 'It seems unfair. Goodnight. I'll see you in the morning.'

Jewel sat for an hour, meditating, watching the sun sink down below the mountains, turning the waters of the creek to deep gold. But strangely it was still light even after the sun had disappeared, a golden glow flickering and lighting up the night sky. How odd, she thought. Not a display of aurora borealis, surely? Can it be seen from here?

And then she heard voices shouting, loud cracks and explosive noises like gunshots, and became aware of an acrid smell. Smoke! Something was on fire. She stood up and pushed the lower casement to its maximum and leaned out. Men were running about and carts and waggons were being hastily trundled out into the road and having horses hitched to them.

She gazed along the valley towards Yeller and saw the bright orange sky lit with yellow tongues of flame, plumes of thick smoke and bright crackling sparks hurling up into the darkness.

'Clara!' she cried. 'Wake up. Yeller is on fire!'

CHAPTER TEN

Clara almost fell out of bed in her haste. She joined Jewel at the window of her room, and gasped in horror as she saw and smelled the smoke. 'What can we do? We must get dressed and see if we can help.'

'Yes, of course,' Jewel agreed. 'The people! The children.'

They rushed to put on gowns and boots. 'I knew it!' Clara said as they ran down the stairs. 'I said the buildings were set too close together. It's a shanty town. A positive fire trap! Mr Crawford!' she called as they reached the hall. The manager was issuing instructions to his staff even as he was hurrying out of the door. 'Is there anything we can do?'

'Stay here!' he said. 'It will be too dangerous to go into Yeller. Perhaps you could help the staff with the evacuees from the fire?' He paused on the steps. 'The news is that the blaze is spreading. People will have lost their homes. They'll need somewhere to stay. Prepare for them to come here.'

He raised his hand and rushed away, and the two girls stared at each other.

'Caitlin – Kitty! Everybody!' Jewel breathed. 'Oh, I do hope they're all right. What if the hotel has caught fire?'

Clara bit on her lip so hard she could taste the blood. 'It might be all right,' she said. 'It's set apart from the rest. There's a space on either side. Room to get round to the back. And they have water barrels.'

Most of the male hotel staff had gone to Yeller and the

female staff were bringing more seating into the lounge area; guests from the hotel awakened by the noise were wandering downstairs, some still in their night clothes; Clara and Jewel found their way to the kitchens.

'Can we put out cups and saucers or tumblers?' Clara asked a flustered maid. 'People will want something to drink when they arrive.'

'Yes please, ma'am,' the maid said. 'I'll get out extra coffee pots and grind some coffee. The crockery is over there.' She pointed to a corner of the room where a huge cupboard stood against the wall. 'Mr Crawford said to do what I could to accommodate everybody.' She wiped her forehead. 'I don't know if he meant the sleeping arrangements or not, but we don't have many spare rooms. Most are occupied.'

'We can share if necessary,' Jewel murmured to Clara. 'But perhaps it isn't as bad as we fear.'

But it was worse. The first waggon rolled up and tipped out its passengers, mainly women with children who came into the hotel weeping and crying that they had lost everything. Many hadn't had the time to grab anything but the barest essentials as they rushed from the scene of the disaster.

'My house has gone,' a woman wailed. 'And our store. My husband's trying to salvage what he can, but it's useless.' She wrung her hands in despair. 'There's nothing left.'

They could do or say little to comfort them. Jewel and Clara took a tray of coffee and cold drinks round and gave the children cake and biscuits.

'Do you know anything about the Yeller Creek Hotel?' Jewel asked someone. 'Our friends live there.'

'Ted and Kitty Allen?' the woman said. 'I saw the fire waggon dousing the building. They're trying to save those that haven't caught fire yet. Some of the others are down to ash already. Even some of the forest is burning.' She gazed curiously at Jewel. 'Are you one of the daughters of Sun Sen? The Chinaman?'

Jewel stared back at her. She shook her head, lost for words.

87

'Some say there'll be a lynching,' the woman continued. 'They're saying the Chinese are stealing from the burnt-out houses.' She pulled a small boy towards her and roughly wiped a cloth across his sooty face. 'Folks always want somebody to blame.'

'I don't know him,' Jewel said hoarsely. 'I'm a visitor. From England.'

'Ah!' The woman nodded. 'Then I guess you're not related. He runs a laundry in Yeller. Or he did. I saw the fire had took hold of his place too. But he'll start up again. They always do.'

James Crawford came back on the next waggon. He said he was superfluous in Yeller and had come back to arrange accommodation for those who had lost their homes.

'Can I have your attention, please?' He stood on a chair so that everyone could see him. 'The church hall is being prepared to take you right now. There will be mattresses to sleep on and food and drink. Some of the residents of Dreumel are prepared to take into their homes those of you with infants, or the elderly. Please go to the church hall now and give your names and say how many there are in your family. We shall endeavour to keep you housed together as best we can.'

As he got down from the chair, they all felt a huge reverberation followed by a rumble. People cheered. 'Thank the Lord,' a woman said, and another shouted, 'Rain! Glorious rain! This'll put the fires out.' But there were mutterings that although the rain would put out the fires, it would also make it difficult to clear up the mess that had been left behind.

James Crawford appeared to be listening intently and glancing anxiously towards the door. A man came rushing in. 'That ain't thunder,' he shouted. 'That's paint and oil drums exploding. The paint shop has just gone up! Blown to smithereens!'

Just about everybody dashed outside. Jewel went ahead and Clara and James Crawford followed more slowly. A huge column of black smoke licked by an incandescent blaze lit the sky. Everyone took a breath; some moaned, others could be heard muttering prayers.

Clara wept. Tears ran down her cheeks as she thought of the people who might be hurt as well as those who had lost everything. She felt a hand on her elbow and turned to see James Crawford looking down at her.

'Everyone had been accounted for when I left earlier, Miss Newmarch,' he said quietly. 'The paint store had already been abandoned.'

'Are you sure?' she whispered.

'As sure as I can be.' He gave her a small smile. 'Don't distress yourself. The people here are of hardy stock. They'll rebuild. Quicker than you might imagine.'

'It will take years,' she said, wiping her eyes. 'Years and years.'

He shook his head. 'Months! If I were a betting man I'd stake my fortune on it.'

She gave a watery snuffling laugh. 'And how much is your fortune worth, Mr Crawford?'

He gazed at her and she saw how dark, almost black, his eyes were. In the half-light of the porch she saw his true self, the Indian.

'Not enough to capture fair lady,' he murmured.

Clara felt herself blushing. Had she made another conquest to add to Robert? Unlike Robert, however, who was just a boy verging on manhood, James Crawford was a most presentable man and she had felt an attraction towards him on their first meeting. Why is that, she thought with a quickening of her senses? Is it because he's handsome? Or is it an appeal of opposites? Perhaps it's because I have never come across anyone like him before.

He kept his eyes on her. 'I wonder,' he began softly, 'if I might ask—'

Clara licked her lips and swallowed. 'Yes?'

'Might I ask if you and Miss Dreumel would assist with setting up the hall? Names must be noted down, so that we know where everyone is, and what help they need. The hotel's administration staff will help in the morning if required, but there are other things for them to do tonight.'

'Of course,' Clara responded immediately, and wondered why she felt disappointed.

'It is perhaps an imposition,' he went on. 'You are a guest, after all, but you seem so level-headed and practical.'

Clara sighed. 'Yes,' she acknowledged. 'I am.'

'Oh, Clara! You're such a do-gooder!' Jewel accused, when her cousin told her what she had agreed they would do. 'I'm exhausted. I need my bed.'

'I know,' Clara agreed. 'I'm like my mother. But it will only take us perhaps an hour, two at the most. Think of those poor people who have lost everything. And unlike them, we can sleep in tomorrow; we have nothing planned.'

Jewel took her arm. 'Come on,' she urged. 'I'm only teasing!'

As they walked down the steps of the hotel, there was a terrific crack of thunder, real thunder this time; the heavens opened and it began to pour with rain and they had to run.

The church hall was large enough to take at least a hundred people and already the residents of Dreumel were bringing in straw palliasses and mattresses, pillows and sheets, as well as food and drink. There were plenty of chairs stacked against the walls and many of the homeless were gathering these up and placing them in groups, making their own small family colonies.

James Crawford had given Clara a sheaf of paper and pencils and they made an attempt to clarify who was who and how many children were with each family, so that if anyone came looking for them the information was to hand.

'You've done this before!' he said admiringly when he came over an hour later to check if they were all right.

'Yes,' Clara admitted. 'I have. A few years ago in Hull, the town where I live, a flax warehouse caught fire. Spontaneous combustion, it was decided. I went with my parents and sister to assist with the evacuation of residents in the area, as it was feared the fire would spread to the neighbouring houses. Fortunately the damage was contained as the fire waggon came very swiftly with the hoses. There are often fires in Hull. Some of the buildings are very old and the timbers dry.'

James Crawford frowned. 'But the houses in England are built mainly of brick, I understand? Brick doesn't burn as fast as timber.'

'That's true,' she agreed. 'But the old houses are packed very closely together, just like in Yeller; the difference being that Hull is a port town on an estuary, and there's plenty of water available.'

'There will be changes in Yeller,' he told her. 'Already the men are setting up a committee to discuss a new town. Ted Allen is heading the committee and says he will insist on fire lanes between the buildings. His son came looking for you, by the way, to assure you that they were all safe.'

'Is there much damage?' Jewel came across to join them.

'The town is destroyed apart from a few buildings,' he said. 'The Allens' hotel is all right and some of the buildings on the outskirts of the town, but the centre is devastated, apparently. We shall know more in the cold light of day.'

'Well, the rain will douse the flames,' Jewel said. They could hear the heavy drumming on the roof of the hall.

He nodded. 'And there will be a sea of mud in the morning! But at least there's no loss of life. As far as we know.'

Jewel and Clara stayed until three in the morning, making lists, helping with drinks and ensuring everyone was comfortable as possible, and then, as people were settling down to sleep in the makeshift beds, they decided that they would go back to the Marius and fall into bed too.

They were both exhausted, but when they arrived back at the hotel they found Isaac talking to Crawford, who was listening to him with a serious expression.

'So I'm danged as to where they are,' Isaac was saying. 'All I know is that they ain't in their beds and nobody has seen them since yesterday at breakfast when they said they were

91

going again to look at land in Yeller that they'd taken a fancy to.'

'I'm sorry,' Mr Crawford replied. 'But I have no idea whether they've been here or not, and don't know why they would. I can't recall anyone mentioning them.'

Clara and Jewel paused. 'Is there something wrong?' It was Clara who spoke and Jewel gazed questioningly at Isaac.

'Why, you gels might remember them,' Isaac said. 'Couple o' folks who said they rode in with you on the coach the day you came. Man and wife; he's middling height, she's what you might call plain, but nice enough to talk to.'

'Yes, we remember them,' Jewel said, and Clara nodded in agreement.

'So what about them?' Clara asked.

Isaac lifted his hat, which he always wore, even indoors, and scratched his head. 'They hired a couple of hosses yesterday and went off towards Yeller, but they ain't come back for their supper or their beds. I've asked around Dreumel but there ain't nobody seen them and I can't get into Yeller to ask about.'

'But it's the middle of the night, Isaac,' Jewel said. 'How is it they were not missed before?'

'Well, they were missed at supper,' he repeated, 'but we guessed that they'd eaten out someplace else, like in Yeller. There's plenty of places they could eat – old Joe's or Mary Lou's or even Ted Allen's place – but it was when the gel went to turn back the sheets and mentioned they weren't there, and then the fire.' He scratched his head again. 'Well, Miss Nellie got kinda worried and said I should go and ask around. And nobody's seen hide nor hair of 'em. They've just disappeared.'

CHAPTER ELEVEN

Hull

'Summer is galloping on.' Georgiana stood looking out of the window. 'It's been very warm today; in another month we'll be in the hottest part of the year.'

They had finished supper and were in the sitting room where they always took their coffee. Wilhelm looked up from his newspaper. He could always tell from Georgiana's voice when something was troubling her, even though she would not admit to a worry. She preferred to think through a difficulty before discussing it with him. She was a strong, determined woman, but since Jewel's departure she had seemed unwell; yet when he asked if she needed a tonic, she had laughed and said no, she was probably suffering a general malaise as women sometimes did, though she had never thought it would happen to her. He knew, though, or thought he did, what it was that saddened her.

'You miss her, don't you?' he said softly. 'Well, so do I. But Jewel hasn't gone for ever. She'll be back.'

Georgiana turned and smiled. 'How well you know me.'

'Of course.' He reached out his hand, and she came towards him and clasped it and then sat next to him. 'After so many years together I know when you're happy and when you're sad.'

He is the dearest man in the world, she thought. So sensitive

93

to my feelings. She gazed at him and saw how his hair was now more silver than brown, and the tiny wrinkles at the sides of his eyes, which showed whenever he laughed, which was often. He was ten years older than she, fifty-five to her forty-five. She had been sad that she hadn't given him a child, but he had said tenderly on many occasions that they did not need a child to cement their love. And they had Jewel, whom they considered as their own.

'And you are restless,' she said. 'I know that about you too. You've been very unsettled since Jewel went away.'

He had been so very edgy that they were no sooner home after seeing Jewel off on the ship than he had insisted that they travel to Amsterdam for a short holiday. It was cold and wet and they were both miserable and returned home to Hull within a few days. A week later he suggested that they go to the south coast and tour the area. But after some time there, he wanted to be home again in case there was news waiting. Which there was, telling them that both Jewel and Clara were having a wonderful time, catching up with everyone and renewing friendships.

'I am restless, it's true,' he admitted. 'When I travelled to America last year I realized how much I had been missing it; oh, I'm not saying that I didn't miss England too, but that was because you were not with me on that occasion. But—'

'England is not your homeland,' she interrupted softly. 'Your roots are over there.'

He nodded. 'They are,' he said, and smiled as he added, 'But I have transplanted very well, and that is because of you and Jewel.'

'And now, because Jewel has gone back to *her* homeland – for that is what it is, even though she perhaps doesn't realize it yet – it has unsettled you again?'

He sighed and picked up the newspaper, which he had dropped to the floor. 'It has. But I'll get over it.'

Georgiana rose and crossed the room to ring the bell. 'Would you like a brandy with your coffee, Wilhelm?' she asked.

94

When he didn't answer but kept his eyes glued to the news-paper, she said again, 'Wilhelm! Brandy?'

He looked up, but his eyes were glazed and his lips parted. 'What? Erm, yes. Georgiana—'

'What is it? Are you unwell?' She was concerned. He was never ill, but he looked decidedly pale and he had put his hand to his face as if in some distress. 'Wilhelm. Tell me!'

He closed his eyes for a second. 'There's news,' he said huskily. 'Of a fire. In Yeller Valley. It says that the town is completely destroyed.'

Georgiana sank down beside him. 'No,' she whispered. 'When? When did it happen?'

He shook his head. 'It doesn't give a date. It says last week. My God! What if they've been caught up in it?'

Georgiana's mouth was dry. 'But – they're in Dreumel. Staying at the Marius.' She put her hands to her mouth. 'Kitty and Caitlin! The girls might have decided to stay with them. What shall we do? *Wilhelm!* What shall we do?'

He got to his feet. 'I'm thinking. I'm thinking! We mustn't panic. We must assume that everything is all right.'

He was interrupted by the maid knocking on the door.

'Coffee, Annie, please,' Georgiana said, and Wilhelm added, 'And please bring my outdoor coat.'

'Where are you going?' Georgiana asked. 'To see Martin and Grace? I'll come too.'

'No. No. I'm going to send a cable.' He ran his fingers through his hair. 'But to where? They'll not get it at Dreumel's Creek. New York! The Marius. Brady will know what's happening and he can send an overland telegraph to Crawford in Dreumel. Or Philadelphia!' He was scratching around for ideas. 'The news office will know.'

Wilhelm still owned the *Star* newspaper in Philadelphia and they had telegraph connection there. Why hadn't they been in touch? They knew of his involvement with Dreumel's Creek and Yeller Valley. Great heavens, they'd announced the finding of gold all those years back. He'd even agreed to an interview, a feature article. Against his better judgement, it had to be said. He wasn't a man to court publicity for himself.

'Will you get through tonight?' She was buoyed up with tension. Sick with fear.

'What time is it? Seven o'clock,' he answered himself and chewed on his lip as he ruminated. 'The Hull Exchange will probably be closed. Perhaps I could catch a train to London and send a cable from there. It might be quicker. London's the hub of communication.'

That's what he had done the previous year during the American financial crisis when he couldn't get through from the Hull telegraph office. Then he had written a hasty letter to Georgiana and caught the next ship to New York.

'Wait, wait!' she beseeched him. 'We must first go to tell Martin and Grace. Martin might know of someone who could arrange for us to telegraph from Hull.'

Wilhelm sat down again and put his head in his hands. 'Yes. Sorry. You're right. He knows many people in authority.'

They cancelled the coffee and the maid brought their outdoor coats and hats and they set off immediately towards town, walking briskly even though each realized that no matter how they hurried they could not influence what was happening thousands of miles away.

They were shown straight into the Newmarches' cosy sitting room. Grace had sewing in her lap and Martin had a leather briefcase on the floor beside him and a sheaf of papers in his hand. They both rose as Georgiana and Wilhelm were shown in.

'No, please. Don't get up,' Wilhelm said. They were old friends and had no need to stand on ceremony. 'May we sit down? We've things to discuss.'

Grace moved up on the sofa to make room for Georgiana and said anxiously, 'Something's happened! What is it? Not the girls?'

'What?' Martin's forehead creased and he put down his reading material. 'What have you heard? We received a letter

96

from Clara only the other day. Everything was all right then.'
He glanced at Grace, who nodded.

'We might be worrying unnecessarily . . .' Wilhelm began.

Georgiana interrupted him. 'We are, I'm sure, but never-theless—' She took a deep breath and fisted her hand, putting it to her mouth.

Wilhelm handed the newspaper to Martin with the short passage about the fire in Yeller facing towards him. 'It's this morning's newspaper,' he said, 'but I didn't read it until this evening. We came straight away.'

Martin read it and then handed it to Grace. 'There was nothing about this in the *Manchester Guardian*,' he said, glancing at Grace, whose lips were moving silently as she read the piece.

'How far is Yeller from Dreumel's Creek?' she asked quietly, when she had finished.

'Boundary to boundary, about two miles,' Wilhelm said. 'The road to Yeller is through the mountain.'

'But it's not the proximity that worries us.' Georgiana's voice trembled. She felt faint with worry, but tried not to let it show. 'It's whether or not Jewel and Clara were staying with Kitty and her family; their hotel is in Yeller.'

Martin got up from his chair and began to walk about. 'Would they do that? I understood that they were staying at the Marius in Dreumel.'

'That's where Clara's last letter came from,' Grace interjected. 'She was telling us about her room, which overlooked the creek.'

'We're probably being foolish and needn't be concerned,' Georgiana said.

'Of course we're not being foolish,' Grace said softly. 'And you'll be anxious about your friends as well as Jewel and Clara.' She huffed out a breath. 'Anything could have happened, and 'chances are that nothing has. But still . . .' Her voice trailed away and Georgiana clasped her hand.

'We need to send a cable,' Wilhelm said. 'But the Exchange will be closed.'

'There'll be someone on duty.' Martin galvanized himself into action and headed for the door. 'I'll get my coat.'

Georgiana and Grace sat waiting. Grace ordered tea for them both and they made small talk. Grace asked how it was possible that a fire could break out and devastate a whole town.

'The gold-rush towns are nothing like the towns we have in England,' Georgiana told her. 'Even nowadays some of them still look like shanty towns, with their boardwalks and mud roads, and of course the buildings are made of timber. Then with the dry summers . . .' She shrugged. 'From what I recall of Yeller I don't know if they even had a fire company.'

'Incredible!' Grace murmured. 'And yet there are such fine cities too, like New York and Philadelphia.'

Georgiana nodded. 'But it's not that long since those cities and others like them were built. It's not like England with our ancient historic buildings. When I first went to New York – oh, when, twenty-five years ago – the city was still being built. Central Park was being laid out.' She smiled. 'I remember Kitty being appalled to see pigs snuffling about in the streets and poor people sitting on street corners. I think she felt that nothing had changed.

'And in some ways, nothing has,' she added. 'Wilhelm said on his return last year that there were even more people begging on the streets following the financial crash.'

'The poor are always with us,' Grace murmured. 'That I know.'

An hour later the two men returned. Martin poured Wilhelm a brandy and then one for himself, before apologizing to the ladies and asking if they would like a glass of sherry. They both refused and waited expectantly for news.

'We've cabled New York and Philadelphia,' Martin said. 'We should hear something soon.'

'Perhaps!' Wilhelm said. He didn't have Martin's confidence. He turned to Georgiana and Grace. 'We've left urgent messages at the *Star* office and the Marius in New York for them to contact us immediately they have any news. We'll go back in an hour.'

But the only news waiting for them when they went back was from the New York Marius to tell them that an overland telegraph had been sent to the Dreumel Creek hotel and that they were awaiting a response. There was nothing from the Philadelphia newspaper.

As they walked back from the Newmarches' High Street home to their own, Wilhelm remarked, 'If there's no news in the morning I shall catch a train to London.'

'Oh, Wilhelm—' Georgiana began.

'No!' He shook his head vehemently. 'I insist. You know I can't abide inactivity. There are several telegraph companies that I can use to send to New York or Philadelphia, or even Boston or Buffalo. Good heavens, I can send a cable via Ireland and Newfoundland if necessary. But it's easier to send from London.'

Georgiana sighed. She found it incredible, not being as up to the mark in technology as Wilhelm was, but she knew that the underground cable which for over ten years had successfully linked Europe and America had thrilled Wilhelm immensely. He had even told her that before very long they would be able to speak to people in other towns or cities, or even other countries, by electronic machine. That, she thought, she would believe when she heard it.

They held each other close that night, each murmuring reassurances that all would be well and that Jewel and Clara would be safe, that they were worrying unnecessarily. But there was no news the next day, and after waiting until midday Wilhelm and Martin were told that the connection to London had failed.

'That's it then,' Wilhelm muttered. 'I'll go to London and find out what's happening. I'll let you know immediately.' He saw Martin's expression change and knew he was going to say he would accompany him. 'There's no reason for us both to go,' he said swiftly. 'I'm sure everything is all right, but if it is not I shall take the first ship out.' He looked steadily

99

at his friend. 'I feel that Jewel and Clara will have already left Dreumel and set off for California, but I am extremely worried about my friends in Yeller. And,' he added, 'if I can help the townspeople in any way, then I will.'

Martin nodded. 'I understand,' he said. 'You helped found the town, I know.'

'I did,' Wilhelm said quietly. 'It took blood, sweat and many tears. Lives were lost, and being with them now is the least I can do.'

He knew that Georgiana would appreciate the reason why he should travel to London; he also knew that if she suspected that he meant to travel out to America, she would want to go with him. Normally he would agree that she should, but there would be arrangements to be made before they could both depart – servants to be advised and people to be informed – and, as he had the previous year, he felt that immediate action was the essential key.

CHAPTER TWELVE

Jewel and Clara went up to their rooms. There was nothing they could do or say about the missing couple, but only hope that they were safe. But it was very worrying, they both agreed.

'Should we delay our plans for travelling, do you think, Clara?' Jewel asked. They were both sitting on Clara's bed. 'I feel that perhaps we should stay, or on the other hand would we be a nuisance if we did so?'

'I'm sure we probably can help,' Clara said. 'But will our rooms be needed?' She shook her head wearily. 'I'm too tired to even think about it.'

'Yes.' Jewel sighed and got up to go to her own room. 'Let's discuss it in the morning.'

They woke at about eight thirty. Clara was up first, and yawning and stretching she wandered over to the window. 'Jewel,' she called. 'Are you up?'

'Mm, no, but I'm awake.' Jewel's voice was husky with sleep.

'Well, it seems that people are on the move.' Clara leaned forward to look down the main street. A snaking line of men, women and children and horse-drawn carts and waggons stretched as far as she could see. Many of them were already moving, waving their arms in farewell; some of the women were crying as they drove off alongside the creek towards the plain.

Jewel joined her and together they stood watching the

cavalcade. Most of the waggons contained families; few carried possessions, and those who did were taking chairs and bundles of what looked like clothing or linen. On top of one waggon was a grandfather clock.

'Where do you think they're going?' she said.

'I don't know,' Clara murmured. 'Let's get dressed and find out.'

There was a hubbub of activity when they arrived downstairs. Hotel guests were waiting in the hall with portmanteaux and trunks at their sides.

'Are you leaving already?' Clara asked one couple, who she knew had arrived only a few days before.

'Sure are, lady,' the man said. 'Just waiting for the coach. We came for peace and quiet and maybe lookin' for a place to live, but ah reckon we'll come back next year and see how things have settled down. If they build a new town in Yeller, well, I guess we'll reconsider, but right now the place reeks of smoke.'

'It might be a good time to buy a plot,' she suggested.

'Not fer me,' he said. 'I'll want to know it's a safe town to live in.'

'Like Dreumel,' Jewel chipped in. 'It's very safe here.'

'I guess it is,' he said. 'But prices in Dreumel are higher than in Yeller, so we'll wait.'

'A mass exodus.' James Crawford came towards them. 'Good morning, ladies. I hope you're rested after your long night.'

'We are,' Jewel said. 'Have you news of the missing couple?'

'Not yet, but a trail has been seen above the tree line.' He smiled. 'I think we'll find they are safe.'

'How do you know?' Clara asked.

He gave her an enigmatic glance in answer and shook his head before going behind his desk to attend to the departing guests.

Jewel and Clara stood on the steps of the hotel to watch the procession of what appeared to be the entire population of Yeller leaving town. Both felt tearful emotion and empathy with the distress and loss which these homeless people must be enduring.

When they returned indoors, James Crawford, seeing their downcast expressions, ushered them into the breakfast room and told them that most of the families were going to stay with friends and relatives, some as far away as Philadelphia, but that the men would be returning to start rebuilding their homes and businesses; of those without anywhere to go, whole families would live in tents or with residents in Dreumel's Creek who had offered to accommodate them.

'Those who are staying are already clearing the area,' he told them. 'But although the storm was welcomed last night at the height of the fire, it's left a quagmire, which is making the work difficult. What's more, some of the buildings are still smoking and too hot to dismantle.'

As they were being served their breakfast, they heard voices in the reception hall and both rose to their feet as Kitty and Caitlin came through to join them. They all hugged and Jewel and Clara wept a little as they told the Allens how worried they had been when they had seen the fire from the window.

'It was like being in a nightmare,' Kitty said, sitting down at the table and accepting a cup of coffee. 'Ted and I had just gone upstairs when we both heard 'crackling sounds and then explosions. We looked out and saw a sheet of flame engulfing the roof of a store opposite and then spreading to the one next door. Luckily we were still dressed and while Ted ran down to get 'fire buckets, I knocked on all 'bedroom doors, Robert and Caitlin first and then all the guests.'

She closed her eyes for a second as if still reliving the scene, and then continued, her voice weakening at the enormity of what had happened.

'Ted has allus been particular about keeping our hotel safe. He says he saw enough fires when he was a lad to know you've got to have water handy; course those houses back home didn't have dry timber like we have here, which catches fire in a minute.'

103

Clara nodded. Just as she had told James Crawford, she thought.

Caitlin took hold of her mother's hand. 'But we're all right, Ma,' she said softly. 'And nobody has been hurt, which is a miracle when you think about it.'

'Yes,' Kitty agreed. 'Except for that couple who've gone missing. Nobody seems to know where they are.'

Jewel and Clara glanced at each other. So how did James Crawford know about the trail above the tree line? Perhaps it was only a rumour, but they hoped not.

Kitty took a sip of coffee. 'I'm sorry your last day has been spoilt,' she said, 'but Caitlin has come over to spend it with you. Ted and Robert said they'd try to come over later, but right now they're busy helping to clear up the debris. Yeller is just a blackened mess, and we feel so lucky that we've escaped without any damage that we must do what we can for those who've lost everything.'

'Ma's set up the kitchen to provide food for everybody,' Caitlin said. 'The guests we were expecting at the hotel won't be coming now, so some of the men will sleep at our place or else here in Dreumel.'

Jewel nodded and thought that the Allen family hadn't completely escaped misfortune. Thanks to Ted's foresight the hotel had avoided devastation, but for a while at least their business would be virtually non-existent. Who would want to stay in a fire-ravaged town? She glanced at Kitty and thought how tired she looked, as if she hadn't slept all night. Which she probably hadn't.

'Could Clara and I stay and help, Aunt Kitty?' she said quietly. 'We don't have to leave tomorrow. There's no urgency at all.'

Kitty gave a wan smile. 'Why, bless you both; it's kind of you to offer, but no. Lots of women have stayed on to help; it's 'younger ones with little bairns who've left. The women here are strong; they're used to a hard, primitive life. They can work alongside their menfolk in rebuilding their homes and cook a meal and wash their clothes at the same time.' She smiled. 'They'll not be set back by a bit of a fire.'

She kissed both girls goodbye and said she was going home to rest for an hour. 'All of our guests have left,' she said, 'which is why we're here. If you come back to Dreumel after your travels, we'll meet again, but if not, then I hope it won't be so long next time before you return.'

'It won't be,' Jewel promised. 'I haven't any plans for after California. I realize now,' she said slowly, 'that we must take life as it comes.'

Clara swallowed. She would be going back to England, no matter what Jewel decided. This country, where everything was so much bigger and wider and higher than anything she had ever known, she had taken to her heart. But it wasn't home.

'Having heard so much about you, it's been very nice to meet you, Mrs Allen,' she said. 'I do hope we'll meet again.'

Kitty grasped her hand. 'So do I,' she said tearfully. 'Take a look at Hull through my eyes, will you, Clara? Look at those mean streets where I once lived, and 'Market Place where I used to shop for my ma afore I went to work for Georgiana's aunt. And Hull Fair,' she said eagerly. 'Does it still come every October?'

'Oh, yes!' Hot tears ran down Clara's face. 'Some things never change. I know the old streets very well. My mother—'

'Of course,' Kitty said softly. 'She knew how it was. She wouldn't forget.'

'No.' Clara shook her head. 'She hasn't. She says she never will.'

Kitty said her final goodbyes and the three girls stood on the porch and watched as she untethered her horse from the hitching rail and jumped lithely into the saddle before waving to them and riding off in the direction of Yeller.

'How does she do that?' Clara asked in admiration.

'What?' Caitlin asked. 'Oh, you mean mount! She learned to ride when she first came out here. It's second nature to her now. She's a better rider than Da.'

Amazing, Clara thought. I must remember to tell my mother!

They sat down on the bench on the porch and Caitlin asked what they would like to do on their final day. Clara waited for Jewel to speak.

'Well,' Jewel said slowly. 'This perhaps will sound very strange.' She took a deep breath. 'What I would like to do is visit the Chinaman.'

Caitlin turned to look at her. 'Which? The one here in Dreumel, do you mean? Old Sun Wa? His son had the laundry in Yeller, but that's burnt out. He'll probably be living here now.'

Jewel shrugged. 'Either of them. I don't mind.'

'Why do you want to see them?' Caitlin frowned. 'Do you need some medicine? There's a doctor here in Dreumel.'

'No. No, I don't need medicine. I'd just like to talk to them.' She glanced at Clara, knowing she didn't have to explain to her, but she told Caitlin that she wanted to ask them something.

'All right,' Caitlin nodded. 'I'll take you. The store is just along the road. Do you want to go now?'

'Please,' she said. 'Will you come, Clara?'

Clara hesitated. At some point Jewel would have to make her own decision about what she wanted to find out about her life. She would value her opinion, she knew, but it was unlikely that she would ask for Caitlin's. The younger girl didn't yet know of Jewel's quest.

'Do you mind if I don't? You won't be long, will you? I'd like to start packing a few things ready for tomorrow.' She smiled. 'And I'm sure that Caitlin would like to have you to herself for an hour or so.'

'Sure would,' Caitlin agreed. 'There's so much I want to ask you before you leave.'

'All right,' Jewel said. 'I'll just go upstairs for my parasol.'

'I'll get it,' Clara said, standing up. 'I won't be a moment.'

She hurried into the hall, almost bumping into James Crawford. 'Sorry,' she said breathlessly. 'I was about to dash upstairs. Not very ladylike, am I?' She laughed.

106

He looked down at her. 'May I have a word with you at some time, Miss Newmarch?' he said quietly.

'Yes, of course. In five minutes if you like. Miss Dreumel is going out and I'm just fetching her parasol.'

She watched Jewel and Caitlin walk down the road, Jewel half hidden by her parasol and Caitlin's red hair tossing and gleaming in the bright sunshine. The weather was not as hot today; the storm had cleared the air, leaving a freshness in place of the stifling heat of the day before.

When she turned to go inside, James Crawford was standing by the hotel door. He had his arms folded in front of him and he looked very serious. Glum, even. Perhaps he's worried about the future of the Marius, she thought. When word got out about the fire, it was possible that people would avoid coming to Dreumel's Creek as well as Yeller.

'Is something worrying you, Mr Crawford?' she asked. 'You look rather anxious.'

He gave her a smile which didn't quite reach his eyes. 'Not anxious, but a little melancholy.'

She nodded in sympathy. 'Because of the people of Yeller who have lost their homes and businesses?'

'That, yes, of course. But in this instance I have become low-spirited because special visitors to the hotel have come to the end of their stay and are taking their leave.'

Clara felt her cheeks flush. 'We have enjoyed our stay,' she said quietly. 'Apart from last night,' she added. She wondered what else he had to say as he ushered her into the hall and asked if she would come through to the office behind the reception desk as he had something to show her.

It was not a large room and most of the space was taken up with another desk and two chairs, but there was a very large window which looked out over the back of the hotel towards the mountains.

'When Mr Dreumel built this hotel, he insisted that whoever used this room to work in must have plenty of light and a view of the mountain range,' he explained, 'rather than just the four walls.'

She nodded. Wilhelm was a most considerate man, but she was still left wondering what that had to do with her.

James Crawford put out his hand for her to come over to the window and when she did so she saw a telescope on the sill. He picked it up. 'You have been curious how I knew about the missing couple.'

'Yes, I was. So you saw them through this?'

'No. I didn't see them, but I saw a signal which told me they'd been found.'

'Oh!' She gave a puzzled frown. 'From them?'

He shook his head. 'From my brothers.'

Clara's lips formed another *Oh*, and then realization cleared her head. 'You mean – your—'

'Yes.' He gave her the telescope and with his left hand turned her to the window. 'Look up to the tree line and then let your gaze search higher.'

She did as he suggested, conscious that his hand was still on her shoulder. 'I can see the tree line,' she said huskily, 'but nothing else, just a dark forest of pines.'

'Can you not see a small rocky area where there are no trees growing?' His head was close to hers and she was aware that her breath had quickened, although she did not feel at all threatened by him.

She searched again, only higher this time, and then she spotted a rocky outcrop jutting out from the side of the mountain. 'Yes,' she said triumphantly. 'I see it.'

In one movement she lowered the eyeglass and turned to find him gazing at her.

'I beg your pardon.' Swiftly he took a step back and turned to glance again out of the window. 'My brothers are often in the forests above Dreumel's Creek and every day I look for a sign from them.'

'Are these your real brothers or members of your – your community?'

He laughed. 'Tribe, do you mean, Miss Newmarch?'

'I don't know what I mean,' she confessed. 'I'm sure that in England we're not given a true picture of the Indian situation.

108

I have heard a little of the Seven Years War, which is now part of history, and of various treaties which guaranteed land to your people, but learned more about the gold rush of 1849.'

'Then I'm impressed,' he said, 'for you appear to know more than might be expected of you.'

She blushed. 'I admit that I did some reading about the founding of America before I left home, but there's little written about the Indians; and in the articles I have seen . . .' She hesitated, not wanting to offend.

Looking down at her, he said softly, 'We are described as wild savages?'

'Yes,' she whispered. 'Which is plainly untrue.'

Quite untrue, she thought. Of him at any rate. I can't begin to consider the rest of his nation. I can only look at him and see someone who is trying to integrate, to make something of his life. But more than that, he is a most attractive man and it's as well that we are leaving tomorrow because when he stands so close I can feel my senses pounding and I wouldn't trust myself to remain in control if we stayed.

CHAPTER THIRTEEN

James Crawford turned again to the window. 'Behind the escarpment is another trail, obscured and rarely used. Mr and Mrs Thompson must have got lost in the forest and come across it by accident. It was fortunate that they were found. They wouldn't have easily come down the mountain by themselves. My brothers do not often venture so far above Dreumel, especially at night, but,' he shrugged, 'perhaps they sensed something; the older men have keen powers of perception.'

'The fire, you mean?'

'Yes. Fire is a forceful element; it affects us all.'

'Do your brothers live near? Is there a settlement here?'

'The nearest settlement is No Name, which is where I was born. My mother is mixed race, my father a true Iroquois.' He gave a wry grimace. 'They lost me for a while after I *came over* to the other side, especially when I went to Philadelphia; but since I've lived in Dreumel's Creek they come regularly to check up on me in the hope that one day I'll return to my rightful place.'

Clara was fascinated and couldn't keep her eyes from his face. He's from another world, she thought. An ancient community so much older than ours.

'The Iroquois confederacy was formed many years ago and the different nations are disbanded, but there are still small groups of Mohawks, Senecas and Oneidas who try to live as our ancestors did and strive to claim their land back.' He was speaking quietly, almost as if to himself.

'And will you?' she asked softly. 'Go back to them? You can perhaps be of use to them: a spokesperson, a bridge between two communities.'

He turned towards her and, as if on impulse, leaned forward and kissed her tenderly on the mouth. 'If I cannot find what I want here,' he murmured and transfixed her with his dark eyes, 'then yes, I think I will.'

A flush suffused Clara's cheeks. She was overwhelmed by his action, but rather than being angry or insulted she felt as if her bones had melted into water. She wanted more than anything to reciprocate, to put her arms round his neck and let him kiss her again.

They gazed at each other, Clara breathing as if she had run up a flight of stairs, not out of breath but exhilarated by the climb. He took hold of her hand and pressed it to his lips. 'I know I am behaving irresponsibly,' he whispered. 'But I am totally intoxicated by you. By your beauty, your manner, your sensibility. Forgive me.' He stepped away from her. 'I don't mean to offend you.'

She put her hand to her throat and felt a pulse throbbing. 'What do you want of me?'

He shook his head. 'Everything – and nothing. That you haven't spurned me is enough.'

He closed his eyes for a second and then, opening them, said softly, 'It is the first time I have kissed a woman.'

There was a silence between them. Clara didn't know what to say or to do and neither did she want to break the spell. A sense of warmth enveloped her, light, protective, and yet at the same time releasing and liberating her. She had always thought of herself as emancipated because she had been brought up by sensible parents, yet she was still bound by convention and propriety. She suddenly thought of Thomas. Though they had been friends since childhood he had never so much as kissed her cheek or her hand, and she would have been astonished if he had.

And it would have been nice if he had done so, she thought, for then I might have been prepared for this. With that experience behind me I would have known that a simple kiss could take me into another place. One of sensuous anticipation of something more.

As they stood close and, though not touching, aware of each other's nearness, a noise from outside brought them from their reverie. There was the sound of hooves and cheering. They both blinked, and it was as if they had awoken from a dreaming state; both stepped back, and had anyone come into the room it would have appeared that there was an insurmountable chasm between them.

'The Thompsons,' he murmured. 'They've been brought down from the mountain. They've come into Dreumel, not Yeller.'

Clara wanted to ask him how he knew, but her tongue appeared to be locked. But then, she thought, why would I ask and what would he say? He just knew.

At the front of the hotel a crowd had gathered around the Thompsons and they seemed overcome by the welcome. As they haltingly told their story, it seemed that they had decided to ride up into the mountains from Yeller and take a look at the town from above, probably following the same track that Jewel and Clara had taken with Caitlin the day before, but then they had continued higher into the forest trail. On turning round to come back they realized that they had taken the wrong path and were quite lost.

It was as darkness was falling and they were still searching for the way out that they heard the crackle of fire and were at first terrified that the forest was alight, and again plunged deeper into the trees; they could smell burning pine and see the columns of smoke, and then they heard the shouts of men. It was a relief followed by dismay when they realized that it was not the forest that was on fire, but the town below them.

'We followed the light of the flames to find our way back to the tree line,' Bert said, 'and saw the whole of Yeller ablaze, but we still couldn't get down. The horses were as nervous as we were; they were snickering and snorting and very restless, so we took them back into the forest and tied them up, and then we sat on the ridge and watched. We couldn't have come down anyway because by then it was pitch dark and we couldn't see the path at all.'

'And then,' his wife said, taking up the story, 'the horses quite suddenly became quiet and when we went back towards them we saw—'

'Indians!' Bert said. 'They were standing by the horses and talking to them and breathing into their nostrils.' He glanced up the steps to the boardwalk and then to the porch, where James Crawford was standing with Clara and some of the hotel staff. 'And,' he continued, 'they said they would bring us down this morning and let someone know that we were safe before a search party was sent out.'

'They gave us food,' Sarah said. 'And water and a blanket to wrap round us. We're very grateful,' she added huskily. 'We might have died.'

'Don't often see Indians in this neck o' the woods.' A man chewing tobacco spat out a stream of brown spittle. He too glanced up at James Crawford. ''Cept tame ones,' he added in a low voice. 'The wild ones mainly stay on their own land.'

James Crawford had heard. He lifted his head, showing his muscular neck, and without a word, though his lips were set in a tight line, he turned round and went inside.

'Why'd ya say you want to meet the Chinaman?' Caitlin asked as they walked down the main street. 'Do you need some medicine? If it's that time of the month I've got aspirin.'

'No. No, it's not that, thank you.' Jewel flushed at Caitlin's frankness. 'I want to talk to him. About the Chinese and how they came to be in America.'

Caitlin frowned. 'Well, I guess they were looking for gold, same as everybody else. Sun Wa came during the gold rush, so they say, but I don't know why he settled in Dreumel's Creek: most of them went to California.' She shrugged. 'He's been here for as long as I can remember, anyway. Sun Sen runs the laundry in Yeller. Well, he did; his middle daughter went to school with me.'

She glanced at Jewel and then, tucking her arm into hers, guided her round a large puddle of water from the previous evening's downpour. 'You don't think of yourself as Chinese, do you, Jewel? Cos you're just such a pure English lady.'

'But I'm not!' Jewel protested. 'I was born in America just as you were. But I had an English father and a Chinese mother, so what does that make me?'

Caitlin blew out her cheeks. 'Well, I had an Irish grandmother and parents from Yorkshire, England,' she said, adding: 'That's in the north of England.'

Jewel hid a wry smile. 'Yes, I know,' she said. 'That's where I live.'

'We're all a mixture,' Caitlin persisted. 'So you don't really need to go searching. Anyway, we're here. This is where Sun Wa lives.'

They stood outside the single-storeyed store. In the window were dusty boxes with Chinese writing on them and dishes filled with what looked like tea leaves. Yes, Jewel thought. I know we're a mixture. Caitlin knows about her ancestry because her mother and father have told her. But I know nothing about my mother or how she came to be in America, because no one knew her. Perhaps my father did, but he's no longer here to tell me.

She swallowed hard. 'Shall we knock?'

'Caitlin! Hello.' A round-faced Chinese girl opened the door to them. She bowed her head in acknowledgement of Jewel and then tilted it as she said, 'Grandfather is not available at the moment. Can I help you? Or my father's here.'

'This is my friend from England,' Caitlin told her. 'Jewel, this is Lucy. I told you we were at school together.'

The girl bowed her head again in Jewel's direction and said hello and then said to Caitlin, 'We were burnt out, did you hear? That's why we're staying with Grandfather.' She had no trace of a Chinese accent.

114

'Could I speak to your father?' Jewel asked, disappointed that she couldn't speak to the older man.

'Of course.' Lucy opened the door wider. 'Welcome.'

They stepped inside the dark interior and needed a moment or two for their eyes to adjust to the dimness after the brightness of outdoors. There was a piquant tang of smoke in the air: not the kind from a wood fire, nor the charcoaled smell of burning which drifted over Dreumel from Yeller, but something more elusive, something sweet and yet potent.

Their eyes opened to reveal a small room; against one wall was a square table covered by an oiled cloth and two chairs beside it. They were invited to sit down. On the opposite wall was an alcove with a half-drawn cotton curtain and another table within it; next to it was an entrance which had no door but a beaded curtain obscuring the room beyond. The beads rattled as Lucy went through them, again delivering to Jewel a half-forgotten memory.

Jewel and Caitlin looked at each other and Caitlin wrinkled her nose; at the aroma, Jewel supposed. After a moment the beads rattled again and Lucy's father, Sun Sen, came through. He wore a spherical cap, a short jacket with a mandarin collar and narrow black trousers.

He clasped his hands together and, bowing low from the waist, asked if he might do anything to assist them.

'Miss Allen,' he said to Caitlin, 'I hope your family have not been inconvenienced by the fire.' He then turned to Jewel. 'I am a herbalist,' he explained. 'Like my father. But I have been making my living in the laundry for many years. Now it seems that I must go back to my original occupation.'

'I'm very sorry to bother you,' Jewel said. 'It must be a difficult time for you and I'm not in need of a herbalist or a launderer, but tomorrow I am leaving for California and intend to search for my mother's history. She was Chinese,' she added, thinking that it was probably unnecessary to do so. 'She died not long after I was born. In San Francisco.'

She gazed into his round face and black eyes, so like his

daughter's. 'I don't know where to begin,' she pleaded. 'Can you help me?'

He surveyed her solemnly. Then he said, 'Thousands of Chinese came to America in search of a better life. Most were men who worked the gold fields or on the railroads. There were few women. The men sent any money they earned back to China to feed their families, which is what my father did. Very few of the families were able to follow them, and many of the men intended to return to China when they had made enough money to afford to do so, but died in the attempt without ever seeing their wives or children again. Thanks to my father's determination, my mother and older brother and sister were the lucky ones able to join him here. Perhaps your mother was from such a family.'

Jewel bit on her lip. 'But how would I find out? Is there a register of some kind?' Even as she asked the question, she realized that even if there were, which was doubtful, it wouldn't help her as she didn't know her mother's family name.

Sun Sen shook his head. 'Not to my knowledge. If you are determined to find out, then you must ask the Chinese community in San Francisco. But prepare yourself for disappointment if they do not tell you anything,' he said, adding kindly: 'You are not Chinese.'

Jewel's eyes suddenly filled with tears. 'I know,' she whispered. 'But I don't know what I am.'

He smiled. 'You are searching for an answer,' he said softly. 'But perhaps there isn't one. Come with me.' He beckoned with his hand.

Jewel followed him through the beaded curtain. Caitlin looked puzzled, undecided whether to go with her, until Lucy appeared and came and sat in Jewel's vacated chair.

'I will take you to see my father,' Sun Sen told Jewel. 'He is old now and very tired.'

They went through another door into a stark room where there was a narrow bed and a fug of the sweet-smelling smoke Jewel and Caitlin had noticed earlier. On the bed lay an ancient-seeming old man; his head was bald but his long

116

white beard came down to his chest. His eyes were closed as he smoked a pipe half the length of his arm. Sleeping on his legs was a white cat, which looked up as they entered and jumped down, disappearing under the bed.

'Father.' Sun Sen spoke in his own language to the old man. 'Here is a young woman who is seeking answers.'

The old man opened his eyes and looked at Jewel; he said nothing but drew heavily on his pipe as he gazed at her.

'I want to know about my mother,' she said softly. 'I have reached a time in my life when I need to know who she was and where she came from.'

The elder Sun took the pipe out of his mouth and spoke to his son and then closed his eyes again.

'What did he say?' Jewel whispered.

'My father said,' Sun Sen spoke quietly, 'that a bird does not sing because it has an answer. It sings because it has a song.'

CHAPTER FOURTEEN

That evening one of the maids came upstairs to help Jewel and Clara pack their trunks. Both girls were subdued. This last day had been significant, and neither had discussed with the other what had occurred. Not yet; the time wasn't right, not until each had assimilated feelings and emotions and come to her own kind of judgement or understanding.

In her head, Jewel constantly repeated the Chinese proverb given to her by Sun Wa in order to make sense of it. That it was profound she had no doubt, but what did it mean to her personally? The answer to that particular question was at present unattainable.

Clara's emotional senses were in confusion; she was attracted to James Crawford by his difference, for he was unlike any other man she had ever met; by his manner, which was polite and courtly and yet, beneath that exterior, undoubtedly passionate; hence his kiss and declaration, which had awakened a response in her that, she decided, must have been waiting, lurking even, beneath the calm and self-possessed exterior for which she was known.

The next morning they were given an early call so that they could finish packing their personal belongings. The coach was due to arrive at nine o'clock and leave at half past. The driver had half an hour to stretch his legs and have breakfast before making his return journey.

Caitlin and Robert were waiting in the hotel foyer to see

them off; Caitlin tearfully asked if they would come back to Dreumel before returning to England, whilst Robert stood dumbly gazing at Clara.

'I don't know,' Jewel said. 'Perhaps. I'm not sure. We'll write,' she said, 'and tell you about California.'

Caitlin wiped away a tear. 'I hope you find what you're looking for, Jewel; you too, Clara.'

Clara smiled. 'I'm not looking *for* anything, Caitlin,' she told her. 'I'm just looking.'

She turned to Robert and gave him her hand. 'Goodbye, Robert,' she said, and impulsively kissed his cheek. 'Don't forget me,' she whispered in his ear.

The staff of the hotel stood on the porch to see them depart. James Crawford came down the steps carrying Clara's portmanteau. Jewel stepped aboard but Clara turned and gave James her hand and he held it for a lingering moment.

'Goodbye, James,' she said softly, so that no one else could hear. 'I'm so glad that I met you. I'll think of you often.'

'And I you, Miss Clara.' His eyes were dark and unfathomable and she saw no hint within them of what he was feeling, until he murmured, 'I will think of you in my dreams and in my waking.'

He bowed then to Jewel, murmuring pleasantries, then turned about and walked swiftly up the steps and into the Marius without a backward glance.

Their companions on the return journey were once again the Thompsons, who were returning home to sell up the possessions they didn't need, having decided that they would buy a plot in Yeller and make their home in the new town. They had not been disheartened by their adventure in the forest; on the contrary, they didn't think they would find anywhere else in the country where there was such comradeship and compassion.

Everyone was quiet for the first few miles, and then Jewel murmured to Clara that perhaps they ought to have written home to tell their parents that they were about to start on the next stage of their journey.

'And the fire!' she said. 'We should have told them about the fire. Will anyone else, I wonder? Not that Papa will be affected by it. I don't think he has any property in Yeller.'

'I wrote home a week ago, saying that we would be travelling on to California very soon,' Clara told her. 'I told them about going up into the mountains and looking down over Dreumel's Creek. I didn't write about the *incident*,' she smiled, 'for how could I explain that we had both sensed something, but knew not what? They won't have heard of the fire in England, so they won't be worried about us. But we can write when we get to New York.'

The New York Marius was to be their first stop before catching another railway train from Grand Central terminus the following morning. When they spoke to other visitors at the hotel they were advised to break their journey into stages, as although they could stay on the train for the whole journey it would not necessarily be comfortable.

'I can't believe that it's possible to travel on a train for so long and so far,' Clara had declared on being told that it would take a week to reach Promontory Point, the historic junction where the Union Pacific from the east and Central Pacific from the west had first met in Utah less than five years ago, joining the railroads from New York and California. The rail route travelled along the old coaching and Pony Express road, which in turn had followed the waggon and pack-horse trail and before that the rutted tracks of buffalo and Indians. Running alongside it was a Western Union telegraph line which after its completion in the north of the country had been a successful aid for communication during the Civil War.

The two girls were up very early the next morning and this time it was Stanley Adams who was on duty and took them in a horse cab to the train, found the porter who would take care of them during the journey and escorted them to their seats in the first-class passenger car.

'Good luck, Miss Dreumel, Miss Newmarch. I hope you have a good journey,' Adams shouted as the engine got up a head of steam and the wheels began to roll. He stood and watched, his hand rising in farewell as the locomotive puffed and chuffed and rattled; thick black smoke issued from the funnel, the guard blew a whistle, there was a series of clanging bells and they were off.

Jewel and Clara sat back and made themselves comfortable, each heaving a gleeful expressive breath. Jewel was buoyant with optimism; at last she was on a journey which might provide her with the knowledge she craved, even though Sun Sen had expressed his doubts; Clara was still animated after what she thought of as a romantic interlude and wistfully remembering James Crawford's words and his swift departure as he left her at the coach.

There were about a dozen other passengers of varying ages in their car and most appeared very pleasant, the ladies greeting them politely and the gentlemen touching their hats before removing them, unbuttoning their jackets and taking their seats. Once they were under way the porter came along and invited them to inspect their sleeping quarters, which were in a separate car.

'Breakfast will be served in the dining car from eight o'clock,' he told them. 'There's a small kitchen with facilities for you to make coffee or cook yourselves a meal.'

They must have looked astonished at this, as he added, 'Some folks like to prepare their own food. Only breakfast is free; at any other time meals have to be paid for, or you can buy supplies from the station houses when we stop to collect coal and water.'

They inspected the beds, which were curtained for privacy, and each agreed that they seemed quite comfortable if a little claustrophobic, with only a minuscule washroom.

'Oh, what *fun!*' Clara declared. 'Oh, Jewel, do let's stay on the train. Let's not break our journey.'

'I agree,' Jewel said. 'But shall we ask the porter what he thinks?'

He took off his cap when they asked his advice and said, 'I guess this is your first journey on the transcontinental?'

When they told him that it was, he said, 'Well, young ladies, this is the finest railroad in America. On that famous day in May 1869 I was on the Union Pacific's 119 when we rolled into Ogden. Proudest day of my life. A tale I shall tell my grandchildren, when the rails joined and made it possible to travel coast to coast. You know, some folks don't like the Chinese,' he went on, 'but I always say that America wouldn't be the same without them. My, but they sure know how to work. They blasted through granite and rock and took us right through the Sierra Nevada to make this journey possible. Don't know of any other race that could do that.' He took a breath. ''Cept maybe the Irish.'

When they managed to turn the conversation back to their original question he nodded and told them that they could break their journey, but that it would add several days to their travelling. 'You'll have to wait for the next connection,' he said, 'and you could be waiting in the middle of nowhere and what's the point in that?'

They agreed that there was no point at all and decided that they would stay on board.

When they arrived in Ogden five days later, they knew that it had been an experience they could never have had in England. They had travelled through narrow rocky canyons which had been blasted out of granite mountain walls; gazed down from terrifying heights on gushing rivers as their carriage rattled over what seemed like flimsy iron bridges; and seen dry and dusty deserts.

From the train windows they had watched herds of wild buffalo roaming the plains; columns of Indians on horseback, platoons of soldiers not far behind; long caravans of covered waggons and trails of Mormons travelling towards Salt Lake City; remote settlements huddled on the banks of tributaries, and isolated rundown homesteads with scavenging dogs and thin cattle and waving children; and always, as a backdrop, the towering lofty peaks of the sierras and soaring, wheeling buzzards in the vast sky.

They had enjoyed the company of their fellow passengers,

played cards with them, sung songs with them and walked along the tracks when the train moved so slowly over high terrain that they got out to stretch their legs and reached the next station house before the locomotive did.

In station dining rooms everyone sat together at long wooden tables and was served meat and vegetables from huge cauldrons, with chunks of dry bread, and declared it to be the best food they had ever tasted.

Hats and bonnets were discarded and Jewel and Clara wore their hair loose down their backs; boots were taken off and slippers were worn, except when descending from the train.

Now, in Ogden, Utah, the home of the Mormons, they had a three-hour wait in blistering heat for the engines to be fuelled with coal and water and to give the drivers the chance to have a sleep before the final two-day leg through the Sierra Nevada mountains and into San Francisco. They took shelter in the station house and at their request were brought cold drinks and beef, and the men of the party drank beer.

Clara looked out of the window and saw the passengers from the second-class car getting off the train. She had glanced through the windows as she'd passed and noticed how ill equipped it was. The passengers were poorly dressed and many of the children amongst them were crying with tiredness. Poor things, she thought. What do they have for food and drink? None of them had come into the station houses so she could only assume that they had no money for food, but only ate what they had brought with them.

The sun was beating down and it must have been unbearable in the train. She took a long drink of lemonade, then put down her glass and went in search of the station-house mistress.

'Could I have a jug of lemonade to take to the children?' she asked. 'Some of them look quite unwell.'

'They've no money to pay,' the woman said. 'They can get water from the outside pump.'

'Yes, I know,' Clara said. She'd seen some of them putting their heads under the pump. 'But I'll pay.'

The woman grudgingly gave her a large jug of lemonade and held out her hand for payment. Clara took the jug outside, to where seven or eight children were standing round the pump. 'Have you cups?' she asked them.

They didn't understand what she meant at first. But then she lifted the jug and said, 'Lemonade!' The youngest of the children, a boy who looked about six, cottoned on and raced back to the train, returning with two tin mugs, one for himself and one for a little girl who he said was his sister. The others then also ran back to fetch a variety of mugs and bowls. All but one, a raggedy dark-skinned child in torn trousers and dirty shirt who just stood and looked at her.

'Don't you have a cup?' she asked, and he shook his head and turned away. 'Wait,' she said. Measuring out the liquid to the eager children, she saved the same amount in the jug and handed it to him. He tipped his head back and drank it straight down.

'Thank you, missy,' he said, and the grin he gave her more than compensated for the discomfort she had been made to feel by the mean-spirited woman at the station.

Three engines arrived clanking and clattering to join the waiting carriages and everyone sent up a cheer. The extra locomotives were required to make the steep ascent over the mountains. The passengers climbed back on board and sat back in their seats for the final leg of the journey to San Francisco.

CHAPTER FIFTEEN

Seventeen years had passed since Jewel left San Francisco as a child and she had virtually no memory of it. She and Georgiana had travelled by clipper into New York, the easiest route at that time as there were no railroads running across the country as there were now. The only other means of travel would have been the arduous overland journey by coach or waggon and then canal boat, which Georgiana had considered too hard for a young child, though for many pioneering women and their families it was the only affordable way.

Jewel and Clara travelled on the last stage of their journey in weary but companionable silence as they passed through scenes of awesome splendour: through dark tunnels of what seemed to be impenetrable mountains, up and over the highest inclines and into the deepest of valleys where the train ran alongside wide and sparkling creeks and wooded slopes led down to rivers and lakes where they saw beavers building dams.

They slept in their shaking beds and rocked giddily as they stood to make pots of coffee and gazed out at the country rushing by. An hour before they were due to arrive, they brushed each other's hair and pinned it up and changed their plain travelling gowns for something more suitable for their arrival in the city of San Francisco.

Jewel chose a grey silk pleated bodice and jacket with a separate apron-fronted skirt and a small padded bustle, whilst Clara wore a tailored leaf-green dress with a short ruched train. They put on their neat flowered hats, and when they stepped gingerly down from the train which had been their cocoon for the past seven days it seemed as if they emerged into a cavernous cacophony of noise: shouting, swearing, roaring men, screaming children and, it appeared, women of easy virtue. Newsvendors yelled incomprehensibly, and foreign citizens of every colour and race swamped the concourse. It was as if they had entered the tower of Babel, for in their confused state they could neither hear nor understand.

Their porter appeared by their side to collect their luggage and find them a horse cab to take them to the hotel which Wilhelm had suggested they use. It was a small establishment set in a quiet street away from the bustle of the centre of the city, and had been recommended to him by someone he knew.

An elevator took them to the third floor. Neither spoke, for, as they discussed later, it was as if they were in a wakeful dream, and each step they took was automatic as they followed the bell boy pushing the trolley with their luggage.

They had been given a suite of rooms with a balcony. The bell boy advised them to use the balcony in the evening only when the weather was cooler; the main room contained two large beds, a sofa, an occasional table and two easy chairs. A separate bathroom with a claw-footed bath and a washbasin, a flush lavatory and a chair holding a pile of soft towels invited them to make bathing their first undertaking.

They tipped the boy and asked him to send up tea and cake. Clara asked him for the time, as she had quite lost track of it and couldn't have said if it was morning or afternoon. Since the sun was hidden behind a thick grey haze, she couldn't tell from that either.

He grinned and told her it was four in the afternoon. 'Afternoon tea time for English ladies, miss,' he said. 'And bread and butter with the crusts cut off.'

She laughed at that and said that would do very nicely, and

126

by the time he had left Jewel was already running a bath, unlacing her boots and rolling down her stockings.

Clara opened a cupboard and found two dressing robes and slippers. She unpinned her hat, unbuttoned her gown and, slipping out of it, said, 'You take your bath, Jewel. I'll lie on the bed until the tea comes up.'

She heard the sound of slapping water as Jewel stepped into the bath and Clara sighed as she put her head on the pillow. Half an hour later she was woken from a rocking, lurching sleep when a maid knocked on the door and brought in a tray of refreshments.

Jewel appeared, pink and rosy, and confessed that she'd also fallen asleep, slipping down into the deep bath and being woken by a mouthful of water.

'You take your bath, Clara,' she said, 'and I'll pour the tea and bring you a cup. How luxurious will that be?'

'Unheard of!' Clara laughed, and happily indulged herself. She considered that after a week without a bath, they had both been in need of one. She stretched back in the water, letting her hair float about her, and thought how lucky she was to be in such surroundings in another country. She let her thoughts drift home, to her sister and her parents, and suddenly remembered that she hadn't written from New York as had been her intention, though both she and Jewel had made copious notes whilst travelling on the train.

'Jewel,' she called. 'Did you write home?'

There was no answer. She's asleep, she thought. We must do it tomorrow. There's no real hurry. Still damp from her bath she climbed into her own bed and felt sleep steal over her. They won't expect a letter every week.

CHAPTER SIXTEEN

Jewel and Clara slept for four hours, then dressed and went sleepily down to supper. They spoke little and ate simply. Both felt shaky, as if they were still on the train.

'Have you realized,' Jewel said, as she spooned tomato soup, 'that it takes almost the same length of time to travel across the country, *coast to coast* as they say, as it does to sail from Liverpool to New York?'

Clara nodded. She could hardly keep her eyes open. 'I know,' she said huskily. 'I can't take in the size of this country. It's so vast compared to our own small island.' She smiled. 'I'm really looking forward to exploring San Francisco, though. Incredible to think it was built on gold.'

'And they're still finding it,' Jewel told her. 'I heard two men on the train discussing gold strikes in Nevada and Utah. They left the train in Ogden, and I didn't see them get back on again.'

'So what would you like to do first?' Clara asked her. 'And when? Shall we find our bearings tomorrow and then—'

Jewel heaved a breath and absent-mindedly crumbled her bread. 'Well,' she interrupted, 'first, I'd like to try and find my father's house. I have a vague picture in my head of where it was, but I don't have an address and Mama couldn't remember it either. I have Dolly's and I wrote to her to say I was coming on a visit and would she tell Larkin and Jed. They were friends of my father's when he first came to America,

I think. Larkin can't read, which is why we used to write to Dolly. She wanted to know about me when I was growing up, but our correspondence grew lax over the years.'

'Do you remember them?' Clara asked.

'Not really,' she said, and then smiled. 'I remember Dolly wearing bright clothes and big hats and sometimes she let me try the hats on, and Larkin used to swing me up in the air, but I can't recall Jed at all.'

'So tomorrow, then?' Clara said. 'Where will we start? At Dolly's?'

Jewel shook her head. 'No. I want to try and find the house for myself. It was at the top of a hill. We'll buy a town plan.'

The following morning, feeling refreshed after a good night's sleep, they ate breakfast and prepared to leave, first asking the desk clerk where they might buy a plan of the town. He directed them further along the street and then asked them where they were heading.

'I can't recall the name of the street,' Jewel told him, 'but I know it was at the top of a hill.'

He looked at her in astonishment. 'Well, ma'am, there are a great many hills in San Francisco and all pretty steep. Have you no idea where it might be?'

She shook her head rather sheepishly. 'The city has grown since I was last here.'

The clerk pursed his lips and then after a moment of pondering he said, 'I'd advise that first you take the cable car up Clay Street.' He seemed to puff himself up, and added, 'Wire rope railway! It's a new invention, fitted only last year. Andrew Hallidie was the inventor – an Englishman, I believe. Pretty soon they'll be all over the city hills; Sutter Street is next, they say, maybe Geary Street. Sure beats walking up them.'

They thanked him and went outside. The weather was foggy and rather warm and damp, but they walked up the street in search of a news store, whilst Jewel wondered whether she should revise her plans and look for Dolly first, rather than wander aimlessly. San Francisco was so much larger than she recalled.

The plan they purchased didn't really help, so Clara, realizing Jewel was becoming despondent, suggested that they journey up Clay Street as the clerk had suggested, so they could find their bearings.

San Francisco was a bustling, noisy city. No one strolled, but all seemed to have an urgent need to get to the next place in the quickest possible time. Horse buses, carriages, carts and waggons flew past them at top speed and they had to pick up their skirts and hurry across the wide roads to avoid being run over.

They entered some of the large stores and made a few purchases, and then wandered up and down the streets and boulevards, remarking on the size of the buildings and on the different types of architecture, which appeared to be taken from every country imaginable. Some of the houses on the hills were built in the English terraced style with steep pitched roofs; some buildings were like French palaces and some had Turkish towers and minarets. Others, possibly Italian, they surmised, had overhanging eaves and balustraded balconies, reminiscent, Clara thought dreamily, of Romeo and Juliet.

They found Clay Street quite by accident, hearing the racket of the cable car before they saw it as it rattled down the hill and deposited its passengers at the bottom. They bought tickets and took their seats in the open-sided cart-like structure; the brass bell rang, the grip man released the lever, the car jerked and up they went, both rather giggly and nervous as the underground cables pulled the car along the rails to the top of the hill.

They hopped off and both laughed at the experience. 'Sure beats walking,' Clara said, mimicking the desk clerk. 'That would be quite a pull uphill and I don't know if I'd have had the breath for it,' she added in her normal voice.

Jewel gazed about her. 'We'll have to find it – the breath, I mean,' she said slowly. 'Because I don't recognize any of this. We'll have to go further up again.'

They walked up the next hill, stopping occasionally to

gaze in store windows or up at the houses, some of which had massive embellishments and were painted in bright colours quite at odds with their architecture. The colours were almost dazzling now that the fog had cleared and sun come out.

They both put up their parasols. Clara had little beads of perspiration on her forehead which ran down her cheeks and off the end of her nose. Jewel on the other hand seemed to remain cool, her pale face contrasting with Clara's pink flush.

'I'll have to stop and sit down,' Clara said eventually. 'I'm desperate for a cool drink. Up there.' She pointed a little further up the hill to where there was a sign for a restaurant. 'Let's go in if it's open.'

The bell clanged as they opened the door and after being greeted by the proprietor, a short dark man with a mass of curly hair, they were shown into a cool dark room with a window overlooking the city below them and brought a jug of iced lemonade.

'I won't be able to find it,' Jewel admitted. 'Papa's house. I really have no idea where it is.'

Papa's house. Papa's house! The words echoed in her head. Wilhelm is my papa; or at least he has been for so many years and yet that phrase rolled off my tongue so easily, and I know who I meant. She felt a sudden rush of warmth and heard a whisper of memory in her head. *Remember I will always love you, my darling.* Was that her father speaking to her? Edward? Not Wilhelm, although she knew that Wilhelm loved her as his own.

'Are you all right, Jewel?' Clara asked anxiously. 'You seem very preoccupied.'

'I am preoccupied,' she answered vaguely. 'I was wondering how I could be so foolish as to think I could remember where the house was after all these years. There have been so many changes, so many new buildings. It is an impossible task.'

Clara nodded and gratefully took a sip of lemonade. 'I fear it is,' she said.

Jewel sat silently, and drank calmly from her glass; already

131

she had made up her mind. Tomorrow they would take a cab and find Dolly. Dolly would tell her where her father's house was and arrange for her to meet Larkin and Jed. She leaned forward to gaze at the panoramic view spread out before them. Then she narrowed her eyes.

'Can you see the church down there?'

Clara's gaze swept the vista. 'The one with a bell tower? Is it a cathedral?'

'I believe it might be,' Jewel said vaguely. 'There's something niggling away at me and I don't know what it is.'

'Something about the church?'

Jewel nodded and then, turning round, she called the proprietor over to her. 'Can you tell me the name of the church down there?' she asked.

'*Si*,' he said, with a strong Spanish or Mexican accent. 'It ees St Mary's Cathedral. Twenty-one years old. The first cathedral of California. Built of granite, cut and brought from China, bricks brought from New England. A church for everyone; all communities, even the Chinese.'

He spoke as if he were a guide showing them around the edifice itself. Jewel thanked him and he moved away to attend to other patrons. Then he turned back. 'Everyone ees welcome,' he said. 'Two blocks north from Chinatown, near the bay on Montgomery Street.'

'Thank you.' Jewel smiled. 'We shall visit. I feel as if I know it,' she murmured to Clara. 'As if I've been. But I don't know when!'

'Then we'll take a look,' Clara said. 'But could we go tomorrow, please? By the time we get back down the hill it will be too late to walk there.'

'All right,' Jewel agreed, realizing that it wasn't the lateness of the afternoon that was troubling her cousin but the intense heat, unused as they were to such high temperatures.

She would have liked to wander off on her own to find the church, but that of course was impossible. Wilhelm's warning that they must only ever do things together rang in her ears. Besides, she was well aware that she would be very much at risk if she were foolish enough to venture out in the streets alone.

They ordered lunch at the restaurant as they hadn't eaten since breakfast and the aroma coming from the kitchen was tantalizing. They asked for a local dish that was not too spicy; the dishes that were being carried towards the other tables looked and smelled very pungent.

A dish of what looked like pale green cream flecked lightly with tomatoes was put in front of them, with warm flat bread shaped like little pancakes for them to dip into it; this, their host told them, was guacamole, made from avocado, chopped white onion and thinly sliced tomato and flavoured with lemon, black pepper and coriander. On a separate plate was a serving of raw fish in lime juice. They declared both delicious and were brought dishes of chicken and rice, black beans, and a plate of a delicious purple vegetable, stuffed with onions and tomatoes, which they were told was eggplant.

To finish, a plate of fresh fruit was brought to the table – melon, mango and banana – and another jug of lemonade.

Both were replete after the food and Clara declared she felt more rested and able to walk back down the hills. 'Perhaps if we bear down towards the direction of the bay,' she suggested, 'we shall get an idea of the whereabouts of the cathedral in relation to our hotel. We can hardly miss it, after all. It's quite a landmark.'

Jewel agreed, but unlike Clara, who had become more energetic, she was now feeling tired and lethargic after eating and pleased to be walking down the hills and not up.

By the time they reached the top of Clay Street, their legs were aching and both agreed that it would be nice to ride on the cable car again. They waited in line with the other passengers to board the car, and as they bought their tickets and stepped on board both felt a sense of smug satisfaction at riding a cable car and eating exotic food as if these were commonplace daily occurrences rather than adding memorable experiences to their lives.

CHAPTER SEVENTEEN

They were up early the next day, aiming to be out before the heat became too strong and dressing appropriately in light muslin dresses and sun bonnets. But when they emerged from the hotel after breakfast the weather was dull and foggy and much cooler.

On stepping off the cable car the previous day they had seen the cathedral of St Mary's in the distance and gulls wheeling in the sky where they judged the bay to be, and this was the direction in which they set off, Jewel having again determined that they should try to find their own way before contacting Dolly. It was a long walk and there were many people dashing about their business, waggons and traps clattering along the road. The two young women clung to each other's arms in fear of being knocked over or carried along in the melee.

'There are lots of Chinese people, have you noticed, Clara?' Jewel asked. 'And they're all heading in the same direction as we are. Perhaps this is the way to Chinatown.'

Clara had observed the Chinese men, dressed in cotton tunics and trousers and wearing hats shaped like wide lampshades, carrying pliable bamboo poles across their shoulders with a basket at each end filled with such diverse contents as laundry or sacks of peas, beans, rice or sunflowers. Many of these porters wore their black hair in a queue which hung halfway down their backs and sometimes to the tops of their thighs. This, Jewel and Clara had learned, was a symbol of subjugation imposed by the Manchu dynasty in eighteenth-century China, and although many Chinese had rebelled against it, there were still those who retained it in deference to their culture.

But the Chinese were not the only recipients of the Englishwomen's curiosity; there were also tall and handsome black-skinned men with their striking exotic wives, and women with honey-coloured complexions dressed in beautiful silk garments, their heads swathed in richly coloured turbans, who were given a second furtive glance. And then Clara gave Jewel a gentle nudge with her elbow to point out a little Chinese girl, as petite as a doll and dressed in gold satin with a wide sash round her waist, her black hair dressed high on the top of her head and adorned by a lily; she was being carried by a man – either her father or her husband, for who could tell in this new and alien country – because her tiny bound feet were too fragile to walk on the cobbled roads.

There were other people who were given a quick glance before eyes were averted: women with coarse and reddened complexions, who sat on cane chairs outside hostelries with a glass of liquor on the table in front of them, a cheroot between their lips and one leg crossed indelicately over the other, chatting in a free and easy manner to men dressed in rough working clothes sporting large-brimmed hats.

After walking for half an hour and not seeming to get any closer, Jewel suggested they hail a horse cab and ride for the rest of the journey to the bay. A high-stepping horse drawing an open surrey pulled up almost immediately. It had a fringed canopy over seating for four, but the driver said he would take them wherever they wanted to go.

'Down to the bay, please, if you would be so kind,' Clara said.

The driver grinned at her accent. 'Sure thing, ma'am. Where exactly? Plenty of coves to choose from. You want Steamboat Point if you're going on a trip. Or Telegraph Hill to see the view, or I can drop you on the corner of Broadway and Montgomery.'

The two girls looked at each other. 'The nearest place to Chinatown,' Jewel said. 'Close to St Mary's Cathedral.'

The driver looked at her and his smile faded. He nodded. 'Montgomery, then. If you're sure. You gotta be careful down there.'

'We will be,' Jewel said stiffly.

Coming from the town of Hull, they had in their naivety thought that the San Francisco wharves would be similar to, though larger than, the docklands adjacent to their homes. They were therefore unprepared for the huge bay full of shipping which shortly confronted them. There were hundreds of tall-masted ships, steamboats, barges, vessels carrying timber and coal and passenger ships sailing to all corners of the world. Other coves they passed by were occupied by numerous shipbuilding yards, lumber yards piled high with timber and a great number of warehouses edging the waterfront.

They both exhaled a breath. 'I had no idea,' Jewel murmured.

Clara shook her head. 'Nor I. Shall we ask him to take us straight to St Mary's?'

'Yes,' Jewel said, and then added in a low voice: 'Will you ask him, Clara? I don't care for his attitude.'

Clara nodded. She too had noticed his change of demeanour when Jewel spoke to him. Was he prejudiced against the Chinese? She had noticed anti-Chinese slogans pinned to hoardings and graffiti written on walls, calling for Chinese immigration to be halted.

Clara called to him and he changed route and took them to the cathedral. As they paid his fare, he pointed in the direction of Chinatown.

'Careful then, miss, if that's where you're heading. Just keep close together and don't try anything they offer.' He looked to where Jewel was waiting. 'And take care of your friend. She's got Chinese in her, ain't she?'

'Thank you,' she said, pointedly avoiding his question, and turned away.

'What did he say?' Jewel asked in a small voice.

'Nothing.' Clara smiled. 'Just said he hoped we'd have an enjoyable day.'

They crossed the road towards the cathedral and Jewel slowed her steps. 'Just a moment,' she murmured, and took a shallow breath as she looked about her. 'There's something—'

'What?' Clara asked. 'Are you all right?'

'I don't know, I'm – I'm remembering something, but I don't know what.'

'Would you like to go inside and sit down for a moment?' Clara took Jewel's arm. She seemed anxious, unsure of herself.

'I think I would,' Jewel said. 'There's some recollection niggling at me; perhaps if I sit somewhere quiet I might remember what it is.'

They went into the cool dark interior and sat in a pew at the back. They were both glad of the respite as the weather was now very hot and once more they were wilting. Clara said nothing, not wanting to distract Jewel, who was gazing round the old church as if gathering up memories.

'I've been here before,' Jewel whispered. 'But not with Papa.' She lifted her eyes up beyond the marble altar and the arches which rode above it to the high vaulted ceiling. 'With Aunt Gianna.'

Clara stared at her but again said nothing. Jewel's voice had taken on a childlike quality as she spoke her adoptive mother's name. The name she had called her before coming to England.

After about ten minutes, Jewel indicated that they should leave and they stepped outside into brilliant sunshine. She looked about her and then said, 'This way. This is the way we should go.'

Clara demurred. 'But this isn't towards Chinatown.'

'I know.' Jewel put up her parasol. It was green, which matched her gown but made her skin look paler and more translucent. 'But this is the way to Papa's house.'

'How can you remember?' Clara was astonished. 'It's so long ago.'

Jewel nodded. 'I'm almost sure.' She led the way towards a steep hill. 'Gianna – Mama – when she first came to visit Papa Edward' – she added on her real father's name so as not to confuse him with Wilhelm – 'used to take me out shopping or looking at places. And one of them was the cathedral. I'd never been before. I suppose my father never thought of taking me. In fact I don't remember going anywhere very much, only that people came to see us. Like Dolly and Larkin.'

They continued up the hill, stopping now and again to catch their breath. 'I hope they put a cable car up here,' Clara gasped. 'I think the city needs more than just one.'

The street was lined on both sides with tall buildings, shops, offices and apartment blocks. Jewel's steps began to slow, not only because of the steepness of the hill.

'I'm having doubts,' she said. 'I don't recall any of these buildings. They must all be new. I only remember wooden houses and shops. Even Papa's house – I think it was a wooden cabin.'

'Such a lot has happened since you were here, Jewel, and remember you were seeing everything through a child's eyes,' Clara reminded her. 'It's a prosperous city now, with so many business people coming here, trading on the back of the gold mining.'

Clara had done her research on California as soon as Jewel had asked her to accompany her, and had read all she could about its history, particularly regarding San Francisco.

'I know,' Jewel said. 'Perhaps it was happening even when I was a child, but I wouldn't have known about it. And now the city is bigger and wider and taller and unrecognizable. I'm looking at it through the eyes of a stranger.'

She became pensive, her emotions mixed. 'Mama said that my father told her he arrived in San Francisco with nothing; just the clothes on his back and a pack of cards which some-one gave him.' She smiled wistfully. 'And he finished up with enough money to buy a saloon and a theatre.'

'And sufficient to leave you a legacy,' Clara interrupted. 'For you to come back here!'

'Yes.' Jewel nodded. 'That too.' She glanced at her cousin. 'Do you think he knew that I would come back?'

Clara took her hand and squeezed it. 'I'm certain that it would have been what he hoped for.'

They were almost at the top now and slowed their steps, both feeling very hot. The hill levelled out and the tall buildings were replaced by single-storeyed ones, some built of timber. They walked on, passing a row of stores and then a plot of land which had been marked out as if to be built on. Next to it was a long low restaurant and simultaneously they drew in their breath as a rich aroma assailed their nostrils.

'Food!' Clara said.

'Tomatoes! Onions,' Jewel added. 'Fresh bread! Is it lunchtime already?' She paused for a moment, gazing at the closed door and the windows, where the blinds were pulled down. Her forehead creased slightly in concentration and she pressed her lips together before moving on.

At the side of the restaurant and set slightly back from it was a timbered cabin. There were clean curtains at the window, though it appeared to be unlived in. In front of it was a small overgrown garden with a neglected flower bed and parched grass in need of cutting.

Jewel stopped and stared and felt a whole range of sensations engulfing her. A pulse in her throat began to throb and she swallowed and licked her lips.

'Clara,' she whispered. 'This is it. I'm sure of it.'

Clara gazed at her, but before she could speak they heard someone singing. It was a loud joyous sound, untrained but melodic, and they both turned their heads towards the restaurant, which now had its door open. Writing on the window in white chalk as he sang was a young thickset man with dark hair loose on his neck.

Jewel walked back towards him. She felt as if she were floating, trancelike, in a dream. Her childish memories battled with present-day reality and her breath quickened as she stood watching him. His profile was familiar. She saw a gleaming white shirt on broad shoulders, the sleeves rolled up to his elbows, and as he lifted his arms to write she saw that they were muscular.

Clara stood beside her, wondering why her cousin was watching this man but remaining silent.

He either sensed their presence or saw their reflection in the glass because his singing ceased and he turned sideways to look at the two young women. It seemed as if he was about to give a merry quip and invite them into the restaurant; but he paused. Their faces were shaded by their bonnets and the parasols which they carried over their heads, but he saw that one was very fair. An Englishwoman, he thought; his mother always said that you could tell an Englishwoman by her skin: like apple blossom, she said. Delicate pink and white.

But the other one was different; not Chinese, at least not like Pinyin, who helped them in the kitchen. Pinyin had a round, moonlike face, with dark slanting eyes which twinkled constantly because of his sense of his good fortune in working for them; this small and petite goddess had sleek black hair coiled behind a slender neck, high cheekbones, wide dark impenetrable eyes and soft lips which parted softly as she spoke almost in a whisper.

'Renzo?'

CHAPTER EIGHTEEN

There was only one person who had ever called him Renzo. But he scarcely remembered her. She had been his childhood friend and they had spent every day of their young lives together. She had eaten at his home – the two rooms behind the bakery which his parents had run – and they had played in her garden next door. He had been devastated when she went away and had cried for days, until his father had said in his strong Italian accent, 'Enough! Be a man. There will be many other girls to weep over in your life.'

But he had remembered his mother crying too, and not just on the day that Jewel . . . *that* was her name . . . had gone away, but on another day some weeks later.

Lorenzo took a step towards them. Bemused, he looked from one to the other, and then his gaze settled on the dark-haired girl and he said softly, 'Jewel? Is it you?'

She smiled. 'You remember me?'

'Yes,' he breathed. 'I do.'

He took another step forward and put out both his hands for hers. She slipped them into his. Such small fragile hands, he thought, and her face – yes, a hint of the Orient. Had he ever known that?

'I can't believe it,' he whispered and kissed her gently on her cheek and then on her hands. 'You went away. Where did you go?'

Jewel could hardly speak and then only to murmur. 'To

141

England; with Gianna, who adopted me. My father was dying, although I didn't know it then.'

He nodded. Yes. That was why his mother had cried the second time, because the man next door had died.

'Lorenzo,' Jewel said, 'I'd like to introduce you to my cousin Clara. Clara, this is my friend Lorenzo, from my childhood.'

Clara dipped her knee and put out her hand, and Lorenzo reluctantly let go of Jewel's in order to clasp it and say how pleased he was to meet her.

'Come inside, please,' he said. 'It's too hot outside for English ladies. You're not used to such temperatures, I'm sure.'

Indeed we're not, Clara thought, as gratefully she sat down inside at a table spread with a white cloth, and mopped her forehead, whilst Lorenzo went off to bring a jug of cold water.

He poured two glasses and then sat across from them. He put his elbows on the table and his chin in his hands and shook his head, looking at Jewel. 'I can't believe it,' he repeated. 'I never thought I'd see you again.'

'I have been back to America,' she told him. 'But not to California. My adoptive father, Wilhelm Dreumel, is American and has property in Dreumel's Creek.' When he shook his head as if he didn't know, she added, 'Above Duquesne? Mountain country.'

He still didn't know and she went on to explain some of Wilhelm's background and how he and Gianna had decided to live in England so that she could grow up with her cousins, Clara and Elizabeth, and get to know her English grandmother.

'But,' she went on, 'when I came of age, I decided I wanted to come here, to visit the place where I was born and where my real father had lived . . . and,' she hesitated, 'try to find out more about my birth mother.'

Lorenzo pursed his lips. 'I don't remember her. I can just remember your father, but only vaguely, and there's another man who comes here sometimes. Larkin,' he said. 'But I don't

142

know the connection. Perhaps my mother knows. She seems to know most of what goes on around here.'

'Your mother!' Jewel said. 'Oh yes!' She gave a sudden smile. 'She used to feed me with pasta!'

Lorenzo laughed. 'She feeds *everybody* with pasta. Would you like to eat? We shall get busy in about an hour, so . . .'

'Yes, please,' they chorused. 'And some of that lovely bread we can smell,' Jewel added.

His dark eyes twinkled humorously. 'Her speciality! People come from miles around to buy her *pane*. She's almost finished baking now. Just putting in the last batch of the day, then I'll fetch her to meet you.'

Lorenzo went off to the kitchen to prepare some food for them, and Jewel looked at Clara. She could barely suppress her excitement and felt all of a quiver. Although she had wanted to find the place where she had lived with her father, she hadn't dreamed that she would meet up with Lorenzo. He was a half-forgotten memory. Now she was buzzing with anticipation of what else might be in store for her.

'He's very handsome, isn't he?' Clara whispered. 'And so – so amiable!'

Jewel nodded in agreement. He was indeed. The dark-haired, chubby little boy had grown into a handsome young man and she felt very strange when he gazed at her from his smiling eyes.

They heard him calling 'Madre', and a woman's voice calling back to him. Presently he emerged again, bringing with him a short, stout, dark-haired woman, who was wiping floury hands on a cloth and speaking excitedly in Italian.

Jewel stood up. 'Madre!' she exclaimed. She had always called her that, following Lorenzo's example and not knowing then, when she was a child, that it meant Mother.

Signora Maria Galli flung out her arms and embraced Jewel in a warm hug. She smelled of yeast and dough, of garlic and tomatoes, and as Jewel breathed in her scent so many memories came flooding back.

'It ees so good to see you again.' Maria laughed and cried

143

and dried her tears on the cloth, spreading flour over her cheeks. 'Your poor papa! I ask him, please let you stay with me, but then the English lady come and he say that you go to England with her.'

Jewel wiped her own tears and said in a choked voice, 'I did. I went to England to see my relatives and Mama – Gianna – decided that we would stay.' She introduced Clara and she too was given a bear hug.

'And now you 'ave come back,' Maria said. 'It ees good! Very good! Now you will eat some pasta and tell me everything.'

Lorenzo brought them each a plate of antipasti: ham, beef and salami, grilled artichokes, pungent and sweet red peppers, tomatoes with garlic cloves and fresh bread with a bowl of olive oil with basil. 'Eat,' he urged them, as they waited for their pasta to be cooked.

The restaurant began to fill up with customers and Lorenzo was kept busy attending them, although most seemed to be old friends who slapped him on the back, laughing and chatting as they drank wine poured from a carafe and rubbed garlic on their bread and dipped it into bowls of oil.

'Is that what we do?' Clara whispered. 'I wondered what the oil was for.'

'Yes,' Jewel said. 'I think so. I don't know; if I ever did, I've forgotten!'

Lorenzo came back to them and sat down close to Jewel. He smiled at them both. 'The bread is good, isn't it?' He broke off a piece and rubbed it with a garlic clove and then dipped it into the olive oil before popping it into his mouth. He grinned at Clara. 'Now if you do the same, you will only be kissed by an Italian, or maybe a Frenchman who has been eating garlic too. Not an Englishman!'

Jewel gazed at him, and followed his example, but she drew in her breath as the pungent flavour hit her taste buds.

Clara looked at them both and laughed. 'Well, I don't ex-pect to be kissed by anyone, especially not an Englishman, so . . .' She tore off a corner of bread and ceremoniously did the same, with gasping consequences.

144

Lorenzo laughed and called out to some people at another table. Neither Jewel nor Clara understood what he said as he spoke in rapid Italian, but the men laughed back and one got up from his seat and came across to them.

He gave a courtly bow and, bending low over Clara, lifted her hand, murmuring 'Buon giorno, signorina' and pressing his lips to it before bowing to Jewel.

Clara put her hand to her throat. She was astonished. How informal everyone was in this country! She had been kissed by James Crawford and now, even though only on her hand, by an unknown man. She swallowed hard and turned to Lorenzo for an explanation.

'I told my friends that the English lady did not expect to be kissed at all today, so Federico volunteered.' He frowned. 'You're not offended? It was meant only as a joke.'

Clara flushed and Lorenzo gave her a gentle smile and lifted his eyebrows. She was indeed a pink and white Englishwoman.

'No,' she said softly. 'Not offended at all. Please tell your friend that I am charmed.'

Lorenzo translated and the men at the table roared and teased Federico. He put his hand to his chest and bowed again before returning to the table, where he was subjected to much banter by his compatriots. As they mimed hands on hearts and handkerchiefs mopping brows he glanced over his shoulder at Clara.

Lorenzo's mother came to sit with them when lunch was nearly over and Lorenzo went to speak to his friends. Jewel saw that he was telling some of them about her for they were nodding their heads or raising their eyebrows. Then she saw a Chinese man come out of the kitchen and begin to clear away the dirty dishes from the tables.

Maria saw her glance at him. 'That is Pinyin.' She shrugged. 'He works for us for a long time.' She leaned towards Jewel. 'Do you know that it ees because of your father that we are here?'

Jewel was puzzled. 'I don't understand,' she said. 'Weren't you always here? But with a bakery, not a restaurant?'

'*Si*, we were,' she said. 'We rented the store from your father. He owned this building and the one next door and the saloon.'

'Oh,' Jewel said. 'I didn't know.'

'Then,' Maria went on, 'after you had left, your papa, he send for us one day and said he was leaving the store to us in his will.' She wiped her eye. 'And the one next door. He was a good man. He saw how we struggled.'

So many things Jewel didn't know about her father. How generous he had been!

'We rented out the other one,' Maria said, 'and when the tenants left about ten years later we expanded.'

'And started this restaurant!' Jewel exclaimed.

'*Si*. But we were halfway through the building of it when Lorenzo's papa died. You remember him, yes?'

Jewel shook her head. She didn't. She couldn't ever recall seeing a man about.

'Lorenzo was sixteen, very young to 'ave responsibility, but he is clever boy,' Maria said proudly. 'He got all his friends to give us help.' She pointed to the table of young men, some of whom were preparing to leave. 'Some of these here today. They help us with their own hands.'

As Maria was telling her story, Clara rose from her seat, murmuring 'Excuse me', and sauntered across to where Federico was standing with his hat in his hands, saying, she thought, goodbye to his friends. All the young men rose as she approached.

'Miss Clara,' Federico greeted her. 'Federico Cavalli.' He looked at her intently and gave a small bow. 'I hope I didn't embarrass you?'

She laughed. 'No. Not at all.' She had been slightly self-conscious, but she wasn't going to admit it. 'So you speak good English after all?' she teased him.

'No ma'am.' He shook his head. 'I speak American.'

'I beg your pardon.' She smiled. 'Forgive me.'

'Anything, Miss Clara,' he said solemnly. 'I could forgive you anything!'

She blushed as she saw the grins on his friends' faces. 'I thought you were Italian!'

He took her by the arm and led her away from the table where the young men couldn't hear them. 'I'm American,' he said. 'Born here in San Francisco. I have never been to Italy where my forebears hail from.'

'I see,' she said. 'And your friends?'

'Italian extraction, just like me.'

He was tall and rather thin for an Italian, with intense dark eyes, she thought, unlike Lorenzo, who was of average height but very broad across the shoulders and had very merry, smiling eyes.

'Are you staying with Lorenzo and his mother?' he asked.

'Oh no! We only met them today. Jewel is retracing the steps of her childhood. We're staying in a hotel near California Street.'

'Ah!' He appeared to be considering, and then said, 'I don't know how you go about things in England, but is it permissible for a man to ask a young lady out for a cup of coffee?'

Clara bit her lip. Well, no, it wasn't, not without consulting her mother first. But then her mother wasn't here.

He saw her hesitation. 'I guess it isn't? But perhaps two young ladies would be all right?'

She shook her head. 'Not really. Not with someone we have just met.'

'But we could meet here? With Mrs Galli? Sort of accidentally?'

She smiled. 'Yes. I think that would be all right.'

'Good.' He nodded. 'About eleven o'clock tomorrow?'

It was agreed, with the proviso that Jewel hadn't made any other arrangements. She felt a prickle of excitement as she said goodbye and turned back to where Jewel and Maria Galli were still talking. Federico was a very engaging man; very civil but with a compelling persona. He would be an agreeable companion with a laconic sense of humour, she thought, excusing herself for her lapse of propriety. Dangerous? She

147

dismissed the idea as preposterous. No harm in it, she mused. Mama would not object at all, though Papa might.

Jewel's normally calm countenance was animated. 'Clara! Mrs Galli says that I can go and look inside Papa's house!' She took a breath. 'I didn't know, and I don't know if Mama is aware of it either, but apparently the house is mine! Mrs Galli has looked after it for all these years, but Papa left it to me!' She stood up, and Clara saw that she was trembling. 'I'd like to go now, please. If I may!'

CHAPTER NINETEEN

Hull

Wilhelm had boarded the first available London train. He had kissed Georgiana goodbye and although they had previously discussed the option of travelling together she realized that this was something he needed to do alone.

She was not a woman under her husband's thumb, ready to defer to his every demand or wish. Theirs was a complete partnership; she followed her own personal aspirations, un-like many married women of her acquaintance, but in this instance knew that she should comply with his instincts. He was a seasoned traveller and with his quiet decisive charm was able to board a boat, ship or carriage at a moment's notice.

The following morning was long but her mind was active; she thought over the possibilities regarding the calamitous fire in Yeller and the potential dangers that might fall or have already fallen on Jewel and Clara. Through her own experience in travelling to America with the innocent Kitty as her only companion, she realized full well that there were dangers for women travelling alone; and yet why should we be denied the adventure of travel, she thought, or the privilege of knowing other lands and the way in which people of other countries conduct themselves and live their lives? It is this comprehension that will help us grow.

And as for Jewel herself, she needs to find out about her

parentage. I cannot tell her anything more about her father, for I knew him for only a short time. And in the years since his departure from England, under a terrible cloud, he had become someone else entirely, someone that even his brother Martin did not know.

During the afternoon, tired of her own company, she put on a silk-trimmed mantle and matching hat and set off across town to see Grace. She walked slowly, for she felt vaguely out of sorts, and paused to look in shop windows in Whitefriargate, though not actually seeing anything, so absorbed was she in her thoughts. She crossed over into Silver Street and glanced towards the Land of Green Ginger, the oddly named street where Ruby had her toyshop, and wondered how Dan and Thomas were coping without their childhood friends, Jewel and Clara.

Thomas was an even-tempered, level-headed, pleasant young man, and she knew that Grace hoped for a match for Clara with the younger son of her best friend. But Dan was different entirely, and although it was obvious to everyone that he was besotted with Jewel, Georgiana hoped with all her heart that he wouldn't ask for her hand, since neither she nor Wilhelm would approve of her marriage to such a volatile and impetuous individual, however charming he might be at times.

Georgiana crossed over Lowgate and cut down narrow Scale Lane into High Street, turning left towards the house where Grace and Martin lived. She hadn't sent a calling card but was sure of a welcome without one.

Grace opened the door herself, having seen her from a window. She looked pale and anxious. 'Is there any news?' she asked, ushering Georgiana inside.

'No.' Georgiana felt relieved to be there and able to share her anxieties. 'It's too soon. Wilhelm will telegraph as soon as he knows anything. He's as worried as we are.'

Grace nodded. 'I hardly slept a wink last night and Martin was pacing about until after midnight. But, as I said to Ruby – she called in this morning – I can't help but think that whatever is done is done. We're so far away we can't possibly help if anything's gone wrong.'

'We can only hope that they were well clear of the area before the fire broke out,' Georgiana said quietly. 'It is out of our hands.'

They sat together, finding solace in each other's company, until they heard the front door open and close.

'Martin,' Grace murmured. 'He's been to 'Exchange again. The second time today, even though he was told that we'd be informed immediately if a message came.'

'Nothing!' Martin exclaimed as he came into the sitting room. 'Hello, Georgiana. Presumably you haven't heard anything either?'

Georgiana shook her head. 'We're worrying unnecessarily, I'm sure. If there had been bad news we would have heard it before the newspaper was told. We must be patient.'

They were brought tea and cake and continued a spasmodic conversation, assuring each other that all was well. Martin got up again.

'Don't go out again, dearest,' Grace pleaded. 'You'll wear yourself out. A message will come.'

Martin ran his hand over his forehead. 'Yes, of course it will, but I hate just sitting doing nothing. The waiting is awful.'

'It is,' Georgiana agreed, and then they all started as the doorbell rang. Martin rushed to the door.

'Telegram for you, sir.' A boy in uniform stood on the step. 'This came just after you'd left.'

'Is this the only one?' Martin asked. 'Are you taking one to Mrs Dreumel?'

The boy hesitated and shifted uneasily.

'It's just that she's here,' Martin explained. 'If you are, it would save you a journey.'

Still the messenger dithered. 'Not sure if I can say,' he finally said. 'It's private, you know. I'm supposed to deliver it to 'house.'

'Then wait here a moment,' Martin said, 'and I'll fetch Mrs Dreumel.'

151

Georgiana came to the door. 'I am Georgiana Dreumel,' she said, and gave her address. 'I'm expecting a telegram from my husband Wilhelm Dreumel.'

'I know you, Mrs Dreumel.' The boy's face cleared. 'I'm not sure this is officially allowed but I'll take a chance.' He fished in his bag and brought out the telegram. 'I'll need a signature, please.'

Georgiana signed his book. 'No one need know that I was not at home,' she said quietly. 'And I'll take the blame if necessary.' She smiled at him. 'This is extremely urgent, and you have done me a great service in allowing me to have it now.'

He tipped his cap and left. Georgiana closed the door behind him and went back into the hall. She felt nauseous as she opened the message from Wilhelm.

All safe, she read. *Both gone to California. Yeller devastated. Catching the next ship out. Will write from New York. Wilhelm.*

Georgiana staggered to the nearest chair against the wall and sat down, heaving a great breath. She had been holding herself together ever since they had read the news and now the release of tension revealed itself in a flow of tears.

'Georgiana!' Martin came through from the sitting room and patted her shoulder. 'All's well, thank the Lord.'

'Yes,' she whispered. 'Indeed.'

They sat for a while in the sitting room, each saying that they had known all along that their daughters were safe. Martin poured Grace and Georgiana a small glass of brandy and water each and they sipped them slowly, savouring the comforting warmth which gradually eased their nervous strain.

'I'd have known if anything had happened to Clara,' Grace said softly. 'And so would Elizabeth, but yesterday I received a letter from her asking if I'd heard from Clara, and saying she was cross because Clara hadn't written since arriving in Dreumel's Creek.' She lifted her eyes to Martin. 'She'd have known,' she said simply. 'They're twins, after all.'

Martin gave her a gentle smile and nodded. 'You're right,

of course, my dear,' he said, and Georgiana felt a small pang of envy at the bond between this couple. She wished that Wilhelm had been here to share with her this moment of ease.

'Did Wilhelm say anything more in your message?' Martin asked. 'He only said that the girls were safe in ours. Did he mention your friends?'

'All safe,' Georgiana told him, 'but Yeller is devastated. Those are the words he used. And,' she added slowly, 'he's catching the first ship out to be with them.'

After a moment, Grace said, 'Will you stay with us tonight, Georgiana? You know that you're very welcome.'

Georgiana shook her head. 'Thank you. I know I am.' She took another deep breath. She felt that she couldn't get enough air into her lungs. 'But forgive me if I go home. I shall go to bed and rest now that I know they are safe; and then – and then tomorrow I shall make arrangements.' She smiled a little tearfully. 'And after that I shall pack a trunk and follow Wilhelm to Yeller.'

'Alone?' Grace asked anxiously.

Georgiana nodded. 'I've done it before.'

'With respect, Georgiana,' Martin spoke like an older, wiser uncle, 'that was over twenty-five years ago.'

Georgiana laughed, her tension easing. 'On my first voyage to America I met a woman from Beverley who was travelling alone. She was nearly sixty and had, as she described it, *upped sticks* for the last time. I am nowhere near that age, and I am used to travelling.'

Martin was silenced for a moment and then said with a smile in his voice, 'You were always formidable, Georgiana. Even when you were young. You always knew what you wanted and set out to get it. Will you come back?'

'Oh, I do hope so,' Grace interjected. Martin had known Georgiana long before she had met her. They were from the same social background, unlike her, a mill girl from the back streets of Hull. 'We'd miss you, Georgiana, if you stayed out there.'

153

'Why would you think that I won't come back?' Georgiana parried. She knew in her heart that she might not. Wilhelm was restless; aching, she knew, to go home. The disastrous fire in Yeller had given him the impetus, a valid reason for going back, but she also realized, with the security of knowing that she was loved, that he wouldn't stay there without her. And she, for him, would stay.

'I don't know,' Martin answered. 'It's just a feeling. Wilhelm is a born traveller. This town is too small for him.'

'Dreumel's Creek is smaller,' Georgiana told him. 'And can't ever grow much bigger because of the mountains. You should come sometime. It's beautiful.'

Grace glanced hesitantly at her husband. She had never been out of Yorkshire. 'Maybe one day,' she murmured. 'When Clara is married.'

'Of course,' Georgiana agreed. 'But what if she has fallen in love with someone in America?' she teased them. 'People there are much freer in their friendships.'

Grace shook her head. 'She'd still come home,' she said quietly. 'That much I know about her.'

At Georgiana's request Martin ordered her a cab; she didn't feel that she had the energy to walk. 'You won't leave without telling us?' he said as he came down the steps with her to the waiting hansom. 'I'd like to help you with your travelling arrangements. I'll come with you to Liverpool, if I may?'

'Martin! Of *course* I will tell you. I wouldn't dream of going without discussing my plans with you.' She put her cheek up to receive his kiss and turned to wave to Grace watching through the window. 'Besides, I have things to do first: the servants and so on. It will be a week – ten days perhaps – before I set off, and I'll wait to hear from Wilhelm first.' She smiled. 'Don't worry about me, Martin.'

He gave a wry grimace. 'I won't. But I expect Wilhelm will when he hears that you are travelling alone!'

CHAPTER TWENTY

Grace met Ruby whilst out shopping in the Market Place the next day. Both to some extent had retained their plebeian roots in spite of having been lifted up into a more urbane society. Ruby didn't consider that anyone could choose better meat or fish than she could, because, she said, she had had so little of it, and could smell rancid meat from a mile away. But she also enjoyed the pleasure of looking the butcher in the eye and watching him bow and scrape as he showed her the best cut and arranged for it to be delivered to her house, the home of a respected tradesman, when once he would have chased her away with his cleaver when she'd begged for a few bones to make broth.

Grace, on the other hand, never wanted to deny her beginnings; by being seen out on the streets of her home town she could be approached by the needy, the sick, and those who had no one else to turn to. Occasionally, she might be taken advantage of by some who had drunk away their wages and belongings, or spent them on an opium habit. But even those inveterate down-and-outs were not refused help. She never forgot that Ruby's mother had been an incurable opium addict and in the end it had killed her.

At Grace's insistence, when she and Martin were first married they had set up a trust fund for the destitute, but it was Martin who looked after the accounts, for he knew that Grace would give it all away.

Now, Grace gave Ruby the news that Clara and Jewel were safe, for Ruby and her family were as anxious as she had been on hearing about the fire at Yeller. Then she told her that Wilhelm had already left for America and that Georgiana intended to follow him.

'I remember when she did it 'first time, don't you, Grace?' Ruby said. 'I think she's ever so brave. She'll be tekking a maid with her, I expect?'

'Apparently not,' Grace replied. 'She wants to go by herself.'

Ruby huffed out a breath. 'But who'll see to her bags and suchlike? And mek sure she's on 'right train and ship and everything?'

'A porter will see to her bags, and Martin has offered to take her to Liverpool. I expect he'll make sure she boards 'right ship.' Grace smiled.

The furthest Ruby had ever travelled was nine miles to the market town of Beverley, when on occasion she had accompanied Daniel or one of her sons in the delivery cart conveying toys or furniture to the shop owners there. It had been a real treat, she declared each time, but she was always glad to be home again. Ruby felt safe and secure tucked into her very own small corner of Hull.

'Dan'll be relieved to hear that Jewel's safe,' she said now. 'And Clara as well, of course,' she added. 'But you know how he is over Jewel. When I told him you were waiting for news he was ready to pack his bags and leave for America himself.'

'And Thomas?' Grace raised her eyebrows. 'What did he say?'

'Oh, you know my Tom,' Ruby said affectionately. 'He just said, "They'll be all right." But I reckon he was worried anyway. He just doesn't show it.'

They parted company and went their separate ways, Grace to finish her shopping and Ruby hurrying home to cook dinner for her menfolk.

'Jewel and Clara are safe,' she declared as soon as they came in to eat. 'I've seen Grace and they've heard 'news by telegram!'

Ruby was amazed at the speed of communication from all the way across the sea. 'They've gone on to California.'

'By themselves?' Dan asked. 'God's teeth!' He ducked as Ruby slapped him for his choice of language. 'Sorry, Ma. But it's not safe for young women to travel across America on their own. It's still a wild country.'

In some respects Dan was very like his mother, but Thomas grinned, relief showing palpably in spite of his previous assertions that Clara and Jewel would be all right. 'How would you know?' he said. 'You're no more travelled than 'chair you're sitting in.'

Dan glared at him but his mother interrupted. 'And 'other news is that Jewel's mother . . . *Georgiana*' – it always seemed impolite to Ruby to call a lady like Mrs Dreumel by her first name, even though she had been asked to do so – 'is going to America. Her husband has already gone to help out with 'town that's burnt down, and Mrs— *Georgiana* is going to follow him. By herself!'

Three pairs of eyes fastened themselves to her face. Her husband, Daniel, a man of few words in recent years, stared at her and then dropped his eyes and continued eating. Thomas blew out his mouth in a silent whistle, whilst Dan stared at her as if mesmerized. Eventually he found his voice.

'Why?' he asked huskily. 'Why's she going?'

Ruby shrugged. 'I don't know. To be with her husband, I suppose, and mebbe to help out. This town – Yeller, it's called – is completely burnt down. Right to 'ground. Except for 'hotel where their friends live. Everything's got to be completely rebuilt.'

'She's a carpenter then, is she?' her husband grunted. 'This fine lady?'

'No,' Ruby said sharply. 'But if you'd gone off somewhere I'd follow you, wouldn't I?'

'Would you?' He fixed his eyes on her face.

'Yes, Daniel,' she said quietly. 'You know very well that I would.'

*   *   *

157

Dan stood outside the kitchen door, whittling a piece of wood. He was trying to imagine what it would be like for a woman, older than his mother, to be travelling on her own. She was an experienced traveller, of course. Everyone knew that Mrs Dreumel had gone to America when she was a very young woman. He admired her for that in a grudging kind of way; but he thought that it would have been easier for her, with the right connections and money, which was a great advantage, than for someone like himself who knew nobody and had no pot of money, apart from what he earned.

I suppose those early pioneers took a chance, he thought. Most of them had nowt to take with them. Just 'price of a ticket and 'clothes they stood up in. Could I have done that? He thought that he probably could have done, but he'd always had the advantage of a regular job, working with his father and brother, and plenty to eat on the table. Comfort and security took away the desire of ambition, he decided. I haven't had hunger in my belly; it has always been full and therefore satisfied, and yet . . . He sat down on the doorstep as he mused. I've never been totally satisfied with my life. I've always felt a bit disgruntled; I'd admit that to myself. Perhaps because my life's been mapped out for me. It was expected that I'd follow Da into his business. And we've built it up, especially when Thomas joined us.

He scratched at his beard. Tom's satisfied with his life. He's a good craftsman. Better'n me. Thomas was the one who came up with the ideas for different products: new toys every Christmas; a special swinging crib for a new baby. I'm a handyman, he thought. Give me a saw, a bradawl, a hammer and chisel and I can fix and build most things, but a designer, a creator, I'm not.

Thomas came out, looking for him. 'What's up?' he said.

'Nowt much,' Dan said. 'Just having a bit of a think.'

'About Jewel?' his brother asked perceptively. 'Is that why her ma's going to America?'

Dan shook his head. 'No. She's not going to see her, is she?

Jewel and Clara have moved on. Mrs Dreumel's following her husband.'

Thomas leaned on the wall and looked down at him. 'Why don't you go with her?'

Dan frowned. 'What? Why'd I do that?'

Thomas shrugged. 'Because you're unsettled. You have been ever since Jewel left. You might or might not meet up with her but it'd be an experience, wouldn't it?' He grinned and added, 'And you could carry Mrs Dreumel's bags. And mebbe do a bit o' carpentry when you got there.'

Dan stood up. 'Why don't you go?' he challenged.

'I don't need to. I like what I do here.' Thomas pressed his lips together, a habit Dan recognized as only occurring when Thomas was bothered about something. 'Besides, I've to wait for Clara coming home.'

'Really?' Dan jeered. 'Are you so sure that she will? She might have met some gold miner or cattle rancher who'll persuade her to stay!'

'Not in New York she won't,' Thomas declared. 'I don't know about 'other places, Dreumel's Creek or California, but one thing's for sure, she'd come back to tell me.'

Dan slapped him on the back. 'Course she will. Come on, let's get back to work or Da'll skin our hides!'

His brother's idea niggled at him all day and the next, as he turned over the possibility of travelling with Georgiana Dreumel; but if I did go, he thought, I'd want to meet up with Jewel eventually. That'd be 'whole point of me going. She'd be sure to go back to this place, Dreumel's Creek, if she thought her parents were there. He pondered over what reason he would give to Jewel's mother for asking if he might travel with her. Would I say that I'd like to help in Yeller? That my father didn't need me here just now; that he and Thomas could manage perfectly well without me, and that I've got itchy feet and am looking for something more out of life?

And – he broke out into a sweat when he thought about it – what exactly would I say to Da?

Dan could never fathom out why his father had taken against

159

Jewel. Even when she was a child he had held back from her, never joking or teasing her as he had Elizabeth and Clara. Yet Dan couldn't believe it was because she was of mixed race. Prejudiced? He could not believe that of his father.

On the third day, when he and Thomas were alone in the workshop, he broached the subject. 'I think I'll ask her,' he blurted out.

Thomas had his mind on other things. 'What? Ask who?'

'Mrs Dreumel. I'm going to ask if I can go with her.'

'Aye?' It had been a proposal made half in jest. Thomas hadn't really expected Dan to take up the idea. 'What'll you say to Da?'

'Shan't mention it unless Mrs Dreumel agrees to it.' Dan chewed on his lip. 'Then I'll think of something.'

He dressed carefully that evening after supper in a clean white shirt and dark grey jacket and trousers, and a light grey waistcoat that he borrowed from Thomas. They were of similar size but his brother was more aware of fashion than he was. Dan hesitated over his choice of headgear and decided finally that he would wear, or at least carry, his father's bowler rather than his own battered soft hat. His father rarely went out in the evening and he could sneak it out without his noticing.

His real worry was that Mrs Dreumel wouldn't agree to see him during the evening but ask him to call the next day. He knew that he would lose courage if he had to wait; besides, he couldn't ask for time off without his father wanting to know where he was going.

Georgiana had made endless lists of things to do in preparation for her departure. She had not yet told the servants that she would be travelling to America, for she was waiting for Wilhelm to write from New York, where no doubt he would hear more up-to-date news. The trouble is, she thought, that I can't make any hard-and-fast plans until I know how long we'll be away. And in any case, we'll have to come home to Hull no matter what is decided regarding where we choose to live. And then there's Jewel.

She was quite concerned about her daughter; Jewel was searching for answers, and whatever she discovered would have an influence on her life. Georgiana sighed. I hope whatever she finds out doesn't make her unhappy. It could well be that some things are better left unknown and undisturbed.

The doorbell jangled and she frowned. She was not dressed for visitors, having dined alone; and what time was it? She leaned to look at the mantel clock. Seven! An unusual hour for callers.

'Beg pardon, Mrs Dreumel.' Her housekeeper knocked and entered the room. 'A Mr Hanson is asking to speak to you. I told him it's rather late, but he said he wouldn't keep you long.'

'Mr Hanson? Senior?'

'Oh no, ma'am. A young man.'

There are two of them, Georgiana thought. I hope it's not Dan. 'Show him in,' she said, rising to her feet.

Dan was very sheepish and apologetic for disturbing her. 'It's difficult to get away during 'day,' he said, hunching awkwardly on a fragile chair when she asked him to be seated.

'I'm sure that it is,' she said calmly. 'What can I do for you, Dan?'

He ran his finger round his shirt collar. 'Well,' he said, 'you might think me very forward, Mrs Dreumel, but – well, I'd heard that you're travelling to America. My ma – mother has seen Aunt Grace—'

'Yes, indeed it's true that I am, but I've not yet decided when, nor told the servants.' Though perhaps word has already got out, she thought, now that Ruby knows. 'So, why . . . ?'

'Fact is, Mrs Dreumel . . .' Dan got up; he couldn't speak to her whilst sitting on a chair that might break beneath him and topple him to the floor, 'I'd like to go to America,' he blurted out, 'and I wondered if I could oblige you in any way on your journey; that is, if I might offer my services – my, erm, assistance to you.'

No matter that he had practised what he was going to say, his words still didn't come out as he wanted them to.

161

He took a deep breath and decided to be honest. 'You'll know already that I'm not well travelled, Mrs Dreumel, but I'm strong and I could manage your trunks and – and you'd not be vulnerable at all if I was there, because, well, I'd guard you and make sure nobody bothered you.'

Georgiana hid a smile. Was she mistaken about him after all? Was he not the arrogant and brash young man she had thought he was? He was obviously embarrassed about approaching her with an offer of help, but at least he had had the courage to do so. He wouldn't know the first thing about travelling, she mused, but she saw his broad shoulders and strong hands and knew he would be useful in a crisis.

But then she wondered about his reason for wanting to travel to America. It must surely be because of Jewel, and that bothered her.

'Are you thinking of staying in America? Are you taking up an occupation? Or is there some other reason for going?' She put her head on one side and raised her eyebrows quizzically.

A slow blush rose from his neck to his cheeks. 'I haven't discussed it with my parents,' he said slowly. 'Only with my brother. He suggested it.'

'Thomas did!' Georgiana was very surprised. 'Why was that?'

Dan sat down again. 'He said I'd been unsettled and thought I should stretch my wings.' Thomas hadn't said that, though it was the sort of thing he might have said, Dan thought.

'And would your father object?' she queried. 'Will he not miss you in the business?'

He lifted his chin and looked at her. 'Probably not, though if I should return home there'd be a place for me.'

'And?' she queried. 'What will you do whilst you're there? It's a big step to take.'

Dan looked down at the floor and chewed on his lips. 'I'll be totally honest with you, Mrs Dreumel. I wouldn't have thought of going if Jewel and Clara hadn't gone.' He raised his eyes to hers and took a breath. 'It's because of Jewel.'

Georgiana nodded. 'I rather thought so,' she said, adding

softly: 'I hate to dash your hopes, Dan, but I don't think that Jewel is ready for a commitment. She has certain matters to sort out for herself. Did she tell you why she's gone to America?'

He shook his head. 'She was becoming bored, I think. She hadn't anything to occupy her.' He tried to recall what reason Jewel had given when she'd first told him she was going away, but he had been so shocked by the revelation that he had only thought of how devastated he would be without her.

'No. That wasn't why,' Georgiana explained. 'Jewel has gone to America to discover her roots. She was a small child when I brought her to England. She barely remembers her father, and her birth mother died soon after she was born.' Have I done right in telling him, she wondered as she added, 'It's important to her that she finds out more about her ancestry.'

Dan was silenced. He'd almost forgotten that the Dreumels were not Jewel's real parents and part of him wondered why it would matter. But I know who I am, he thought, therefore it's not something I've ever considered. I suppose everybody wants to know their back history.

'It wouldn't make any difference to me,' he murmured. 'About Jewel, I mean.'

Georgiana gazed at him. 'This concerns Jewel alone,' she said quietly. 'It isn't about you, Dan.'

'Yes,' he said humbly. 'Sorry. So would you consider it, Mrs Dreumel? Would you consider allowing me to accompany you?'

CHAPTER TWENTY-ONE

San Francisco

Maria apologized for the unkempt state of the overgrown garden. 'Pinyin cuts the grass at the end of summer,' she explained.

Jewel wasn't listening, at least not to Maria. She was listening to other voices, the ones in her head. To Renzo laughing as he chased her round the yard, the garden which in her child's memory had been so large and now was minuscule.

Maria unlocked the door with a flourish and beckoned Jewel to step inside her father's house. It was as if she were the proud caretaker showing a visitor round a stately home or museum. She indicated to Clara that she should follow Jewel, but Clara laid her hand gently on Maria Galli's arm and motioned that they should wait.

Jewel stepped over the threshold and memories came rushing back. She recalled the mirrors on the wall, which she had never been tall enough to reach. Her father had to lift her up to see her reflection. A rocking chair, a small sofa, bookshelves, two easy chairs. No table; wasn't there once a table? She took a breath; there was a faint odour, not of damp as there might be in a house in England that had been shut up for years, but of a slight mustiness, like crisp autumn leaves just fallen from a tree, or the faint scent of sandalwood, reminiscent of the wooden balls kept in the bottom of a blanket box. A sound, too, which seemed to be haunting her, one she had heard before. A clatter, like dried peas in a baby's rattle.

She lifted her eyes; the draught from the open doorway was blowing the beaded curtain that hung over the middle door and it was swinging gently, one string of wooden beads slapping into another. She walked towards it. This was where the aroma came from. How strange that the scent had lasted so long. She clutched a handful of beads, holding them to her nose and opening up elusive dreams of the room beyond. This room, then, was where all her childhood memories were kept, waiting for her to set them free and give her the answers she was looking for.

She parted the curtain and slipped through. There was the bed, and a chair and a small table.

Lift me up, Papa. Her voice was a childish treble. *Lift me up.* He had picked her up to sit on the bed beside him. Or wait! Had someone else lifted her? A pair of steady hands. But whose? Someone who had clasped her fingers and walked with her down the hill. Someone who had taken her into the church and had sat with her hand over her eyes as if she were praying. Her? She? *Gianna?* A small kernel of resentment unfurled itself inside her. Had Gianna stolen her away from her father? Her beloved Papa, who had read to her whilst she was tucked beneath his arm, so cosy and secure, and who had tried to show her how to write her name. You're named after a beautiful English lady, he had said, but she had never met anyone else with the same name. She sat down on the chair at the side of the bed and closed her eyes and tried to remember.

He'd sat with her and kissed her cheek; and then he had said, 'I have to go on a long journey. A journey only for grown-up people.' He had explained that she couldn't go with him. And of course now she knew why.

A tear ran down her face. He had loved her, of that she was certain. She felt the warmth of that love as she glanced round the room, the room Maria had tended over the years, leaving most things exactly as they had been before.

She could hear the whispered voices of Maria and Clara and she rose from her seat and lifted the curtain. 'Thank you for waiting,' she said. 'I needed to be alone.'

'It ees the same, yes?' Maria asked. 'Just as your papa said. He said, in case you came back. All but the table,' she added. 'He said that we might have that.'

Jewel wiped her eyes and nodded. So he did hope that one day she would come back. 'Did you ever meet my mother?' she asked.

'I think not,' Maria mused. 'We had been 'ere only short time when we heard the bambino cry. It was the first time we heard it; it was you,' she added, smiling. 'But I no see your *madre*. I would 'ave remembered. Pinyin say you 'ave a Chinese mother.'

'How did he know?' Jewel asked eagerly. 'Did he know her?'

Maria shook her head. 'I think he saw you and know you 'ave Chinese in you.' She seemed embarrassed and gave a little shrug. 'I think she die.'

How could Pinyin have seen me from next door, Jewel wondered? Did he come into the garden, and why don't I remember him?

'Has Pinyin always worked for you?' she asked as they walked back to the restaurant. 'At the shop, I mean?'

'*Si*.' Maria nodded. 'Sometimes he work for me when I bake the bread. He come to wash the baking things and the oven. Maybe once, twice a week. We 'ave no money to pay him for more, but still he like to come. Then after your papa die and we build the restaurant he come more.' She laughed. 'We 'ave more money then.'

'I think I might speak to Pinyin,' Jewel confided in Clara as they walked back down the hill. They had said goodbye to Maria and to Lorenzo, who insisted they come back the next day as he had been too busy to have a proper conversation with them. He held tightly to Jewel's hand before they left.

'I mustn't lose you again,' he had said earnestly. 'Promise me that you won't disappear.'

Jewel had blushed. 'I promise,' she whispered, and knew with certainty that she wouldn't.

'Why?' Clara asked. 'Why do you wish to speak to Pinyin? You can't speak to every Chinese person that you meet, Jewel, in the hope that they might have known your mother!'

'How old do you think he might be?' Jewel asked, completely ignoring her cousin's advice. 'Forty, do you think? If he is,' she went on without waiting for an answer, 'that would make him in his twenties when he first came to work for Maria, and so he would remember me when I was a baby.' She paused for a moment to take hold of a fence as they negotiated a particularly steep part of the hill, which they had elected to walk down rather than take a cab. 'But I don't remember him at all.'

'You don't remember Maria's husband either,' Clara reminded her. 'So there's nothing strange in that.'

'That is true,' Jewel agreed. 'I recall Maria because she often fed me at their house and sometimes she brought food to ours.' She gave a little frown as she searched her memory. 'She – she brought dishes of pasta to Papa when he was ill, I think, and I used to eat with Renzo in their kitchen.'

Clara smiled. 'There you are, then,' she said softly. 'It's all coming back. Don't rush the memories. Give them time. By the way,' she added diffidently, 'I agreed to meet Federico at the restaurant tomorrow, if you intend – erm – to be there?'

Jewel turned to her with a look of astonishment. 'Federico? Is that the man who came across to the table?' When Clara nodded, she said, 'But you don't know him, Clara! You haven't been introduced. You don't even know his family name.'

'I do. It's Cavalli. And he's Lorenzo's friend, isn't he?' Clara said defiantly. 'So I have been introduced and it's not as if I'm going elsewhere with him.' She blushed. 'I only said I would meet him to have a cup of coffee. And I agreed only because you would be there, and Mrs Galli,' she added sheepishly.

'Well,' Jewel said, as they trod carefully down some steep

steps and at last gained the lower pavement, 'I suppose it will be all right. But you know, Clara, we neither of us would be meeting anybody in such circumstances unless our parents were with us, and we must remember what Papa said about never going anywhere unless together.'

'I haven't forgotten,' Clara told her. 'That's why I agreed to meet Federico at the restaurant. I knew we'd be chaperoned there.'

Jewel gave a giggle. 'How wayward we are!' she said.

'But how silly it is,' Clara answered. 'We are both sensible young women and know when not to take chances; besides, we often see Thomas and Dan without our parents present.'

'Oh, but that's different,' Jewel declared. 'They're our friends and we've known them all our lives. We know that we're perfectly safe with them.'

As they entered the hotel they heard a rumble and both turned back to look outside. 'Thunder,' Clara said. 'Perhaps it's going to rain.'

'The air is heavy,' Jewel agreed, 'but it's still sunny.'

Another rumble, and two large vases standing in the reception area wobbled. A bell boy rushed up to them and put a hand on each, steadying them.

'What was that?' Clara said. 'Not an—'

'Earthquake!' Jewel said. 'They have them often, apparently. If there's a big one, Papa – Wilhelm – said we must go outside immediately.'

'Goodness!' Clara said. 'Should we go outside now?'

'Miss!' The desk clerk called over to them. 'It's all right. It's only a tremor. We get them frequently. Nothing to worry about. We haven't had a big one for a long time. Not that I can remember, anyway.'

'So is it safe to go up to our rooms?' Jewel asked him.

'Sure,' he said. 'Perfectly safe.'

But they were a little apprehensive and that night they both lay very still in their beds, waiting expectantly for the beds to shake and the pictures on the wall to shift. However, nothing happened and eventually they drifted off to sleep.

The next day they took a horse cab up to the restaurant. 'San Francisco is so *huge*,' Clara said, looking about her as they moved out of the quiet street where the hotel was situated and into the busier thoroughfare. 'I overheard someone at the desk saying that it's one of the largest cities in California. I find it quite overwhelming, and very noisy.'

'Do you?' Jewel said. 'I think it exhilarating! It's exciting and lively.' Her eyes sparkled as she spoke and Clara wondered if there was some other cause for Jewel to be so enthusiastic. Like meeting a handsome, charming Italian by the name of Lorenzo.

Lorenzo was again writing on the glass and singing as the cab drew to a halt. How happy he seems to be, Jewel thought. I've never heard a man singing out in the street before. He turned to greet them with a beaming smile and kissed their hands, lingering longer over Jewel's dainty fingers, Clara thought with amusement.

'I've created a special dish for luncheon,' he declared. 'And my mama has made a cake! It is a *jewel* of a cake!'

They both laughed. 'A jewel of a cake?' Jewel asked.

'Yes. Come and see.'

He led them into the restaurant, where cups and saucers and plates were set on a white-clothed table. In the centre was a glass cake stand with a splendid cake on it. They both bent over it.

'Oh, look!' Clara enthused; she was a keen cake baker, unlike Jewel, who had never made one. 'Gemstones! Candied orange and lemon for amber, golden sultanas, angelica – what could that be? Opal perhaps? And cherries of course for rubies. How wonderful!'

'How very kind of your mother,' Jewel said shyly.

'Ah, she is so pleased to see you again,' Lorenzo said, adding softly: 'Back where you belong.'

The door behind them was pushed open and they all looked up. 'Fed!' Lorenzo said. 'Didn't expect to see you again so soon!'

Federico took off his hat and gave a slight bow to the young women. 'I had hoped,' he said, 'to see these charming ladies again and guessed that they might be here. And as I was passing I thought I would look in.'

So he hadn't told Lorenzo that he was going to call, Clara mused. Why was that, I wonder?

'I'm about to make coffee,' Lorenzo said. 'Perhaps you'd like to stay and also enjoy a piece of special cake?'

'Indeed I would.' Federico threw his hat on to the hat stand and came to greet Clara and Jewel. 'Mm.' He sniffed appreciatively. 'Fruit cake. Maria's speciality.'

They sat down and Maria came in to slice the cake. Jewel thanked her for her generosity. Maria patted her on the shoulder and said it was the least she could do to show how pleased she was to see her. 'To see both of you.' She included Clara within her big smile.

'I was thinking.' Federico stretched his long legs. 'How would the ladies like to take a ride along the coast? I've got the buggy outside and it's a lovely day now that the fog has lifted. Perhaps we could take a picnic?'

'You know I can't get away during lunchtime,' Lorenzo told him. 'Not all of us exist only for pleasure.' His tone, though jocular, had a slight edge to it. 'Some of us work for a living.' He disappeared into the kitchen to make the coffee.

Clara glanced curiously at Federico. Surely he must do something with his time? Yet he couldn't have a regular commitment, she thought, as he hadn't hesitated over the suggestion of coming to meet her this morning.

'Do you have a profession, Mr – Federico?' she asked, and added with an engaging smile: 'Or are you a gentleman of leisure?'

He nodded and grinned. 'That's what I am, much to the chagrin of my friends.'

Clara raised her eyebrows but said nothing. It was neither her business nor polite to enquire about his fortune.

'Federico is very rich,' Maria said, putting a slice of cake on each plate and handing them round, first to Jewel, then to Clara and lastly to Federico. 'But not by his own hand. His papa give 'im too much money. It make 'im lazy.'

The two girls were astonished by her openness. It was not done in their social circle to talk about money in such a lax way.

Federico shrugged and took a bite of cake. He blew a kiss to Maria. 'Delicious,' he mumbled. 'One of your best.'

The cake was moist and fruity, and tasted of rum. Lorenzo brought the coffee to the table.

'So you can't come?' Federico said. 'That's a pity.' He glanced at Clara and then Jewel and smiled. 'This is a beautiful coast-line. If we can't persuade Lorenzo to leave his dishes, perhaps I might be permitted to escort you myself?'

CHAPTER TWENTY-TWO

There was an awkward silence. Jewel broke it with an apology. 'Thank you very much but I'm so sorry,' she said. 'Lorenzo has invited us to have lunch, and we have accepted. Perhaps some other time, when he is free?'

Clara leaned forward. 'I'm curious,' she said. 'Is a buggy large enough to hold four passengers? In England a buggy is a two-wheeled vehicle, like a gig or a curricle.'

'No ma'am,' Federico said. 'A buggy such as mine is a four-wheeled surrey. It's quite new, well upholstered, and has a canopy to keep the sun off the passengers. It's outside if you'd care to take a look.' There was a touch of pride in his voice which was apparent to everyone.

'You can go,' Maria said suddenly to Lorenzo. 'I can manage. Pinyin will help me.'

Lorenzo opened his mouth to protest, but Clara spoke first. 'Excuse me, but couldn't we go after lunch?' she suggested. 'Lorenzo has said that he's making a special meal in Jewel's honour.'

Lorenzo looked at her gratefully and glanced at Federico. 'You can stay and eat with us.'

Federico appeared doubtful; he looked as if he was used to having his own way, but then he said, 'Well, thanks. That would be really good.' He pushed back his seat. 'Excuse me. I'll just check that the mare is secure.' He grinned. 'Don't want her setting off home without me!'

Lorenzo cooked a delicious meal for the four of them, his mother declining to eat but insisting she served. They started with a small plate of prawns tucked into a thin pastry parcel on a bed of spinach. Then Maria brought in a large dish of just tender fettuccini pasta in which Lorenzo had tossed thin strips of succulent chicken breast, garlic, herbs, red pepper and a creamy white wine sauce, topped with grated Parmesan cheese. He then served Jewel and Clara and invited Federico to help himself.

'Delicious!' Jewel said, wiping her mouth on a crisp white table napkin. 'I remember eating pasta with you, Lorenzo, when we were children, but I don't recall it tasting like this.' She put her hand over her mouth as she realized that Maria might think her remark a slight on her cooking.

Maria lifted her hands. 'No!' she exclaimed. 'I no cook like this for bambinos. Only pasta with butter or olive. Or mushroom, or basil sauce.'

'I'd never eaten pasta before I came here,' Clara said. 'It's lovely.'

'*Tch!*' Maria said. 'It is peasant food.'

They finished the meal with a board of different cheeses, and then were brought a plate of crisp biscotti made with almonds and pistachio nuts, which Maria urged Jewel and Clara to dip into small glasses of sweet wine.

Pinyin, in the meantime, had been clearing dishes from their table, and although he kept his eyes lowered Jewel felt that they were straying towards her. I must speak to him, she thought. He might have known my mother, or met her at some time. She resolved to have a conversation with him as soon as she could. Perhaps, she mused, he could advise me, and maybe better than Sun Sen or his father.

Federico seemed anxious for them to take the drive as soon as they were finished. At his mother's insistence that he should take the afternoon off, Lorenzo changed into a jacket and donned a cream panama hat, which Jewel thought very dashing.

173

'Will you come and sit up front with me, Miss Clara?' Federico asked. 'Plenty of room for two!'

She agreed that she would and he helped her up, then, sitting beside her, took the reins whilst Lorenzo assisted Jewel into the buggy, giving her a smile which made her feel very warm inside. She knew that she wouldn't want to take her leave of him and go back to England. *Whatever am I thinking of? How can I have such ideas? Papa and Mama would be devastated if I didn't go home.*

Federico drove them back down into the heart of the city, turned towards the bay and then climbed once again to show them the view from the topmost height possible.

'What a sight, eh?' he said. 'There's nowhere to beat it. Just take a look at those ships. They come in from all over the world.'

'We live in a port town,' Clara ventured and suddenly felt homesick. 'Not as large as this by any means, of course, and we don't have hills like these, or such a view, but—'

Federico turned and flashed a smile. 'You'll never want to go home, Miss Clara, not after being here in this wonderful city.'

'Oh, but I will,' she remonstrated. 'Of course I will! There's nowhere quite like home.'

She turned, expecting Jewel to back her up, but Jewel was not even looking at the view. Her eyes were cast down and her hand was being clasped in Lorenzo's.

Goodness, Clara thought. *Is Jewel falling in love? Whatever will we do?*

They got out on a grassy area to gaze at the view and Federico, with one hand holding the reins, put the other on Clara's shoulder. 'See that clipper out there?' he murmured in her ear.

'Yes indeed,' she said. 'The three-masted. It's a fine ship.' She put her hand to her forehead, both to shade her eyes and to edge away from such close proximity. 'Built for speed and originally to transport tea from Asia.'

'Oh!' he said. 'You know about ships, do you?'

174

'As I said,' she was now convinced that he hadn't listened to her, 'we live in a port town. My home overlooks the Old Harbour which leads into the biggest dock in England.' Then she took pity on his crestfallen expression and added, 'The ships there are not so numerous as here, and are mostly fishing vessels, trawlers, barges, schooners and the like. But the transport ships come in from all over the world. And we export our wool and import cotton. It's a very busy commercial port, but for passenger ships we mainly travel to Liverpool or London.'

'Really!' he said. 'Well, shall we move on?' He called to Lorenzo, who had climbed higher up a bank with Jewel, the better to admire the bay. 'You'll have food to prepare for this evening, I expect?'

Which he had: a large party was expected that night. Jewel and Clara tried to decline Lorenzo's request that they should come for supper, thinking that they would be a distraction, but when they got back to the restaurant he and Maria insisted that they would keep a table free for them. Lorenzo didn't include Federico in the invitation and Clara didn't know whether to be pleased or sorry about the omission.

Federico, however, seemed indifferent to what might have been a slight, and asked if he might drive them back to their hotel.

'Would you be so kind as to take us as far as Chinatown?' Jewel asked him as they stepped into the vehicle. 'There's still time to look round before we need to go back to the hotel to change.'

He hesitated. 'You're not thinking of going alone? Just the two of you?'

'Why, yes,' Jewel said. 'We did in New York. It's perfectly safe.'

'Not here it's not,' he answered tersely. 'There's always trouble with the Chinese. There are too many of them, that's the top and bottom of it.' He gazed openly at Jewel. 'I don't mean to offend, Miss Jewel, and I'm not including you in

175

what I say, for you're a visitor to our country and not wholly Chinese, but—'

'I beg your pardon, Mr Cavalli.' Jewel's voice was icy as she broke in. 'I must advise you that I was born in this country just as you were, and my mother was Chinese, as perhaps your mother was Italian. I may not have been to California for many years, but I do not consider myself to be a visitor.' She lifted her chin defiantly. 'This, in a manner of speaking, is my homecoming.'

He had apologized profusely and humbly. 'It's a great weakness of mine,' he'd said, standing by the surrey with his hand to his chest. 'I may appear arrogant, I admit. I have too much money, as my friends are always at pains to remind me.' He gave a dismissive shrug. 'I often wonder how I keep their friendship, but somehow I do. Forgive me.'

Clara immediately did, for he seemed quite penitent, but Jewel remained aloof even when he offered to escort them into Chinatown. She had coldly refused, and reluctantly he had dropped them close by with the warning to take great care.

'I do believe he's quite used to apologizing,' Jewel said cuttingly, when he had driven off. 'The words roll off his tongue with consummate ease and don't mean a thing.'

Clara said nothing. She was bitterly disappointed. He had seemed so charming, an amusing companion; but it was plainly true that he was condescending and self-important and appeared to have done nothing with his life except spend his father's fortune. But why should we judge, she thought? We don't know him or anything about him.

'He's a wastrel,' Jewel said.

'That's rather strong, cousin,' Clara protested. 'He may well have qualities that we're not aware of, and it's quite right that he should warn us of danger.' She looked down the narrow street and the many smaller streets and alleys that led off it. 'We are strangers to this area, after all, and we are women. Perhaps we're being foolish to go alone.'

Jewel took her arm. 'Nonsense,' she said firmly. 'We will not do anything to endanger ourselves. We'll simply observe, and then when I speak to Pinyin, as I intend to do this evening if there is an opportunity, I shall ask him if he would be willing to escort me so that I can make enquiries.' She cast a glance at Clara, who had a bright spot of colour on each cheek and was pressing her lips together. 'You don't have to come with me, Clara,' she said in a softer tone. 'When I come again, I mean. But I won't go without you now, if you don't want to come.'

'Of course I'll come,' Clara said. 'We'll look at the stores as other people are doing.' She had noticed that there were many sightseers wandering about the streets, looking in shop windows and handling the silks and satins which were displayed on the stalls. It's odd, she thought, that Jewel considered herself to be a visitor when we were in New York's Chinatown, and yet here in San Francisco she claims to belong. What has brought about that change, I wonder? Was it seeing her father's house and remembering that she spent part of her childhood here? And more to the point, will she come home with me, or will she want to stay?

They wandered arm in arm down the centre of the main street, at first keeping a watchful eye on those around them, but, as they became more confident, looking up at the colourful unintelligible signs above the stores. Gradually they drifted towards them, curious to see what items were being sold. Each time they stopped, a shopkeeper appeared in the doorway, bowing deeply and inviting them in broken English to come inside. Politely, they declined and moved on.

All around them were sounds; of tinkling bells and flutes, rattling beads and voices like the chattering of small birds, none of which they understood.

On the corner of an alley was a stall piled high with rich materials: scarlet satin, inky-black silk, deep red brocade with decoration of oriental patterns and flowers imprinted on them; Jewel and Clara were drawn towards them. A musky scent of incense and spice wafted on the air and they glanced beyond the stall to the alley. There was boarding above the entrance, painted with Chinese characters in black and blue, telling them they knew not what; they glimpsed a crowd of men, some Chinese but mainly Caucasian, entering doorways above which young girls peeped out from behind curtained windows.

'No look, laydee.' The stallkeeper stood with his back to the alley entrance, blocking their view. 'Bad men. You come look at my things. All good. Genuine from China.'

He wore a tunic of rough cotton twill and a round cap of the same material on his head; when he turned to pick up a length of material from the stall they saw that his black queue reached below his waist. He held the sample towards them, inviting them to feel the quality.

Clara put her fingers to it. 'Silk,' she murmured. 'Quite wonderful. I might buy some later to take home to Mama and Elizabeth.'

Jewel stood back and shook her head when the stallholder proffered it towards her.

He bowed low and said softly, 'Welcome back to China, missy.'

Jewel took a breath. Was he welcoming her or was there a threat in his small dark eyes? But he was smiling and bowing in an obsequious way which made her feel embarrassed.

'Come, Clara, we must move on. There's so much to see,' she urged. Clara thanked the man and took her arm.

'What is it, Jewel?' she asked, for she thought that Jewel had become quite pale.

'Nothing. Nothing at all. But I think perhaps you're right, as was Mr Cavalli: we should bring someone to escort us next time. Shall we turn about and go back?'

'You said that you would ask Pinyin,' Clara began, and then hesitated as a distant rumble began. 'Thunder,' she said. 'At least—'

It was not thunder, though the air was hot and dusty. The locals seemed to know what it was as they grabbed their valuables and began to hurry down the street, calling urgently to each other. People rushed out of the buildings, pushing one another out of the way as the ground began to shake.

'Earthquake!' Jewel and Clara stared at each other. What to do first? Run! But to where? The main street was suddenly a seething mass of escaping humanity, a throng of jostling bodies pushing and shoving into them. Wooden stalls collapsed and a chimney pot crashed to the ground in front of them.

'We must try to stay together,' Clara shouted, for they were being pushed apart by the onrushing crowd.

'Which way? Which way should we go?' Jewel shouted back and then screamed as the front of a building collapsed, scattering bricks and glass. A cloud of choking dust enveloped them, filling their mouths and nostrils.

'Jewel! Jewel! Oh, watch out!' Clara put her hands up to her face as the ground opened up in front of her, the cobblestones parting into a long slicing gap. People tripped and were trampled on in the melee as others fell over them in their attempt to escape the danger. The street was so narrow that as the tremors continued and doors and windows collapsed on either side, there was nowhere to hide from the falling debris. Clara saw a fleeing scantily clad girl, no more than twelve or thirteen, being followed by a man who grabbed her arm and pulled her along with him as she screeched and wriggled to escape him. Both fell headlong as they were hit by falling masonry.

'Jewel! Jewel!' Clara screamed as she was swept along by a river of people, all intent on saving their own skins. She could smell burning and saw that some of the dilapidated buildings were on fire as their chimneys collapsed and their blazing hearths, open now to the street, were fanned into flames.

She was carried by the fleeing crowd, pushed and shoved and hardly able to keep on her feet, until she reached the other end of Chinatown, the opposite end from where she and Jewel had entered. Just as quickly as they had begun, the tremors quietened and people began to turn back, their voices raised to screeching fever pitch. It was less than five minutes since the earthquake had begun and it was as if they knew it was all over, but Clara felt no such certainty. She was close to a low, sturdily built wall and chose to sit on it to get her breath

179

back, examine her hands and arms for scratches, for she had been hit by falling debris as she'd raised her arms to shield her head and face, and wait for Jewel, in the hope that she too would have been propelled this way.

After about a quarter of an hour Clara decided to walk back. She felt no fear now of being alone, as everyone's concern seemed to be to gather up what remained of their businesses and homes and get back to some kind of normality, although what would be done about the devastated buildings she had no idea.

She was covered in grit and her hands were filthy, as she knew her face would be too. Her eyes prickled with dust and her nostrils were clogged. She took a handkerchief from her pocket to blow her nose and looked about her as she walked, calling out Jewel's name until she reached the area where they had been looking at the material on the stall. The boarding above the alley had fallen to the ground but she saw that the young girls were being shepherded, seemingly unwillingly, back into the building. That is not very savoury, she thought. I do believe that they are there under duress.

She saw the stallholder picking up the remains of his broken stall and ventured to speak to him. 'I beg your pardon,' she said, 'but I wonder if you have seen my companion. We were separated.'

He looked at her and, crossing his hands in front of his chest, gave a low bow and shook his head. 'I no see her. She not here.'

Clara walked on, looking in every corner and down every alley in case Jewel had been injured and was waiting for her. But she wasn't there. She reached the end where they had come in and looked about her. Some of the other streets were damaged, yet others had not been touched by the quake. But of Jewel there was no sign.

CHAPTER TWENTY-THREE

Hull

Before leaving London Wilhelm had sent a cable to Ted informing him of his plans, which he hoped would reach Dreumel's Creek before he arrived in New York. Sure enough, on his arrival at the Marius a letter from Ted was waiting. It outlined the devastation in Yeller but sounded remarkably upbeat about it. *It's a chance to rebuild a new town,* Ted wrote. *Some of the men have started on their homes already but we need a town plan, wider streets, firebreaks and a proper fire brigade for a start. I'm glad you're coming,* he'd added. *We need your keen mind.*

Wilhelm relayed this information in a letter to Georgiana, waiting at home. *I must go to them,* he wrote. *They are my people and I want to help as much as I can. Forgive me, my darling Georgiana, for leaving in such a hurry, but as I know you, then I also know you will understand.*

Georgiana gave a wry smile as she read his letter. Well, of course she had known that he would go to Yeller. That was apparent right from the start. The inhabitants of Dreumel's Creek and Yeller were indeed his people. His determination and perseverance had made their lives possible. Without Wilhelm there would have been no towns. And without Lake, she thought, the half-breed trapper who had shown Wilhelm the valley and subsequently stolen her heart, there would have been nothing.

I'll follow him, she decided. I'm halfway ready. But should I allow Dan Hanson to travel with me? She thought that she would perhaps be glad of having someone to accompany her; to find porters and take care of her luggage and perhaps ward off lone male passengers who might make a beeline for her. But on the other hand, what kind of companion would he be? He was not at all worldly or experienced. And would Jewel be cross if he followed her? Jewel, Georgiana was convinced, was not at all interested in Dan in a romantic way.

She was deliberating thus over afternoon tea, when her housekeeper knocked on her door. 'Apologies for disturbing you, Mrs Dreumel,' she said. 'But Mrs Hanson is asking if she might see you.'

'Mrs Hanson?' Georgiana was puzzled for a moment and then her head cleared. Ah! Ruby. 'Yes, of course. Ask her to come up, and bring more tea, please.'

She rose to greet Ruby, who was highly embarrassed when Georgiana offered her tea. 'I'm so sorry,' she began, 'but I – well, I don't know what to do and I asked Grace and she said I ought to come and see you. So I did before I changed my mind.' She took a deep breath. 'It's about Dan and his da.'

Georgiana raised her eyebrows and waited, her hands folded on her lap.

'They've had an almighty row – a quarrel,' Ruby explained. 'Dan told his da that he's thinking of going to America and Daniel hit 'roof. He said that Dan was only going cos of Jewel and if that was 'case then he needn't bother coming back.'

Georgiana was nonplussed. 'Why would he say that?' she asked. 'Has your husband some antipathy towards Jewel?'

'Oh, it's not Jewel,' Ruby hastily explained. 'It's because of me, and what happened with Edward all those years ago. Daniel's somehow got it into his head that Dan will ask Jewel to marry him, and every time Daniel sees Jewel he thinks of when I was – when I was—' Ruby's eyes filled with tears. 'When I was Edward's mistress,' she whispered.

Georgiana leaned across the sofa and clasped Ruby's hand.

182

'But Jewel has nothing to do with you! And besides, you were so young then.'

Ruby nodded. 'Sixteen,' she snuffled. 'And poor! Daniel's forgotten how poor we all were; how desperate. And he should remember,' she said, quite fiercely. 'For he had it hard too.'

'He's still jealous,' Georgiana said softly. 'After all this time, and Edward long dead!'

Ruby took the handkerchief that Georgiana proffered. 'And so you see,' she wiped her eyes, 'even though Daniel'd be angry if Dan went away, I think it might be for 'best. It would clear 'air and it would be good for Dan cos he's very frustrated.' She gave a watery smile. 'I know that Jewel won't have him anyway. She's a class above him and I think she regards him only as a friend; but Dan can't see that cos he's obsessed by her. Allus has been.'

The housekeeper brought in more tea. Georgiana thanked her and said she would pour.

'But if Dan travelled,' Ruby continued, looking appealingly at her hostess, 'he might get over her and it'd do him good to see something of another world; his da would have him back, there's no doubt about that. He's a good man is my Daniel,' she said wistfully. 'He's just lost his way a bit.'

Georgiana poured the tea and waited patiently. So what was coming next?

'So I wondered, Mrs Dreumel,' Ruby licked her lips, 'and you might think it a proper cheek and not 'right thing to be done or asked for; but I'm onny Dan's ma and want 'best for him, so I wondered – if you'd mind if – that is, if he decided to go to America, could he travel on 'same ship as you? I think he'd be very helpful towards you, but I'd have peace of mind cos he's inclined to be a bit hot-headed, and he wouldn't really know what to do if he was on his own; not that he'd ever admit it.'

So she doesn't know, Georgiana mused. Ruby doesn't know that Dan has already been to see me to ask the same question. But she's right. It probably would clear the air if Dan went away, and Daniel Hanson might come to his senses when he discovers that his own feelings are not more important than his son's – or his wife's either, for that matter.

'Well,' she said, taking a sip from her cup, 'I don't see why not. He's an adult, so of course I couldn't be responsible for him. Jewel won't be in New York or in Dreumel's Creek, which is where I'll be going. I don't know where she is, but probably in San Francisco.'

Ruby opened her mouth. 'Oh!' she exhaled. 'But aren't you worried? Grace never said. Just that they weren't staying in that place where there was a fire.'

Georgiana shook her head. 'Anxious, yes. But Jewel and Clara are both level-headed young women. They won't take any chances.'

It seemed then that Ruby grasped what Georgiana had said. That she hadn't disagreed with her request.

'So – so you wouldn't mind if Dan went with you?' Her face flushed and she smiled so widely that her cheeks dimpled. 'Oh, that'd be wonderful, and I'd mek sure it'd be all right with his da. I know how to bring him round, and especially if I tell him that Dan's not going anywhere near where Jewel is.'

'Nothing to stop him going on, of course,' Georgiana said wryly. 'And I'd have no control over that.'

'I wouldn't expect it, Mrs Dreumel – Georgiana,' Ruby protested. 'Thank you so much. Is it all right if I tell Dan that he should come and speak to you?'

'Yes.' Georgiana smiled. 'You may. If that is what he wants to do.'

That evening, just after she had finished her supper, Dan called on her again. He seemed subdued.

'My mother said she'd been to see you, Mrs Dreumel,' he said uneasily. 'And that you wanted to talk to me. I don't understand why she came.'

'She came to ask if you could travel to America with me. If you decided to go there, that is.' Georgiana smiled reassuringly. 'I didn't tell her that we had already discussed the matter.'

He was astonished. 'Ma did that? I can't believe she'd do such a thing.'

'She's very concerned about you,' Georgiana told him. 'Mothers always look for ways to help or protect their children.'

'Yes, but – Ma, she's not like that! She's not pushy, or forward, and – well, it'd have taken a deal of effort to come here to speak to you.'

'Am I such an autocrat? Do I have a sinister reputation that I'm unaware of?'

He laughed, realizing that she was teasing him. 'No, ma'am. Not that I know about, but Ma's nervous of those she calls society folk.'

'Then she has been very brave,' she told him. 'She's a mother to be proud of.'

'Aye, and I am,' he said sincerely. 'And can I ask what your answer was, Mrs Dreumel? Was it yes or no?'

Georgiana looked him in the eyes. She saw honesty there, a frank and direct though slightly anxious gaze right back at her. *He's like most young men, I suspect. Slightly arrogant, with a belief that he knows best. But in spite of that* she thought *she could trust him.*

'I said yes.'

Ruby hadn't given Georgiana the whole story regarding Dan and his father. Daniel had decided to go out on the evening that Dan had visited Georgiana and had searched for his bowler. Ruby too had looked for it, and when Thomas saw his father getting more and more irritated by its loss he suggested that perhaps Dan had borrowed it, immediately raising his father's suspicions. When Dan returned home after visiting a hostelry, Daniel, who had waited up after Ruby had gone to bed, had demanded to know where he had been.

Dan had at first replied that he was old enough to go out of an evening without his father's permission.

'But why my bowler?' his father had asked. 'Who were you meeting that you wanted to impress?'

In a fit of temper, Dan had replied that it was none of his father's business but that if he really wanted to know, he had been out for a walk and a drink while he considered the possibility of travelling to America.

When he saw his father's angry expression he knew what was coming next and before Daniel could speak he spat out, 'And if I do go, I'll follow Jewel Dreumel and ask her to marry me.'

His father's face was red and contorted. 'Jewel Newmarch!' he'd spluttered. 'A bastard child of a libertine. Then marry her, but don't ever show your face here again.'

It was to Dan's credit that he'd turned on his heel and walked out of the house. If he'd stayed he knew that he would have struck his father, and that would have been the end of their relationship for ever.

Ruby, on hearing the shouting from upstairs, had come down and demanded to know what was going on. Daniel, shamefaced, had related what he had said.

'Daniel,' she'd said slowly. 'You'll rue this day and your temper and your suspicions. You might not mind losing your eldest son, but I do.' She gazed at him steadily. 'You've forgotten.' Her voice dropped. 'Your ma and da drove you away from home and when you returned your ma was dead by her own hand.' She shook her head sadly. 'She must have had so many regrets over what she'd said in anger.'

Daniel had wept. 'I'm sorry, Ruby. So very sorry. But I can't help it. I don't know what gets into me when I hear Newmarch's name, and when I see his daughter it's like a knife in my heart.'

Ruby looked at him but made no effort to console him; she simply turned away and went back upstairs, climbed back into a comfortless bed and sobbed.

CHAPTER TWENTY-FOUR

What am I to do, Clara wondered as she stood in the middle of the destruction. Do I go back in and search again? Is Jewel injured? Suppose she's lying beneath a pile of rubble? She felt panic enveloping her. She looked about and saw only unfamiliar Chinese faces, oblivious of her. She tried to quell her terrifying thoughts and be positive. These people are as anxious as I am, she told herself. There was shouting and crying, and people were calling in a language she couldn't understand.

Then she heard a voice calling her name. 'Miss Clara! Miss Clara! Over here.'

She looked about her urgently. Who? Who knew her here? 'Miss Clara!'

Clara looked beyond the immediate crowd, stretching her neck to see above them, and to her relief saw Federico Cavalli. She waved and hurried towards him as he did towards her. He grasped her hand.

'Thank God!' he said. 'I came back as soon as I could. There's such a panic in the streets I found it difficult to get here. Everyone was running the other way. Where's Miss Jewel?'

To Clara's dismay she burst into tears. The shock of the quake and not being able to find Jewel suddenly hit her, making her feel vulnerable.

'I don't know.' Tears streaked her dusty face. 'I can't find her. We were pushed to the other end of Chinatown by the crowds and I've walked all the way back. But I can't find her!'

Federico took her arm. 'We'll look again,' he said decisively and to his credit did not mention that he had warned them against coming into Chinatown alone. Clara was glad to let him take charge. She felt weak and helpless, which is ridiculous, she told herself. I'm not some feeble, dependent female, incapable of making a decision. But her knees buckled as they walked and without his hand on her arm she would have fallen.

They reached the stallholder again and Clara pointed him out to Federico. 'I spoke to him,' she said, 'and asked him if he'd seen Jewel. He said he hadn't.'

'Well, begging your pardon, Miss Clara,' Federico murmured. 'But he might not have noticed her in the confusion, whereas he would have noticed you with your fair hair and fine complexion.'

Clara flushed, but admitted to herself that he might be right. Jewel's hair was as dark and glossy as that of most of the young Chinese women who were thronging the streets now, and although her features were not wholly Oriental she looked Chinese, except of course for her European dress.

Federico approached the stallholder and spoke to him haltingly in his own language. He shook his head and replied in English. 'I no see her,' he repeated, and Federico turned away, muttering tetchily.

'Can't get any sense out of the fellow,' he grumbled. 'He'd never tell me anyway. Damned heathens.'

Clara was shocked at his language, but was too distraught over Jewel's disappearance to remonstrate with him. She needed his help, not his antipathy.

She saw Federico glance up the alley and then usher her away. 'We mustn't hang about here,' he told her. 'It's an unsavoury area, not for a young woman such as you. That's why I didn't want you to come alone.'

'I'm not entirely unworldly,' she told him. 'There are undesirable places in my home town where I would not venture.

I am circumspect at all times.' She didn't bother to tell him that she lived in the heart of Hull and would not venture into some of the streets after dark except with her father as escort, although her mother did. Grace always said that there was nothing in life to be feared, only to be understood, and it was true that her mother had never been accosted by anyone.

They searched up and down the streets and alleys, and to Clara's surprise Federico seemed to know some of the Chinese people. He stopped them to ask if they had seen Jewel, but none had.

Eventually Clara said, 'I must go back to the hotel. Maybe Jewel is waiting there. She might be as worried about me as I am about her. And if she is not there, then I'll go to Lorenzo's as arranged and speak to Pinyin and ask if he can help.'

Federico considered. 'Yes,' he agreed. 'I'll escort you back to the hotel, and if Jewel isn't there I'll drive you up to Lorenzo's and we'll organize a search party.'

Clara felt sick with apprehension. Please be there, Jewel, she thought. Please, please, please!

But she wasn't. Clara asked the desk clerk, who shook his head at her query, and then she went up to their room. It was as they had left it, except that the staff had made the beds and tidied up. Clara washed her hands and face and changed her gown, for the one she was wearing was filthy. She brushed her hair and put on a clean shawl, then went down to Federico, who was waiting in the lobby.

The desk clerk called to her and came round to the front of his desk. 'Beg your pardon, Miss Newmarch. I forgot to say that a letter came for you.'

He handed her an envelope on which she recognized her mother's handwriting. Vaguely she thanked him and slipped it into her pocket.

'I'm so sorry to inconvenience you,' she told Federico. 'I could order a cab.'

'Nonsense,' he said. 'The evening is getting on; it will soon be dark. You can't be going about on your own. It wouldn't be safe.'

There, she thought. He's doing it again. Making decisions for me. But perhaps he's right: Jewel and I promised Uncle Wilhelm that we would be careful at all times and the one time when we weren't Jewel disappears. So she allowed Federico Cavalli to escort her to his horse and surrey, which were in the stable yard behind the hotel.

'I came back here as soon as I felt the quake,' he said, handing her up to sit next to him. 'I heard that it was worse in Chinatown and was worried that you might be hurt.'

'You're very kind,' Clara murmured. 'I very much appreciate your concern.'

He smiled and, holding the reins in one hand, clasped her hand with his other. 'It's the least I can do,' he said, and Clara couldn't understand why, although she was grateful, she was also uneasy.

They travelled in silence up towards Lorenzo's and Clara eventually extricated her hand on the pretext of using a handkerchief to wipe her eyes.

'Try not to worry,' he said. 'I'm pretty sure we'll find your friend safe and well.'

'How can you be so sure?' she said. 'I'm afraid that she might have fallen into hostile hands and be in danger.'

He didn't answer at first and she glanced at his profile and saw his frown and the way he was pressing his lips together in concentration. 'We'll find her,' he said.

The restaurant was full and buzzing with talk of the earthquake, although Clara heard odd bits of conversation which seemed to indicate that it was only a small tremor that had not done a great deal of damage except in Chinatown.

Lorenzo came from the kitchen bearing a huge platter and gave a big grin when he saw Clara, which dropped when Federico closed the door behind him.

He deposited the dish on a table and came over to them. 'Where've you been?' he asked. 'I thought you'd be here long ago. Where's Jewel?' He searched their faces. 'You didn't get caught up in the quake? They're saying there's not much damage, although we felt it up here – lost some crockery . . .'

His voice faded away as he saw Clara's face crumple. '*Where's Jewel?*'

She shook her head and began to weep. 'I don't know,' she gasped. 'We can't find her. We were in Chinatown when the earthquake began. We were separated.'

Lorenzo glanced at Federico for confirmation. 'I advised them against going in there and after the quake I went back to see that they were safe,' Federico said. He shrugged. 'We went in again to look for Miss Jewel but couldn't find her.'

'*Pinyin!*' Lorenzo bawled through the kitchen door. 'Come here!'

Pinyin scuttled out of the kitchen, followed closely by Maria. 'What's wrong?' she said. 'What happened? What did Pinyin do?'

'Nothing,' Lorenzo said sharply. 'Pinyin has done nothing. Pinyin,' he said urgently. 'My friend Miss Newmarch is missing in Chinatown!'

Clara noticed that Lorenzo called Jewel Miss Newmarch, not Miss Dreumel, and that Pinyin responded immediately. He looked sharply at Lorenzo. 'There has been an earthquake in Chinatown,' he said.

It was the first time Clara had heard Pinyin speak, and although his voice was of a higher tone than a European's and he had a slight difficulty with his r's, he spoke good English.

'Can you help us find her, please?' she begged.

Pinyin looked at Lorenzo, and then he clasped his fingers together and bowed.

'You must!' Lorenzo demanded. 'Pinyin! You must help. How else can we find her?' He sounded distraught. 'God knows what might have happened to her.' He turned to Federico. 'Are you sure you looked everywhere? Did you ask anyone?'

Then he turned to his mother who was standing wringing her hands. 'Everyone is served. Can you manage alone? I must go and Pinyin must come with me. You will, won't you? We can't go without you, Pinyin.'

Pinyin bowed again. 'Of course. I have many uncles and

relatives in Chinatown. I will speak to them. If she is still there they will know of it.'

If she is still there, Clara thought? Of course! Jewel might have been concussed by the falling debris and be wandering about anywhere, not just in Chinatown.

Lorenzo hurried across to all the tables and gave his apologies, explaining that a friend had become caught up in the earthquake and he had to leave. He asked his mother to put a complimentary bottle of wine on each table, then he took off his apron, grabbed a coat and ushered them out, with Pinyin following close behind. Suddenly he stopped. 'Sorry, Miss Clara. You don't have to come with us. Please! Stay here with Madre.'

'Oh no!' Clara protested. 'Of course I must come. Perhaps Jewel is injured, or – or . . .' Dire imaginings of what might have happened to her cousin filled her mind and she shook her head to try to banish them. 'No. She might need me. I have to come.'

'It is best that Miss Clara comes,' Pinyin said, 'in case Miss Newmarch needs another woman's assistance.'

Federico glared at Pinyin in a patronizing way, as if he shouldn't have spoken, but he didn't say anything. But as Clara and Lorenzo climbed into Federico's surrey, Pinyin said, 'I will see you at the entrance to Chinatown,' and holding on to his round hat, his wide trousers flapping, set off at a run down the hill before Federico had gathered up the reins.

Lorenzo turned to Clara. 'I don't wish to alarm you, Miss Clara, but I don't like to think of Jewel being there alone. Most Chinese are fine people, like Pinyin, but there are those who are not and some places in Chinatown where it is wise not to go.'

Clara swallowed. 'That's true of many people and places,' she said in a small nervous voice.

'Yes,' he agreed. 'But we might recognize certain traits in Americans or English and know when to be wary, whereas the Chinese are inscrutable and don't show expression as we do. But if anyone can find her it will be Pinyin.'

Clara nodded. She felt a hard knot of anxiety inside her. Whatever would she say to Aunt Gianna and Uncle Wilhelm if anything bad had happened to Jewel? She took a breath. Should she cable them? How long would it take for a cablegram to reach England? But no, she was being ridiculous. They would find Jewel, of course they would, and besides, what was the point in worrying them? There was nothing they could do from such a distance.

They passed the cathedral of St Mary and Lorenzo looked out into the street. 'Slow down, Fed,' he called to his friend. 'Look out for Pinyin.'

Federico muttered something they didn't catch, but he slowed the horse as they reached the top of Chinatown.

'There he is!' Lorenzo said. 'Just on the corner.'

The surrey stopped to allow Clara and Lorenzo out, and Federico said he would stable the horse and vehicle nearby and catch up with them.

'How will he know where to find us?' Clara asked as they hurried towards Pinyin. 'It's a big place.'

'He'll find us,' Lorenzo said. 'Fed knows Chinatown; better than most.'

Clara glanced at him. He sounded crabby, irritated somehow, and Clara felt sure that his displeasure stemmed from annoyance with Federico rather than anxiety over Jewel.

'Pinyin!' Lorenzo called, and now he did sound anxious. 'Have you spoken to anyone yet? Has anyone seen Jewel?'

Pinyin bowed his head to Clara and then turned to Lorenzo. 'There has been much damage in Chinatown,' he said. 'People are injured. Everywhere is confusion.'

'Dammit, man, I know that,' Lorenzo bellowed. 'But has anyone seen Jewel?'

Pinyin shook his head. 'No. I have asked,' he said patiently, unperturbed by Lorenzo's outburst. 'People remember seeing the English lady and her companion, but not since the quake. I am about to speak to my uncle. He sees much of what happens in Chinatown.'

Clara and Lorenzo hurried after Pinyin, who moved at a

quick and nimble trot, and Clara saw him stop by the stall-holder they had spoken to earlier. 'I have asked him already,' she said, 'and Mr Cavalli spoke to him too.'

Federico came up behind them. 'I'll take a different direction,' he told Lorenzo; he was slightly out of breath, as if he had been running. 'It's better if we split up. There are so many corners in which to look. I'll try asking in the gambling dens; the doormen generally know what's happening.'

Clara held her breath. Chinatown was taking on a differ-ent atmosphere now that daylight had gone. Lanterns had appeared outside the buildings, giving an eerie glow to the street, and there was a potent smoky aroma which was coming not from the burnt-out buildings but from some of the base-ments.

People were taking up positions outside the houses and stores. Men sat on stools, smoking vile-smelling pipes and watching the passers-by, and women stood by screened door-ways or on balconies, their blue-black hair dressed with flowers and fancy combs. Some were wearing richly embroidered sacque dresses and gold-coloured shoes on their tiny feet, whilst others were dressed in long, wide trousers of brightly coloured satin and played twanging music on small stringed instruments and sang in high-pitched voices.

It seemed that the earthquake had not affected the usual night-time activities, and indeed there appeared to be more people milling around now than there had been during the day.

Federico turned on his heel and headed off in another direction and Clara saw that Lorenzo's lips were tightly clenched as he watched him turn down an alley. He said nothing to Clara, but took her elbow to guide her towards Pinyin, who was still talking to the stallholder.

'Well?' Lorenzo asked Pinyin, and Clara was confused by their manner towards each other. Pinyin was a servant, an employee of Lorenzo's, and yet he was treated almost as an equal.

'Nothing,' Pinyin said. 'It is very strange. My uncle, Soong Zedung, says Miss Newmarch has not passed this way, but he will ask others.' He gave Clara a small bow. 'Please do not worry. We shall find her. Everyone will look.'

CHAPTER TWENTY-FIVE

The journey to New York took just over a week. Georgiana and Dan travelled together by train to Liverpool and caught the evening tide. Georgiana was quite glad to have his company, for he was adept at finding porters and whistling for a cab to take them to the ship when they arrived at Liverpool railway station.

Dan's mother, Ruby, had sent him off with a parcel of home baking as if convinced that he would starve before they arrived at the western port, and Dan, embarrassed by this, was all for throwing it out of the window as soon as the train departed.

'Don't do that,' Georgiana had said. 'You'll find when we reach Liverpool that there'll be many poor folk who'll be glad of your mother's cooking.'

They travelled in a first-class carriage; Georgiana had paid the extra for Dan's ticket. 'If we are to be travelling companions,' she murmured, 'you must travel at my standard, not I at yours.' She smiled. 'You can pay me back in kind by taking care of my luggage.'

On board ship Georgiana had a first-class cabin, but here she considered that at Dan's tender age he was not yet ready for such luxury, and a little discomfort would do him no harm at all.

For Dan it was no hardship. He was sharing a four-bedded cabin on a lower deck with one other passenger, who was a frequent traveller and able to advise him on the behaviour that was expected on board. Dan stretched out on his bunk, put his hands behind his head and heaved a sigh of utter contentment. *Freedom!*

He and his father had to some extent made up their differences, and he rather thought that was due to his mother's influence. He felt sure that his mother would have warned his father that he was in danger of losing contact if he didn't meet Dan halfway.

Daniel had taken him on one side. 'I can't say I approve of 'motive for you going to America,' he'd said gruffly, 'but 'fact that you've made 'decision to spread your wings is summat I can understand. You're a young man with ambition and I hope you'll use your time wisely while you're away and not go chasing moonbeams that you'll never catch.'

Dan had listened but made no comment. His father would take his time saying what he had to say, and although it was obvious that he didn't approve of Jewel, for whatever reason, he was at least giving him tacit permission to travel.

Daniel had put a thick envelope on the table and pushed it towards him. 'Tek this,' he'd muttered. 'I'll have no son o' mine behodden to anybody. Spend it wisely. Money doesn't come easy.'

Dan had had a lump in his throat as he picked it up. 'Thanks, Da.' There was no need for any fancy speeches; his father would know that he was grateful.

'And,' his father had added, 'you can tek my bowler!'

Now as he lay on his bunk he was filled with excitement, and it wasn't wholly due to the possibility of meeting up with Jewel. It was simply because he realized that he had been stifled by his commitment to working in the family business, which although profitable gave him little chance of achievement through his own endeavours.

He heard the juddering of engines below him, the muffled shouts of seamen, and the movement of the ship which told him they had cast off and were on their way. He couldn't help but grin and jump off the bunk to make his way on deck, to watch the departure from the shore into what for him was unknown territory.

Georgiana Dreumel joined him, which surprised him, as he thought she might have preferred to stay in her cabin. But she leaned on the rail beside him and told him of the time when she too had made her first journey to America.

'Kitty and I travelled from London,' she said. 'We took a packet boat from Hull and disembarked at London Bridge and boarded the ship, the *Paragon*, in the Thames.' She smiled as she remembered. 'I was about your age and it was so exciting,' she said. 'It was a great adventure!'

He looked at her admiringly. He'd been concerned that Jewel and Clara were travelling alone, but he thought that for two women to do the same thing twenty or more years ago was very brave, and he told her so.

She laughed. 'If I told you some of the things that Kitty and I did when we were there, I doubt whether you'd believe me.'

As the voyage went on he didn't see much of her. He took his meals with his cabin mate and assumed that she was probably dining with the captain, until one morning he saw her in a deckchair, wrapped in shawls and blankets and looking very pale.

'I'm not the best of sailors,' she said, 'and I have been un-well. The heavy swell is worse for me than a storm.'

Dan was astonished to hear that, as he thought it had been a tranquil voyage. But the Atlantic swell had been deep as the ship ploughed through the vast waters, dipping and plunging into troughs so yawning and bottomless that only the greenness of massive waves could be seen above them. He had found it exhilarating; that, and the darkest of skies covered in a million sparkling stars.

'Come and sit down,' she said, 'and we can talk of what you'd like to do when we arrive in New York.'

He drew up a chair beside her and she motioned to a pass-ing steward to bring coffee for Dan and a cup of mint tea for herself.

'First I shall stay in the Marius,' she said, 'and hope there will be a letter waiting for me from Wilhelm; then I shall travel on to Dreumel's Creek.'

'And 'town that was burnt down – will you go there?'

'Yeller. Yes,' she said. 'But it's only through the mountains. They are what you might call sister towns. If the mountain didn't divide them they would have become one large town. I'm pleased that they haven't. They have quite separate identities and it will be interesting to hear what plans are being made for Yeller's rebuilding.'

'Interesting indeed,' Dan agreed, and thought that to be in at the beginning of such a project might be very satisfying.

'So what would you like to do, Dan?' Georgiana sipped her mint tea. 'Jewel won't be at Dreumel's Creek. She and Clara have already left for California. They might or might not return to Dreumel; I know nothing of their arrangements.'

Dan considered. The original point of his journey had been to see Jewel. But what if she was displeased with him for following her? She had her own reasons for being in America. Perhaps if she had been able to solve her own questions, she might be happy to see him again.

'I have already told you that I don't think Jewel is ready to make promises or vows, Dan,' Georgiana said softly. 'She's on the verge of making discoveries for herself. You will, I feel, have to exercise patience.'

'I think you're right, Mrs Dreumel,' he confessed. 'I've always been so obsessed by her that I haven't been able to think of anything else but to be with her. Perhaps it might seem ridiculous, but it's not infatuation. I really do care for her.'

'It doesn't seem ridiculous, Dan. I understand exactly how you feel, but if you really do care for Jewel, you will allow her the freedom to do whatever she wants without trying to influence her.'

He nodded. She really was a most understanding woman. You'd almost think that she'd experienced such emotions herself. 'I will,' he said. 'Thank you for your advice – I'll tek it. If you've no objection, I'd like to travel with you to Dreumel's

Creek and to Yeller, and if I can be of any help in rebuilding 'town, then perhaps I could stay there for a bit afore moving on.'

They stayed two days in New York, and whilst Georgiana rested after the voyage, for she said that it had tired her, Dan explored the city. He was impressed by the wide roads, or boulevards as the locals called them, and the fact that not all streets were given names, so some had numbers instead. Tall buildings were going up, taller than he had ever seen. Towers, they were, soaring high into the sky, with elevators to take people to the top floors. He strolled in Central Park with its immense green areas, flower beds and lakes, and knew that there was nothing he could possibly compare it with; not the People's Park or the Zoological Gardens in Hull, for neither was anything like this vast and landscaped space.

Carriages and pony traps swept along the wide paths and he heard the sound of music as an afternoon concert began, but he realized that only the wealthy and those with leisure time were enjoying the pleasures of this oasis in the middle of the city; he was disheartened to discover later that many of the poorer residents of New York had been moved out of their homes so that this garden of delight could be created.

When he returned to the Marius in the early evening Mrs Dreumel was seated in the hotel lounge. Her head rested on the back of the chair and her eyes were closed. A pianist was playing something soothing and Mrs Dreumel was nodding her head gently in time to the music.

'Mrs Dreumel!' Dan spoke softly so as not to startle her. 'Are you sleeping?'

She opened her eyes and smiled. 'No,' she said. 'I was reminiscing.'

'I'm sorry if I've disturbed you,' he said awkwardly.

'Not a bit,' she said. 'Did you enjoy your excursion?'

'I did,' he said earnestly. 'It's so different from anything we've got at home.'

'Yes,' she agreed. 'And it's changing and growing constantly.

I can see a difference from when I was last here, even from the hotel doorway.'

'Are you well rested?'

She sighed. 'Yes, I think so. I have never felt so exhausted after a voyage before. It's so unlike me to be sapped of energy.'

Dan nodded. Perhaps she wasn't quite as intrepid or enterprising as he had thought, but then she was older, so perhaps it was to be expected that such a journey would now tire her. He would take care of her, he decided. After she had given him such a chance to travel, it was the least he could do to repay her.

Over supper she told him that Wilhelm had sent a letter to the Marius from Yeller. *There is much to do*, he had written. *So much planning. I will be pleased when you arrive. I know what an innovative mind you have, and besides*, he'd added, *I miss you.*

And I miss him too, she thought. And I need his reassurance and steady disposition, for I feel somehow insecure. I am unwell, I think; not at all myself. She had always been robust, yet now she felt vaguely frail and rather weak and had been very sick on the ship. It surely cannot be my age, she decided, even though I am coming up to the time of life when there are changes in women's bodies. But I'll not be a party to that. I will not be feeble about such a natural occurrence!

But her insecurity came from the worry that there might be some other reason why she felt unwell. She had heard lately of women who had taken to their beds with undiagnosed illnesses, and their families, mainly daughters, were running ragged about them. Well, that is not for me either, she fumed. If I am ill I will tell no one, except Wilhelm.

They departed for Dreumel's Creek early the next morning and Dan could hardly contain his excitement, although he tried his best to appear casual and blasé. They were to be travelling almost the whole day by train and coach until reaching their final destination.

Dan fetched and carried for Georgiana: tea, coffee and whatever she wanted at the station stops. He arranged the safe transfer of their luggage when they changed trains and finally on to the coach, but mainly he watched from the windows as they travelled over wide plains, through mountain passes and alongside vast lakes; he gazed at the rich colours of the trees, for they were now into autumn, and marvelled at the immense expanses of land, water and hills. He was, without any doubt whatsoever, completely bowled over by the landscape. I cannot imagine ever wanting to go home again, he reflected, and wondered if he had spoken aloud, because Mrs Dreumel gave him a winsome smile as if she completely understood.

It was dark when they reached Dreumel's Creek and lamps were lit over the hotel porch and outside some of the buildings. The town seemed sleepy, as if it had put itself to bed. Wilhelm was waiting to help Georgiana down from the coach, and he shook hands with Dan. He knew him and his family, although not well. But he welcomed him and thanked him for looking after his wife, and added that he looked forward to showing him round the town the next day.

'But now you must have something to eat and drink, and I know that Georgiana will want to rest. Come along in,' he said, holding Georgiana firmly by her arm as he guided her up the steps. 'Welcome to Dreumel's Creek.'

CHAPTER TWENTY-SIX

Strangely enough, Dan wasn't tired. His body ached because of the motion of the train and the jolting of the carriage along the potholed road, but his mind was whirring with all that he had seen. What a country, he thought as he stood in the hotel porch breathing in the mountain air; he considered the Native Indians whose home it was until the settlers began to arrive in their waggons, followed by the miners who came looking for gold.

It's every man for himself out here, he pondered. He'd eaten supper with the Dreumels, and then Mrs Dreumel had declared that she was very tired and would go up to her room. Dan said goodnight to them both and strolled outside. Although there was no moon, he could see the blackness of the mountains rising up into the sky and hear the rush of the water in the creek, and felt again the rising sense of excitement he had known in New York.

I won't make any plans just yet, he decided in his enthusiasm. I'll wait awhile, but I get 'feeling that I'll like it here. I'll have to work, though. There'll be no place for slackers, so thank heavens I've got a trade. He thought guiltily of his father, who so often had to hound him to finish a piece of work, or would give back some item which Dan had thought was reasonable enough and tell him to do it again. *Perfection is what we're looking for, lad.* Dan could almost hear his father's voice. *Not just 'it'll do'.*

I'll have to do things right out here, he mused. My work will reflect on me. There'll be so many others waiting in line, mebbe better craftsmen than me and all eager to earn a living in this land, and I won't have my father or brother to back me up. I'll be on my own.

He had been leaning on a wooden pillar as he reflected, and now he stood up and stretched, just as a figure ran swiftly up the steps.

'*Jaysus*, but you scared me!' It was a woman's voice. A young woman, who he saw as she came into the lamplight had a mop of flaming red hair tied back loosely with a ribbon. She wore a simple skirt and bodice and a shawl flung about her shoulders. 'What are you doing skulking here?' She scowled at him and her tone was accusing. 'Who are you?'

'Sorry,' he apologized. 'I didn't mean to frighten you.'

Caitlin Allen put her hands on her hips. 'You didn't frighten me,' she said. 'I said you scared me. Jumping out like that.'

'I didn't jump,' he retaliated. 'I was stretching 'cause I was stiff, and about to go inside.'

She frowned again and then asked in a more polite manner, 'Are you a guest here?'

'In a manner of speaking, yes I am.'

'In a manner of speaking? What's that supposed to mean? Are you or not?'

Dan laughed. She was certainly forthright. 'Yes. I've just arrived with Mrs Dreumel.'

If he had thought that by giving the name of Dreumel he might win some respect he was mistaken, for she squealed and pushed past him. 'Aunt Gianna! Is she here?'

Dan followed her into the hotel. 'Yes, but she's gone up to bed. She's very tired after her journey.'

'Oh.' She seemed deflated. 'I've been looking forward to seeing her again.' She recovered her manners. 'Sorry for the little tiff just now, but I wasn't expecting to see anybody loitering there. I'm Caitlin Allen, by the way. I'm from Yeller but the town's burnt down and I'm living here at the Marius for now. Living and *working*,' she emphasized. 'Paying for my keep.'

'I'm Dan Hanson.' He was a little miffed at being accused of loitering as well as skulking, but added, 'I'm from England. I live in 'same town as Mr and Mrs Dreumel, and Jewel.'

'Oh, sure. I think I heard your name. So are you taking a vacation or planning on staying?'

Dan shrugged. Tiredness was creeping up on him. 'Don't know yet. I wanted to travel and when I heard Mrs Dreumel was coming to America I asked if I might come with her.'

'Are you sweet on Jewel?' Caitlin asked perceptively.

What a lot of questions she asks, he thought. Little busybody. 'Jewel's a friend,' he said. 'I've known her since we were children. Since she came to live in England.'

'She's not here, you know. She and her cousin have gone to California.'

'Yes, I know,' he said. 'Clara and her sister are friends of ours too. I've known them all my life. Our mothers have been friends since they were young.' He felt that he had thus fully established his credentials.

Caitlin looked at him speculatively. 'Would you like me to show you around? Not that there's much to see in Yeller. Our hotel is about the only building left standing. My mother's from the same town as Aunt Gianna,' she told him. 'And my pa is from the north of England too. He came to America with Jewel's pa but they got split up somehow. There's a long story about them.'

Dan nodded. 'Yeh. I've heard some of it.' He suddenly felt a wave of tiredness wash over him. 'I'm sorry, Miss Allen. I'll have to go up to my room. I'm beat.'

'Sure,' she said again. 'And you can call me Caitlin.' She smiled. 'We don't worry too much about being proper out here. Everybody knows who's who anyway. Good night.'

'Good night!' He walked up the stairs to his room. He was perplexed by her. He'd never met anyone who was so open or candid. Even Clara and Elizabeth, although they would discuss or argue about things with him, were generally civil and polite. He gave a wry laugh. Caitlin Allen, he considered, would tell you what she thought straight to your face. Was this what life in America was like? No pretence? No division between the haves and have nots?

He slept soundly as soon as he climbed into bed and was woken the next morning by the sun shining into his room and the sound of gushing water. For a second he forgot where he was and thought he was still on the ship. Then came the realization that this was a much comfier bed than the bunk he had occupied in the ship's cabin, and he sprang out of it to look through the window at the road below.

The creek was in full flow, the water sparkling in the sunshine as it rushed down the valley. On the opposite bank, cattle grazed on pastureland and beyond that thick scrub led into a tree line which grew denser as it led up the mountain range.

Dan stared and stared. He was town born and bred and had never had any desire to move away from cobbled roads into the muddy tracks of the country, but this was overwhelming and he caught his breath. The mountains reached into the blue sky and the shrubs below the tree line were ablaze with rich rusty brown colour. The trees – cottonwood, Georgiana Dreumel had called some of them – reached maybe forty feet high and were lit with yellow-gold shimmering leaves. Others, he thought, were maybe ash, and he was sure he recognized pine.

He narrowed his eyes. On a rocky plateau something moved. Something black which nosed around on the ground. He heaved a breath. Bear! He'd seen his first bear. He wanted to rush out and tell somebody the news. But who would he tell? The folk who lived here were probably used to seeing bears in the same way as back home they'd see a stray dog.

He washed and dressed and went down to breakfast and found Georgiana already at the dining table drinking coffee. She invited him to join her and asked if he had slept well.

'I did,' he said and then in a sudden rush said enthusiastically, 'This is a wonderful place! I've just seen a bear!'

Georgiana smiled. 'Have you? Where? On the mountain?'

'Yes. There's a sort of rocky shelf jutting out from the

mountainside and it was on there. It was nosing about as if it was looking for something. Food, mebbe?'

Georgiana's eyes flickered for a second and Dan thought she took a shallow breath. She was still pale but didn't look quite so strained.

'How are you this morning, Mrs Dreumel?' he asked. 'Are you rested?'

'Yes.' She nodded. 'Much better today after a good night's sleep.' She took another breath. 'It's good to be back. The air is wonderful here, so fresh and clean. What are your plans? Are you going to take a look round the town?'

'I've been promised a personal tour,' he grinned. 'By Caitlin Allen.'

'Ah!' She smiled. 'The incorrigible Caitlin. She's just been in to see me. Be careful how you tread or she'll skin you alive!' She laughed again. 'She's fearless. She reminds me of how her mother was when we first came to America. Kitty was courageous and optimistic, but not as audacious as her daughter. But then Caitlin has had more advantages than Kitty had ever had.'

As Georgiana finished speaking Caitlin popped her head into the dining room. 'Ah, good morning, Mr Hanson. Would you like breakfast?'

'Yes, please,' Dan said. 'I'm really hungry.'

'Would you like steak and eggs, sausage, bacon, coffee?'

Dan licked his lips. 'Yes, please, and then are you free to go out?'

Caitlin's cheeks flushed. 'If Mr Crawford doesn't need me,' she said. 'This is a working day. I said I'd put in the time to pay for my keep.'

'I'm sure there's really no need,' Georgiana began, but then added: 'You could perhaps make it up on another day.'

Caitlin nodded. 'I'll ask him. Today would be a good day to go out. It's going to rain tomorrow.'

'Dan said he saw a bear on the mountain this morning,' Georgiana told her.

Caitlin paused on her way out of the door. Her lips parted.

207

'Yes,' she said softly. 'I've seen him too. Several times. He sits up on the ridge.' She gazed at Gianna. There was something she wanted to say to her, but she didn't know what it was. It was about a memory, but the memory was hazy, as if a mist was hovering over her thoughts. But the thoughts had some connection to Gianna, and, oddly, with the Indian trapper Lake.

Georgiana could see that Wilhelm was in his element. In the short time he'd been back in Dreumel's Creek, he and Ted had organized a committee to plan a new town in Yeller. Democratically they had asked the townsfolk to come to a meeting and they had both been elected to choose other members of the committee; this they had done from those who put their names forward, mainly tradespeople but also the parson, a lawyer and a doctor who had only recently come to live in Yeller. A good cross section of the community, Wilhelm had said.

'And women?' Georgiana had asked, and he'd grinned and said: Of course. Kitty Allen and Nellie O'Neill.

'Perhaps you'd like to be involved too, Georgiana?' he had asked tentatively. 'You're good on committees.' He'd rubbed his fingers in his beard as he spoke and she knew there was another question to be asked, but perhaps not yet.

She said that it wouldn't be right. She would have to be voted on to the committee. 'People will ask if I am staying. If *we* are staying,' she added, and then quickly said: 'I hope that we hear from Jewel soon. Grace sent Clara a letter to tell her that we were coming to Dreumel and I wrote from New York to say the same to Jewel.'

Wilhelm nodded contemplatively. 'Yes,' he said quietly. 'We mustn't rush into anything. Just take our time over decisions.'

'Wilhelm, this doctor who has come to Yeller. What is he like?'

'A good fellow, so everyone says, and his wife is a nurse midwife, so will be most useful. Why?' he asked anxiously. 'You're not in need of him, are you?'

'I don't think so,' she said. 'But I was very ill on the boat, and the train journey was very tiring.'

'Surely not!' he exclaimed. 'Not when you consider how we used to travel! My darling—'

'It's nothing. I'll feel better after walking in the mountain air and getting plenty of sleep. I've been troubled over Jewel and Clara, but now that I know they're safe I shall soon pick up again.' She patted his cheek and whispered, 'It's a woman's thing, I expect. I'm approaching middle life, Wilhelm. It's what happens. Some women take to their beds and enjoy ill health, or have fits of the vapours.' She smiled. 'You know that I won't do that.'

'But I shall worry!' His face creased apprehensively. 'I think you should go to see Dr Fox. I'll make an appointment for you.'

'Not yet,' she said. 'A few days of rest and a walk along the creek, and I'll be right as rain.'

But she too was a little anxious, though she tried not to give in to her fears. She had never been sickly and had always had a robust constitution. Wilhelm will take care of me, she thought, if indeed I do have some malady. I'll give myself a week and if I don't feel any better, then I'll visit the doctor.

CHAPTER TWENTY-SEVEN

Jewel woke in a dark room lit only by a lamp and a small fire. Her head ached and she touched her tender forehead, which was covered with a damp cloth. 'Clara,' she whispered. 'Where are we?'

A woman came and knelt beside her and it was then that Jewel realized she was lying on a mattress on the floor.

'Clara!' she said again. 'Clara! Where are you?'

She heard whispering voices but they were speaking in a language she couldn't understand. She was frightened and began to shake. Her body felt limp, and when she tried to sit up her head swam at the effort and the room began to spin.

A cool hand gently pushed her down again and a voice murmured something. Jewel, trying to focus, saw a small dark-haired woman gazing at her. It wasn't Clara. Where was she? And where am I, she thought, trying to recall where she had been and what she had been doing. Something had happened. What was it?

She must have fallen asleep again, for the next time she opened her eyes the dizziness had eased a little. The woman still knelt beside her; she was bent double, her head touching the floor as if she were asleep. Jewel risked a glance round the room. The fire had died to a mere flickering flame, but she could make out other figures sitting cross-legged and leaning against the walls: three young women, and a young man by the door. She frowned and felt pain on her forehead. Who were they? They were all dark-haired but it was difficult to see their faces in the gloom.

One of the girls lifted her head to look at her; it seemed as if they were on watch. Seeing that Jewel was awake, she spoke to one of the others. This girl leaned forward and touched the woman by Jewel's side, waking her instantly. The woman glanced at Jewel and gently patted her cheek; Jewel flinched. The woman was tiny and dressed in white cotton trousers and shift. She was Chinese.

'Do you mean me harm?' she whispered, as fear and apprehension wrapped round her. Rumours of kidnap and slavery came to mind. How did she get here? Was it a dream from which she would shortly awake?

But no, the woman was now patting her arm and repeating something. Jewel strove to make out what it was she was saying.

'Keepsafe. Keepsafe. Nofraid. Nofraid.'

What does she mean? She glanced at the other people in the room. At an apparent signal from the woman by the bed, the young man came closer. He was probably about her own age, she thought. He gave a slight bow with his hands folded together and spoke.

'My mother asks me to say that you are safe and need not be afraid,' he said in almost perfect English. 'You were hurt in the earthquake and we brought you here to our home.'

The earthquake! Of course. She had been with Clara when the ground shook. They had run, but she remembered no more. So where was Clara? Had she too been hurt?

'I must go,' she said, raising herself, but then fell back again as dizziness overcame her. 'Please,' she said to the man. 'I was with a friend. Is she here?'

He shook his head. 'No. You were alone when we found you. You were unconscious.'

'Oh!' she said tearfully. 'Thank you. It was very kind of you to take care of me.'

He translated for his mother, and then he said to Jewel, 'When we found you my mother said that we must bring you to our home because there are some bad people who would take a foreign young lady and . . .' He hesitated, but Jewel knew what he was trying to say. That she might not have got home again.

'I must tell my friends where I am,' she told him haltingly. 'They will be worrying.' No matter how kind these people had been in rescuing her, she thought there was no harm in telling him that she had friends who would be looking for her. 'They will have set up a search party.'

He gave an enigmatic smile. 'In Chinatown,' he said, 'not everyone gives an answer to a question, or at least not the right answer.'

Jewel took in a breath. What did that mean?

He answered her even though she hadn't spoken. 'We will ask the right people. You will give us your name, please, and we will ask someone to find your friends.'

'My name is Jewel Newmarch-Dreumel,' she said, 'and my friends are the Gallis. Lorenzo Galli and his mother Maria.'

She had no sooner spoken than his mother began to speak rapidly in a high-pitched voice, throwing questions at her son, who held his hands up towards her as if trying to calm her, at the same time glancing at Jewel and nodding. Then the young women joined in until there was such a cacophony that Jewel cowered beneath the blanket that covered her, pulling it above her ears.

Within the shrill discourse, however, she could make out a repeated word. *'Pinyin. Pinyin.'* Was it a name they were saying, or were they words that sounded like Pinyin? And if the former, did they mean the Pinyin who worked for Lorenzo, or was it a common name?

She peered above the blanket and glanced from one to another. The older woman was wiping her eyes on her sleeve. Her black hair was plaited in a long pigtail; the other women wore cotton trousers and smocks like hers, but the young man wore a European-style shirt with his wide floppy trousers.

212

He came and stood over her. 'I will go now, missy, and try to find your friends,' he said softly. 'Please rest now and take some nourishment. I will be as fast as possible.'

Jewel swallowed. She was still afraid. 'What is your name?' she asked.

'Soong Chen,' he said. 'My mother is Soong Daiyu.'

'H-how do I address her?' She was sure there was a formal way but didn't know what it was.

'You may call her Mrs Soong. She will be happy with that. We are not in China, after all.' He turned to the young women, who were clustered in a group. 'These are my sisters.' He smiled. 'I will not tell you their names as you will not remember them.' He gave a formal bow. 'You are very welcome here, Miss Newmarch.' Turning, he left the room.

Mrs Soong came and knelt by the bed again and began swaying back and forth, whispering to herself and occasionally glancing at Jewel. Presently she called to one of her daughters, who went out through a curtained door, returning shortly with a bowl of soup; she knelt at the other side of the mattress and offered it to Jewel. Jewel pulled herself up and couldn't believe how weak she felt. Her body still ached but her headache had gone, though her forehead felt sore. As she sat up the cloth on her forehead slipped off and she saw that it was stained with blood.

Mrs Soong retrieved it and nodded at Jewel. 'Better now,' she said, and motioned that she should take the soup. The aroma was fragrant, and although the broth was thin and Jewel couldn't have said what flavour it was, it was very satisfying. When she had finished, she handed the bowl back to Mrs Soong and slid down beneath the blanket again.

She sighed. Whatever was happening was out of her hands. She could only trust Soong Chen to find Clara and Lorenzo, and if he didn't . . . well, if he didn't – she felt sleep stealing over her – there was nothing she could do about it right now.

'Try not to worry,' Lorenzo said, although by now he was clutching Clara's arm so hard that she knew he was worried

213

even though he beseeched her not to be. 'We must rely on Pinyin. He knows many people.'

They followed Pinyin up the street, though they couldn't keep up with him. Each time he stopped to speak to someone they thought they would catch up, but then he was off again, his heels flying, dodging in and out of the milling crowd. They could hear him too as he called out to people up in the windows of the buildings, who either shook their heads or pointed back the way he had come.

Then Clara saw another flying fellow, a younger man and taller than Pinyin who shot past him; Pinyin shouted to him and about-turned and chased after him, and they both skidded to a halt in front of the stallholder and bowed to each other. The young man grasped Pinyin's hands and although neither Clara nor Lorenzo could understand, even had they been able to hear what they were saying, Pinyin bowed and bowed and clasped his hands together as if in supplication.

As Clara watched, a slight hope rising, they spoke to the stallholder. They again bowed low but began to back away from him. Pinyin came hurrying back towards Clara and Lorenzo. 'Good news.' He bowed to Clara. 'Miss Clara, you will come with me, please? Miss Jewel is safe.'

'Oh.' Clara breathed out a sigh of relief. 'Thank goodness. Where is she?'

'I must come too,' Lorenzo declared. 'Is she with friends?'

'She is,' Pinyin said. 'She is with my sister and her family. You must wait nearby,' he told Lorenzo. 'I will take Miss Clara to her.'

'Why can't I come?' Lorenzo demanded. 'I need to find out if she is injured or hurt.'

Pinyin nodded. 'Of course you are anxious, but she is in a house of women and you must wait outside.'

'A house of women!' Lorenzo's voice rose. 'What's that supposed to mean?'

'You are mistaking my meaning.' Pinyin sounded aggrieved. 'I mean *my* family of women; at present there are no men there. Miss Clara must enter alone.'

'I'm sorry,' Lorenzo said. 'You know best.'

They walked together until they reached a corner, where Pinyin asked Lorenzo to wait. Then he turned towards a building that looked like a tenement block, stopped outside a door, opened it and invited Clara inside. She looked over her shoulder and saw Lorenzo standing forlornly on the corner, watching her.

The room smelled of herbs and something aromatic and as Clara's eyes adjusted to the dimness she saw several young Chinese women and an older one who was kneeling by a low bed. She rose when Clara was ushered in by Pinyin, who stayed outside the door. In the bed and apparently sleeping was Jewel.

'Oh,' Clara gave a low gasp. 'Jewel! Is she all right?'

The older woman came towards her and bowed low. She was very tiny, hardly reaching Clara's shoulder. She said something that Clara didn't understand and one of the young women came forward and translated in hesitant and broken English.

'Your friend is recovering. She was hurt in the earthquake. Please. You will speak to her.'

Clara moved towards the bed and knelt down beside it. 'Jewel,' she said softly, touching her cheek. 'It's Clara.'

Jewel stirred. 'Clara!' she whispered. 'Is it really you? Am I dreaming again?'

'No, dear cousin. I'm here. You're quite safe. You were injured in the earthquake and these good people have looked after you. It's Pinyin's family.'

Jewel raised her head. 'Pinyin! How – where is he?'

'Just outside the door, and Lorenzo is waiting out in the street. He can't come in because there are only women in here.'

'Will you help me up, Clara?' Jewel murmured. 'I feel so dizzy.'

Clara did so and noticed that Jewel was wearing a white cotton nightdress, buttoned up to the neck; not one she had seen before. Jewel's gown and bonnet were laid neatly on a chair beside the bed.

A pillow was brought and Jewel settled back against it. 'Mrs Soong,' she said to the older woman. 'Thank you, thank you very much. You have been so kind.'

Mrs Soong nodded as if she understood and then put her hand to her forehead and bent low, murmuring something they didn't understand. The young woman who had spoken previously said hesitatingly, 'My mother wishes to speak to you, but her English is not good. Please, you allow Pinyin to come inside?'

Clara took off her shawl and wrapped it round Jewel's shoulders. 'You are quite respectable, Jewel,' she murmured. 'And these are exceptional circumstances. I think you should allow Pinyin to come in.'

'Of course,' Jewel said without hesitation. 'I would like to thank Mrs Soong properly.'

Pinyin was brought in and Mrs Soong spoke rapidly to him and then knelt on the floor, touching her forehead to the wooden boards several times. At a word from Pinyin she got up again and came to stand by Jewel's bed.

Pinyin cleared his throat. 'Soong Daiyu wishes me to tell you that they found you injured in the street. You were brought here to her home so that no further harm should befall you.'

'Please thank her for me, Pinyin,' Jewel murmured. 'I'm so grateful.'

Pinyin nodded. 'There is more,' he said gravely. 'Soong Daiyu is my sister.' He waved his hand to indicate the young women. 'These are my nieces, and Soong Chen, whom you saw earlier and who came to find me, is my nephew.'

'Please thank them all,' Clara said. 'If we can do anything to repay their kindness—'

Pinyin gave a slight bow. 'That will not be necessary, Miss Clara.' He took a breath. 'There is more.'

Jewel gazed at him with parted lips. She did not feel well. Her head ached and although she longed to leave, more than anything she wanted to lie down again and sleep.

'What, Pinyin?' Clara asked. 'Is Miss Jewel not well enough to leave?'

216

'My sister thinks one more day of rest and then she will be ready.'

Soong Daiyu again spoke to Pinyin and he answered impatiently, then adding, 'Yes. Yes. In a moment.'

'Is there something wrong, Pinyin?' Clara asked softly. 'Something troubles you.'

'Oh, no, Miss Clara,' Pinyin gave her a rare smile. 'Not at all. On the contrary. I am only thinking of the best way in which to impart the knowledge that I have.'

'What knowledge?' Jewel asked, and looked at Soong Daiyu, who had come closer. 'What is it?'

'Only that this is a great time for rejoicing.' He nodded his head gently as he spoke.

'I don't understand,' Jewel said faintly. 'What is it you're saying? '

Soong Daiyu took Jewel's hand in her own. '*Little Gem,*' she said softly, and her English was quite clear. '*Little Gem.*'

Jewel gazed with wide dark eyes at Pinyin. 'What does she mean? Pinyin! What do you mean?'

CHAPTER TWENTY-EIGHT

'I don't understand,' Jewel repeated. 'My name is Jewel. Who named me? My mother died when I was a baby.'

'Yes,' Pinyin agreed. 'She did. There is a long story to tell. Will you permit for Lorenzo to come in, please?'

Jewel glanced from one to another and wrapped Clara's shawl tighter about her. 'I'm not sure. Is it all right to do so, Clara?'

'No, I think not,' Clara answered steadily. 'He is a friend, but of only a short acquaintance. It would not be seemly.'

Pinyin bowed. 'I understand. I ask only because Lorenzo is part of the story.'

'Then we'll tell him of it at some other time,' Clara said firmly and wondered if she was being absurd, but better to be cautious, she thought, than regret it later. It was different for Pinyin because he was part of this family.

'How do you fit into this story, Pinyin?' she asked, encouraging him to begin.

He sat cross-legged on the floor and Soong Daiyu sat on the edge of the bed like a small bird waiting to be fed.

'I met your mother Tsui when she was straight off the ship from Hong Kong,' he said to Jewel. 'I was working on the docks as a coolie and saw her trying to come down the gang board. She had stowed away and was edging through the passengers. One of the seamen saw her and shouted for her to stop but she fled off the ship on to the dock side. I called to her; she ran towards me and I took her and hid her. There were many young girls in those days who came without a ticket. They didn't know how dangerous it was to be on their own. Sometimes it was worse for them here than in China.'

Jewel put her fingers to her mouth and nibbled on them. Mrs Soong, almost automatically, took hold of them and clasped Jewel's hands with her own.

'I kept her hidden until I had finished my shift and then brought her to my sister's house. I knew she would keep her safe.'

Keepsafe. Keepsafe. Those were the words Mrs Soong had used, Jewel remembered.

Mrs Soong spoke to Pinyin, who nodded. 'My sister says to tell you that Tsui was like one of her own daughters. She – Tsui – told me of her life before coming to America. She was from a poor family living in the village of Shenzhen in Guangdong province, where they worked in the paddy fields and barely earned a living. It was very hard for them and so her father could perhaps be forgiven for what he planned to do.'

'Which was?' Clara breathed.

'This is how Tsui told it to me,' he explained. 'Her father was always involved in politics. He thought that it was the only way to rise above poverty. He obtained work in the capital of Guangzhou, where he met a gang master who was involved in rebellion against the West. The Taiping rebellion took place in Guangdong province,' he added. 'This man promised Tsui's father heaven and earth and, especially riches; the price to be paid was for him to give him his daughter, Tsui, in marriage. She was fourteen. The man was fifty.'

Jewel drew in a breath and licked her lips. 'And what happened?'

'When her father came back to his village to tell her to prepare herself for marriage, she ran away. The first time she was caught and beaten. The second time she was brought back, he threatened that if she didn't marry this man he would sell her to the highest bidder and she would not have the privilege of marriage. The third time she ran away she

219

dressed in her brother's clothes and headed north towards Hong Kong.'

Pinyin became pensive. 'It must have been very difficult for her,' he murmured. 'It is a very long way.' He sighed. 'But she couldn't stay in Guangdong as her father would have had people looking for her. She spent a year and a half travelling, working for her food, and eventually reached Hong Kong. She had heard as she travelled of the many men who had headed for California to work in the gold fields and on the railroads, and although she couldn't do that kind of work she thought that perhaps there would be something she could do if only she could reach America.'

Jewel felt as if she couldn't breathe. How brave Tsui had been! She couldn't think of her yet as her mother, for she had been so young, not much more than a child.

'She was such a little thing,' Pinyin said softly. 'I recall the first time I saw her, I thought she was only a child. She was so frail; she had had so little to eat. And yet she was strong in spirit. And so—' He lifted his head and looked at them. It was as if he had been away on a journey and had just returned. 'She asked at Hong Kong about the ships and heard of one sailing to San Francisco; she managed to smuggle herself on board.' He shrugged. 'The rest you know.'

'No,' Jewel said. 'I don't know. What happened after you found her and brought her to Soong Daiyu?'

'She got work,' he said. 'Mainly in hotels and bars. As a cleaner,' he added. 'Never behind the counter. She always wanted to be – unobtrusive. I think she was afraid of being found out and shipped home again.'

Jewel shook her head. How sad. She looked up at Pinyin and thought that although he seemed impassive, there was a yearning on his face.

'And then,' he said softly, 'and then she met the Englishman.'

Soong Daiyu broke in and Pinyin apologized. 'Excuse me. Soong Daiyu says that I tire you. I must finish the tale another day.'

'Oh, but—' Jewel began, and then realized that they were right. She was very tired. It was enough for one day. 'Will you stay, Clara, or will you go back to the hotel?'

Clara looked round the small room. 'I think if you don't mind, Jewel, I will ask Lorenzo to take me back to the hotel. I feel quite exhausted. It has been such a long day. You'll be all right, won't you?'

'Yes.' Jewel smiled. 'Mrs Soong has been so kind that I think I should stay. I don't want to rush away and hurt her feelings; and I feel there is much more to be told.'

And Mrs Soong told her of things which she couldn't understand. She gave her a cup of fragrant tea and held her hand and murmured in her sing-song voice while she smoothed her hair and cheek until finally Jewel drifted off to sleep, a dreamless sleep, deep and satisfying, unlike any sleep she had had before, in which she felt at ease and sheltered as if she were a child again.

Lorenzo was sitting on the doorstep waiting for them and jumped to his feet when Pinyin opened the door.

Clara told him that Jewel would be staying the night with Mrs Soong, and some of what they had gleaned. 'There is much more to know,' she said. 'Not everything has been told to us. Lorenzo, would you be kind enough to escort me back to the hotel?'

'You must come back with me to the restaurant,' he said. 'We have plenty of room and my mother would be upset if you didn't. And you must be hungry. When did you last eat?'

'I can't remember,' she said. 'But I can't stay. I have no clothes with me.'

'*Tch*, as my mother would say.' He smiled. 'Besides, I am desperate to know what was said behind closed doors that I wasn't privy to.'

'If you're sure your mother won't mind.' Although Clara was tired, she was quite glad to be going back to some friendly company rather than an empty hotel room.

'She won't mind,' he promised. 'And then tomorrow we can come back and fetch Jewel back home.'

Clara agreed. 'Pinyin has disappeared,' she said as they walked back down the main street of Chinatown. 'And so, it seems, has Federico.'

'Yes,' Lorenzo said shortly. 'Pinyin has gone back to the restaurant.'

'And Federico?'

'Who knows?' Lorenzo shrugged. 'Who cares? It doesn't matter, we can get a cab.'

As they sat in the cab taking them back up the hill to the Gallis' restaurant, Clara felt the rustle of paper inside her skirt pocket. In the flurry and disorder of the evening she had forgotten her mother's letter. She clutched it with her fingers but decided she would read it later.

Maria Galli received her exuberantly, yet anxiously. *'Avanti. Avanti!'* To Lorenzo she let forth a stream of voluble Italian that Clara couldn't understand; Lorenzo replied as they were hurried in and Clara heard Soong Daiyu's name mentioned several times, to which Maria exclaimed, *'Grazie a Dio. Molti grazie.'* Turning to Clara, she clapped her hands together and said, 'Mrs Soong, she is good woman.'

Clara nodded and sank down into the nearest chair. 'Yes,' she said. 'I believe that she is.'

A glass of red wine was brought to her and she sipped slowly, being unused to alcohol, but she felt the warmth of it trickling down her throat and slowly relaxing her.

'Where's Pinyin?' she asked Lorenzo when he came to sit beside her, bringing with him a plate of titbits for her to eat.

'Back in the kitchen.' He grinned. 'There are very many dishes to wash.' He heaved a great sigh. 'I just can't tell you, Clara, how very relieved I am to know that Jewel is safe. Pinyin is such a good fellow. I knew he wouldn't let us down.'

'Yes,' Clara said thoughtfully. 'It was incredible that he should find her so quickly.'

'It was Soong Chen who found her,' Lorenzo reminded her.

222

'I know him slightly. He comes here sometimes to speak to Pinyin, but I didn't realize they were family.'

'And how odd that they recognized Jewel's name,' Clara said.

Pinyin seemed to appear out of nowhere, but suddenly he was there in front of them bearing a large bowl of soup. He placed the bowl on the table and bowed low to Clara.

'Tomorrow,' he said, 'Miss Jewel will hear the full story, but we have always known her English name, Miss Clara, and she gave it to Soong Chen when he asked her, so that he could trace her friends.'

'Of course,' she said faintly, but that seemed too simple; how, she wondered? How had they known Jewel's English name?

She ate the soup and fresh bread and shortly afterwards asked if she might go to bed; a room had been hastily prepared for her by Maria and she was aching to lie down and rest. Her head was buzzing with the day's events and also she wanted to read her mother's letter and learn the news of home.

She undressed and put on the voluminous nightgown that Maria had put out for her; a soft white towel, warm clean water in a jug and a basin stood on an old-fashioned washstand.

She climbed into the bed with a deep sigh. Propping a pillow behind her, she began to read the letter.

My dearest Clara, it began. *So much appears to be happening both here and where you are. My news is that Uncle Wilhelm has left for America. He was very concerned about the fire in Yeller and to know that you were both safe.*

Clara turned over the envelope to look at the date on which it was sent, but it was obscured. She continued reading.

On hearing from him that you and Jewel had left to continue your journey to California, Aunt Gianna decided that she too would travel to Dreumel's Creek to be with him. Her escort on the journey was Dan Hanson.

Clara gasped. How cross Jewel would be!

However, I think it's not all to do with Jewel, but that he and his father had quarrelled and Dan decided to strike out for himself and

*asked Gianna if he could travel with her. Aunt Ruby, of course, is
very anxious about him.*

She went on about other happenings in the town and ended
by saying that she was expecting a visit from Elizabeth that
afternoon and so would write again soon.

'Mama may consider that Dan's journey is not all to do with
Jewel,' Clara murmured to herself. 'But I would say that it is.'

She heaved a sigh and slid down beneath the sheets. Jewel
will not want Dan here, especially not now when she is on the
verge of finding out more about her background. But, most
especially, not now that she and Lorenzo have rediscovered
each other. Dan is the last person on earth that Jewel will want
here.

CHAPTER TWENTY-NINE

Hull

The day after posting the letter to Clara, Grace put on her bonnet and took a warm shawl from the cupboard. The days were getting colder, autumn leaves were falling fast and there was a tang in the wind as it blew in from the estuary, a sharpness which gave a tingle to the nostrils, a reminder of the saltiness of the sea from whence it came. Winter will soon be upon us and the year will be gone, Grace thought. A slight smile played around her mouth. And what will the New Year bring?

Something good. Ever optimistic, Grace felt a fluttering of excitement. An excitement which had begun the day before with the news that Elizabeth had brought with her. And Clara will surely be home by then, she thought. She will be able to share in the joy.

She walked across town to visit Ruby, for she had to tell someone and Elizabeth had said that she might, knowing that her mother would want to confide in her oldest and dearest friend.

But Ruby wasn't in. The house and shop were shut. A notice on the shop door said that it would be open at two o'clock.

So where is she, Grace wondered? Shopping? Or at the workshop helping with the orders and the packing as she sometimes did? She turned away from the corner of the Land of Green Ginger, retraced her steps and headed for Trinity House Lane and the warehouse close by Holy Trinity Church where Daniel and his sons built their toys and nursery chairs and tables and anything else that small children required.

She pushed open the door and went inside. Grace had been a regular visitor since the very early days when Daniel had first set up in business, so there was no need to knock or make an appointment. She was a welcome caller at any time.

At first no one seemed to be about, but then she heard someone whistling. 'Hello,' she called. 'Is anyone there? Daniel! Thomas!'

Ahead of her was an office partition, built of plywood but with large windows so that anyone within could see out into the warehouse space. A head popped up. Thomas. She smiled. He must have been sitting down and not seen or heard the door open.

'Thomas. Hello. I didn't mean to disturb you. I'm looking for your mother. She's not at home.'

He came to the office door to greet her. 'No, she's not. She's gone to Beverley with Da. I said she should let him go alone, let his misery keep him company. But you know Ma.' Thomas grinned as he spoke. 'He'll have to come out of his strop sooner or later. Will you come in and sit down for a bit?'

She smiled and agreed. Thomas was nearly always cheerful. If he had any worries he kept them to himself.

'Is he still cross about Dan going away?'

'I think he's angrier with himself,' Thomas said thoughtfully. 'Reading between 'lines, I reckon he wishes he'd been more understanding.' He pulled a chair away from a drawing table and invited her to sit down. On the table was a sheet of paper with drawings on it.

'I've disturbed you,' she said. 'You're busy.'

'No. No, it's fairly quiet at 'minute. Apprentice is out at 'back making up some boxes for 'next delivery and I'm just thinking of what we might do for Christmas. We need to have something a bit different so I'm just doodling – well, trying to boost trade if I'm honest. Da seems to have tekken a back seat since Dan left.' He grinned again. 'Lost 'will to live if you ask me. No, I'm joking,' he said, seeing her frown. 'But he doesn't seem to have his heart in 'business any more.'

'I'm sorry,' she began, but he interrupted her. His face was serious.

'Why?' he said. 'Why is Da so set against Jewel? He told Dan that if he married her he needn't come back home.' His face creased with anxiety and puzzlement. 'He's always been against her, but more so since we grew up.' A torrent of words tumbled out. 'This'll sound daft, but it's as if he's scared of her for some reason, and more scared that Dan might ask for her. Not that she'd have him, of course,' he added.

Grace gave a sigh. 'I think we're all agreed on that. But as for why . . .' She hesitated. 'Have you spoken to your mother about it?'

He gave a small shrug. 'Not really. I don't like to interfere. But it's Ma who takes 'brunt of his bad humour, and lately she hardly talks to him. It's as if she's given up trying to coax him any more.'

'He never used to be like this,' Grace said softly. 'He was the kindest, gentlest man you could wish to meet.'

'Well, you knew him better than anybody, Aunt Grace. Why do you think he's changed so much?'

Grace knew why; she'd always known the reason for Daniel's discomfort when Jewel was around, but it wasn't her place to tell his son.

'You'll have to ask your ma and da, Thomas,' she said. 'I really couldn't say.'

He nodded, and changed the subject. 'Have you heard from Clara? I've only had one letter.'

'Not since they left for California, but I've written to her to tell her about Dan travelling with Georgiana.' She frowned a little. 'Georgiana wrote to tell Jewel, but she was unsure what his plans were, whether he would go to Dreumel's Creek or travel to San Francisco . . .' Her voice tailed away. 'What do you think, Thomas? What do you think he'll do?'

'I hope he'll be diverted from thinking about Jewel by being in another country and seeing different things,' Thomas said. 'He'd be devastated if he travelled to San Francisco and Jewel didn't want him there. I just hope that there'll be so much for him to do and see that she won't be 'chief object of his thoughts. She's always distracted him from 'true purpose of his life.'

'Which is?'

'Why, being happy and satisfied with what he does. He's a fine wood worker. He never really enjoys making small crafts as I do; but he could build a house if he'd a mind to.'

'And what about you, Thomas?' Grace smiled. 'Do you never get distracted?'

'Oh aye!' Thomas's cheeks took on a rosy hue. 'All the time. But 'difference between me and Dan is that I have hope, and I'm prepared to wait for what I want. And in 'meantime, while I'm waiting, I'm busy. Busy thinking and making plans.'

He took a breath and chewed on his lower lip, and Grace realized that he wasn't as confident or self-assured as he made himself out to be. 'But what I need is somebody to say I'm doing 'right thing.' He swallowed. 'And that somebody isn't here right now.'

Ruby called round to see Grace later in the day. 'Thomas said you'd been whilst I was out.' She slipped off her shawl when Grace asked her to sit down and rang for tea. 'Did you come for owt in particular?'

Ruby always slipped into her local dialect when she was with Grace or people she knew well, although she tried her hardest to modify her voice when she was with customers, even though Grace told her that she should always remain true to her real personality.

'I did,' Grace said, unable to keep a beam from her face or her voice. 'Elizabeth visited us yesterday. She has some news and she said that I might tell you.'

'Oh!' Ruby put her hand to her mouth. 'She's expecting?' she breathed. 'Is she?'

'Yes. Isn't it wonderful? I'm so pleased.' Grace clasped her hands together. 'I was bursting to tell you and you weren't there! I didn't say a word to Thomas, of course; it's early days and Elizabeth'll want to make the announcement herself once they've told Patrick's parents.'

'Is he pleased? Patrick, I mean.' She leaned forward and whispered confidentially, 'He seems such a cold fish. I wouldn't know what to say to him; not that we're likely to mix in 'same circles.'

Grace laughed. 'I think he's better for knowing. Elizabeth says he's very witty, but I can't say I've noticed. But yes, Elizabeth says that he's delighted and of course he's hoping for a son.'

Ruby preened, having two sons of her own. 'Well, he will be.' Then she smiled. 'And you'll want a little girl.'

'As long as it comes safely, I shan't mind what it is,' Grace answered softly. 'But it'd be rather nice to have a little boy to play with. I haven't told Clara yet. I'd only just posted a letter to her when Elizabeth called. She'll write to tell her herself, of course.'

'I won't breathe a word, I promise,' Ruby said, and then looked rather disconsolate. 'I wish my lads would shake themselves up in that department. I don't know what Dan'll do if – when Jewel spurns him.'

'Ruby, you ought to speak to Thomas,' Grace said earnestly, and then waited as the maid brought in a tray of tea and left it on a side table for her to pour. 'Tell him why his da's acting in 'way he does over Dan and Jewel. It would clear the air.'

Ruby took a sip of tea and nodded. 'I know, but I can't. I'm too embarrassed and ashamed, if I'm honest.'

'Oh, Ruby!' Grace exclaimed. 'It was such a long time ago. We were living a different life then. Your sons and my daughters have no idea what we went through, although I've told some of it to Clara and Elizabeth. Martin and I did that when they were small children; we took them to see 'courts and alleys where 'poor still live, to give them some understanding that life is not always fair.'

Ruby took out a handkerchief and wiped her eyes. 'I know you did; but you pulled yourself up, Grace. I fell into 'gutter, and sometimes,' she gave a huge sigh, 'sometimes I feel as if that's where I really belong.'

As she walked back home, Ruby huddled into her shawl. Grace had told her that she shouldn't feel any shame. That what she did was her means of surviving, but Ruby couldn't see it that way. I was wicked, she thought, and that's why Daniel acts in 'way he does. He just never forgets that he wasn't 'first.

She went into the house by the side door. There was a fire burning brightly. Somebody was home and had added more coal. I'll never get used to seeing a fire burning in 'hearth, she mused. It's one of my greatest pleasures; that and having food on 'table every day.

She called out 'Hello', and two voices answered. Daniel and Thomas. 'You're both home, then,' she said with forced cheerfulness as she went into the kitchen. 'That's good. I've got some nice chops for supper. I'll put them on in a minute.'

Her boots were nipping her toes and she sat down to take them off.

'Here, let me do that.' Daniel knelt on the floor beside her and began to unfasten the laces. He pulled off her boots and tenderly rubbed her toes.

Ruby gazed at him in astonishment. They had travelled to Beverley and back in virtual silence. No topic of conversation she instigated had brought any more response than a brief yes or no. So what had happened since then to make a change in him?

'Da and me have been having a bit of a chat while you were out, Ma,' Thomas piped up. 'We've got summat to discuss.'

'Have you?' Ruby said nervously. 'What?'

'Mainly about Jewel and why Da's set against her. When I asked him he promised he'd discuss it when you came home.'

'Nay, lad,' Daniel broke in, getting to his feet. 'I've nowt against Jewel personally.'

Thomas gave a grunt. 'You could've fooled me.'

'No,' Ruby said slowly. 'He hasn't. It's me. It's me and our Dan that your da's got a concern about. He's scared that Dan will ask Jewel to marry him and that she'd be family – not that she'd have him, but your da can't see that any more than Dan can.'

'I don't understand,' Thomas said. 'Will somebody please explain?'

'Yes,' his mother said. 'I will. It can come out in 'open and then you, Daniel, once I've spoken of my shame, can decide what you want to do. We can live in harmony as man and wife or I can just become somebody who cooks and cleans for you.'

'Ruby!' Daniel protested. 'Don't say such a thing.'

She ignored him, even though she could see tears in his eyes. 'When I was young, Thomas, I was as poor as 'proverbial church mouse—'

'I know that, Ma,' Thomas said.

'But I reckon that 'church mouse had more to eat than I did.' She went on as if he hadn't spoken. 'Or Grace did or any-body that I knew, including your father, did. Church mouse at least had a bone or two to chew on. Grace sold a few things in 'market. Do you remember that, Daniel? After you'd left to go to sea, she sold some of 'carvings that you'd left behind for her to burn on 'fire. Me and my ma, we didn't have a hearth so we had no fire. Nothing,' she said bitterly. 'We had nowt but a mattress on 'floor. Not even a chair to sit on.'

She took a breath, and when she began again her voice trembled and Daniel put his hands over his face.

'But I got an offer,' she said. 'From a gentleman; and I accepted it. This gentleman fed me and clothed me, gave me a room of my own with a hearth and furniture – and a bed. It's that bed that's causing your da such a problem. Oh yes,' she added. 'And this fine gentleman was so besotted with me that he left his wife and asked me to go away with him to America.'

Her face was awash with tears but she didn't brush them away. 'But do you know what, Thomas? Even though this gentleman said that he loved me and would look after me . . .'

Her voice was choked and Thomas bit his lip but didn't move to touch her or say anything, for he felt that she would break in two if he did.

'Even then,' she continued, 'even though I could've had so much, I refused to go. I refused because I loved Daniel – your da – and I couldn't bear to leave him.'

She looked up at Thomas, standing so still. 'It was Edward Newmarch who was my lover. Jewel's father.'

Thomas was silent for a moment, then he glanced at his father sitting with his head in his hands. 'I see,' he said. 'And so – am I right, Da, in thinking that every time you see Jewel . . .' he frowned as if puzzling it out, 'when you see her, you think of him?'

Daniel nodded and blew his nose hard. 'Aye.'

'But – he went on to have a different life, just as you and Ma did, and surely you were both young at 'time and fighting to survive?'

Ruby gave a hiccuping laugh. How simple it sounded.

Thomas shrugged. 'Well,' he said, 'I reckon that Edward Newmarch saved Ma's life by being there, and if all he got in return was her virtue and not her love, then I'd say that he was the loser.'

Daniel looked at his son and blinked as if he had suddenly come out of darkness into the light.

Thomas gazed at them both in turn. 'Well,' he said again, 'if that was what all 'fuss was about, then think on this, Da. Edward Newmarch was, as I understand it, 'brother of Martin Newmarch, Aunt Grace's husband and Clara and Elizabeth's father.'

'I've nowt against Martin—' Daniel began.

'It's just as well, Da,' Thomas said tersely. 'And even if you had it wouldn't mek any difference. Because when Clara comes home, I intend to ask for her hand in marriage; and if she'll have me there'll be a Newmarch in 'family after all. So you can put that in your pipe and smoke it.'

CHAPTER THIRTY

Georgiana borrowed a mount from the hotel stables, a steady ancient mare which would do little more than plod and trot if urged. A stable lad helped her on; she hadn't ridden for a long time, and she accustomed herself to the mare's gait as they ambled down Dreumel's main street.

There was a slight breeze and the water of the creek gushed and surged as it raced down the valley. Mmm, she breathed. That's good. I'm feeling so much better after these few days in the mountain air. Her spirits were lifting and the lethargy which she had felt for some weeks was slipping away.

Wilhelm had gone to Yeller this morning. Although he had spent time with her since her arrival, sitting outside the Marius, talking of plans or escorting her on gentle walks through the town, she knew he was itching to get back to his project, that of rebuilding Yeller. He'd taken Dan with him that morning as the young man had expressed an interest in helping if he could, and so she was alone, to do with the day whatever she wished, but with Wilhelm's warning not to over-task herself ringing incessantly in her ears.

'I won't,' she'd told him. 'I'll be very sensible and take it easy with a good book.' She hadn't told him that she intended riding out towards the mountains.

She patted the mare's neck as she approached the bridge. 'I used to ride out here on Hetty, you know,' she murmured, and the mare snickered and pricked her ears. 'She knew the way all right, we'd done it so many times.'

The horse increased her stride and trotted over the bridge. 'So you know the way too,' Georgiana murmured. 'I suppose new people are curious and come and look at Dreumel from the other side of the water.'

After they'd crossed she reined in and looked back. The town looked much as it had always done, as if it had grown into the valley. True, there were more buildings, stores and houses than there had been when she was last here, but the town hadn't lost its sleepy character, in spite of the activity which she knew went on within it.

She took in a deep breath of satisfaction. It was so very good to be back. She wheeled the mare's head round to face the mountain and the track running up it to the plateau where Dan had seen the black bear. She gazed up. There was nothing there this morning, just the pine trees gently swaying and white clouds scudding across the blue sky.

Georgiana lifted her chin, and with her lips parted slightly and her nostrils flaring, she sniffed. With her tongue pressed to the roof of her mouth, she sniffed again. It was what Lake had taught her to do. 'It takes practice,' he had said. 'A lifetime of practice.' He was a master of it, despite having only had a short lifetime.

'You can smell the weather,' he had told her. 'You can smell the snow even if it's across the mountains. You can smell bear and wolf, and you can smell danger when it's coming for you.'

She dug her heels into the mare's flanks and urged her up the track. Had Lake been able to smell the danger that was coming towards him, she wondered? Did he know it and yet face it head on?

She had first met him at an Iroquois settlement on the long journey between New York and Dreumel's Creek in the days before the railroad crossed the country. Lake was a hunter and trapper, a half-breed; his mother was an Iroquois Indian, a descendant of Handsome Lake, who had brought together

234

Indians and white men to live in peace; his father had been a French trapper. It was Lake who was entrusted with seeing her and Kitty safely though the mountains to visit Wilhelm Dreumel, and it was during that journey that they had each recognized a kindred spirit and eventually learned to love one another.

But he was a man of the mountains who lived beneath the stars and earned his living trapping beaver, both for their pelts and for the meat. A city life wouldn't suit him, walls wouldn't contain him, and neither could she live the life that he did, brought up as she had been amongst gentlefolk, and with the earnest desire to be independent, which was why she had gone to America in the beginning. And then, whilst she was away in San Francisco, rendezvousing with the dying Edward and rescuing his daughter Jewel, Lake was killed by his sworn enemy, his half-brother.

It was Wilhelm who was waiting to tell her. Wilhelm, who comforted her and eventually told her that he loved her, that he had always loved her.

They eased their way up the track, the mare sure-footed as if she knew the route. It was another lifetime. And would I change it if I could? No, she thought. I wouldn't. Not one single part of it. I loved Lake then as he loved me, but we could not have lived together. I couldn't have lived a life in the wilderness and I would have been a constant worry to him. He would always have been watching over me, keeping me from danger, from wolf or bear or enemy. I would have ruined his life.

She reached the plateau and dismounted, tying the reins loosely to a branch. How well I remember it, she thought, looking down at the valley. I recall so well the first time Kitty and I came here.

'It's a secret valley,' she had proclaimed to Lake and he'd agreed. Unknown, then, except to Indians and the chosen few who had come here because of Lake. Wilhelm was the first, the visit his reward for saving Lake's life the first time his murderous half-brother attacked him. Wilhelm brought Ted

Allen, then old Isaac; Pike, who was killed blasting through to Yeller and whose name was given to the road; the young Jason; Ellis, a man of few words; and others who could see the potential of the valley, not just for the gold they were sure was there, which cost them life and sweat and tears before they found it.

It's still so beautiful, she thought, her gaze traversing the lush meadow, the green uplands, the gushing creek and the rocky mountain range; and the town itself, looking as if it had always been there.

She leaned her back against a pine tree as she contemplated. Why would anyone ever want to move from here? Not Wilhelm, and – would I? I should be torn, there is no doubt, but would I be beset by old memories? She closed her eyes and breathed in steadily the smell of pine needles, the fresh cold air and something else, something musty like sweat or something animal.

She kept very still. Imaginings, she told herself. The horse would be disturbed if there was a bear or wolf; and yet she recalled two occasions when there had been both, once when Lake had been distracted by her presence and a lone wolf had come upon them. Lake had killed it, the animal's blood spattering them both. The other time she had been with Kitty and a female black bear had strayed into their territory. She had kept her nerve then and it had gone away.

Opening her eyes, she gazed around without moving. The mare had her head down, nosing amongst pine needles. Georgiana turned her head slowly; a shadow, a rustle amongst the trees, a faint aroma of old leather. She swallowed. *I am at one with the elements of nature*, Lake had told her; and the very last thing he had said to her was that she should look for him on her return and he would be there.

But I don't believe in ghosts, she thought, and it was such a long time ago; besides, I love Wilhelm. But I loved Lake too, there's no denying that. She felt a warmth stealing over her. A tender sweet happiness to have known such a man. She took a breath and turned to catch the reins and it was then that she saw the bear. He was large and standing on a ledge above her, half hidden by the trees. Gently she clapped her hands so as not to frighten him. They were timid creatures and only attacked if disturbed. The horse whinnied and pawed the ground and instantly the bear turned and disappeared into the forest.

She felt quite calm, gathered up the reins and led the horse towards the track, where she stood on a fallen log and mounted. Enough, she thought. I will not ride out alone in the mountains again. I'm no longer young and foolhardy. I'm a mature woman who should know better. Carefully, the mare eased down the route as if carrying a fragile load, and then halted as Georgiana brought her to a standstill to look back. The bear was on the plateau where she had just been, looking down at her. He lifted one foot; Georgiana gazed, her lips parted, and then raised her hand in farewell. I was in his special place, she thought. That is his lookout.

She rode down towards the bridge and it was there that she was struck by a sudden thought. I *am* a mature woman, but I'm not old by any means. This malaise that has been bothering me since before I left England, the seasickness I experienced, is not a mid-life malady after all. She felt curiously elated. I do believe that I'm expecting a child.

CHAPTER THIRTY-ONE

Dan had been lent a pony to ride into Yeller beside Wilhelm. He'd mounted easily and was relieved that he had, for Caitlin had watched them move off and he didn't want to make a fool of himself in front of her. She would have laughed, he was sure of that.

As they rode Wilhelm told him something of Yeller and the fire and how they wanted to rebuild it. As he spoke, Dan picked up on the enthusiasm in his voice. This is a man of vision, he thought. There's no wonder that a town was named after him. Without him there would have been no Dreumel and no Yeller either.

'I'd like to help,' Dan said. The words popped out, surprising even him. What an opportunity, he thought. To be in at the beginning. To put my mark on some aspect of the new town. 'I'm a qualified joiner,' he said. 'Served my apprenticeship.'

Wilhelm turned to him. 'Well, if you're as good as your father then you'll be welcome,' he said. 'We'd need a commitment, as far as you could give it, that is, and there might not be much money to begin with. Most folks have lost everything and need to start again. They might not be able to pay right away.'

Dan nodded. 'I'd only need to earn my bed and board,' he said. 'I can manage otherwise.' He gave silent thanks to his father, who had given him enough money to get by on. He could live on that.

They rode into what was left of Yeller and Dan was aghast at the devastation and yet also amazed to see buildings going up, windows and doors being fitted. There was the sound of hammering and sawing and the shouts and whistling of men as they worked, and a general air of purpose. Dan felt a buoyancy, a sense of enthusiasm and eagerness to be part of the scene.

'Hi there, Bill,' somebody called out.

Wilhelm turned in his saddle and, touching his hat, greeted a man on the road. 'Jason! How you doing?'

Bill, Dan thought? I'd never have thought of Wilhelm Dreumel as Bill.

'I'm doin' jest fine,' the man said, and came over towards them, raising his hand for Wilhelm to shake. 'Got my house jest about finished. On the outside, that is.' He laughed. 'Rose's got some fancy ideas for indoors.'

'Dan, this is Jason,' Wilhelm introduced him. 'Jason was here right at the start of Dreumel's Creek. Before we had any kind of town.'

'No more'n a shanty town.' Jason reached up to shake Dan's hand too. 'A few tents and wooden shacks.'

He must have been young, Dan thought. He can only be late thirties now.

'You jest arrived? Is it you that's come over from England with Miz Gianna?'

'Erm, yes,' Dan said. 'That's right.'

'You got a trade?' Jason bit on his lip. 'We sure need tradespeople.'

'Yes,' Dan said again. 'I'm a wood worker. Time served.'

'Uh huh! Well, if you're staying there'll be plenty of work.' Jason touched his hat. 'Be seeing you.'

Wilhelm smiled as Jason left them. 'He's a good sort is Jason. Made his mark here. He was only young when he arrived, maybe eighteen or nineteen. He stayed on even when there seemed to be no hope of finding gold. He teamed up with Pike – Pike who was killed when we blasted through.' He nodded thoughtfully as if he was thinking about the past.

'It was Jason who called this Yeller Valley, after we found gold.'

'I'd like to stay,' Dan said.

Dan was introduced to Isaac and Nellie. Isaac too had been here at the beginning and Nellie O'Neill had come soon after to run a saloon. Together they now ran a rooming house and it was here that Dan found lodgings. The Dreumel Marius was too expensive, he decided; he needed something simple and cheap.

Caitlin found out and came to see him. He was sitting on the front steps of the porch. 'Here,' she said. 'Why don't you stay with my folks? They've plenty of room.'

'I expect they will have,' he said. 'But I can't afford to spend much until I earn some money.'

'You intend staying a while, then?' She put her hands on her waist as she surveyed him.

He grinned. 'I thought I might. Any objections?'

She shrugged. 'Please yourself. You gonna look fer work?'

'Yeh! Why don't you sit down a minute?' He moved up on the step to make room beside him. 'I'm sure you'll know 'best people for me to ask.'

She hitched up her skirts and sat down. 'Sure. I know everybody in Yeller and everybody in Dreumel's Creek too. Lived here all of my life.'

He gazed at her. Her red hair gleamed and she had a bright freshness to her cheeks and full red lips. He could just imagine—

'What you lookin' at?' she demanded. 'Ain't you seen a red-head afore?'

His eyes scanned her. 'Not like you,' he said. 'Are you, erm – seeing anybody?'

'Wadd'ya mean? Seeing anybody? I see folks all the time.'

'Erm, no, I meant – you know, a feller, a man, somebody special?'

She blushed. 'What's it to do with you if I am?'

240

'I wouldn't want to muscle in; you know, stand on anybody's toes.'

She got to her feet and defiantly stared him out, her hands planted firmly on her hips. He too rose to his feet, standing over her.

'You've got a nerve,' she said, her eyes flashing. 'You've not been here five minutes. Is this what happens in England? Some guy comes on to a woman the minute he sets eyes on her?'

'Depends on the woman,' he said, grinning.

'Well, you can wipe that smirk off your face,' she snapped. 'Cos I ain't jest any kinda woman.'

Dan laughed. 'I can see that.' Afterwards he wondered what on earth had got into him as he leaned towards her, put his hands on either side of her face and kissed her full on the lips.

He held his hand to his smarting cheek and gazed after her as she ran down the steps. Life in the new world, he decided, was going to be very interesting.

'Crawford is leaving,' were the first words Wilhelm said to Georgiana later that day as he washed and changed for supper. 'He'd told me that he'd be going soon, but I'd hoped that it wouldn't be yet. He's going back to his tribe. He said that their need was greater than ours. '

'I'm sure it is,' she replied. 'As an educated man he'll bring much to their confederacy.'

'Yes,' he sighed. 'He'll be able to speak for them. But I fear that their settlement is being moved on again. He also told me that it was time he took a wife.'

Georgiana smiled. 'He'll have no difficulty there. I need to speak to you, Wilhelm.'

'Yes,' he said absently. 'But we'll be lost without him at the Marius. We'll manage over the winter period, for there won't be many visitors, but we must find someone to start in the spring. I was wondering, what do you think about asking Caitlin to cover for him? She's young, I know, but very efficient—'

'Wilhelm! I saw the doctor today. I'm expecting a child.'

'And then if— What did you say?'

She smiled. She had his attention at last. 'I said, Wilhelm, that I'm expecting a child.'

CHAPTER THIRTY-TWO

Maria Galli brought a cup of strong coffee to Clara's bedroom the next morning.

'You sleep well, yes?' she asked.

'Yes, thank you.' Clara sat up and took the cup. 'I feel quite rested.'

'Good.' Maria nodded. 'Lorenzo, he is anxious to fetch Miss Jewel, but I say he must let her rest a little longer. She will be quite safe with Pinyin's sister.'

But Clara too was anxious to collect Jewel and bring her back, either to the Gallis' or to the hotel, so as soon as she had finished breakfast and Pinyin had completed his morning duties they set off once more to Chinatown, this time walking down the hill, for the early-morning fog had cleared and the sun was warm.

'We'll take a cab to come back,' Lorenzo said, his stride much longer than Clara's so that she had to hurry to keep up with him. She stumbled and he caught her arm. 'I'm sorry,' he apologized. 'I'm rushing you.'

'Yes,' she said breathlessly. 'You are rather.'

Soon, however, they reached the cathedral and saw Pinyin waiting for them.

'I beg your pardon.' Pinyin bowed, clasping his hands. 'I have taken the liberty of asking my uncle Soong Zedung to come to my sister's house. I wish to say something to him regarding Miss Jewel.'

243

Both Lorenzo and Clara frowned. 'Is that the stallholder we have seen?' Clara asked, whilst Lorenzo shook his head. He didn't know who he was.

'Yes.' Pinyin bowed again but said no more, though as they passed through Chinatown, where the stallholder was arranging the silks and other materials on his cart, Pinyin looked towards him and raised his hand, opening his fingers wide.

Jewel was up and dressed in her own clothes when they arrived and said she felt perfectly well. Her headache had gone and the cut on her forehead was healing and barely discernible, except as a small red wound.

Soong Chen was there with his mother, but his sisters were not. It seemed that they had all gone out early, sent off on errands by their mother.

'My mother wishes to speak to you privately,' Chen said. 'My sisters are chatterboxes. If you should wish to speak of your experiences, Miss Jewel, then that is your right, as it is your right to have your friends present.'

Jewel gazed at him. What was there to say that couldn't be said in front of Soong Daiyu's daughters or Clara and Lorenzo?

'If you'd rather I didn't stay, Jewel . . .' Lorenzo began.

'Why, no,' Jewel said, 'I'd like you to stay whilst I give my thanks to Mrs Soong for taking such good care of me.'

The door opened and Soong Zedung came into the room. He bowed to everyone present and Soong Daiyu spoke briefly to him before indicating that he should stand against the wall, not offering him a chair. He gazed at her and then round the assembled company. 'What is the purpose of this meeting?' he asked tersely.

'Honoured uncle.' Pinyin bowed. 'It is to right a wrong.'

'What wrong?'

Pinyin turned to Jewel. 'I must first tell you that my uncle Soong Zedung was the brother of my sister's husband and after his death he assumed position of elder of the family.'

'Oh, really,' Jewel murmured, wondering what that had to do with her.

'When I first brought Chang Tsui to my sister,' Pinyin went on, 'she lived with us as family, but always worked and gave all of her money to my brother-in-law; she was told by him and Uncle Zedung that she must do this or leave.'

Jewel, watching Soong Zedung, saw him straighten himself up and murmur something to Pinyin.

Pinyin went on speaking. 'Then Tsui met the Englishman and went to live with him.' He paused for a moment. 'After a time she became with child and came back to my sister, asking if she would take her in. She thought the Englishman wouldn't want her if he found out about the child.'

Jewel took a breath and sank into a chair. Not want her! Was that true? But her father was a loving man; she remembered that he was.

Daiyu broke in and said something and Pinyin nodded. 'Yes. Yes,' he said. He looked at Jewel. 'That child was you, Miss Jewel.'

There was an intake of breath from Zedung, who spoke rapidly in Chinese to Pinyin and then to Daiyu, who seemed to cower.

'Your mother died shortly after your birth, Miss Jewel,' Pinyin said softly, not responding to Soong Zedung. 'She was sorely missed.' He swallowed hard. 'Tsui was a beautiful, kind and caring young woman and we loved her.'

Jewel felt her eyes filling with tears and she glanced at Clara, who had her hands pressed to her mouth. 'Then who . . .' she stammered, 'who took care of me?'

Pinyin put out his hand to Daiyu, who came towards him and put her hand in his.

'Daiyu had also given birth to a child only a few months before. Chen.' Pinyin looked towards the young man leaning in the shadows against the wall opposite Soong Zedung.

'Miss Jewel,' Pinyin murmured, 'Soong Daiyu was your milk mother.'

Jewel, as if stunned, sat silent as stone in the chair; then Daiyu came and knelt beside her, bending her head low and murmuring words Jewel couldn't understand.

'My mother says that she has ached for you since you went away.' Chen came to stand by her. 'And I have always known that there was someone missing from my life.' He touched Jewel softly on the head. 'We shared my mother's milk,' he said. 'She said that I cried when you were gone.'

Jewel reached out to lift Daiyu's chin that she might see her face. 'You took me to my father,' she murmured.

'Yes,' Pinyin answered for her. 'Soong Daiyu's husband and his brother said that once you were weaned you must be sold. There would be a good price for a mixed-race child. My sister did not want this to happen, for she loved you as her own. She took you to your father, Edward Newmarch, and begged him to take you, telling him of the fate waiting for you if he didn't. She didn't tell her husband or his brother. She told them that the child had been snatched by a foreigner when she was out.'

There was silence in the room for a moment and then Soong Zedung began berating Soong Daiyu in harsh words, shaking his fist. Chen strode across the room to him.

'*Enough!*' he shouted. 'You have no authority here. I am old enough to be the master of this household. We are in America, not in China!'

His mother bent into a curled-up ball beside Jewel's chair, but Chen put his hands beneath her arms and pulled her to her feet.

'My mother is within my care now,' he told his uncle. 'She is a free woman. She does not have to ask your advice for anything. And,' he added, 'you are no longer welcome here.'

Soong Zedung stared long and hard at Chen and then at Soong Daiyu. His glance took in Pinyin, who simply folded his hands together and bowed as politely as ever. His gaze crossed to Jewel, who was holding Mrs Soong's hand.

'You were a very pretty child,' he said. 'But you were not of our family. You had an English father, not Chinese, therefore you had no place with us. If I mistreated you by my actions I apologize. I act only to keep our traditions and culture pure.'

Jewel shook her head. 'It was unkind of you to think of

selling a child,' she said softly. 'But at least by Soong Daiyu's actions I was united with my father and subsequently my English family.' She took a deep breath. 'Now I am reunited with my Chinese one.'

He bowed low to her and without another word he walked to the door, opened it and departed.

'Mrs Soong,' Jewel said, but looked up at Pinyin. 'You called me Little Gem.'

Soong Daiyu nodded, smiling. 'Little Gem,' she said.

'Little Gem was your milk name,' Pinyin said. 'Your mother named you that. Later, your given name was Lili. Tsui was also called Lili. In English she was Lili Tsui Chang.'

'Did my father know that Little Gem was my milk name, I wonder?' Jewel said as they drove in the cab back up to the restaurant, having told Mrs Soong they would come back to see her again. 'Is that why he called me Jewel? There are still so many things I need to know.'

'There will be many questions that will go unanswered, I suspect,' Clara said. 'But now you know who you are, which is why you came back, isn't it?'

'Yes,' Jewel said. 'It is.' She smiled shyly at Lorenzo, who was sitting opposite them. 'No other reason.'

When they reached the restaurant she was received exuberantly by Maria, who ushered them into the living quarters and would have called to Pinyin, who arrived just behind them, to bring coffee for everyone, but Jewel interrupted.

'Excuse me, Mrs Galli, but might I ask Pinyin something?'

Maria shrugged. 'But of course.'

'Pinyin!' Where to begin, Jewel thought.

'I know what you ask, Miss Jewel,' Pinyin said. 'How do I know your name? We are not at the end of the puzzle.'

'No, we're not.' Jewel shook her head. 'There is more, I think.'

Pinyin clasped his hands together. 'When my sister brought you to your father, she said he was very sad about Tsui, but so happy that he had a daughter he could love. But Daiyu was very lost without her Little Gem and worried too that she might never know anything more about you.'

He glanced at Maria, who pressed her lips together and nodded, and went on. 'A few weeks later she came up here, hoping that she might see you, and saw a notice in the Gallis' window. It was a bakery then, and they needed someone to wash the dishes, and my sister sent me to apply so that I could hear any news about the child.' He gave an inscrutable glance towards Lorenzo. 'And Maria found that I was good with Lorenzo, and, although you wouldn't remember, I used to bring him to play with you, until the English lady came, just before your papa died.'

'I cried,' Lorenzo said suddenly. 'When you went away I cried for days. Pinyin was the only one who could console me.'

'You were just a bambino,' his mother said. 'But we all cried when she was gone.'

They heard the door bell of the restaurant jangle and Pinyin went to answer it. 'Tell them we serve lunch in an hour,' Maria called after him.

He came back a few minutes later. 'I serve them coffee,' he said. 'It is Larkin and a friend.'

Jewel went through into the dining room. A grey-haired man of about sixty wearing a checked shirt and heavy twill breeches and holding a large-brimmed hat stood biting his lip and looking slightly nervous. Beside him was a large woman, younger than Larkin, with dyed hair and flamboyant clothes.

'Larkin?' Jewel whispered. 'Is it really you?'

'Sure is, Miss Jewel.' He ran his fingers round the brim of his hat and took a step towards her.

She gazed at him, trying to recall. He used to swing her up in the air, that much she remembered. He put out his hand, formally. It was rough as if he did manual work, though spotlessly clean.

'Oh, Larkin,' she said. 'I can't believe I'm seeing you after all this time.' She held out her arms and he put his round her

248

waist to hug her. She knew it was him; he smelled the same, of tobacco and carbolic soap.

'Guess you won't know who this is,' he said gruffly. Clearing his throat, he cast his thumb towards the woman.

'Dolly?' she said. 'Is it Dolly?'

'It sure is, m'darlin,' Dolly said, and tears streaked her powdered face. 'Why, I knew you'd be a looker, but I never guessed how beautiful you'd be.'

Jewel went to her and again she was given a bear hug. She instantly recognized the scent of perfume and powder and remembered too how Dolly used to let her try on her hats and scarves and totter about in her shoes.

'I'm overwhelmed,' she said. 'It's too much to take in all in one day.'

Larkin raised his bushy eyebrows enquiringly.

'I have found out about my mother,' she said. 'I've been in Chinatown.'

They all sat down and Larkin said, 'I met her once at the house. Tiny little thing she was. Eddie missed her a lot. Searched all over San Fran, he did, and in Chinatown, but he couldn't find her. Never knew what happened to her till you were brought by the Chinese woman.'

'How did you know I was here?' Jewel asked.

'We didn't,' Dolly said. 'But we've been coming up here most weeks since we got your letter to say you were coming home. Jest checkin'.'

Coming home, Jewel thought? Yes, I suppose that's how it appears. And is that so? Now that I have found out about myself and about my mother?

'Larkin,' she said. 'Dolly! There's so much more I need to know about my father.'

CHAPTER THIRTY-THREE

They talked and talked and Jewel listened. Larkin told her about meeting her father in the Mississippi Basin and their trek to California; he told her of their friend Jed, whom she barely remembered. Jed and his family had left San Francisco but still kept in touch; he'd bought some land, Larkin explained, saying, 'I guess he wuz always a farm boy.'

Dolly told of meeting Jewel's father when he was working in the bar in San Francisco where he had met Tsui, before he opened his own saloon. 'He left it to me, did you know that, honey?' Dolly wiped her eyes. 'He was a real gentleman, your pa; I wish you could have remembered him.'

Jewel nodded. She wished she could too, but she was piecing together his life, bit by bit.

She introduced Clara to them and then they all sat down to lunch of antipasti and a steaming bowl of pasta with salad, served by Maria.

After they had finished, Larkin and Dolly stood up to take their leave. They were promising that they would meet again in a few days' time at the downtown hotel where Jewel and Clara were staying when the restaurant door opened and Chen peered cautiously in.

'Excuse me, please. I must speak to Pinyin and Mr Lorenzo.' He beamed at Jewel, but then apologized. 'I am very sorry,' he said, on realizing she had guests. 'But it is most urgent.'

Pinyin was summoned and Chen spoke a stream of

unintelligible sentences, while Pinyin's usual enigmatic expression changed to a frown and a torrent of questions.

'What is it?' Lorenzo asked. 'Is something wrong? Why has Chen asked for me?'

Pinyin whispered something to him. Lorenzo started, and muttered an involuntary, though hushed, curse.

Larkin bade them goodbye and ushered Dolly outside to where a pony and trap were tethered. They both gave a cheery wave as they left.

'I'm sorry, I must go on an errand immediately,' Lorenzo told Jewel. 'I won't be long. Please wait.'

Jewel said she and Clara would go back to the hotel and they would meet later in the day.

'Come for supper,' he urged, pulling on his jacket. 'Please come! I must go. Pinyin, come.'

Chen rushed across to Jewel. Taking her hand, he murmured, 'Little sister, I am so pleased to have found you again.'

'Chen.' Jewel pressed his hand. 'What has happened? Something is wrong!'

'Not for you,' he assured her. 'It is not a worry for you or for us. Perhaps for Mr Lorenzo. That is why I came.' He rushed out of the door, following Lorenzo and Pinyin.

Maria watched them racing down the hill and shook her head. Then she shrugged. 'Some Italian in trouble! They always send for my boy.'

Jewel and Clara left then, saying they would walk down the hill and that they would benefit from the exercise and the fresh air.

'And I need to talk to you, Clara,' Jewel said, tucking her arm into her cousin's. 'There is so much to discuss.'

'Indeed there is.' Clara smiled. 'I too have things to tell you.'

'What?' Jewel asked. 'What has been happening to you? Oh, Clara,' she sighed. 'I am so happy! I just can't tell you how much. Has something nice happened to you?'

'Well, of course I was worried sick after the earthquake

251

when I couldn't find you, and just as I was wondering what on earth I could do next, and where I could go for help, Federico Cavalli turned up. He'd come looking for us when he felt the quake.'

'That was kind of him,' Jewel murmured.

'Yes,' Clara agreed. 'He's a strange man of so many temperaments. Charming – and yet arrogant too. We went back into Chinatown and he asked various people, including the stallholder whom we now know as Soong Zedung.' Clara frowned. 'He was quite rude about him actually,' she added. 'Mr Cavalli, I mean, was rude about Soong Zedung. He called him a heathen and although we know he's not a very nice man, I don't think he should have said that.'

Jewel shook her head. 'I agree,' she said. 'So then what happened?'

They picked their way down the steep hill as Clara described what had followed, and then said, 'But what I wanted to tell you, Jewel, was that on the same day, when I went back to the hotel, there was a letter from my mother waiting for me.'

'Oh!' Jewel said. 'Perhaps there will be one waiting for me from Mama and Papa. What a great deal I have to tell them!'

'Ye-es, indeed. But I haven't finished telling you about my letter.'

'Sorry,' Jewel apologized. 'I am so taken up with my own affairs. Please go on, Clara. I promise I won't interrupt.'

Clara laughed. 'There might be some who would offer a wager on that, but this is what Mama said.' She pulled the letter from her pocket and began to read. *'My news is that Uncle Wilhelm has left for America. He was very concerned after the fire in Yeller and to know that you were both safe . . .* Oh, here.' She handed the letter to Jewel. 'You'd better read it for yourself.'

She propelled Jewel to a low wall and they sat down and Clara waited for the outburst that she was sure would come when her cousin read that Dan had also come to America.

'I can't believe it!' Jewel exclaimed, looking up. 'Mama and Papa have travelled all this way to be sure we're safe!'

Clara raised her eyebrows expressively, but remained silent, and Jewel turned back to the letter.

'What? Clara! Dan has travelled with Mama!' Jewel hadn't taken in the significance on the first scan of the letter. 'Dan! He'll be in Dreumel's Creek! Oh, no, Clara! This will ruin everything. He'll come here and – and – I don't want him to. I want—' Her pale cheeks flushed. 'Clara – I'm very taken with Lorenzo. Is that very bad of me?' Her voice dropped to a whisper. 'And I think he's—'

Clara put her arm round Jewel's shoulder. She could sense how confused she was, probably not thinking straight after her ordeal in the earthquake and all that had followed.

'I think that Lorenzo is totally captivated by you, Jewel. Anyone can see that! But there are many implications which you must think about and prepare for if' – she gazed at her cousin – 'if he should ask for you.'

'Yes.' Jewel's voice trembled but there was a hint of excitement in her dark eyes. 'Yes, of course.'

'Let's move on,' Clara suggested. 'We'll go back to the hotel. You can bathe and change and then we'll sit for a while in the hotel lounge and talk about the ifs and buts if such a circumstance should arise.' She squeezed Jewel's shoulder and beamed. 'Which I'm sure it will!'

They were approaching St Mary's and the entrance to Chinatown. Clara, who was looking about her, suddenly caught Jewel's arm.

'Wait!' She spoke in an urgent, quivering whisper. 'Look!'

Coming out from the Chinatown entrance and hailing a cab was Chen. Behind him were Lorenzo and Pinyin and between them, with an arm draped round each of their shoulders, they were trailing a dishevelled and unsteady Federico Cavalli.

'Oh! He's drunk!' Jewel exclaimed in horror.

Or worse, Clara thought, considering where he has been. Has he been in Chinatown since he came in with Lorenzo and me to look for Jewel? She recalled how she'd asked Lorenzo how Federico would find them and he'd shrugged and said that Fed knew Chinatown better than most.

She swallowed hard and took a breath as she watched them haul him into the cab. How humiliating for Lorenzo. *I rather feel that Federico has been in the opium dens. And if he has, then there is little hope for him.*

They hurried on to the hotel and there was a letter waiting for Jewel in Georgiana's handwriting. She tore it open and discovered that it had been written before her mother had left Hull.

You will be surprised to discover that Dan Hanson has asked if he might travel with me and I have agreed. He will, I feel sure, be very useful to me on the voyage. Please don't be alarmed, my dear, for I think he has other reasons for travelling apart from seeing you – I have forewarned him that you have moved on to California and that in any case you are not ready for any kind of commitment and he seemed quite content with that. It appears that he has had a disagreement with his father and wants to stretch his wings, as any young man might.

There were other pleasantries, and Georgiana closed by saying that she was hoping to be useful in helping to rebuild Yeller and with the fervent wish that Jewel and Clara in discovering America were learning what a wonderful country it was.

'I think Mama's pleased to be coming back,' Jewel said thoughtfully, 'and I know Papa will be.'

'Do you think they will stay?' Clara asked. 'It is Uncle Wilhelm's home country, after all.'

'I don't know.' Jewel stretched out on her bed. 'Clara, would you mind terribly if I rested for a while? I know we said we would chat, but—'

'I don't mind at all,' Clara said at once. 'I'll go downstairs and write my letters there so as not to disturb you. I must send a long overdue one to Elizabeth. Come down when you feel rested. There's no hurry at all for us to do anything strenuous.'

She felt sure that Jewel wanted to quietly mull over the events of the last few days and to consider not only her new-found family but also the prospect of a relationship with Lorenzo. I hope I'm right in saying that he is of the same mind as she is, Clara thought as she quickly changed her dress and shoes and brushed her hair. I would hate to see her heart broken. But oh dear, it will mean that I will lose her.

The writing desk in the hotel lounge was by a window overlooking the street, and Clara looked up from her letter to see Lorenzo striding towards the door. He went to the desk clerk, who pointed to where Clara was sitting.

'Miss Clara,' he began. 'I'm so pleased to see you alone. I know that you are aware of the ghastly scene outside Chinatown, for as we drove away I saw you and Jewel there. I'm so sorry that you were witness to such a degrading and shameful spectacle.' He sat down at Clara's request. 'I hope that what you and Jewel saw has not soured your opinion of either our society in San Francisco or values which my family hold dear.'

Clara shook her head. 'Please do not trouble yourself on our account,' she said softly. 'You are not responsible for your friend.' She hesitated. 'I must say that although I found Mr Cavalli very charming and, shall I say, attentive, that in itself made me rather guarded. Jewel and I are learning that manners and traditions are different here in America from what they are in England. I'm not saying that that is a bad thing by any means – in some instances it is very refreshing – but I did have some doubts about Federico's disposition and attitude. Particularly regarding the Chinese.' Her voice dropped. 'He has, I think, a dark side to his nature.'

Lorenzo called to a passing bell boy and ordered coffee for them both. 'You've hit the nail on the head, Miss Clara. It's most perceptive of you, but I'm worried that Fed is set on a downward path.'

'Does he frequent the opium dens in Chinatown?' she asked quietly and observed with wry humour the gaping astonishment on Lorenzo's face.

'I – I wouldn't have thought that an English lady would have known about those places,' he said.

Clara smiled. 'There is much that you don't know about me,

255

or Jewel either for that matter, although I doubt that Jewel knows much about opium addicts. I'm aware of them because of my mother's work in our home town. The opium habit isn't only confined to Chinatown, you know!'

'That I realize,' he admitted. 'But let me tell you about my experience. When I was twelve years old, my father decided that he would educate me in the ways of men. He told me that there are many temptations in San Francisco, perhaps more than in most cities because there are so many cultures, so many nationalities who came here thinking it was Eldorado.'

'Because of the gold?'

He nodded. 'That, and the chance of a new life; perhaps escaping from a life of poverty in their own country. That was the case with my own parents. However, my father saw that I was running wild and so he took me on a tour of the city. He brought me to Montgomery, down Washington and Stockton, and showed me the down-and-outs who had squandered what little money they had on women, bars and gambling and sat on the sidewalks begging for a crust.

'It opened my eyes and yet in the cold light of day it made little impact on me, except that to see the thriftless men and the loose women hanging about the street corners was fascinating to a youth of my years, and I believe my father saw that.'

Lorenzo heaved a breath as he continued. 'And so he took me, against my mother's warnings, to Chinatown at night. There are many good people living there, as you have already discovered, but at night it's a different place altogether and decent citizens close their doors and curtains.'

'There must be many places like that,' Clara interrupted. 'Not only Chinatown.'

Lorenzo agreed, but went on, 'My father had a friend who was a policeman and he came with us, though not in his uniform. Pinyin came too, and they took us to a gambling den. We were allowed to enter even though I was so young and I was offered liquor. The air inside the room was blue with smoke, from tobacco I assumed, though it had a strange sweet smell. The room was filled with men dressed in black: these were the bankers and completely disguised by their robes and hoods. The customers looked like country boys just down from the farm, or miners from the diggings; most of them were already drunk and were throwing money on the table as if it grew like leaves on trees. When they lost their bets and made a great fuss, they were ejected from the room and put out into the street.

'Next I was taken to another house. At the time I wasn't sure of the purpose of this visit, but it dawned on me when I was a little older. There were young girls there, some perhaps the same age as me, others younger, but they had colour painted on their faces and their hair dressed like women, which made them look older, although I could tell that they were not by their immature figures beneath their thin and gaudy clothing. They looked very sad, frightened even. There was music playing and one of these girls came up to me and stroked my arm and asked if I'd like to dance with her. Pinyin then insisted that we'd seen enough and must leave. I recall him saying that it was too dangerous to stay any longer.'

'How dreadful,' Clara murmured, and thought of the young girl she had seen fleeing after the earthquake.

'Yes,' Lorenzo said quietly. 'And that was not the worst of it. I was shown the opium dens, the places where Federico spends his time and money.' Lorenzo paused for a moment and then plunged on, as if pursued by demons. 'I must tell you, Miss Clara, that Fed has told me that he's very attracted to you and wishes to take your friendship further. *Please*, do not listen to him. He has a very persuasive manner in his sober moments, but I'm sorry to say that he's a hopeless case. I speak as a friend to him, and I hope to you.'

The realization came to Clara as Lorenzo spoke. 'I've no intention of allowing my friendship with Mr Cavalli to go any further,' she said. 'Indeed, I'd rather not speak to him any more if that is his purpose.' She smiled. 'If he should broach the subject again you might tell him that I already have a commitment.'

'Oh.' Lorenzo's face brightened. 'Is that so? I'm very pleased to hear it. This is someone in England?'

'Erm, yes. At least, that is what I hope for.'

Lorenzo laughed. 'You mean he hasn't yet spoken? What's the matter with the man?'

Clara wouldn't be drawn, but turned the tables on him by asking, 'And what of you, Lorenzo? Do you have plans?'

He stared at her in astonishment. 'Can you not tell? I thought it would be written all over my face. I adore Jewel! I feel as if I have been waiting for her all my life! But we've known each other such a short time. I can't tell her of my intentions yet, as she'll surely not wish to hear of them.'

Clara hid a smile. 'Perhaps you're right, and how sensible you are,' she said wryly. 'And perhaps I should tell *you* that her parents, her adoptive parents, have arrived in America and are presently in Dreumel's Creek.'

CHAPTER THIRTY-FOUR

'Are you sure!' Wilhelm whispered.

'Absolutely,' Georgiana said. 'And so is the doctor.'

'Oh!' Wilhelm breathed out; it was as if he was lost for words. He put his arms round Georgiana and closed his eyes. 'I can't believe it.' He kissed her cheek. 'I must take great care of you. Is it safe? What did the doctor say?'

'He said it was fairly unusual to have a first child at my age, but not unheard of, and,' she said reassuringly, 'he said I was very fit and therefore he foresaw no difficulty.'

Wilhelm gave a sudden whoop and picked her up and swung her round. 'I'm going to be a father,' he cheered. 'I'm going to be a *papa*! Oh!' He stopped suddenly. 'Whatever will Jewel think? We are giving her a brother or sister when she is old enough to have a child herself.' He put his hand to his mouth. 'Will people think we are too old?'

'It doesn't matter what other people think, Wilhelm,' Georgiana said softly. 'It's what *we* think that matters, and *we* are delighted,' she added.

'And another thing, my darling,' Wilhelm said slowly. 'Another thing that we must think of—'

She put the palms of her hands on either side of his face. 'I have already thought of it, Wilhelm. Is it not strange that after all these years of wanting a child and now – we're here, in the land of your birth! You'll want our child to be born here? In Dreumel's Creek?'

259

He nodded mutely, too full of emotion to speak.

Georgiana smiled. 'I know. I've already spoken to the doctor's wife. She'll take care of my confinement. I think that we won't announce the news just yet, not until we've written to Jewel, and then perhaps, when she has discovered all she needs to know about her birth mother, she'll come back here to be with us. Then we can tell Kitty and Grace. The doctor thinks the birth will be in the spring, but he can't be sure.'

'Perfect,' he said contentedly. 'It's the time of rebirth. When the dark soil gives forth green shoots and the birds nest.' He heaved a deep sigh and held her close. 'I cannot believe my good fortune.'

Dan had been talking to Jason and had been invited to supper with him and his wife, Rose, a plump, pretty woman. They had four children, all girls, two of them now married.

'I wished for a son,' Jason said, 'but I was blessed with daughters. What about you, Dan? You got a wife or a gal back home?'

'N-no,' he said. 'I don't seem to have much luck with the ladies.'

'No?' Rose said. 'Why not? A handsome buck like you? Well, we've got two daughters left over. Or maybe you're not the type to settle down? Or maybe not ready?'

'I think I'm probably ready,' he said. 'But mebbe I look beyond my station.'

'I don't know what that means,' Rose said. 'Surely you're as good as any other man? You've got a trade?'

'Yes, I've got a trade, but I guess I'm too plain-spoken and I like my own way. The women I've met so far don't like that.'

Rose laughed. 'Of course they don't. But there's the fun of it. If you can find a young woman who can stand up to you, then she's the one for you.'

'Do you think so?' Dan gazed at her over his coffee cup. 'Well, I'm not so sure.'

'What kinda gal do you like?' Rose asked inquisitively. 'Dark or fair? Plump or slender? Quiet or merry?'

'Well, I did like them dark, but lately I've discovered a partiality for redheads.' He smiled. 'Somebody with a—'

'Ah'm looking fer a business partner,' Jason interrupted, cradling his cup. 'Ah'm lookin' to build up a new business. There's a deal o' work ahead and I need tradesmen and somebody who can organize them. I'm not a tradesman myself,' he explained. 'I came to Dreumel when I was jest a young feller and did whatever was axed of me – dug shafts, panned fer gold, blasted through rock – but I feel the need to do more, build up sump'n permanent so I'll be remembered; sump'n my wife and daughters, aye, and grandchildren too, will be proud of.'

'Why, you old silly,' Rose said. 'We're proud of you now, Jason. Don't you be thinking we're not.'

'Ah, well, you know what I mean, Rose. I need to have my name up on a hoarding so's that folk will look up and say *yip, I remember him.*'

'What sort o' business?' Dan asked. 'I'm a wood worker though I can turn my hand to other crafts, but I've no money to put into any company.'

'Well, the way I look at it,' Jason mused, 'folks round here want to rebuild after the fire, and most of them haven't any money either; majority of them put all they had into their homes and lost everything. And folks'll be coming from far and near once they know that a new town is going up. I'd like to build some nice new houses, not fer sale but to charge a fair rent so's that them folk can get back on their feet again and then they can have the option of buying once they're good'n' ready.'

Dan shook his head and grinned. 'You'd need a deal o' money to do that, Jason. Or to know a friendly banker!'

Jason leaned back in his chair. 'Why, I know several of them,' he drawled. 'Fall over the'selves to have me bank with them. "Yes, sir, no, sir, what can I do fer you today, sir?"'

Dan listened, astonished. Jason and his wife had a nice

house and comfortable furniture, but they were far from pre-
tentious. Rose had obviously cooked the supper herself. Was
Jason boasting? Or did he really have wealth?

'But there's no sense in having money,' Jason went on, 'if ya
can't spread it around.'

He looked at Dan, who was staring at him open-mouthed.
'Whatcha lookin' at, boy? Did Bill Dreumel not tell you of the
time we found gold?'

My darling Jewel, I hardly know how to begin this letter, Georgiana
wrote. *You will know by now that Papa and I are in Dreumel's
Creek. We were so worried over you and Clara, as were Aunt Grace
and Uncle Martin, and of course concerned about all our friends
when we read of the disastrous fire in Yeller. Papa took ship immediately, although by then we had heard that you were safe and had
left for California.*

She went on to describe the journey and how she had been
unwell and how very helpful and considerate Dan Hanson
had been. *He seems to be settling into life here and has joined forces
with Jason in a building project in Yeller. He has said nothing about
travelling to California!*

Georgiana thought long and hard about how to tell of the
most important news of all and wondered how Jewel would
react to it; but there was nothing for it, Jewel must be the
first to know. She gave her the glad tidings and concluded by
saying that she and Wilhelm were absolutely delighted at the
prospect of a child and also of seeing Jewel again soon. She
put a postscript at the bottom.

*I'm sorry to say that James Crawford is leaving the hotel. He has
been an excellent manager, but now feels that it is time to return
to his roots. He asked if, when writing to you, I would send his
very good wishes to you and Clara and say what an honour it had
been to meet you. He said, in particular, that he would never forget
the pleasurable conversations he had with Miss Clara. What a very
agreeable man he is; he reminds me so much of someone I used to
know. We shall miss him here in Dreumel's Creek.*

Your ever loving Mama.

CHAPTER THIRTY-FIVE

Jewel and Clara spent the next two weeks travelling around San Francisco and areas beyond. Larkin and Dolly took them into the hills in his trap, as Jewel had said she was keen to see the city as her father had seen it when he'd first arrived.

'By rights we should've died on that journey.' Larkin chewed thoughtfully on a wad of tobacco. 'I don't know how we ever made it. Just a gang o' Mississippi swamp suckers we were; greenhorns, and your pappy was greener than most. A city gent we called him, but he proved to be as good as anybody. We walked across plains, got buried in the snow, and crossed the Old Spanish Trail and over the Sierra Nevada.'

He pointed down to the city below them. 'It's changed in the twenty-five years since we came. Back then it was full of bars, cheap hotels, farmhands like us with hayseed in their hair, card sharps, and a bay full of ships disgorging men who were greedy fer gold. We pitched our tents and pondered on what to do.'

'Did you never want to go back home?' Clara asked. 'To see your family?'

'Nope,' he answered laconically. 'Don't have any. I've gotta nice little place here. I've got Dolly to talk to, she's bin a good friend, and, well,' he cast an eye towards Jewel, 'I guess I allus wanted to hang around in case this little lady came back.'

Jewel felt very touched. She felt as if she had suddenly acquired many members of a family that she had barely known about. Dolly too was thrilled to have her here, just like a warm and friendly aunt, and together they were all fitting together the pieces of the jigsaw of her life to make her whole.

Federico Cavalli appeared at their hotel, enquiring if he might be allowed to show them around San Francisco. Clara came down to meet him in the foyer. He seemed to have recovered from his excesses and made no mention of the fact that he hadn't been seen at the Gallis' restaurant. In fact, from his smiling face it was as if he had only seen them recently. He did not mention the earthquake or Jewel's disappearance, and appeared genuinely disappointed when Clara refused his offer on behalf of them both, giving him the explanation that they had already done a tour with a friend.

'Oh!' he said in a high-handed manner. 'But I'm very familiar with the entire city. I was born here; I'm a true San Franciscan.'

'Thank you, but no,' Clara said calmly. 'And forgive me, Mr Cavalli, but it would not be proper for us to do so without an escort.'

He laughed. 'What nonsense! You came once before, and' – his eyes narrowed – 'I also escorted you into Chinatown.'

'Lorenzo came too, and it was only a brief visit.' Clara hesitated, embarrassed that he should point it out. 'And with hindsight even that was perhaps unwise, although it was an emergency.'

He clicked his tongue. 'You're not in England now, with its pious ways and conventions.' His eyes searched Clara's face. 'I do believe you are making an excuse.'

She gazed back at him. 'I do believe you may be right.'

'Clara!' He reached for her hand. '*Please!* I want to see you. *Must* see you! You've heard, haven't you, that I became involved with some villains in Chinatown? They plied me with drink and took my money. Who told you?' His voice rose. 'That Chink Pinyin.'

Clara lifted her chin. 'I don't wish to discuss anything further with you. Your manners are a disgrace. Excuse me.'

She turned to leave, but he grabbed her arm. 'Clara! I'm

mad for you. You're perfect. Beautiful! I adore you. You alone can save me from myself.'

Clara pulled her arm away. 'Don't be so dramatic. You need help, Federico,' she added, 'but not from me. I'm sorry.' She took a breath. 'And besides, I shall be leaving soon to begin my journey home.'

She didn't know why she had said it, but the second the statement popped out of her mouth she realized that that was what she wanted to do. She wanted to go home. Home to be safe; to be away from temptation and to be with those who really did care for her.

'You can't,' he pleaded. 'Don't, please! Don't deny me. I'll do anything. Anything to keep you here.' His eyes searched her face and she saw the entreaty there and something else: bafflement, she thought. He's not used to rejection or conflict. He is only accustomed to having his wants and needs indulged. 'What is there in England that you can't find here? There is everything and more that anyone can want.'

Clara turned on her heel. 'Not for me!' She walked swiftly away from him and up the stairs before he could say anything more, though he rushed after her to the bottom stair. She reached the top landing and ran along it and into her room, where she leaned against the door, panting, not with exertion but with exasperation.

There came a sharp tapping on the door. 'Go away! Leave me alone,' she called. 'I don't wish to speak to you.'

There was a hushed silence and then Jewel's voice said softly, 'Clara? Are you all right? It's only me.'

Clara cracked the door and saw Jewel's anxious face. 'Sorry,' she said, opening wide to admit her. 'I thought it was Federico Cavalli.'

'What? Here? At our door?'

Clara explained what had happened. 'I suppose I was rather rude and rushed away. I really didn't want to discuss anything with him. He's so persuasive, Jewel. I feel sure that he would talk me out of my better judgement and persuade me to meet him again.'

Jewel raised her fine eyebrows. 'What temptations, Clara! But you are quite right,' she said seriously. 'He's very handsome and I admit he can be charming, but there is something about him that makes me uneasy; something dark and moody and, dare I say it, rather sinful.'

'Yes,' Clara agreed, and walked to the window. 'Jewel!' she said, turning round. 'I need to talk to you.'

'And I want to talk to you!' Jewel waved the letter she held in her hand. 'This is from Mama! Such news you'd never believe!' She gave a little hop and skip and danced round the room, a whirl of skirt and petticoats.

'Good,' Clara said. 'Jewel. About going home—'

'Yes, but not yet. Mama and Papa are both in Dreumel's Creek.' Jewel beamed.

'Yes, I know.' Clara felt thwarted. She really did want to discuss the journey home and whether or not Jewel would be making it with her.

Jewel shook the letter in her hand. 'I *must* tell you the news. It's central to any decisions we might be contemplating.'

'Really?' Perhaps Aunt Gianna and Uncle Wilhelm have decided to stay in America, Clara thought, and if so then so will Jewel, and in that case how will I get home? I'll travel alone, she decided, before Jewel had time to say another word.

'Clara.' Jewel sat on her bed and spoke softly. 'Mama was ill coming over in the ship. She thought she was seasick. But she wasn't. She's *expecting* a *child*!'

Clara sank down beside her. 'Oh!' she breathed. 'Oh, how wonderful!'

'Yes!' Jewel was ecstatic. 'But will she be all right, Clara? She's quite old to be having a first child.' She bit on her lip. 'I couldn't bear it if she—'

'I'm quite sure she'll be all right, Jewel,' Clara assured her. 'Mama knows women older than her who have had children. Not their first, admittedly, but then neither were they well fed or under a doctor's care as I'm sure Aunt Gianna will be.'

'Mama says she hopes to see me soon; oh, Clara, I must go to her,' Jewel spoke earnestly. 'I must look after her. She's my mother, after all.' Her eyes flooded with tears. 'How must she feel? I've been selfishly pursuing my birth mother, when Gianna has brought me up and been as much my mother as anyone could be. And Wilhelm too – he has been my father in every sense of the word.' She began to sob. 'I've been so self-absorbed. I never thought that I might have hurt them by leaving on this mission.'

Clara put her arm round her shoulder. 'They won't have been hurt. They have always spoken about your birth parents. They've never hidden from you that you were born in America to two other people. And they are the ones who have brought you up to question and enquire, and never objected when you said that you were ready to come here and discover your past.'

Jewel wiped her eyes. 'Yes, you're right. I do know. It's just that I suddenly felt guilty; but, Clara, I've been so happy since I came, except of course when I was caught up in the earthquake and even that turned out so well. And what will Mama and Papa expect of me now? I shall be torn.' She swallowed hard, and put her fingers to her mouth. 'And then there's Lorenzo!'

Ah, Clara thought – Lorenzo is the issue. He is the cause of all this emotion. 'Has he spoken of his feelings for you?' she asked.

Jewel shook her head. 'No, he hasn't, and I don't think that he will, not yet. I believe that he has been brought up in a traditional manner, rather as we have. It's too soon – but if I go away—'

'If he cares for you, then he'll wait,' Clara said patiently, 'and if you tell him the reason—'

'That's just it,' Jewel broke in. 'I can't. Mama has asked me not to write of the news to anyone back in England – not that I would; or to speak of it, except to you of course. She'll write to your mother herself in a week or two. I suppose she wants to get used to the idea first,' she said, with a watery smile. 'So what will I say to Renzo when I tell him we're leaving?'

Clara contemplated. 'I have just now told Federico Cavalli

that I'm going home soon, so if he sees Lorenzo first he's sure to tell him.'

Jewel slipped off the bed. 'Then I must go and speak to him immediately. Will you come with me, Clara? I shall think of some reason to explain why we are going.'

Perhaps Lorenzo might be galvanized into action when he learns Jewel is leaving, Clara thought. But it is too soon for her to make a lifetime's decision. How goes the old saying – *marry in haste, repent at leisure?*

When they arrived at the restaurant in the early evening, Lorenzo was singing as he set the tables, and from the kitchen they could hear Maria joining in.

'How he loves to sing,' Jewel whispered to Clara. 'It reminds me of something.'

'What?' Clara asked, but Jewel didn't answer as Lorenzo came towards them, his hands outstretched to them both in greeting but his eyes only for Jewel.

'You've come at last!' he cried. 'I've missed you – both. Where have you been?'

'Sightseeing,' Clara answered for them. 'Seeing the city.'

His eyebrows rose in query.

'With Larkin and Dolly,' Jewel said.

'Ah.' He smiled. 'I see.' He gazed at her and said, 'Madre was asking when you might move into the house next door.' He saw Jewel's hesitation. 'You will come to live there, won't you?'

He looked from Jewel to Clara and it was as if he was suddenly struck by the possibility that perhaps she wouldn't, that neither of them would stay, and the idea was totally appalling to him.

Pinyin came through from the kitchen and his face lit up in a beam of delight. 'Miss Jewel, Miss Clara. Very good to see you! Miss Jewel, my sister would like to come and talk to you. Would that be possible?'

'Yes, that would be lovely,' Jewel said. 'When?'

'Tomorrow. Chen will bring her. It is his day off. He works at a restaurant in Chinatown.'

They agreed on a time and Pinyin went back to the kitchen. Lorenzo then suggested that maybe they should open the house next door and light a fire and make it cosy. Clara was sure that he was suggesting it so that Jewel would become used to the idea that the house was hers. But when Jewel took him to one side to tell him that they would shortly be leaving for Dreumel's Creek, Clara saw his face drop and his hands catch hold of Jewel's as if in earnest supplication, and realized that his intentions were real and trustworthy.

'Why?' he asked Jewel. 'Why now?'

'Not immediately,' she responded. 'Perhaps in a week or two. I'm sorry,' she said miserably. 'I'll come back just as soon as I can.'

'But how long will you be away?' His expression was anguished as she shook her head. 'I shall miss you, Jewel.'

'And I shall miss you too, Renzo.'

The use of his childhood name seemed to convince him that she really was going, and yet still he pressed for the reason why, which she couldn't give, except to say that her parents were in Dreumel's Creek and she was needed there.

'And I need you here,' he groaned. 'Yet we have only just met. You don't know me. We are almost strangers. We need more time to get to know one another again.'

'I don't,' Jewel said, and saw his sudden smile.

The next day Maria lit a fire in the house next door. Although the weather wasn't cold, it was foggy, and the fire in the hearth gave the house a welcoming atmosphere. When Chen arrived with Soong Daiyu, it was here that they came. Jewel had plumped up cushions and tied back the beaded curtain and Maria had brought a kettle, a teapot, tea and china cups and saucers so that she could make refreshments for her guests.

Soong Daiyu gave a low bow from the waist. 'I bring you gift,' she said, and handed Jewel a parcel wrapped in soft paper decorated with Chinese lettering.

Jewel unwrapped the parcel and found inside a red silk brocade cheongsam and matching slippers. The svelte fitted

269

dress was sleeveless and had a mandarin collar and slits at each side of the skirt. Also in the parcel were several silver and jade bracelets, two of which were for Clara, and a silk flower for Jewel's hair.

'How beautiful,' Jewel whispered, and impulsively kissed Soong Daiyu's cheek.

Soong Daiyu clasped her fingers together, obviously quite overcome by the gesture, and murmured something Jewel couldn't understand. Chen was hovering by the door and Jewel turned to him questioningly.

'My mother says: now you are real Chinese daughter.'

CHAPTER THIRTY-SIX

They were persuaded to stay another month. It seemed churlish to refuse, and an opportunity not to be missed, when Larkin offered to show them more of California and took them on a trip to the tree-lined city of Sacramento.

Sacramento had been a trading colony on the Sacramento river when gold was discovered by John Marshall at Sutter's Mill in nearby Coloma and the city was inundated by miners. In spite of being half drowned by floods twenty years before, it had now grown into a city of fine buildings with parks and riverside walks.

They travelled on to meet and stay with Jed and his family at his farm; then they rode towards the Sierra Nevada mountains, where Larkin told them more of his travels with Jewel's father and how they had been trapped in the winter snow.

The trail up to the high passes was more defined now but still rutted and difficult. The air was fresh and sharp and they looked down from jagged rocks into the green valleys and sparkling lakes below; the Colorado river glinted in the far distance and they imagined how hard it had been for those travelling on foot or by waggon.

They stayed one night in a small mountain hostelry lit by lamplight and roaring pinewood fires and the following morning, with one last look down the mountain, they set off on their return to San Francisco. Then Jewel and Clara made ready to depart.

Jewel had tried on the cheongsam and it fitted perfectly. She wrapped it up again in the soft paper and put it carefully in a cupboard in her house. 'So that you know that I will return,' she said to both Soong Daiyu and Pinyin. 'But I must go to see my English mother.'

'I think she needs you,' Pinyin said, and Jewel didn't know if it was a question or a statement, but she answered, 'Yes.'

Soong Daiyu clasped her hands and spoke, and Pinyin translated. 'Soong Daiyu says that you are right to go, and that she knows you will return. She says that to forget one's ancestors is to be a brook without a source, a tree without a root.'

'I won't forget you, ever,' Jewel said softly. 'And I will return. The winter is long and hard where I am going, but come spring or early summer I'll be back.'

She said the same to Lorenzo and his mother, and Maria said, 'So long? My son will be unhappy.'

Jewel whispered, 'And so will I.'

'Your *madre* is sick, yes?' Maria asked and when Jewel hesitated, she raised her head and opened her eyes and mouth wide and breathed out, *'Aah!'*

Federico came to the restaurant on the day before they were due to depart. 'I must speak to you, Clara.' He looked pale and ill. 'Please don't go away.'

'I must,' she said. 'Everything is arranged.'

'Then cancel!' he said urgently. 'I'm sorry, I've been a fool. Please believe that I don't usually behave in this way. My intentions are sincere. Ask anyone.' He grasped her hands. 'I can give you so much. Wealth, your own carriage, anything that you desire.'

Clara eased from his grasp. 'But I don't need any of those things,' she said calmly. 'And you haven't mentioned love.'

He shrugged. 'That goes without saying. You are beautiful. I shall be the envy of all men with you on my arm.'

She turned away. Another possession, she thought, something else to boast about. 'I'm sorry, Federico, I am already committed. And as I told you before, I'm going home to England.'

He was angry and yet his tone was icy cold as he spoke. Again she had the feeling that he wasn't used to being crossed. 'On our first meeting I was given the distinct impression that you were inclined to be more than friendly. Is this the way English women normally behave?'

Clara drew in a breath of astonishment. Had she? By approaching his table that first day at Lorenzo's had she indicated something more than mere sociability? She wouldn't have been so forward in England with an unknown man, but had assumed, wrongly it now seemed, that amiability was allowed here between unmarried men and women.

'I'm sorry if I unwittingly gave you the wrong impression,' she told him. 'You are a friend of Lorenzo's and I did not think that a little banter and conversation would be considered to be more than conviviality.' Her voice was now as cold as his, though she was hot and furious inside, not just with him but with herself for being so foolish as to trust him. 'I beg your pardon for my mistake.'

He stormed out, not speaking or acknowledging anyone. Maria shook her head and then, catching Clara's eye, pointed her finger to her forehead, indicating an unhinged disposition. She came over.

'Don't be concerned about him,' she whispered. 'Federico has set his own path. No one can move him from it.'

Clara swallowed down her fury. She was sure that Maria was right, but she felt both sad and furious about Federico. But it's my fault too, she realized. I had thought that here in this new country men and women could be equal. And perhaps they can, but not with Federico. Charming as he can be, he'll always want to be master. He is so assured of his own importance. Could I ever love him? Thoughts of home flitted through her head and she knew that she couldn't. That very morning she had received a letter from her sister, Elizabeth, with news which made her even more determined to return.

Lorenzo and Maria, Soong Daiyu, Pinyin, Chen and two

273

of his sisters came to the railroad station to see them depart, but not Federico, and Clara didn't know whether to be glad or sorry. Lorenzo was steeped in gloom and seemed to be on the brink of tears.

'I can't bear to lose you again, Jewel,' he whispered to her. 'I'm bereft. My heart is breaking.'

'Please don't say anything more,' she pleaded. 'I must go. If I leave it too late I should never forgive myself.'

He nodded. 'The weather; I know. I wouldn't want you to be in any danger. The rail journey is hazardous in winter.'

'Not the weather,' she said. 'Although the valley becomes closed in winter.'

'Then wait here until spring,' he said urgently, clutching her hand. 'It's not too late to change your mind.'

She gently squeezed his hand. 'And what of Clara? She wants to go home to England. She misses her family. This is the first stage of her journey. Besides, I have written to my parents to say that we are coming.'

He swallowed. 'Then I must be patient, but I don't know how.' He gazed at her. 'Is there someone else you care for who makes you rush back, apart from your mama and papa, I mean? Someone else?'

'No.' She smiled. 'No one.'

There came a sudden screech of steam and they all jumped. Clara moved towards the carriage. Chen carried their hand baggage, packed with everything they would need for the week-long journey. Pinyin carried a box of food: tea, bread, biscuits and cake which Maria had baked early that morning; ham and smoked sausage to supplement the food they could buy at the station houses. She had also provided knives, forks and spoons and snowy-white table napkins.

Clara kissed Maria, offered her hand to Chen and Pinyin, and climbed the high steps on to the train. Lorenzo was still holding Jewel's hand, unwilling it seemed to let her go.

'I'll write,' she said softly. 'Don't forget me.'

'Never,' he said, pressing her fingers to his lips. 'And not a song will pass my lips until you come back. Not a single note. There's a Chinese proverb—'

'Yes,' she said, taking a sudden deep breath, recalling Sun Wa's phrase. 'I know it. *A bird does not sing*—'

'*Because it has an answer,*' he finished for her. '*It sings because it has a song.* I have no song now. Nor will I have till you return.'

'Jewel!' Clara called urgently. 'Come quickly! We're getting under way.'

Jewel saw the head of steam from the engine and the guard waving his flag. 'But I have an answer,' she told Lorenzo, and drew her hand from his and touched her lips. 'All I'm waiting for is the question.'

There were fewer passengers on the return journey and they had a car to themselves, although they joined others in the minuscule kitchen when they went to make tea or coffee or to prepare a meal. They were both quieter and introspective, lost in thought, Jewel more so than Clara.

'I have something to tell you,' Clara said to Jewel as they climbed into their cots on their first night. 'I've received a letter from Elizabeth. She's expecting a child. She thinks it's due in January.' Jewel heard the joy in her voice. 'I'm going to be an aunt!'

It was Jewel's turn to be thrilled. 'How lovely! I hope she'll be all right and doesn't suffer too much pain. That's what worries me about Mama, whether or not she can bear the agony of childbirth.'

'They can have chloroform if it gets really bad,' Clara said practically. 'Or ether. I'd really like to be home in time for the birth, Jewel. Will you mind terribly if I leave for home soon after we arrive in Dreumel?'

Jewel sat up and leaned on her elbow, and Clara saw her pale face and dark eyes framed by her loose silky black hair by the dim light of the lantern.

'Of course not. I understand perfectly. It's such an important time and Elizabeth will want you to be there.' She leaned back on her pillow. 'I wonder what it's like, having another being growing inside your body. And how difficult must it be to be totally confined to the house during pregnancy! Some say the woman must remain completely secluded.'

'Not all women do,' Clara murmured. 'Some women, who have to work for a living, stay working right up to the day the child is delivered. It's not healthy, of course,' she added, turning over on to her side. 'But then neither is staying in bed for the whole time, for that makes the mother weak.' Her voice grew sleepy. 'But both Aunt Gianna and Elizabeth will have doctors and midwives in attendance and will be guided by them.'

During the night Jewel woke. She lay for a while listening to the clang and clank of the wheels, the snorts and hiss of the engine, the rattle of the windows and the strident snores of someone further down the corridor.

'Clara,' she whispered, 'are you awake?'

There was no answer, but Clara turned over with a mutter.

'I just wondered if you've missed Thomas whilst we've been away.'

'Mm,' Clara murmured. 'Yes.' She turned over again. 'I have.'

'Will you be all right travelling home alone?'

Clara considered for so long that Jewel thought she had fallen asleep again. 'I will,' she answered at last. 'There's no other option. Unless some other person decides to travel home again too.'

'Yes,' Jewel said. 'That's what I was thinking about.'

The thought of Dan was causing her considerable disquiet. Had he really travelled all this way because of her, or because he had decided to break free from the constraints of home? If he has come because of me I must tell him straight away that I could never love him enough to marry him; I know now that I can only ever care for him as a friend. She felt a pleasurable warmth steal over her. I have only just rediscovered Lorenzo, but I know – I feel sure – that what I feel for him is love.

276

The train was cold and both declared that it was as well they had decided to travel now rather than later. They wrapped up in shawls and scarves, warm stockings and gloves. The weather outside was dreary, with only an occasional shaft of sunshine breaking through the grey cloud. After two days they reached Ogden in the pouring rain and waited in the chilly station rest room to begin the next stage of their journey, remarking on the difference in temperature from when they had been there previously. When they were on the move again they read books until both complained of headaches. They missed the camaraderie of other passengers and although the view from the windows was still spectacular, they were both busy with their own thoughts and didn't appreciate it as they had done on the journey in the other direction when everything was fresh and new and exciting.

'It was such fun travelling out, wasn't it?' Jewel said softly. 'So thrilling to be going alone on an adventure and not know-ing what was in front of us. And now, although I am really looking forward to seeing Mama and Papa again, I am also rather sad.'

Clara nodded. 'I know; but you're sad because of the people you are leaving behind. And have you thought, Jewel, that if Lorenzo should propose and you should accept – that's always supposing that you care enough for him – then you would un-dertake the outward journey again, and perhaps not go back to England?'

'I'm torn, Clara,' Jewel said miserably. 'I do care for Lorenzo and can't bear to think that I shan't see him again. Yet I feel bound to Mama, especially now, and although I'm sure she will stay in Dreumel to have the baby – she surely won't travel – they might decide to return to England afterwards.' She swallowed hard. 'And then I won't know what to do.'

Clara smiled. 'I think you will, Jewel. I *know* you will.'

The following day the journey was slow, with the train stopping from time to time for no apparent reason. Then the porter came along and, apologizing profusely, told them that they must stop at the next station to change the engine.

'You may stay aboard if you wish, ladies, but you might find it more comfortable in the station house. The weather's not good but at least there'll be a fire.'

They decided they would get off the train and since in spite of the murky weather it wasn't raining they were able to walk about the platform for some much-needed exercise and chat to the few other passengers, before eating a bowl of broth and a plate of sausages. An hour later they were on their way again.

'The journey seems so long this time,' Clara said and thought with a sinking heart of the journey from New York to Dreumel's Creek and then back again before her voyage home. 'I'll spend a week at Dreumel,' she told Jewel, 'then ask Uncle Wilhelm to book a berth for me.'

'Only a week?' Jewel asked. 'Oh, Clara, how I'll miss you! Must you go so soon?'

'You said that the valley becomes closed in because of the snow. I don't want to be trapped until the spring.' And Clara realized that now she had decided to go home, she didn't want any delay.

'But it won't snow yet! What month are we in? I've quite lost track of the time.'

'We left England in June, and we are almost at the end of October already!' Clara said. 'By the time I'm home I shall have been away for six months. Such a long time,' she said pensively. 'Oh, I'm not saying that it hasn't been wonderful – it has; but now I'm ready to go home.'

'Yes,' Jewel replied, but she had a catch in her voice and wondered where home was for her.

The journey had taken longer than anticipated, and when they descended from the train, stiff and weary, they were delighted to see Wilhelm waiting for them on the platform and wearing a huge smile of welcome. They were more than pleased to let him take charge of their luggage and hand them into the waiting chaise to be whisked off to the New York Marius, where tea and cake were waiting. When they had finished, a warm bath was run for them.

'So nice to be independent,' Clara remarked, as they changed for supper. 'But lovely to be cosseted too.'

Wilhelm assured Jewel that Georgiana was very well and looking forward to seeing her again. 'It has been a long time without you,' he said, and stroked her cheek. 'We missed you.'

His words comforted her, but also troubled her. How would they feel if she left again? They wouldn't try to detain her, she knew that, but how would they feel if she left to live in San Francisco? Would they be so bound up with the new baby that they wouldn't make any objections, and if that was the case how would she feel, when they had always been such a big part of her life?

On the journey towards Dreumel's Creek, Clara watched unobtrusively as Jewel nestled into Wilhelm's shoulder. She is going to be so divided between longing for Lorenzo and her loyalty and love for Wilhelm and Aunt Gianna. She'll want to be in two places at the same time. But she has to make a choice. Whereas I – she thought fleetingly of Federico, then lingered longer and with some tenderness over James Crawford, who with his ancient culture was so much more remarkable and enlightened, and gave a contented sigh – I have decided on my choice.

CHAPTER THIRTY-SEVEN

Georgiana was waiting on the porch of the Marius when they drove into Dreumel's Creek. She was wrapped in shawls but they could see that she was plumper, and looked fit and happy.

She gathered them both up in her arms and led them into the hotel lounge and vowed that she wanted to know everything about what they had been doing. 'But not all at once, of course. You must take your time, and you must be very weary after your long journey.'

'It was wonderful, Aunt Gianna,' Clara declared. 'This is such a *wonderful*, wonderful country. And I should be so happy to come back again some time.'

Gianna raised her eyebrows. 'Does that mean that you are leaving us soon?'

'Yes,' she said, and told her about Elizabeth.

'Then of course you must go home; Elizabeth will want you there to share the joy, as will your mother. And what about you, my darling?' Gianna asked Jewel. 'Did you find what you were looking for?'

'Yes, Mama, I did.' Jewel smiled at her. 'And I also discovered what I already had.'

Gianna nodded. 'Yes,' she said softly. 'That is so important. To be grateful for what we have. I discovered that many years ago when I was at a crossroads in my life.'

'And now you are about to produce another life,' Clara said

softly, though boldly, knowing that many women never spoke of their impending confinement.

But not Georgiana. She smiled and smiled. 'I am *so* lucky,' she said. 'After so many years of thinking that we would never give birth, a miracle has happened. We have Jewel, of course' – she took hold of Jewel's hand and intertwined their fingers – 'who has brought us such joy; but one day she'll leave us for someone else, someone she loves, and have children of her own.'

Jewel's eyes filled with tears as she realized that she should have known that her parents would never hold her back. 'Mama,' she said. 'I have already met someone. I'd like to tell you about him. And I want to tell you about my birth mother, Chang Tsui, and Soong Daiyu, my milk mother; about Chen and his sisters and also about Pinyin, who is at the heart of the story.'

Clara had noticed that James Crawford had gone from the hotel and when they were alone asked Georgiana about him. 'I liked him very much,' she confessed. 'He told me that he would return to his people one day.'

'That is what he has done,' Georgiana said. 'He spoke of you, Clara, and wished you happiness in your life. He also said,' she paused, 'and I have not spoken of this to anyone else, that he would always remember you with great affection.' She gazed into space, as if thinking of times past. 'The Iroquois are very special people,' she said softly. 'We should be honoured to have their regard – and love,' she added in a whisper.

'Thank you, Aunt Gianna,' Clara murmured. 'I am. I feel it has been a special privilege to know him. He opened my eyes to know myself.' She felt that Gianna too had experienced something remarkable, something secret and cherished in her life which she wasn't prepared to share, but would keep locked in her heart for ever. As I will also.

Georgiana went on to tell her that until they found some-one else to run the hotel, Caitlin was acting as temporary manager. 'She's doing very well,' she said, 'but we don't feel that she is quite ready to take on the responsibility completely. She's fairly experienced, as she helps Kitty in their Yeller hotel, but they're not busy just now, nor will they be for some time until the town is rebuilt, so they can spare her.'

She gazed at Clara quizzically. 'I haven't yet told Jewel that Dan is working in Yeller. He's teamed up with Jason, who needs someone with wood-working skills. How do you think Jewel will react to that?'

Jewel had wandered down by the creek on her own, telling Clara that she would catch up with her later in the morning. She paused halfway down the Dreumel road to Yeller to gaze into the sparkling rushing water, and then lifted her eyes to the changing colours of the trees on the mountainside. Most were clad in a showy dappled mantle of colour now that autumn was in full swing: a rubicundity of scarlet, a tincture of blood red and the warmth of russet and creamy gold. The air was crisp and sharp, a complete contrast to San Francisco, where the days had been hot in the summer, but also dank and foggy sometimes when the rolling mist had obscured the bay.

She heard a horse and waggon approaching from the direction of Yeller and idly looked up. The driver lifted his whip as he passed but then swiftly turned his head, reined in and jumped down.

'Jewel! Great heavens! Is it really you?'

'Dan!' Strangely enough, she was pleased to see him and not anxious or embarrassed, as she had thought she would be. 'Dan. How lovely to see you here!'

He put his arms round her and gave her a smacking kiss on her cheek, which really did unnerve her. He wasn't usually so demonstrative.

'It's really good to see you, Jewel.' He grinned. 'When did you arrive? I didn't know you were coming, which is surprising considering the drumbeats we hear when anything's happening round here.'

'Only last night,' she said, and listened. *We?* He sounded most proprietorial. Had he settled here? Was that why? Is he happier than he was? He seemed more relaxed, not as intense as he usually was in her presence. Can we at last be true friends, she thought, without any hindrance between us? For I would like that above all else.

'Dan,' she said, as he at the same instant said, 'Jewel. There's something I must tell you.'

They were interrupted by a loud 'Hello' and a thud of hooves as a rider came fast towards them. Jewel saw Dan's face light up in a grin. Caitlin, she realized, and knew at that instant why Dan had changed.

Caitlin slid off the horse. 'Jewel! I've only just heard you've arrived at last.'

'Did you know she was coming?' Dan asked querulously. 'You never said.'

'Didn't I?' Caitlin turned up her nose. 'Well, since when did I have to tell you anything?'

'Only because Jewel is one of my oldest friends!' he retorted. 'Of course I'd want to know when she was coming.'

She shrugged. 'You know now,' she answered coolly, and tucking her arm through Jewel's said, 'I want to know about everything you and Clara have been doing whilst you've been in California,' she said. '*Everything*, cos nothing happens here that's worth talking about.'

Jewel laughed, more at Dan's expression of incredulity than anything. 'You had a fire in Yeller before we left,' she said. 'I should have thought that was enough to last a long time. And then,' she said mischievously, 'you have English visitors.'

'Have we?' Caitlin said nonchalantly. 'I hadn't noticed.'

Dan shook his head in exasperation and turned towards the waggon. 'I'll catch up with you later, Jewel,' he said, raising his hand. 'Maybe we can have a chat alone without fear of interruption.'

Caitlin watched him go and Jewel saw that she pressed her lips together and frowned as if wishing she'd held her tongue.

'Do you like him?' Jewel asked her and watched in amusement as Caitlin assumed an expression of disinterest.

'He's all right,' she said. 'Don't really know him.'

Jewel smiled. 'Don't you? I would have thought that you knew each other very well.'

Caitlin shook her red curls. 'No. Not really. He's working with Jason, you know. They're building houses in Yeller.'

'Are they?' Jewel watched Dan's retreating back. 'So does that mean he's staying?'

Caitlin stroked her horse's neck. 'Guess he might be. He says he likes it here.' She turned to Jewel and again she bit on her lip. 'Has he ever kissed you, Jewel?' She blushed as she spoke.

Jewel took a breath. 'No!' she said, even though he just had, but she knew that Caitlin didn't mean that kind of friendship kiss. 'Dan would *never* do anything like that. Why do you ask?'

Caitlin lifted her shoulders. 'I just thought that you and he were . . . you know.' She shrugged again.

'Were what?' Jewel said in mock indignation. 'You're not saying that Dan has – has romantic feelings towards me?' She lifted her eyes to the sky and then closed them. 'And I never guessed,' she said softly. 'What a fool I am.'

Dan hitched up the horse and waggon and ran up the steps into the Marius. 'Is Mrs Dreumel here?' he asked the desk clerk, and was directed into the hotel lounge, where Georgiana was sitting with Clara.

He welcomed Clara enthusiastically when she stood up to greet him. 'I can't believe we're meeting here,' she said. 'So far from Hull! Is everyone all right at home – your ma and da?'

'Yes.' He laughed. 'And Thomas is too, in case you were wondering, and so are your ma and pa, and I don't know about Elizabeth, as I hadn't seen her in months before I left, but I'd have heard if she wasn't.'

'Would you like to have coffee with us, Dan?' Georgiana asked him. 'You can hear of some of Clara's and Jewel's adventures.'

'Oh, thank you but no, I'm on my way to 'wood yard. I've just seen Jewel and had a few words with her, but I'd like to talk to her, and you too, Clara, when you've settled back in.'

He appeared to hesitate, and Georgiana asked, 'Was there something else, Dan?'

He nodded and fiddled with his shirt neck. 'There was: I wanted some advice. But it'll wait.'

'Shall I leave? Did you want to speak privately to Aunt Gianna?' Clara half rose from her chair.

He licked his lips. 'Erm, no. I shouldn't be here really. I've a job to finish; but when I met Jewel, I came in on 'off chance of speaking to you, Mrs Dreumel.'

'Then you'd better tell me. Get it off your chest, as they say,' Georgiana said brightly, though there was a slight tenseness in her voice.

'Will you stay, Clara? Please,' Dan urged. 'You know me as well as anybody, I'd say, and I'd value your opinion.'

'If you're sure.' Clara too felt uneasy. Was he going to speak about his feelings for Jewel? Was he going to declare himself to Aunt Gianna? But if that was his intention, why would he want her there? And surely he'd want to speak to Wilhelm?

'You'd think, wouldn't you, that I could mek my own decisions.' Dan began to pace about. 'But I'm in another country and it seems to me that there're not as many restrictions as there are back home when your ma and da want to know all 'ins and outs; well, not *want* to know exactly, but you feel obliged to tell them.'

'What are you trying to say, Dan?' Georgiana asked quietly. 'And are you sure that it is a question you want us to hear?'

'Oh yes.' He stopped his pacing and stood in front of her. 'I want to know if I'm likely to mek a fool of myself; although,' he added, 'I don't really care if I do.'

Georgiana felt a sinking feeling coursing through her. Poor fellow, she thought. He's still carrying a torch for Jewel and she has told me that she cares for someone else.

'It was just now when I saw Jewel again that decided me,' he said in a rush. 'Cos you both know how I've felt about her.

But my head's been in a whirl ever since I came here and – well, to be honest I've never felt like this before. I can't sleep. I break out in a sweat when I think about her, even though I've not known her long; she drives me crazy with her temper but 'worst thing is that I don't think she even likes me very much cos we're allus at loggerheads whenever we meet, and she's so offhand and scathing and hardly ever has owt pleasant to say to me.'

Clara and Georgiana glanced at each other and both wore a puzzled frown. Then a small smile touched Georgiana's lips.

'Am I right in thinking that you're speaking of Caitlin, Dan?' she asked solemnly.

'Why, aye,' he said bluntly. 'Who else is there that answers to that description, Mrs Dreumel? Thing is, I don't know what to do about it.'

'You should ask her to marry you, Dan.' Jewel's voice came from the doorway. Dan turned, open-mouthed in astonishment.

He went towards her and took her hand. 'You know how I've cared about you, Jewel,' he said softly. 'Since we were just bairns. How can I love someone else so soon? It's as if a thunderbolt's struck me, or I've been run over by a team of hosses.'

'I do know,' she answered in a whisper. 'But it wasn't grown-up love you felt for me. You were attracted to me because I was different.' She smiled. 'And I can tell you that Caitlin is *so* jealous because she thinks that you care for me and not for her. Go and tell her,' she urged, 'and put her out of her misery.'

He grinned and rushed out of the room. Clara and Jewel went to the window and watched him taking the hotel steps in one giant leap. He looked up and down the road and then as if shot from a spring ran down the road to where a rider was coming towards him. They both craned their necks and Jewel stood on tiptoe as they tried to see.

Caitlin looked down at him, but tossed her head and rode past him as if coming towards the hotel; but Dan about-turned and grabbed the reins. They couldn't hear what was said, but saw Dan reach up to Caitlin and her lifting her hand as if to slap him. He wasn't deterred and grabbed her with both hands and physically lifted her down.

'What's happening?' Georgiana asked from her chair. 'Is it resolved?'

Jewel and Clara both glanced over their shoulders at her, smiling broadly, and then turned back to the window.

'Yes,' Clara said gleefully. 'He's swinging her round and kissing her.'

Jewel took a breath. 'And she's kissing him back.' She laughed. 'And what's more, there seems to be half of Dreumel's Creek watching them and cheering!'

CHAPTER THIRTY-EIGHT

'She's too young,' Ted objected when Dan, with Caitlin by his side clasping his fingers, asked for her hand in marriage.

'I'm not, Pa,' Caitlin argued.

Her mother agreed. 'She's 'same age as I was when we wed,' Kitty reminded him.

'It's not that I've any objections to you personally, Dan,' Ted said. 'But you've only just come to Yeller; we hardly know you. Besides which, Caitlin's not met many young fellers and won't know her own mind.'

'Sure I do, Pa. There are all the young lads I was at school with. I've hung around with most of them.' Caitlin linked her arm in Dan's. 'Kissed a few too,' she added, blushing to her hair roots as Dan turned to look at her with his brows raised.

'What!' her father said, but Kitty only laughed.

'Wish I'd done that before I met you!'

'I'll think on it,' Ted said. 'It's not something I expected for a while. Caitlin's still a bairn as far as I'm concerned.'

'I'm almost nineteen, Pa.' Caitlin left Dan's side to stand by her father. 'Jenny Mathews is married and expecting,' she said, 'and Katy Thompson's getting wed in a fortnight. They're both younger than me.'

Ted grunted. 'Like I say, I'll think on it. We don't know if Dan intends staying in Yeller.'

'I do, sir,' Dan said earnestly. 'Though I'll want to go home to see my ma and da at some time and tell them all about this place, and about Caitlin too!'

'Oh!' Caitlin took Ted's arm. 'And I'd be able to go with him!' she said. 'I'd love to do that. To go to England and see where you and Ma came from.'

Ted glanced at Kitty. 'It's nothing like here,' he said. 'That was a different life.'

'It still is, Mr Allen,' Dan told him. 'You made 'right decision when you travelled to America. Some things don't change. There are more opportunities for folk here than there'll ever be in England.'

'Mebbe so,' Ted agreed. 'But it doesn't mean to say that it's an easy life. You get nowhere without working hard and there's as much poverty in America as there is in England. I saw it for myself when I first came.' He pursed his mouth. 'I realize now that without Edward Newmarch, Jewel's father, I might not have made it. But that's another story. I'll give it some thought.' He shook his head. 'Can't think of my little girl getting wed.'

Caitlin reached up and kissed his cheek. 'I'll always be your little girl, Pa, no matter how old I am.' He grinned and pushed her away.

Jewel and Clara walked with Georgiana every day along the side of the creek so that she might take her daily exercise, and then in the afternoon she went to her room for a rest, although she strongly objected, saying that she wasn't an invalid and that childbirth was as natural as breathing.

'But you know that it's Papa who insists,' Jewel said, to which Georgiana laughed and said that she knew that it was a conspiracy between the three of them.

'I'm so pleased that you're here to take care of Georgiana,' Wilhelm said to them both. 'It means that I can concentrate at this very critical time on making sure all the early planning is in place at Yeller. We want to make it a city to be proud of.'

'I hope the new Yeller won't have very tall buildings like those in Sacramento or New York, Uncle Wilhelm,' Clara said.

'It won't seem right somehow, not in the middle of the mountains.'

'My view entirely,' Wilhelm agreed. 'We want a modern city, of course, and to be progressive, but in my opinion sky-high buildings would spoil the very nature of Yeller. It is after all a mountain valley and we want to attract people here who will appreciate its beauty.' He paused. 'New Yeller, you said. That's a good name, Clara. I might put that to the committee. I think it will appeal; show the difference between the new and what went before.'

Clara was thrilled to think she had contributed to the project with her chance remark, but she hoped that the planning business wouldn't take too long. Wilhelm had insisted that he would make the journey back to England with her, but that he couldn't go until the planning was concluded.

No matter that she had said she could travel alone if he would take her as far as New York, and although Georgiana had looked at him wryly and shaken her head, he would brook no argument and said that in any case he had things to arrange in England.

'You realize, don't you,' Georgiana said to Jewel and Clara one evening, as they sat in the small sitting room at the rear of the hotel which had been designated as their own private place, 'that even after the birth we might not return to England for quite some time.' She glanced from one to the other. 'I don't think that I can drag Wilhelm away from his beloved mountains.' She paused for a moment and then added, 'And I'm not sure that I want to. We both want our child to be brought up here.'

'I know, Mama,' Jewel said. 'I've thought that ever since you told me you were expecting a child. And Papa only stayed in England because of me; because of my father's family.'

'I didn't know that!' Clara exclaimed.

'It's true,' Georgiana said. 'When I brought Jewel to England we were very torn as to where she should be brought up, and we decided that it should be in England. Your grandmother welcomed her, as did your father and mother, and then her cousins, you and Elizabeth. You were her family more than I was back then.' She smiled. 'We've no regrets about that, none; but now it's time for Wilhelm to come home.'

'But what about you, Aunt Gianna?' Clara asked. 'What do you want?'

Georgiana hesitated for only a moment. 'I shall miss everyone in England, of course, and by that I mean you and your sister and your parents, but I want to stay.'

'Jewel?' Clara questioned.

'It's odd,' Jewel said, 'but when I began to consider that I'd like to come to America to uncover the facts of my birth, I hadn't given thought to what I would do if I discovered nothing, or if by chance all the circumstances were revealed. I didn't anticipate that my life might change because of either situation.'

She hesitated. 'But it has, and I realize now that there is no going back to how things were, but only forward.' She gazed wistfully at Clara, and said softly, 'And so, my dearest friend and cousin, I too will stay.'

Ted relented and said that Caitlin and Dan could consider a courtship. It was Caitlin who did the persuading, but Kitty also told him that she knew their daughter had been attracted to Dan from the moment she'd met him. 'She's so contrary,' she said. 'I knew by her offhand manner with him that there was a spark there.'

'It needs more than a spark to start a fire,' he'd grumbled.

'But we don't want a conflagration,' she'd warned. 'Not afore they're wed.'

But Caitlin was impatient. She wanted Dan to build them their own little house in the new town and wandered around the valley looking for the best sites before they were all snatched up. Dan soon caught her enthusiasm, though tempered by the fact that he had no money.

'Not enough to build a house,' he explained. 'I need to get on my feet first.'

She'd pouted at that and then cajoled her father. 'It makes

291

sense,' she said, 'to buy a site now, even if we don't build on it straight away.' And Ted's instincts told him that his self-willed daughter was also level-headed, just like her mother, and was probably right.

'All right,' he agreed. 'The pair of you look for a site, which I'll want to approve,' he warned them, 'and I'll loan the money to Dan until such time as he can earn enough to pay me back.'

Dan demurred. 'My da allus told me *neither a lender nor a borrower be,*' he said. 'And I never have been.' He'd scratched his stubble. 'Reckon I'll have to think on that afore I tek up your offer, Mr Allen.'

On which, Ted Allen, mighty pleased with his circumspect response and with some prompting from Kitty, decided that a gift of land would be a suitable wedding present, now that without his actually realizing it he appeared to have given his consent.

Another week went by and then another. Clara was becoming more and more restless. There had been a slight scattering of snow, the air was fresher and cooler and fires were built up for the darker evenings. Householders were beginning to bring out their warmer shawls and winter bedding; Georgiana wrapped herself up in furs and sat on the hotel porch watching the people of Dreumel walk by.

'I'm sorry,' she said to Clara. 'I know that you want to be going home. I'll do my best to persuade Wilhelm that the matter is pressing and you need to be on your journey before the weather closes in.'

'I don't like to bother him,' Clara said. 'I know how important this project is to him; if only he would agree that I'm perfectly able to travel alone.'

Georgiana shook her head. 'He won't,' she said wryly. 'He knows how anxious your father would be if you were travelling by yourself.' She mentioned the problem to Kitty during their conversations. Kitty's hotel was quiet because of the fire and the subsequent building work in Yeller, so she came most days to chat with her friend.

Caitlin had asked Clara if she was going to stay until the spring. 'You could be a bridesmaid,' she said eagerly. 'And I want Jewel too.'

Clara replied that although she would be sorry to miss Caitlin and Dan's wedding, above all else she wanted to go home to be with her twin sister, who, she told her, was expecting a child.

'Oh, of course you must go,' Caitlin exclaimed and promptly told Dan, who came to see Clara to proclaim his enthusiasm at the news.

'Elizabeth going to be a mother!' he declared. 'If onny Caitlin and I were already wed, I'd be happy for us to escort you. Caitlin longs to see our home town. But it's a question o' money. Work is slowing down; Jason says it allus does this time of year. Everybody finishes off all 'big projects afore 'winter sets in and then do all 'indoor jobs. Da and Thomas and me allus had plenty of work over 'winter. That's when we did all our big orders. Rocking horses and dolls' houses, trains and waggons and furniture for 'bairns. All that sort o' thing.'

Caitlin laughed. 'You sound just like my ma and pa. *Bairns*,' she mimicked, and then said, 'You could do that here. We don't have a toy store in Yeller or Dreumel.'

Dan had told her about the toyshop in the Land of Green Ginger and she was enchanted by the name, not really believing it until her mother had confirmed that it was true.

He looked at her and she gazed back at him. 'Why not?' she gasped. 'Why not? A winter project! And I could run a store, just like your ma.'

He stared at her. 'Thomas is 'one with ideas,' he said. 'I'm not much good with design but I can follow his plans. He's a wizard is our Thomas. He's got such an eye for detail.'

'He has,' Clara agreed. 'Years ago he made me a small wooden box for my birthday and carved such an intricate design on the lid.' She fell silent with her thoughts. How I long to see him again.

Caitlin and Dan were still arguing. He was telling her that special tools were needed for toymaking.

'You can't use 'same tools for toys as you would for building a house,' he said. 'We've allus used Hirsch chisels and planes; they're made in Germany and 'best you can buy. I'd need a whole selection of them. It's not possible just to tek a piece o' wood and start carving without 'right equipment.'

'Well, we can get them,' Caitlin said eagerly. 'There'll be tool catalogues.'

He caught hold of her hand. 'Course there are; but *money*!' he said. 'You can do nowt without money.'

'I'll ask my Pa,' she said eagerly.

'*No!*' Dan was adamant. 'I've been under my own da's rule. I want to be my own boss and I'll not go running to your pa every time you want summat.'

Clara remained silent. Dan was right. He had to make his own decisions about his and Caitlin's future. Caitlin was obviously used to twisting her father round her little finger for all that she wanted. Dan, she was sure, would be quite different.

CHAPTER THIRTY-NINE

'I'm sorry, Caitlin,' Dan said. 'But that's 'way it is.'

He and Caitlin had come out of church on Sunday morning; Caitlin wanted him to meet the parson who would marry them when the day was set. Dan was uncomfortable about it; he'd never been much of a churchgoer, but when he went inside the simple wooden church in Dreumel's Creek he hadn't felt overawed. But he was amazed when the parson turned towards them and he realized he had met him before. Jason had taken Dan into the timber yard and introduced him to a man called Mark, only a few years older than he was. Mark had been sawing a length of timber which he said he needed for a pillar. The timber pillar was now one of two on the church porch.

'I'd expected him to be a parsimonious old preacher,' Dan exclaimed, at which Caitlin had laughed and asked why would that be. They needed young blood in the town. The parson had only recently arrived in Dreumel's Creek and had a wife and children.

Dan and Caitlin had walked by the creek into Yeller and begun the climb up the mountainside to see the town from on high. Except that there wasn't much to see at the moment, only piles of timber, some blackened from the fire, and plots staked out where houses once were and would be again.

Dan was sweating, not because the weather was warm, for it wasn't – the air was crisp and sharp up here – but because he wasn't used to walking up hills. Hull was in one of the flattest parts of England, he told Caitlin, but he was also hot and bothered as she had once again asked why they couldn't borrow the money from her father and take a trip to England. He was fast coming to realize that his parents' teaching of thriftiness had bred caution into him.

'It's 'way I was brought up,' he said. 'You don't spend what you haven't got. And right now I've got hardly owt.'

Which wasn't quite true, since he still had the money his father had given him, but he regarded that as emergency money.

'Phew,' he groaned. 'I'll have to sit down, I'm jiggered.'

He dropped on to the rocky ground and stretched out, heaving out a breath. 'I can't believe we've climbed so high.' Then he sat up again to survey the view and saw the dips and humps and blackened crags where men had once sunk shafts and blasted rock in their search for gold. Caitlin sat beside him. 'This is 'highest I've ever been.'

'Never,' she said. 'We're not even halfway up. Next time we'll come on horseback.'

He glanced about him at the rugged outcrop and the rough uneven track they had ascended and then the towering mountain behind. 'No. I think I'd feel safer on my own two feet.'

She gave him a little push. 'You're just a city feller,' she scoffed.

'I am,' he agreed. 'Was! I could get used to this place, though.' He nodded thoughtfully. 'Yeh. I really could. It's grand.' This was praise indeed from a taciturn Yorkshireman not inclined to compliments or pretty phrases. 'We could build up here,' he murmured, 'and see this view every day, though it'd be a long hike down to work.'

Caitlin leaned towards him. 'Give me a kiss, Dan, and don't talk so much.'

He put his arm round her, pulling her towards him and kissing her gently on the mouth.

She fingered his shirt buttons and began to undo them, running her fingers inside and on to his chest.

'Hey,' he said, catching hold of her hand. 'Cheeky! Don't get me going.' He kissed her again and breathed softly into her ear. 'Or it might be a shotgun wedding.'

'I wouldn't mind,' she whispered. 'Then Pa would have to let us get married now rather than wait until spring. Anyway,' she giggled, 'Ma was expecting me when they got wed.'

Dan drew away. 'How do you know?'

Caitlin laughed and snuggled into his shoulder. 'I worked it out.'

He patted her gently on the nose. 'You are a very naughty girl.' He looked down at her. 'I hope you haven't been practising all these naughty things with anyone else?'

She drew herself up and away from him. 'No, I haven't. I've been waiting for someone special to come along.' She glanced down at him from under her lashes in a provocative way. 'And then you did.'

He laughed and grabbed her. 'Then don't tease,' he said. 'Or I might not be able to wait either.' He jumped to his feet and stretched, looking around him. 'I'm thirsty. We should have brought some water.'

Caitlin stretched out and put her hands behind her head. 'Plenty of water up here; can't you hear it?'

Dan cocked his head to one side and listened. 'Yeh! Is it a stream?'

'Sure it is,' she said. 'How do you think the creek gets filled? The water runs down the mountainside.'

'Not all of it, surely,' Dan said. 'There'll be a source somewhere higher than here.'

'My pa says that the headwaters come from pack ice, probably from thousands of miles away. And every mountain stream contributes to the rivers and creeks and lakes. After the winter snow melts, the streams are fast-flowing and the creek becomes really full.'

'So we couldn't build up here,' he said. 'We'd get washed away.'

'Yes,' she agreed. 'Or crushed by an avalanche.'

'So why doesn't the town get washed away?

She pointed up the mountain to the banks of pines which covered the rock. 'The trees,' she said. 'When Dreumel's Creek was being built, some of the city men cut down the trees for timber and they cut too many, not realizing that the trees would protect them, and there was a flood the following winter. Now there's some kind of law in Dreumel and Yeller that the trees can only be thinned and not cut down at random.'

Dan nodded. I've a lot to learn, he thought as he wandered over to the nearest trickling stream to take a drink from the icy water. He hunched down and ran his hands through it to cool them and scraped the gravel at the bottom. Imagine the excitement of finding gold, he thought, recalling what Jason had told him, of how Wilhelm and Ted Allen were on the point of giving up searching for gold in this second valley; they had found some but not much and many miners had left. Then one day as Jason was wandering along the side of the creek he saw something glinting in the water. It was gold washed down into the creek. They'd blasted deeper into the bedrock, and Jason had had a grin on his face as he told him, 'We had a lucky strike. We hit the lead!'

The gravel glinted as Dan ran it through his fingers. How did they tell, he wondered? How did they know it was gold? I suppose they'd seen some; enough to know, anyway. He held a handful of gravel in his palm. I wouldn't know; this could be gold. It's shining like gold anyway, and there's a seam on this lump of rock that's glinting.

'Hey, Caitlin,' he called. 'I've found gold!'

'Oh yeah? Tell me another!' She turned over towards him and lay with her head propped on her elbow.

He went over to her with the cube of rock in his hand. 'What's that, then?'

She took it from him and turned it over. She shook her head. 'Don't know. They've always said that the seam was played out up here. But who knows? It might be.' She smiled at him. 'If it is we could go to England after all.'

He gave a deep sigh. 'You don't give up, do you?'

'No,' she said softly. 'And now would be such a good time to go, to escort Clara and see your ma and pa.'

'I know.' He sat down and contemplated. It would be nice to take her, but I've not been here five minutes. It's too soon to go back and yet in another way it makes sense. I could ask Da and Thomas what they think about me starting up a toy store here. Better to explain face to face than in a letter. This'll soon be a good-sized town and families will come to live here. I could buy tools, and I could tell Ma that I'm staying here for good but that it doesn't mean she'll never see me again.

'Come on.' He jumped to his feet and held out his hand. 'I'll talk to your pa again.' He jiggled the piece of rock in his hand. 'And he can tell me if we've found gold.'

'Fool's gold,' Ted told him, when he was shown the rock. 'Pyrite. It's a mineral and looks a bit like gold, though it's more of a brassy yellow, and see this greenish streak? You don't get that in gold. But,' he added, seeing Dan's look of disappointment, 'it does sometimes show that there's gold or copper in the vicinity, so mebbe I'll go up with Jason and we'll take a look. But don't get your hopes up.'

'There was some gold-coloured gravel in 'stream where I found this rock.'

'All right. We'll have a look in a day or two. There's no hurry, is there?'

Dan gave a wry laugh. 'No, onny for Caitlin. She thinks we can get wed straight away and sail for England if it's gold.' He hesitated. 'I suppose you wouldn't consider letting her travel before we were married, sir? Clara wants to go home but Mr Dreumel is too busy to go yet, but won't agree to her travelling alone; and, well, I could escort her, and Caitlin would be a companion.'

Ted gazed at him. 'And what about the return journey?'

'Ah!' Dan said. 'I hadn't thought o' that!'

Ted patted his shoulder and grinned. 'You've got to learn not to give in to her.'

'Like you, you mean!' Kitty said sarcastically when he told

299

her that evening of their conversation. 'You don't spoil Robert in 'same way as you do Caitlin. Do they have to wait? We didn't.'

He laughed. 'We were in a hurry.'

'So are they.' She smiled back at him. 'So why not?'

'He's only just arrived,' he argued. 'Yet they want to go to England now, or at least Caitlin does; they're making the excuse that they can escort Clara.'

Kitty put down her sewing. 'It'd be nice for her to go,' she said pensively. 'Clara would show her around Hull and she'd meet Dan's parents and his brother. She'd know what kind of family they are.'

'And see how we once lived?'

'Yes,' she said softly. 'And how Dan's parents once lived – and Clara's mother, though not her father. She'd see 'difference in society there as compared with here. There's no shame in our background, Ted. None at all.'

He leaned over and kissed the top of her head. 'You're right, of course. As usual.'

Caitlin raced down the main street of Yeller the next morning. She should have been at work at the hotel but this just couldn't wait. She charged into Jason's yard shouting Dan's name. A carpenter looked up and pointed towards a shed and she ran towards it. 'Dan,' she called. '*Dan!*'

The door flew open and Dan came out. He was wearing a bowler hat, a rough cotton jacket and a wool scarf wrapped round his neck. 'What in heaven's name – what's up? What's happened?'

She flung herself at him. 'Oh, it's wonderful news! Pa said we can be wed straight away if we want. And we do want, don't we, and then we can go to England with Clara and – and – aren't you pleased?'

'Of course I'm pleased, but we need money, Caitlin!' Dan pushed the bowler back and scratched his forehead. 'Haven't you thought of that?'

She nodded. 'Yes, but Pa showed the piece of rock to Wilhelm and he said it might be worth taking a look at the site where you found it, and so Pa is going to put up the money to sink a small shaft in *your name*, cos he knows how to go about it, and even if it isn't gold you can still sell the pyrite!'

'I'll be for ever in his debt,' Dan said doubtfully.

'You've got to have faith, Dan,' she said earnestly. 'You do want to marry me, don't you?'

He gave a sudden grin and threw his hat in the air. 'Course I do.'

CHAPTER FORTY

Everything is moving so fast, Jewel thought. Dan and Caitlin were immersed in wedding plans, and she was both delighted and relieved. I hope he never tells her of his obsession with me, she thought. That would not be a sensible thing to do. She wanted to keep Caitlin's friendship, and Dan's too, for ever.

And now I'm losing Clara. They had spent nearly all their time together since they had come to America and she knew how much she would miss her.

'You've been like a sister to me,' she told Clara, and couldn't help the tears which welled in her eyes. 'But I realize that you must leave and how much you wish to see Elizabeth, your real sister.'

Clara put her arms around her. 'I do long to see Elizabeth, especially now at such an important time for her; but I cannot find words to say how much affection I hold in my heart for you. When I reflect on the time we have spent together, with never a harsh word between us, I know that our friendship has become even more than a sister's could be. We have shared so much, Jewel, but what comes next in our lives must undoubtedly be shared with others.' She smiled. 'Have you heard from Lorenzo?'

Jewel wiped her eyes. 'Yes. I wrote to him and Maria to tell them we had arrived safely, and then wrote again once Mama had given permission, to say she needed my company at the present time, thus giving him the reason for our hasty departure. He has written twice since then and says he hopes to see me in the near future.' She blew her nose. 'But that could mean anything, Clara. It could be just his abiding politeness. I've yet to recognize any sign of passion.'

'But he's written twice,' Clara said. 'And when we were in his company, I saw his tenderness towards you. You must be patient, Jewel. In your absence his love will grow; I have no doubt at all that he'll be missing you.' She searched Jewel's face. 'You have changed, cousin, since we came to America. Of all of us, you were always the one who was self-assured and confident—'

'And now I am not,' Jewel interrupted. 'I know. I think it was because, back in England, I knew who I was, or I thought I did; Gianna and Wilhelm gave me the security of a loving family and a good home life. But when I came to the land of my birth I discovered I was someone else entirely. It takes some getting used to – the new me.' She smiled. 'But it will come, I'm sure of that, and especially if . . .' She left the sentence unfinished.

Clara knew what she meant without her saying it. Especially if Lorenzo really did love her. 'Will you go back to San Francisco after Aunt Gianna has her child?' she asked. 'Will you return regardless of Lorenzo, and live in your little house, the house your father left for you?'

Jewel wondered. What a dilemma! To leave her beloved parents and their child: it would break her heart. Would she live alone in her house, next door to the man she loved and close to her Chinese family? For that is how she felt about them, even though she barely knew them.

She shook her head and confessed, 'I don't know.'

There was still a week to go before the wedding of Caitlin and Dan. Many of the locals whispered behind their hands at the haste, but others said Dan was just what Caitlin needed; somebody to calm her, for she had always been a wild child with odd ideas.

Jewel and Clara were to be Caitlin's attendants and Dan asked Robert if he would be his best man.

'I'd have asked my brother, Thomas, if we'd been wed in England,' Dan told him. 'But as Caitlin's brother I'd be pleased if you'll do me that honour.'

Robert was proud to be asked, even though he felt that he hardly knew Dan, for he was inclined to be a romantic at heart and thought of this union as a true whirlwind romance. He still had slight yearnings towards Clara, but whilst she and Jewel had been away he had observed how pretty Jason and Rose's youngest daughter was – something he hadn't noticed before, even though he had known her all her life. He hoped she'd be impressed when he was decked out in his best on the day.

Clara had almost finished packing her trunk for the journey home. Dan and Caitlin's wedding feast and their honeymoon night was to be at the Marius, a wedding gift from Wilhelm and Georgiana. The following morning the three of them were to set off by coach and train to New York, where they would spend two days before sailing to Liverpool.

Clara had written to her parents to give an estimated day of arrival but she had not told them that Dan and Caitlin would be accompanying her, having been pledged to secrecy by Dan.

'I want to see Ma and Da's faces when I turn up as a married man,' Dan said gleefully, and although Clara was rather unnerved by the prospect, she went along with it.

I shall be travelling with two companions, she wrote home, *and will be well chaperoned for the whole journey. Uncle Wilhelm is still very busy and also, although he hasn't said so, I know that he would be uneasy about leaving Aunt Gianna at this critical time.* She knew her mother would understand, as Gianna had written to Grace to tell her her happy news.

I am so pleased to be coming home again, Clara continued, *and not after all having to wait until the spring, and I hope that Papa will be able to meet me in Liverpool so that my companions may be relieved of their duties.*

The wedding day dawned bright but sharp and cold and everyone agreed that winter would soon be upon them. Logs were stacked against the houses, under porches and along-side the stores and warehouses, ready for the inevitable snow. There had been a further scattering of snowflakes and there was a nip to the nostrils when a breath was drawn in.

Caitlin walked on her father's arm down the aisle of the church where her parents had been the very first to marry. She wore a cream organza gown with a separate apron front, trimmed with bows and long sash ends, with a short train which Kitty had hurriedly made on her sewing machine. In her red hair she wore a headdress of cream lace which had been her mother's. Dan wore his best and only suit and had brushed away the wood shavings from his father's bowler; Ted had lent him a cravat and matching handkerchief for his pocket.

Because there had been so little time to prepare, Jewel and Clara wore gowns they had bought in New York, Jewel's sheath-like with a low-set bustle in peach and Clara's in pale blue satin, half-hooped with a bustle pad; they wore ribbons in their hair, which they dressed in chignons, Jewel's glossy black and Clara's soft and fair.

'What a lovely day it has been,' Georgiana said to Kitty as they sat and watched the young people dancing during the evening. Georgiana wore several lacy shawls over her full-skirted gown and a beaver cape over her shoulders.

'Yes,' Kitty sighed. 'I can't believe I've seen a daughter wed. It seems like no time at all since you and I came to this country. Where have the years gone?'

'For you they have gone in bringing up a family, start-ing a successful bakery and running the Yeller hotel. You've achieved so much, Kitty,' Georgiana told her.

'Yes.' Kitty nodded. 'Who would have believed it? Will you stay after your baby is born?' she asked suddenly. 'Or will you go home to England?'

'When our child is born, this will be our home, Kitty,' Georgiana said softly. 'It's where Wilhelm wants to be.' She placed her hand over Kitty's. 'We shall stay.'

'I'm so pleased.' Kitty's eyes welled up with tears. 'I've missed you all these years. In spite of having Ted and Caitlin and Robert, I've missed our chats and our – our . . .' She paused to feel for the words.

'Our links with the past?' Georgiana smiled. 'We went through so much together, didn't we? Now, my dear Kitty, we can catch up again.'

The next morning the travellers were up early for the coach to take them to Woodsville, where they would catch the train to New York. Caitlin looked flushed and sleepy as they climbed aboard, but she was very excited to be going on such a journey. The furthest she had ever travelled was to Philadelphia with her father. Both her parents and her brother were there to see them off but Kitty was in tears as she gave her last-minute instructions about what to do and what to see when she arrived in England and her home town of Hull.

The luggage was loaded. Dan helped his wife and then turned to Clara to assist her aboard, but she was still taking her leave of Jewel, Gianna and Wilhelm. They were in floods of emotion, not knowing how long it would be before they met again.

'I'll write,' Clara and Jewel said simultaneously, and both wiped their eyes. 'I'll come again one day,' Clara said, sniffling. 'Aunt Gianna, you must write to tell us of – of your happy event, and we'll tell you about Elizabeth.'

Georgiana smiled. 'We'll send a telegram. We're to have a telegraph office here in Dreumel!'

With that Clara was ushered aboard. Dan got in, closing the door behind him. The driver lashed his whip and shouted, 'Ho up!' The two greys snorted and skittered on the dusty road and they were off, two pale handkerchiefs and one bowler hat waving from the window.

The start of the sea voyage was rough. There had been a heavy storm and the waves were still running high, the troughs deep. Clara and Caitlin kept to their cabins, Clara's single, being hot and airless, adding to her discomfort. Dan took a brisk walk round the deck every morning, and apart from mealtimes, when he ate heartily, and mostly alone, in the dining saloon, he spent the rest of the day administrating to Caitlin, giving her cool sips of water and holding her hand.

When the sea became calmer, Clara and Caitlin and the other passengers finally emerged, pale and unsteady, to drink in the cold invigorating air; they had only three more sailing days to Liverpool. I can't wait to get home now, Clara thought as she leaned on the deck rail whilst Dan took Caitlin on a walk round the deck. I want to see my mother and my sister and my darling papa. And Thomas, of course. Will he be changed, she wondered? Or will he be his steady, sweet self? Dear Thomas, the nearer I come to seeing him again the more I realize how much I've missed him.

She looked out over the ocean, where there was as yet no sign of land. Nothing in the distance but more of the same lashing white-crested waves topping the blue-green watery waste. But will Thomas have missed me? For the first time ever she began to have a flicker of doubt. They had always had a rapport, drawn together by a common bond even when they were children. She thought they had had a special, affectionate relationship, but did Thomas think that too, or did he consider her only as his childhood friend? Precious as that relationship was, was she right or wrong in thinking that there could be more than just companionship in his feelings for her?

Her confidence had been broken by Federico's anger – no, scorn – being directed towards her, by his mistaken presumption and conceit that she had encouraged him. And yet – I'm confused! What is expected of a woman? James Crawford – she touched her mouth as she recalled how he had tenderly kissed her. There was no boldness or arrogance in his actions, and he had then humbly begged forgiveness. He was a natural gentleman, yet driven by a compelling emotion.

She sighed and turned her back on the restless waves, and saw Caitlin and Dan walking towards her.

'Would you like something to eat, Clara?' Dan asked. 'I'm trying to persuade Caitlin to come for something, a slice of beef or ham mebbe.'

Clara shook her head. 'I'm not hungry,' she said. 'I've had

porridge this morning; maybe something later.' She glanced at Caitlin, who still looked pallid and washed out. 'Why don't you go, Dan? Caitlin and I will sit out here for a while and wait for you.'

Dan eagerly departed and Clara called a passing steward to bring two chairs and blankets and put them in a sheltered spot so that they might enjoy the pale sunshine and recover from the seasickness.

'Clara,' Caitlin said softly, 'can I ask you something?' She sighed and gazed wanly at Clara, who nodded. 'Do you think that Dan's mother will like me?'

Clara gave an astonished murmur. 'Whatever makes you doubt it?'

'Well, you hear that mothers are protective of their sons, and Mrs Hanson won't be expecting Dan to have married so soon after leaving home. It worries me that she'll think I've ensnared him.'

Clara hid a smile and thought that that would be the last thing that Aunt Ruby would think. She was more likely to think that Dan had caught and captivated Caitlin. As for Dan's father, he would perhaps be pleased that his eldest son was settling down at last. But as she sat and looked and listened to Caitlin, she realized that Caitlin's unrestrained manner and boisterous ways had diminished over the last few weeks and she had become calmer; yet she was obviously very happy.

How could that have happened in such a short time, she wondered; I would never have thought that Dan of all people could have had an influence on anyone, especially someone as volatile as Caitlin was. There again, she thought, Dan too seems less brash and antagonistic, more caring and thought-ful than I would have thought it possible for him to be. They are good for each other, came Clara's enlightening discovery. They have opened their hearts and minds to each other and found friendship as well as love.

'Caitlin,' she said, 'Ruby will love you. Once she overcomes the shock of hearing that Dan is married, she will think of you as the daughter she always wanted.'

CHAPTER FORTY-ONE

Clara could see her father waiting on the quayside, his hand to his forehead as he searched for her in the crowd of passengers waiting to disembark, and she waved her arms frantically. Finally he spotted her and enthusiastically waved back. She was one of the first down the gangway and fell into his outstretched arms.

'Oh, I'm so pleased to see you,' she said, and burst into tears.

'And I you, my darling girl.' Martin kissed her wet cheeks and hugged her. 'I can't tell you how we've missed you. It's been so long.' He looked about them. 'Where's your luggage, and where are your travelling companions? I must thank them for accompanying you.'

'Oh . . .' Clara fluttered her hand about. 'The porter will bring it, and – and – they'll be here in a moment. A last-minute hitch. Papa,' she said breathlessly, 'it's a surprise. Something quite unexpected.'

'Really? Will I like it?'

Clara laughed. 'I think so. Everyone else does.'

Her father looked puzzled and raised his eyebrows. 'I hope they won't be long; we have a train to catch. I thought you'd like to go straight home rather than wait until the morning.'

'Oh, I would,' she said. 'I really would. I just can't wait to see everyone.'

Her father was gazing towards the ship's gangplank.

'There's a fellow there the image of Dan Hanson,' he murmured. 'How is he?' He turned back to Clara. 'Has he settled? And more to the point, how is Jewel? Oh, you can tell me everything once we're on the train. There must be so much to say.'

'There is,' she agreed, and saw Dan and Caitlin walking towards them. 'Papa! Here are my travelling companions.'

Martin turned and his jaw dropped in astonishment. 'Dan? It is you! But . . .' He glanced at Caitlin and then Clara and his lips formed a question.

'Uncle Martin! Sir.' Dan gave a hesitant grin. 'Yes, it's me, and I'd like to introduce you to my wife, Caitlin. Caitlin, this is Clara's father, Martin Newmarch. Not really my true uncle but allus considered as good as.'

Caitlin dipped her knee. 'How do you do, Mr Newmarch? I'm really pleased to meet you.'

Martin took her outstretched hand and gave a polite bow. He was obviously astonished. 'Married! Erm – I'm lost for words, but delighted to meet you, erm, Caitlin, is it? Mrs Hanson!'

Caitlin's cheeks dimpled and Clara knew that her father would be won over. 'I'm not used to being Mrs Hanson yet,' she admitted. 'It's only been just over a week since our wedding day.'

'Indeed! Well!' Martin was unusually taken aback and Clara could see that he was trying to work out all the whys and wherefores.

'Dan and Caitlin very kindly brought their wedding day forward so that they could escort me home,' Clara explained. 'I would have been there until the spring if I'd waited for Uncle Wilhelm.'

'And we really wanted to get married,' Caitlin said eagerly and without preamble. 'Even though there was no need to hurry, as some folks seemed to think; but I wanted to meet Dan's ma and pa, and he wants to discuss something with his pa and brother, so as winter is coming on in Dreumel and there ain't a great deal of work right now for Dan, we decided to come with Clara.'

310

She smiled as she finished her breathless explanation and Dan put his arm round her shoulder and said, 'What Caitlin's really saying is that I was talked into it.' He gazed indulgently at his bride, and then kissed her cheek. 'And I've no regrets about that, none at all.'

'Goodness!' Martin huffed out a breath and shook his head. 'Well, well.' Then he laughed. 'You'll certainly wake up the neighbourhood when you get home with this news.' He took hold of Caitlin's hand again and gently squeezed it. 'Welcome, Caitlin. Welcome to England.'

Martin had booked a first-class carriage to take them home and quickly changed the tickets to accommodate two more. In between sleeping, or in Caitlin's case gazing out at the passing countryside, they talked of Dreumel's Creek and Yeller and occasionally Clara spoke of California, though not too much, as she wanted to share the experience with her mother and Elizabeth too. And, she thought, best not to say too much about Jewel in front of Dan and Caitlin.

'So do you plan to return to America?' Martin asked Dan. 'You've only been there a short time.'

'Oh, yes!' Dan exclaimed. 'It's my kind of country. It's 'sort of place where anything can and does happen. There's every opportunity open to anybody and though I'm not saying it'll be easy – it certainly won't be, cos you've got to be prepared to work – it's a young country and there's no class divide. Every man is as good as 'next one.'

I could take issue with you over that, Dan, Clara mused. There's arrogance there regarding wealth – she was thinking of Federico – and there's a division in culture. She considered Jim Crowfoot, who in order to fit in with the new order had changed his name to Crawford. She remembered the anti-Chinese slogans she had seen on walls and hoardings in San Francisco, and thought there was also an abhorrence of those who were different. But she didn't raise the subject, for part of her agreed with Dan that it was a country where dreams could be realized, or dashed, according to your luck; where opportunism and opportunity went hand in hand. Dan was tough enough to face

311

that challenge, and with a ready-made family to shield and advise him, she thought he would do well.

Clara and Caitlin were exhausted when they finally arrived at Hull Paragon railway station. They had had an early-morning call when the ship had docked at Liverpool and both staggered slightly as they stepped down from the train. Dan, though, was bullish, eager and excited to be coming home to show off his new bride.

Martin signalled for a cab and the driver tipped his top hat when he saw Clara. 'Welcome home, miss,' he said. 'Did you have a good trip? Left somebody behind, I see!'

'Yes, thank you. Most enjoyable.' She recognized the regular driver, but didn't respond to the mention of Jewel. Time enough for news of her, and of Georgiana and Wilhelm's decision to stay in America, to filter out.

'Papa,' she said, 'we're all tired, I know, but I wonder if we could go the long way home. It will only take another five minutes.'

Martin smiled down at her. 'By the pier, you mean?'

'Yes. Do you mind, Dan?'

He didn't and said that they could then be dropped off at the top of Silver Street. 'I'll pick 'trunks up later.' He grinned. 'I want to just turn up at 'door and see Ma's face.'

'I'll bring them round in the trap,' Martin agreed. 'After supper?'

The driver was given his instructions and instead of turning for home he turned right for Queen Street and the pier. He reined in, lit a pipe and waited whilst Clara and her father, then Dan and Caitlin, walked to the rail and looked down into the Humber.

'It's not like your creek,' Dan said. 'It's a mighty estuary.'

'It's a lot wider than our creek,' Caitlin said, and shivered as a sharp wind blew. 'What's that land across the water? Is that Hull too?'

'No. That's Lincolnshire,' he told her. 'Another county.'

Their conversation washed over Clara as she watched the rich brown turbulent waters. It was nothing like the waters

312

of the creek, she agreed with Dan; nor was it as vast as the blue waters of San Francisco Bay. She heaved a sigh. But it was so familiar and comforting; she had always known it and its different temperaments. It seemed capricious now, the white-capped waves tossing against the wooden pier and then rushing off as if in a mad dash to reach their destination: the estuary mouth off Spurn Point, where they would join the salty waters of the German Ocean.

'Good to be back?' Her father put his arm round her shoulder.

'Oh, yes!' she said on a breath. 'So very good.'

Five minutes later, Dan and Caitlin were set down in the Market Place at the top of Silver Street. Caitlin, wide-eyed, looked about her at the numerous shops. It was now quite dark, but there were still people going about their business; the shops were lit by glowing gas light, as were the street lamps. 'This is so quaint,' she said. 'All the buildings are in brick or stone!'

'Aye,' Dan laughed. 'We don't have as many trees as there are in Yeller to build timber houses; nor any mountains or even hills round here. No hills in Hull,' he joked.

She clung to Dan's arm. 'It's so different from home.' She pulled him closer as he led her down the narrow Land of Green Ginger. 'All the buildings seem to be on top of each other.'

'Aye, well, this was once a very small town, an ancient town enclosed by walls and gates to keep out any enemy; it's spreading wider now,' he told her. 'The Dreumels live in the newer part of town, but there's still a lot of folk living in 'old town, like my folk and Clara and her family. I'll tek you tomorrow and introduce you to Aunt Grace, Clara's mother. She's my ma's best friend. Here we are.' He was standing in front of a bow-windowed shop. 'This is it.'

Caitlin was enthralled by the toys in the window and pressed her nose to the glass.

'I think we'll have to go round 'back,' Dan said. 'Looks as if Ma's shut 'shop up early.'

He led her to a side door and winked at her as he knocked,

then gently pushed her to one side so that she wouldn't be visible as the door was opened.

His mother stood in the doorway. 'Good evening, madam.' Dan lifted his father's bowler. 'Could I interest you in a gift from America?'

Ruby squealed. 'Dan? Dan! Oh, Daniel – Thomas! It's our Dan.' She opened the door wider. 'Whatever brings you back so soon?' She threw out her arms to embrace him as his father, frowning slightly, and then his brother, Thomas, appeared behind her.

Dan drew Caitlin towards him. 'Here's what brings me home. Ma! Da! Thomas. Please meet my wife.'

The cab rattled down High Street and stopped outside the house. 'Go on.' Her father smiled. 'I'll see to everything here. Your mother's waiting.'

The door opened before Clara reached the steps and her mother was waiting with open arms. 'At last!' Grace cried. 'This has been such a long day. Come along, give me your hat and shawl. Nancy,' she said to the young maid hovering behind her, 'take Miss Clara's things and tell Cook we'll have supper straight away.'

'Oh, wonderful.' Clara laughed. 'Some things never change!'

'Of course they don't.' Her mother hugged her. 'Welcome home, my dearest girl. We've missed you so much. And guess who's waiting for you in the sitting room?'

'Elizabeth?' Clara was overjoyed. 'Elizabeth's here! Is she well? I can't wait to see her.' She rushed off down the hall, her mother and then her father, both wreathed in smiles, bringing up the rear.

Her sister was sitting on the sofa, propped up on cushions with her feet on a footstool, looking plump and pretty. Her face lit up when she saw Clara. 'Come here, you naughty girl,' she said, with a catch in her voice. 'Come here and give me a hug and don't ever leave me again.'

Clara sat beside her and put her head on Elizabeth's shoulder. She gently put her hand on Elizabeth's rounded belly. 'I won't,' she said softly. 'Never.'

CHAPTER FORTY-TWO

Only Dan chatted through supper, which Ruby had been about to dish up when he'd knocked on the door. His family seemed stunned by the fact that he was home, and with a bride.

Ruby was being as accommodating as she could possibly be with a stranger who was now family sitting at her table. Thomas had hastily brought two more chairs to the table and politely pulled one back for Caitlin.

'Perhaps, erm, Caitlin would like to change or tidy up first, or . . .' Ruby stumbled over her words, not really knowing what one was supposed to do with a visitor who had travelled such a long way. 'Dan,' she said. 'Tek Caitlin up to your room. Mebbe she'd like to put on her slippers, or . . .' Her voice tailed away.

Caitlin glanced at Dan. 'Yes, please,' she whispered. 'I would. Except that my other clothes are in the trunk.'

'Uncle Martin is bringing our trunk later,' Dan explained when he came down again, leaving Caitlin upstairs to compose herself.

'Dan!' his mother said *sotto voce*. 'I hope you haven't got that girl into trouble. Marry in haste—'

'I haven't, Ma.' Dan gave her a smacking kiss. 'Don't worry. I wouldn't have done that. I just fell overboard 'minute I met her.' He glanced at his father. 'There's just nobody else in 'world like her. She meks me laugh and she's that merry and full of energy for whatever she does that she teks my breath away!'

His father nodded, and then smiled. 'Glad to hear it, son.'

'This is 'oddest thing,' Dan said. 'Although Caitlin is American born and bred, her ma was born in Hull and went out to America with Georgiana Dreumel all those years ago, and her da – you'll never believe this – used to be valet to Edward Newmarch, Jewel's real father, who was, of course, brother of Martin, Clara's da! Isn't that amazing?'

Caitlin's footsteps were heard on the narrow staircase as she came carefully down.

Ruby and Daniel glanced at each other, and then Daniel's face creased into a slow grin. 'Incredible,' he said. 'Who'd ever think that 'world was so small!'

When Caitlin came in, Dan explained that they had married in a rush so that they could come home with Clara, but Thomas interrupted. 'Was that 'only reason? I'd have thought that Clara was capable of coming home by herself if she wanted to.'

'Sure she could,' Caitlin answered. 'But Uncle Wilhelm wouldn't allow it. He reckoned he was responsible for her whilst she was over there, but he had so much on with the re-building of Yeller that he ran right out of time, and we knew that she didn't want to wait.'

'She didn't?' Thomas queried.

'Guess not,' Caitlin said. 'Don't know why, but she just wanted to come home.'

'But it was a good excuse for Caitlin too,' Dan said indulgently. 'She wanted to come and meet my folks, so she twisted my arm behind my back so that I'd agree. And she talked her pa into agreeing too, but what really clinched it was that I thought I'd found gold!'

'What!' Ruby gasped.

Dan raised his hand. 'Onny it wasn't, Ma. It was pyrite; fool's gold it's called, cos it's yeller and looks like gold.'

'My ma says you can buy jewellery made from pyrite,' Caitlin chipped in. 'It's not as expensive as gold but nearly as pretty. If there's a good seam we could mine it.'

'And so did Clara like America?' Thomas persisted in changing the subject again. 'And California – she and Jewel travelled there specially to find out about Jewel's mother.'

This time, Dan and Caitlin looked at each other. They had been so wrapped up with one another that they had barely questioned Jewel and Clara on their return from San Francisco.

'I guess Clara will tell you all that happened there,' Caitlin said, blushing. 'Jewel did find out about her birth mother but we were so busy planning the wedding that we hardly had a chance to talk. Sounds silly, I know, but that's the way it was.'

'There was another reason for coming home,' Dan said, 'although you might think that I could've written to ask. I want to discuss ideas about starting a toyshop in Yeller. Caitlin would like to do that, Ma. Just like you.'

Clara spent the whole of the following day telling her parents and Elizabeth about her time in America, and about Jewel and the earthquake which had so frightened them, and the revelations which had followed, until Patrick came to collect Elizabeth and take her home with the promise that he would bring her back again soon.

'We need a town house,' Elizabeth complained. 'I dearly want our child to be born in Hull, rather than in the country. I need to be near Mama and Clara.'

'We're only half an hour from town,' Patrick said. 'Cottingham is very close.'

Clara drew in a breath. 'I know just the place,' she said, thinking of the Dreumels' house in Albion Street and their decision to remain in America. 'I will enquire for you.'

She kissed her sister goodbye and Patrick pecked her cheek, and after an hour or so of chatting to her mother she said she would like to take a walk.

'Do, my dear, and why not call on Ruby?' her mother suggested. 'She'll want to hear all about your adventures

317

with Jewel, and Georgiana and Wilhelm too. Is it official that they're all staying in America?'

'It's a fact that they're staying, but whether we can spread the news I don't know. But, Mama, perhaps Elizabeth and Patrick could rent their house – at least until after the baby is born.'

Grace's face creased into a smile. 'That would be perfect,' she said. 'I'll write to Georgiana straight away and ask her. Off you go then, Clara. Ask Dan to bring Caitlin to meet me, and give my love to Thomas – if you should chance to meet him!'

Clara assumed nonchalance. How astute her mother was! Was that something which came with experience or maturity, she wondered?

It was a cold, damp and rather foggy day, but Clara was hardly aware of it. What she did notice was how small the town appeared to be after the wide open valleys and mountainous country she had become accustomed to in America. But it did not dismay her; rather she felt comfortable and safe within its familiar confining embrace. She met and greeted many people she knew as she walked down Scale Lane into the Market Place, and down Silver Street towards Whitefriargate and the Land of Green Ginger.

She hesitated at the top of the street for only a moment and then swiftly turned back and crossed over into Trinity House Lane in the direction of the warehouse, where she was almost sure she would find Thomas.

The door knob turned noiselessly and as she stepped over the threshold she saw Thomas leaning over the work bench. His fair hair hung over his forehead and he was concentrating on a piece of wood. He had an adze in his hand, so she held her breath and didn't speak in case he should spoil whatever he was doing.

'You can come in, you know,' he said quietly. 'I shan't cut myself.'

'Oh! I didn't think you'd heard me.' She gave a low laugh. Of course he had heard her; and probably seen her too, as he was facing in the direction of the door.

He looked up and smiled his slow smile, and she felt as if the sun had suddenly come out.

'How are you, Thomas?'

He pursed his mouth and nodded. 'Better'n I was five minutes ago. You?'

'Yes,' she said, and wondered why she felt so breathless. 'I'm well.'

He put down the adze and she went towards the bench. 'What are you making?'

'A crib. It's for a friend o' mine who's expecting a happy event.'

'Good. You heard, then? Are you – keeping busy?' She felt the need for small talk until she had accustomed herself to his nearness and they were back on their old easy footing.

'Aye. I've been working on a new idea.'

'Oh? What sort of idea?'

'I'd like to set up a larger warehouse; a business where other craftsmen and toymakers could either work alongside us, or send their work to be displayed. Sort of like a large shop where 'public can come in and watch us work and buy our products. I've been thinking about it and planning while you've been away. No distractions, you see.'

'Did I distract you?' she asked, almost holding her breath.

'You know that you did; just as Dan was distracted by Jewel, except that he now loves somebody else, whereas I . . .'

She gazed at him. 'What will you call this idea of yours?'

'Toy Town Incorporated.' He came slowly round the bench towards her.

'TTI,' she said softly. 'The children will love it.'

He took hold of her hands and gazed at her. 'This has been 'longest time of my life.'

'Has it?' she whispered. 'And yet you let me leave without saying anything?'

He continued looking at her, his eyes sweeping her face. When he spoke his voice was warm and sure. 'You had to go on this journey, Clara, in order to know yourself. It wasn't only Jewel who was looking for answers. If I'd spoken earlier to say I loved you, you'd never have known if there was someone else that you might have loved more than me.'

'But there isn't and never was,' she whispered.

'Are you sure?'

She thought of Jim Crowfoot and the impossibility of loving him and Thomas seemed to sense the hesitation. 'Not someone you *might* have loved?'

'More than you?' Clara smiled. 'No.'

'Can I kiss you?' he asked, fingering her cheek.

'Do you need to ask?'

'Aye, I do. I tek nothing for granted.' But he bent forward before she could reply and gently kissed her lips. 'I've wanted to do that for so long,' he whispered into her ear as he drew her close.

Clara closed her eyes. 'And I've been waiting,' she murmured. 'Longer than I even knew.'

He held her at arms' length. 'I'm not like our Dan, all hot air and exuberant passion. My love for you has been smouldering for years.' He put his head back and laughed. 'A red-hot fire beneath a volcano!'

She laughed too and they rocked in each other's arms. 'And I have no means of putting out the fire!'

'We'd best get wed then as fast as we can,' he said, kissing her again. 'Or else we might burn.'

CHAPTER FORTY-THREE

Jewel sat in her room at the Dreumel Marius and reread Clara's letter. It was the second she had received from her cousin since she had left for England and home. The first was to tell her about her engagement to Thomas and their wedding plans for the summer, and the new business that Thomas was planning. This one was to tell her of the safe arrival of Elizabeth's son, born in January in the house in Albion Street.

Jewel smiled and heaved a sigh. How lovely. She recalled her own happy childhood in the house and was pleased that once again there would be the sound of a child's voice echoing round the rooms. Now she was about to write to give Clara the news from Dreumel's Creek.

I have delayed writing, she wrote, *as the doctor told Mama that he thought the baby would be early, and she was. Three weeks ago, Mama was safely delivered of a daughter. Mama was quite weak, but the doctor says she is now making a good recovery and she is deliriously happy. The babe is to be named Clarissa after the aunt who brought Mama up when she was a child. She's the most adorable baby ever, so tiny and sweet, and it's going to break my heart to leave her. Oh, now I'm giving away what I am about to write!*

As I look out of my window I see Dan going by, driving a horse and waggon. The snow is still very thick here but he is clearing the site in Yeller where he and Caitlin are to build a house. Caitlin is still managing the hotel but come spring Mr Adams is coming from the New York Marius to take over from her. Then Dan and Caitlin have plans for their toyshop, which I'm sure will be very popular, and I understand they will also sell small items of furniture suitable for children. Dan's hopes for a gold or pyrite strike came to nothing, unfortunately, although he seems quite unperturbed about it. I think he feels lucky with what he has.

The winter has been exceptionally hard here and we were completely cut off for several weeks, but eventually the men from both towns were able to dig a track through, with just enough room for a horse and waggon to pass along.

But as I speak of the winter snows, I come to the most important part of my letter, and yet I don't quite know where to start. But perhaps at the beginning, which was in San Francisco about a month ago . . .

Maria and Pinyin were together in the kitchen behind the restaurant. Maria was leaning on the pastry table, her knuckles clenched into fists and her mouth set in a pinched line. Pinyin had both hands on his slim hips, but one also held his wide chopping blade. Had it slipped it would have sliced through his foot.

'What am I to do with him?' Maria muttered. 'That boy is driving me crazy.'

'I've told you. Tell him to go!' Pinyin gazed expressionlessly at Maria, yet his black eyes flashed. 'He's no good to anyone right now.'

Maria straightened up and looked at him. 'How will we manage?'

'We'll manage.' Pinyin put down the blade and started to empty a basket of onions, carrots, garlic and tomatoes on to a chopping board.

Maria gave a little smile and reflected on how often she had sought advice from Pinyin. She remembered the first time he had come to the bakery begging for a job. She had given him the chance against her husband's wishes, for he was willing to work for next to nothing and she badly needed help. It wasn't until some time later that she had realized he was watching

322

over the baby next door. He'd taken the toddler Lorenzo to see the little girl and Edward had handed her to him. From behind the dividing wall in the yard she had seen Pinyin gently kiss the top of the baby's head.

At the time she had thought it an unusual thing for a young unmarried man to do, but now and again his sister Soong Daiyu had called to see him and Maria had noticed her too glancing across to the house next door; she put two and two together and realized that there was a slender link between them and the motherless child. But by then Pinyin had become inseparable from Lorenzo. He was the only one who could tame the tyrannical toddler, as he was then, moulding him to be the sweet-natured boy and gentle man that he was to become.

'How?' she asked him now as with deft fingers and swift movements he began chopping and slicing. Then she shrugged. 'Not that we are so busy just now.'

'Exactly so.' Pinyin never paused for a moment and she marvelled at his dexterity. He had never, to her knowledge, cut himself. 'I can cook and serve, you can cook and my sister can wash the dishes. If necessary my nephew Chen will help. He has worked in a restaurant.'

Maria stared at him, her mouth parted. 'But then it will be a Chinese restaurant!'

'Italian and Chinese, yes.' He didn't lift his head but looked up at her from beneath his dark raised brows. 'You may have a half-Chinese daughter one day. She might like Chinese food.'

Maria sat down on the nearest stool. Lorenzo had not smiled since Jewel had left and even his friends had remarked on it, except Federico, who no longer came to visit. Christmas had been dismal and the two of them had eaten together after their customers had left with hardly a word passing between them.

'If it makes him happy,' she said, 'then that is what we must do. Otherwise he may never sing again.'

And so Lorenzo was dispatched from San Francisco on the

long journey towards the young woman whom he so desperately loved. Jewel had written to tell him of her journey to her home in the mountains and how much she was missing all her friends, Italian and Chinese, more than she could possibly say. He knew now what his mother had guessed, that Jewel's mother was expecting a child and that this anticipated event had precipitated her early departure.

She had written again to tell him of Clara's engagement to someone she had known all her life, and he thought he had caught a sense of yearning within her words. Yet whenever he began a letter to her he was barely able to string a sentence together. In each one he wanted to tell her of his affection, yet dared not write the word *love* in case she should reject him, even though he felt she had given him some cause to hope by her sweetness towards him when she had been in his company. So instead he wrote of the weather, and about the restaurant, and of Soong Daiyu's occasional visits, *and oh, yes*, he had added in one, hoping that she would read the hidden message between the lines, *Madre has begun lighting a fire several times a week in your house; she says to keep it aired for when, or if, you should return, which I hope with all my heart that you will.*

Jewel had described the snow in the valley, and so before he began packing warm clothes for his hurried departure he wrote a hasty letter to her to say that he was travelling to New York and would like to call at Dreumel's Creek to see her, as if it were a mere street away rather than another day's journey.

'Madre!' he said, kissing his mother's cheek as he left. 'I might not return alone, do you realize that? Can you manage without me? It could be some time before my return.'

'Go!' She gave him a push towards the door. 'Do whatever you must. Take care. Be happy again.'

He smiled at that and climbed into the cab. Pinyin ran alongside, planning to help Lorenzo with his trunk at the station and make sure that he got on the train and didn't have second thoughts about his mission.

The first two days of the journey passed pleasantly. Lorenzo played cards with other passengers in his carriage, of which there were six, two of them being elderly ladies. He joined in the singing and was commended for his fine voice. They arranged a duty roster for cooking so that they didn't all crowd into the tiny kitchen at the same time, and Lorenzo was very popular as his mother had sent him off with enough food to last a week, which he shared. Others had brought ready-cooked joints of beef and chicken, which were sliced and handed round. Some had brought jerked meat, which he found almost inedibly tough; others distributed tinned fruit and sweet cake.

He watched from the windows as they followed the route through the high sierras, two additional engines enabling them to travel at reasonable speed through the long snow sheds, but when they came out of them, even with the additional engines they travelled so slowly through the high terrain that he and two of the men left the train and walked for an hour, savouring the exercise and the clean sharp air. Lorenzo marvelled at the beauty of the peaks and the white clouds which drifted above them and saw in the far distance herds of buffalo crossing the plain.

As they neared Ogden, the sky darkened and it began to rain, which turned to sleet and then snow. Lorenzo peered out of the rattling window, feeling the draught blowing in, and saw that the high ridges were white with snow. He fished around in his travelling bag for a warm scarf to wrap round his neck, and went towards the kitchen to make a hot drink.

One of the other men, Henry, was doing the same and the kettle was already steaming. 'Here,' he said. 'I've just made coffee, enough for two.'

Lorenzo thanked him and asked if he travelled this route often.

'Sure. Do it three or four times a year, though I try not to come in winter. The snow gets pretty bad on the other side of Ogden. Hope you've got some sturdy boots!'

'I haven't,' Lorenzo confessed. 'I've never seen snow. I've

lived all my life in San Francisco, seen fog and rain and felt earthquakes, but never seen snow.'

Henry took a gulp of coffee. 'Then you've sure got an experience coming. Be warned.'

They shivered in the station house in Ogden, though there was hot food to eat. A train with another crew was due in two hours, but by now there was a blizzard blowing and Henry reckoned it would be late, which it was. Three hours later they were taking it in turns to sit or stand near the stove. The second-class passengers stayed on the first train, for they had no money to buy food and were therefore not invited by the railroad porters or conductors to share the fire.

Another hour went by and the ladies in their party were becoming distressed by the cold. The men gave up their places by the fire and Lorenzo and another man went out to forage for more wood to burn and to persuade the railroad men to come out of their hut and bring more coal, which they did, although reluctantly.

When the train finally arrived, they were told that the delay had been because of an overturned engine on the line, which had to be moved before any other transport could get through.

'There are snow drifts six foot high,' one of the drivers said. 'Never seen such snow before! We'll need all the manpower we can get.' They organized a work train with another six railmen on board to accompany them back down the line; the passengers piled back in the carriages, the ladies deciding to take to their beds in an attempt to get warm.

They all agreed that the next two days were a nightmare. The train stopped and started and the railroad men were kept constantly busy clearing the line of snow, which they shovelled to the side of the track. A blizzard was blowing and it seemed that as fast as they cleared the snow more came down. The railroad men from the work train grumbled at the extra labour, complaining that their wages didn't cover situations like this. Lorenzo, Henry and another man from their carriage put on their coats and volunteered to help in order to keep moving, clearing the snow with shovels and pieces of wood.

They moved on for another two hours before once again coming to a halt. By now it was dark and the railmen were exhausted and unwilling to continue; the volunteers came back on board, their clothing wet through, the ladies gave them hot soup to warm them and they all took to their beds. From the safety of their bunks they heard the howl of wolves.

'This I do for you, Jewel,' Lorenzo murmured as he huddled beneath his blanket. His ears were burning from the driving snow. 'Never in my life have I been so cold.'

The next morning the blizzard was still blowing and the line was blocked by snowdrifts. Other passengers volunteered to help clear it; it was at least a way of keeping warm. Henry said they were about an hour's walk from the nearest town and he was willing to go for supplies if someone else would come too in case of difficulty.

Lorenzo agreed to go with him but by now his leather boots were soaking wet; another passenger offered to lend him his waterproof galoshes if they would fit, which they did, and he and Henry set off in the face of a blinding gale-force wind. It took them nearly two hours to get to the town, but they bought enough bread for everyone in their carriage, as well as extra tea, coffee, biscuits and muffins. Both men were warm though tired when they returned to find the line had been cleared and they had another two or three miles of walking as the train had moved on without them.

And so it continued for two more days and nights and it seemed as if the journey was never going to end, but the conductor came to tell them that they would move much faster once they reached the state of New York, which they should do in two days. This cheered everyone immensely until the following afternoon, when once more they were beset by blizzards and a blocked line. Lorenzo and Henry were dispatched to the nearest town to ask for extra men to help clear the snow, and a gang of twenty came back with

327

them, armed with shovels and spades. Within two hours they were once more on their way.

As they rolled into New York Grand Central everyone shook hands and it felt as if they were parting from dear friends. Lorenzo asked about accommodation and was directed to an establishment close by the station. He paid for a meal and a hot bath, fell into his bed and slept for twelve hours whilst the laundry service washed all the clothes he had been wearing and dried out his boots.

When he felt human again, he enquired of the desk clerk at the railroad terminus regarding trains to Dreumel's Creek. The clerk shook his head. 'Never heard of it. Is it in the Appalachians? Up Ohio way?'

'I guess so,' Lorenzo agreed, but he'd never thought to look on a map. He only knew that Jewel had travelled by way of New York.

'Hey, buddy,' the clerk called to a colleague. 'You ever heard of Dreumel's Creek up Ohio way?'

The other clerk came over. 'Isn't that somewhere near where they had a fire? Where a town got burnt down?'

'Yes,' Lorenzo said eagerly. 'It is. The town's called Yeller.'

The second clerk pursed his lips and shook his head. 'We ain't got a line going that way.'

'Why d'ya want to go there if it's bin burnt down?' the first clerk asked quizzically. 'You planning on building there?'

'No,' Lorenzo said patiently. 'I don't want to go to Yeller. I want to go to Dreumel's Creek.'

'Best go by Woodsville then,' the two men agreed. 'Then by coach,' said one. 'But if it's the place I think it is, you might not get through,' said the other. 'They get a good deal of snow up there.'

Lorenzo sighed and said he'd buy a ticket anyway, but was told he'd have to wait until morning as the last train to Woodsville had already left and there wasn't another that day. He went back to the hotel, booked for another night, ate another mediocre meal and went back to bed.

CHAPTER FORTY-FOUR

Lorenzo did not think it possible to have another such gruelling experience of rail travel. But the journey to Woodsville almost equalled that of the Transcontinental in its arduousness. It took a whole day to Fort Duquesne, where they were due to change trains for the final trek to Woodsville, but again the line was blocked in several places by deep snow which had to be cleared before further progress could be made. The train they should have caught had already left without them and so passengers slept on board until the morning, huddled into their coats and blankets. When the next train arrived it was cold and draughty and there was no food, only tea and coffee, and Lorenzo had omitted to buy any supplies whilst in New York.

There were just three people in Woodsville wanting to travel on to Dreumel's Creek; the other two were inhabitants of Yeller who had been away on business and were now trying to get back home. One of these was Ted Allen, the other a victualler. Ted Allen introduced himself to Lorenzo and asked him what brought him to Dreumel's Creek at this time of year.

'I'm visiting a friend,' Lorenzo told him, unaware of how small Dreumel's Creek was in comparison with San Francisco, or that Ted would know everyone who lived there, being one of the first inhabitants.

'I hope we can get through,' Ted said. 'We opened up a track before I left, but it might well have closed again.'

The victualler nodded gloomily and said that he wished now that he had waited until spring before travelling.

'No use waiting for the weather,' Ted said. 'Life and business must still go on. Somebody will keep the track open, but we might have to walk through. The coach, if we can get one, will only go as far as the mountain pass. Does your friend know you're coming?' he asked Lorenzo. 'If he does, he'll no doubt get a party together to clear a way.'

'Erm, no,' Lorenzo said. 'And it's a young lady I'm visiting, not a gentleman.'

'Ah!' Ted said quizzically. 'Perhaps I know her? I know most folk in Dreumel. She could even be a friend of my daughter's. She got wed recently to an Englishman. They went straight off to England and have only just returned home again.'

'Are you an Englishman, sir?' Lorenzo asked. 'I don't recognize your accent.'

'I was,' Ted said. 'But I've lived in America longer than I ever lived in England, so I regard myself as an American now. And you? Italian, are you?'

Lorenzo shook his head. 'Extraction, yes, but I was born in San Francisco, so I'm an American.'

'And the young lady you're visiting? What did you say her name was?'

I didn't, Lorenzo thought, but I don't suppose it matters. 'Jewel Newmarch,' he said. 'We knew each other when we were children. Her father, Edward Newmarch, lived next door to us in San Francisco. I don't remember him, but my mother said he was a fine and generous man.'

Lorenzo felt Ted Allen's gaze on him intensify. Then Ted took in a breath. 'I know Jewel,' he said. 'And I once knew her father.'

They had to search out a driver willing to take the road to Dreumel's Creek and they asked several before finding one who would undertake the journey. They paid him twice the normal fare but all three regarded it a necessity and worth the price.

The road was thick with packed snow and Lorenzo wondered

330

how the coach didn't turn over, but the driver was adept and the pair of greys steady and sure, and six hours later they were headed for what seemed to Lorenzo to be a mountain wall. The driver slowed and then stopped. 'Can't go any further,' he called down to them. 'I don't want to get stuck in the valley for a week. This is where we say goodbye.'

But first of all they helped him turn the team and coach round so that he was facing back to Woodsville and his long return journey. Ted Allen offered him refreshment if he would like to walk into the valley with them but he declined and said he'd rather get back. The horses, he said, would be fine knowing they were on their way home.

The three men shouldered their bags and set off through the mountain pass, which had been kept clear as Ted had predicted.

'Are you staying at the Dreumel Marius?' Ted asked. 'They'll have vacancies, but you can come and stay with me and my wife if you'd care to. It's a bit further to walk to Yeller. We've got a small hotel too, but there's nothing else much in the town as it was burnt down last year.'

'Yes, I heard about that,' Lorenzo said. 'May I keep my options open, sir?'

'Sure.' Ted smiled. 'You'll want to know what kinda reception's waiting for you first!'

'Yes,' Lorenzo said hesitantly. 'I certainly do.'

An hour later they were standing in front of the Marius hotel and on the porch was a man, not too tall but sturdily built, who was gazing out at the creek, which was full to the brink, the water lapping over the edge. He saw Ted and lifted his hand in greeting, and then came down the steps.

'The creek's very full,' he said to Ted. 'I think we might have to break through the bank into the meadow on the other side to let it flow out. It'll come on to the road if we don't.'

Then he noticed the newcomer and gave a smile. 'How do you do, sir? You're a stranger here?'

'I am, sir,' Lorenzo said.

'This is Wilhelm Dreumel,' Ted broke in. 'Founding father

of Dreumel's Creek. This is Lorenzo Galli,' he told Wilhelm. 'He's come in search of Jewel.'

Wilhelm invited him in, in his customary welcoming manner, and Ted and the victualler went on their way to Yeller. 'Jewel has spoken of you,' Wilhelm said, 'but she didn't say that she was expecting you. At least not to me.'

'I wrote to say I'd like to call,' Lorenzo said. 'But I didn't give a time or date, which was just as well because I've had a most horrendous journey. I'd no idea that I should encounter such snow! There were times when I thought I'd never get here.'

Wilhelm laughed. 'You live in San Francisco! My wife remembers you from when you were a child.'

'Oh!' Lorenzo suddenly remembered. 'Of course. It was your wife who took Jewel away to England. How is she, sir? Your wife, I mean.'

'She is very well indeed.' Wilhelm beamed. 'As is our infant daughter. Come, take a seat and rest yourself.' He led him into a small sitting room and signalled to someone to bring a hot drink and food. 'Jewel is sitting with Georgiana now to ensure that she rests, and I suspect watching over the baby, Clarissa.'

'You must be very proud.' Lorenzo offered his congratulations, thinking despondently that Jewel wouldn't want to leave this happy family to return with him.

'I am,' Wilhelm said, drawing up a chair beside him. 'We never thought that it would happen.'

When the maid brought hot coffee and bread and chicken, he asked her to slip upstairs and ask Miss Jewel if she would come down. 'Please just tell her that I wish to speak to her urgently. Don't say anything about a visitor.'

The girl glanced at Lorenzo and gave a little grin. 'No, Mr Dreumel. I won't.'

They heard Jewel's voice calling to someone on the top landing and Wilhelm, rising swiftly, said, 'Excuse me a moment. I've just remembered that there's something I must do.' He headed in the direction of the reception area.

'Papa! Where are you? Papa?'

From his seat Lorenzo saw Jewel come down the stairs into the hall and look about her. The maid who had brought the coffee appeared and pointed towards the sitting room. Jewel turned to come in and saw Lorenzo, who rose from his chair, almost knocking over the small table which held the crockery.

She stood stock still in the doorway. 'Lorenzo?' she whispered. 'How – how did you get here?'

He walked towards her and held out his hands for hers, drawing her into the room. 'By railroad. By walking. By coach. Through snow and blizzards. And it was worth every minute of discomfort, every chilblain, each and every frozen finger, every snowdrift and icy blast just to see you again. I've missed you so much,' he added softly. 'I haven't smiled since you left, nor uttered any glad word; and yet I couldn't write what was in my heart. Words on paper were not enough to convey what I feel for you.'

'Lorenzo!' she breathed. 'I've missed you too, so much, yet could not be so forward as to say so without some word of affection from you. How could I? It's not for women to display their feelings, no matter how strong.'

He drew her close and kissed her cheek. 'That must change immediately, for I want – need – to know what you feel for me. I need to know that you love me as much as I love you. That you've thought of me every day since you left me, as I have thought of you.' He swallowed hard. 'I cannot wait to make you my wife so that I can show you every day how much I care. Tell me that you feel the same.'

'I do,' she murmured. 'I think I have loved you for ever, and I never knew that you were always there, waiting for my return.'

CHAPTER FORTY-FIVE

And so, my dearest Clara, I come to the conclusion of my letter. My darling Lorenzo has asked me to be his wife and I have so joyfully accepted; we are to be married in two months' time here in Dreumel's Creek. Papa gladly gave his consent and will give me away, and Mama said how strange life is, and who would have thought that all those years ago when she and I left San Francisco and Lorenzo and I both wept at the losing of a childhood friend that we would come together again so happily.

You'll be pleased to hear that at last I know who I am! I am Jewel Newmarch-Dreumel, born in America of an English father and a Chinese mother, adopted daughter of the dearest parents in the world, and soon to be the wife of a beloved Italian American, who, after our marriage, will take me home to San Francisco, where we will have another wedding. We shall be blessed in St Mary's Cathedral and I will wear my red Chinese cheongsam in honour of my Chinese mother and family; Pinyin will stand by my other side for my father, Edward Newmarch, and my mother, Chang Tsui.

I wish you could be here with me, my dear Clara, as I also wish that I could be with you when you wed your faithful Thomas in St Mary's Church in Hull. But we will be together in spirit as we each celebrate our homecoming.

Yours for ever in love and friendship,
Jewel.

ABOUT THE AUTHOR

Val Wood was born in Yorkshire, where she still lives. Her first novel, *The Hungry Tide*, was the first winner of the Catherine Cookson Prize for Fiction.